T0356318

DROWN ME
WITH
DREAMS

ALSO BY GABI BURTON

Sing Me to Sleep

DROWN ME WITH DREAMS

GABI BURTON

BLOOMSBURY

NEW YORK LONDON OXFORD NEW DELHI SYDNEY

BLOOMSBURY YA
Bloomsbury Publishing Inc., part of Bloomsbury Publishing Plc
1385 Broadway, New York, NY 10018

BLOOMSBURY and the Diana logo are trademarks of Bloomsbury Publishing Plc

First published in the United States of America in August 2024 by Bloomsbury YA

Bloomsbury books may be purchased for business or promotional use. For information on
bulk purchases please contact Macmillan Corporate and Premium Sales Department at
specialmarkets@macmillan.com

Library of Congress Cataloging-in-Publication Data
available upon request
ISBN 978-1-5476-1041-9 (hardcover) • ISBN 978-1-5476-1042-6 (e-book)

Book design by Yelena Safronova
Typeset by Westchester Publishing Services
Printed and bound in the U.S.A.
2 4 6 8 10 9 7 5 3 1

To find out more about our authors and books visit www.bloomsbury.com
and sign up for our newsletters.

For Black girls growing in the ashes of our stolen past

C'RYNN

BELLEHAVE

TELLU

WYSTMEREN

THE FELL

THE BARRIER

TAMSIN'S PEAK

ENFORCEMENT CAMP

MIDKA

AUNTIES' HOUSE

KETZAL
WITCHES

KEI

SINU
HUMANS

IDRIS
AIR FAE

JEUNE RIVER

GREYSN RIVER

SAOIRSE'S HOME

VANIHAIL
WATER FAE

PALACE

HARAYA HALL

BARRACKS

BHAIRI SEA

MOERUS

ALKARA

ASTRINE

LYRCANA

URYEFELL

CALAMID

PENNEX

NIRI

DOOR
WAY

KRILL
WITCHES

SZEIRYNA

RDRE

KURR VALLEY
EARTH FAE

LAKE RY'ANNEN

PHYDAN
FIRE FAE

SERINGTON
MIXED FAE

SAFE
HOUSE

BLIDDON
EARTH FAE

DROWN ME
WITH
DREAMS

CHAPTER ONE

A NEW MARK

I have two faces. Both are wanted criminals. I'm meant to stay hidden—safely tucked away in my room until the new King deigns to summon me—but tonight, after days trapped indoors, I finally have a new mark.

Is it dangerous? Sure. But the thrill is worth the risk.

I feel clumsy as I scramble out my window. It's been a while, but some instincts never fade. My fingers send ripples across the glassy surface of the Palace wall. I'm not sure what it's made of, but I heard from a trusted source that it reflects the mood of the reigning King. Tonight, it's smooth and still. Which means the King is either sleeping or deceptively calm.

I land softly on the ground and pause, listening to the night: soft coos of nearby birds, low whines of crickets, and rustling tree branches in the wind.

Missing from the blanket of sound: footsteps. Alarmed shouts that a fugitive siren just climbed from a Palace window.

Good. I'm alone.

I take a running start from the base of the Palace toward the surrounding gate. I leap and catch the metal bars to pull myself up and over.

In the process, my hood slips. For the briefest moment, I'm

exposed. As soon as I'm on the other side, I pull it back up. Look around.

Nothing. It's past midnight. The streets of Keirdre remain deserted, and I remain shrouded by the velvety night and dark fabric of my navy cloak.

I creep through Vanihail in the periphery of the streets, making my way to my mark for the evening.

One week ago, I was informed I'm leaving Keirdre. Traveling to the other side of the impenetrable barrier I've been trapped inside my whole life. Since then, I've been separated from my family, given a secluded room in the Palace, and told to stay put.

For one week, I obeyed, sitting still and docile, waiting for vague updates from a King who used to confide in me without reservation.

Tonight is blessedly different. Tonight, I shirk rules and embrace the exhilaration of a few fleeting hours of freedom and a fresh mark.

This part of Vanihail—South Vanihail—is a collection of short, navy-bricked buildings and shop signs faintly illumined by chaeliss torches. The cobblestones are perfectly even, with alternating shades of muddy brown and cloudy gray.

My pulse quickens as Haraya comes into view, towering over the rest of Vanihail. My tongue toys with the groove carved behind my false tooth. A habit. Useless now. I used to keep *keil* beads there, but they're rarer now than they used to be. Besides, everyone in Keirdre already knows who and what I am. I'm a fugitive no matter what face I wear.

Moonlight and starlight flicker like torches as clouds swoop in and out, intermittently blanketing the sky. I hide in the shadows their light creates along the building. Haraya is home to Vanihail's sentencing chamber—a foreboding hall where lawbreakers are tried and sentenced. The sentencing chamber is empty this time of night, but what I'm after lies underneath. The dungeons. Where the accused wait to stand trial and the guilty go to rot.

Keirdre is not in the business of freeing the accused.

Haraya's front doors and locking mechanism are made of marble—too heavy for normal lock picking.

Fortunately, the doors aren't the best point of entry for what I have planned.

I trace a hand over the crevices of the outer wall. My fingers dig into the grooves in the rough mortar as I start to climb. Wind bludgeons me from all sides. Its attack grows more vicious the higher I scale.

My arms burn when I reach my destination: the massive glass clockface on the front facade of the building. It's made of blue stained glass with metal clock hands on the inside and outside.

Working quickly, I grab the smaller of the two clock arms with one hand and reach the other into my pocket for my knife. A harsh breeze billows my cloak and shoves the hood off my shoulders. I don't let it distract me.

I wedge my knife's blade between the glass of the window and the stone of Haraya. Back and forth, over and over . . .

Recently, I learned a few secrets from a trusted source about Haraya Hall.

Fact one: its clock is cleaned regularly.

Fact two—

I yank on the knife and the clockface swings inward.

—the clock is on a set of hinges. Apparently, it makes it easier to clean. And, right now, it makes it easier for me to duck inside.

Fact three: there's a ledge *just* inside the window. Also used for cleaning. Also making it easier for me to enter.

I balance on the stone ledge and push the clock closed with a soft *thud*.

Pause. Catch my breath. Wait for someone to come sprinting.

All I hear is the steady *tick, tick, tick* of the clock.

I'm on edge as I pivot to face the sentencing chamber. Rows and rows of deserted benches facing a wooden stage at the front of the room.

For a flash, I see a spatter of red in my mind's eye—the haunting memory of human blood splashing across the stage. Hear the raucous cheers in response.

I shiver. It has nothing to do with the cold.

The chaeliss chandeliers have been snuffed for the night, but there's the faintest orange glow coming from under a door beneath me.

Homed in on that light, I climb down from the ledge and make my way to the door. I lean forward on the balls of my feet to absorb the sounds of my footsteps. One hand clutches my knife, the other seizes the erstwyn door handle.

The old wood creaks as I eke open the door. Which means I should assume the guards on the other side can hear it and are aware of my arrival.

My lips part. A song flows out like a stream. The melody starts slow but builds until the door is fully out of the way and I come face-to-face with two guards. Both frozen like ice. Their eyes are already glazed over from the sound of my singing, and when they catch sight of me—of my face, left eerily perfect without the disguise of a *keil* bead—they tremble from a combination of bone-chilling fear and aching desire.

The flavor of their want for me invades my senses, bathing my tongue in something sweet like honey and spicy like powdered chilis.

Lune above, I've missed this. Missed the feeling that accompanies reducing marks to drooling lightbrains, desperate to do as I command.

I survey the room. Small. The walls are decorated with wanted posters. Some are yellowed at the edges and have clearly been here for years. Others are fresh, like the one of a girl split in half. Half her face is monstrously beautiful. The other has her hair pulled back, revealing a burn on her cheek.

Both faces—both girls—are me.

There are two doors. The first is the one I came through, and the second is behind the guards. *That* is my destination—it leads into the deeper fortress of Haraya's dungeons.

A tingling sensation in my fingers mixes with a hum in my heart—there's water in this room. It's above me, suspended in a large basin, ready for the guards' use. A benefit of having a King—*former* King—who overvalued water fae: a steady supply of water on hand.

The guard on the right has one hand stilled over his belt. The fight must've seeped out of him when he caught sight of me.

I look into his eyes. Smile. Still singing, singing, singing.

The water overhead sings me a deliciously tempting song. Its tune is as soothing to me as my voice is to the guards. It entreats me to reach for it—use it, wield it, *unleash* it on the men before me.

Kill.

But now isn't the time for that.

I grit my teeth against the water's plea and move closer to the guards.

Their bodies are immobile but their eyes dart over my face, soaking it in like fresh honey on warm cornbread.

The guard on the left speaks first. "Y-you're—"

Beautiful? A criminal? Both are correct, but the guard's voice trails and he doesn't finish the sentence.

Conflict wages in the man closest to me. He's torn between his duty to capture me and his desperation to please me.

The guard on the right never stood a chance. As his partner eyes me, fighting himself, the one on the right stares in enraptured awe. From the moment he heard my voice, loyalty to Keirdre became an exasperating afterthought.

I focus all my attention on him. Smile wider. It's cruel and taunting, but he doesn't notice. Can't see anything but me through the fog of his desire.

My song builds. I move closer. Hold his gaze with flashing silver eyes.

His companion watches, but I know he won't strike me. He's stronger-willed than his partner, but he's under my spell just the same.

The water sloshes in the basin above us. *Kill.*

It would be all too easy and blissfully familiar to tell them to plunge their blades through their own hearts, keep pushing until they keel over, stone dead. I swallow the urge.

No kills tonight. No matter how refreshing it would feel after the past week cooped up in the Palace with no one to sing to.

I'm half a pace away from the guard on the right. He holds his breath, as though afraid if he releases it, I'll blow away in a cloud of smoke.

"Hi," I say softly. "I need to take a peek into the dungeons.

Let me pass?" I sing a few more low and haunting notes. Place a hand on his shoulder, so gentle it's barely a touch at all.

His body wracks with shivers. Without a word, he lurches aside, granting me access to the door behind him.

I square my shoulders so I brush him as I pass. I smirk as he tenses from the brief contact.

Was it necessary?

No.

But damn it all if it wasn't *fun*.

Torches bracketed to the stairwell walls light my path as I descend into the dungeons. The door thuds closed behind me and I pick up my pace. I only have so much time before the effects of my Siren Song fade and the guards sound the alarm to apprehend me. It's not an exact science, but I give myself seven minutes before the Palace is alerted to my presence.

Including, of course, Keirdre's new King.

I reach the base of the stairs. Three stone corridors branch from where I stand, each lined with small, dimly lit cells more befitting caged animals than people.

I start down the middle path. My eyes scour each cell for my mark. Above each set of cell bars is a number carved into a wooden plaque.

321, 322 . . .

Prisoners move to the front of their cells and stare as I pass, jaws unhinged.

325, 326 . . .

A man reaches for me from between his cell bars.

I ignore him.

329, 330, 331 . . .

I stop. A familiar figure is tucked in the back of cell 332.

His back is pressed against the far wall of his cell, head ducked to obscure his face. Not that it matters. I could pick his silhouette out from a wall of shadows.

It's odd to see him reduced to a prisoner. Throughout our years of friendship, he struck me as some kind of invincible. Or, at the very least, above the law. He lied to the Keirdren military for years and lived to tell the tale. As far as I'm concerned, for a time, he *was* invincible.

Until he betrayed me—took my sister, threatened to kill her, and shattered my heart in the process. He's mortal. I know that now. Just as disappointing as everyone else.

He doesn't look up as I approach, but his breathing changes—he knows I'm here.

The last time I saw him, I hated him—wanted him dead. I still do.

I've spent my life fighting myself. Over the past few lunes, I've gained a bit of stability over my instincts. Still, restlessness and anger are my enemies. After a week of silence, with nothing but fury and memories that burn like acid to keep me company, my impulses are on edge. Singing to the guards above was thrilling. Seeing my biggest heartbreak now is infuriating.

Temptation prickles my senses, and I'm all too aware of how easy it would be to kill him.

It makes me even angrier. Seeing him reminds me how volatile I am. How easy it is to slip back into violent habits.

I dig my fingernails into my palms, forcing myself calm.

He's a mark tonight, yes. But I'm not here to spill blood. I'm here for answers.

I crouch in front of his cell. "You look cozy. I like seeing you like this."

"Saoirse." His head is still ducked.

It irritates me—feels like a dismissal—so I mimic his tone and say, "Spektryl."

His eyes snap up. Brilliant green and flooded with hurt he hasn't earned. The look dissolves, like sugar in tea, almost instantly, but the brief flash was unmistakable. There was a time those eyes were comforting. A time when seeing them flicker with pain would move me. Now, they make me cold and I savor his displeasure.

"What are you doing?" he asks. "Does your Prince know you're here?"

"He's a King now." *And about as far from "mine" as he could be.* I shove that thought aside.

Carrik's face twists with disgust and his emotions sour on my tongue. "He's a boy with a crown. Doesn't make him a King. Certainly not mine. You didn't answer my question. Does he know you're here?"

"I don't answer to you. I'm out here. You're behind bars."

"For now." He smirks. "But what is your Prince going to do when he discovers you here? Who knows? Maybe you'll join me."

"I have questions about the other side of the barrier." I ignore his questions about Hayes. I'm trying *not* to kill Carrik right now. Thinking about Hayes—and all the jumbled emotions that come with it—isn't the best way to do that. "I suspect you have answers. You work with the Resistance, and at least some of you have contact with the other side. Laa'el told me, so don't bother denying it."

"Who says I'm denying it? But why are you—" His smug expression warps into wide-eyed fear. "Is he— He's not thinking of sending you there, is he?" Carrik's on his feet, gripping the cell bars and staring at me with chilling intensity. "He is, isn't he?"

I don't confirm or deny the accusation, but he can read my thoughts clearly enough without me breathing a word.

Carrik scowls. "That *lightbrain*. What the hell is he thinking, putting you in danger like that?"

"Don't pretend to care about my safety," I say. "Why do you say the other side is dangerous?"

"They *hate* the Royals. Anyone from Keirdre, but especially Larster and his family. Anyone affiliated with them will have a target on their back. There's a hierarchy in Keirdre, and fae are on top. It's not like that over there. There are other creatures."

"What kind?" I try to mask my interest. I'm here for answers about the other side. I'm here because I need to know where the doorway to cross over is, what dangers I might face over there, and how to prepare myself.

But I have another secret, maybe irrational reason for traveling to the other side: hope that Larster *didn't* kill all other sirens. Maybe it's silly, but I came from somewhere—someone. Someone else who's unbearably beautiful but terrified of mirrors. Someone with a constant war waging inside.

I want to find someone like me—someone *better* than me. Someone who learned to quiet the raging storm of their desires. I managed it briefly on the deck of the *Sea Queen*, only for it to be immediately shattered the moment I was angry again.

I've been inhaling chaos like I breathe underwater, and I want it to stop. Want someone to tell me it *can* stop. Somewhere out there, there's someone like me. I know it.

Carrik's eyes soften, and he answers the question I refused to ask outright: "I don't know if there are sirens, Saoirse."

I feel the cold sting of crushed hope. I shove it aside. I don't want him to see. "I didn't ask about that. What *do* you know? Do you know where the doorway is?"

He wavers for a tick before shaking his head. "No. But even if I did know, I wouldn't tell you."

"Why not? I thought you wanted me to forgive you?"

"I do." He meets my eyes with sincerity so raw I hope he chokes on it. "And I'll keep apologizing for however long it takes. But you have to be alive to forgive me. I'd rather you live long enough to hate me forever than die absolving me. If your Prince asked you to go to the other side of the barrier, tell him no. Please."

"He's not *my* Prince," I say, annoyed.

"Actually," a deeper, huskier voice speaks from behind me, "he's not a Prince at all."

I go rigid. I hadn't heard his approach, but I sense him now—feel his glare on the back of my neck, scalding enough to rankle my nerves.

I half turn. "Your Majesty." I bow. This should be familiar, but it feels awkward now.

His eyes, blue like the ocean and somehow even more captivating, are uncharacteristically blank as they look me over. The look is brief—just a swift once-over to ensure I'm upright and breathing—before they shift to Carrik.

I hate myself for missing the way his gaze used to linger.

"What are you doing here?" Hayes's words are directed at me even though he's no longer looking.

"I—"

"This was reckless." He asked the damned question but he talks over my answer. "If it was *anyone* else who responded to the alarm, you'd be locked up. Maybe even dead."

"I wanted answers," I say.

He scoffs. "You're fortunate I told the guards to contact me directly if they saw you."

I raise my brows. "You thought I'd come here?"

Hayes finally looks at me again. His expression is dripping with derision. "You think you're complicated, but I've got a foolproof way to figure you out. Just think of the last possible thing I'd want you to do—the most *reckless* thing you could possibly do. It's a safe bet that's exactly what you've already done twelve times over."

His words are so harsh, even Carrik flinches.

I stand my ground. "Your Majesty—"

"Never mind." He turns on his heel and starts back down the hall. "We should go." He doesn't motion for me to follow or even ask. Just assumes I'll trail behind him like a well-trained ox.

Carrik watches him leave with a scowl. "You're really going to risk your life to keep *that* asshole happy?"

"It's not about him. It's about my family. I need proof that whatever is over there is better for them than Keirdre. But since you won't help . . ." I turn away. Manage a single step before—

"*Wait!*"

I smirk to myself before schooling my features and facing him again. "What?"

"Saoirse, *please*. Don't cross the barrier."

"Why? You haven't given me a reason not to."

He pauses.

I sigh. "If you're just going to waste my time—"

"It's one-way," he blurts.

That's not what I was expecting. "What?"

"Once you leave Keirdre, you can't come back. Not unless the barrier comes down."

I'm freezing. Like I plunged headfirst into the Jeune River in the dead of winter. "I don't believe you." My words feel hollow.

"I'm telling the truth," he says. "If you go over, you'll be trapped. You'll never see Rain, your family, me, or that damned Prince you like so much again."

CHAPTER TWO

WEIRD, COLD SPACES

My feet are heavy as I drag them down the dungeon corridor. I barely register the prisoners who call for me as I pass.

I'm numb to it all. I don't even feel a rush as I wait outside the door at the top of the stairs. *Feel* for the water in the basin above the guards on the other side. *Grab* it with my mind, *wrap* it around their faces like scarves. Wait until they pass out—stop before they're dead—and ascend from the dark depths of the dungeons. I step around their unconscious bodies, still feeling nothing.

It's child's play. I'm so dead to it all, I'm not even tempted to kill them. Not tempted to do anything but curl up and cry. Or scream. Maybe both.

I pull up my hood as I leave Haraya. Keep it up as I climb into the carriage waiting outside. Hayes sits on one side, looking down as I slide onto the bench across from him.

It's not until the carriage rocks to life and we begin the journey back to the Palace that he finally looks at me with a single raised brow. "What do you think? Was I convincing?"

I force a smile I don't mean. I should be pleased. Our feigned spat successfully softened Carrik's resolve and loosened his tongue. We know more about the barrier than we did before. Still, my victory feels more bitter than sweet.

For one thing: Carrik's words are an echo I can't unmute. *"Once you leave Keirdre, you can't come back."*

He might be a liar and a traitor, but I believe him.

I could cross over the barrier and be trapped forever. In a world I only learned existed a few weeks ago. Without my sister, my parents, my aunties, my . . .

My eyes land on the frowning King sitting across from me. *Hayes.*

That fear alone is enough to send my stomach sinking to the carriage floor. But I can't linger on it because of the second concern consuming my thoughts: our "feigned" spat felt all too real.

Each word he hurled at me felt targeted. Not like manufactured anger for the sake of a convincing show. More like festering honesty, finally unleashed.

I want to ask him how much was real and how much was fabricated, but I can't because we have bigger issues. Can't because I'm secretly a coward and I'm not sure I want to know the answer.

So, I tuck my fears behind a smile so strained, it's painful, and pretend the wall between us—made of secrets and lies and heartbreak—doesn't exist. "Should I be concerned? Your acting was so impeccable, you even had me convinced." My words are true, but my tone—light, teasing, and unbothered—is a lie. A half-truth. My specialty.

Hayes's smile is, like mine, frayed and vacant. He only manages to hold my gaze for a tick and a half before even the fake grin drips away like melting candle wax. He rests his head against the carriage seat. I think he means to seem relaxed, but there's too much tension in his shoulders to fool me. "Did it work? Did Spektryl say anything after I left?"

"He told me the doorway is one-sided. Once I go through, I can't come back."

Hayes sits up, eyes sharpening. *"What?"*

"It's fine," I say quickly. "I'll find a way."

"What if you don't?"

"I will," I insist. "But if I can't, I'll neutralize whatever army the Resistance has waiting for us so it's safe for you to bring down the barrier." I keep my spine rigid and shoulders straight, arming myself with confidence I don't feel.

There's still so much we need to accomplish before I can leave. We need to actually *find* the doorway. I need to get my *lairic* beads runed again. We need the potion that will unlink Hayes's and Ikenna's lives from the barrier. And now there's not even a guarantee that if we find the doorway, I'll be able to come back.

Over the past week, Hayes and I have been strategizing.

First, we read through every letter Larster received from Reyshka Harker. We have one last unsent letter in Larster's hand we found in his office and dozens from Reyshka over the past five years.

They were useful enough. She wrote detailed instructions about where she is on the other side, so I know how to find her when I get there. Unfortunately, nothing she wrote hinted at *where* the doorway is. Or what she's doing over there. Every few years, the top Deltas from the Vanihailian Barracks are sent to the other side to train under her—but we have no idea what they're training *for*.

After that, we contacted Auntie Drina. She made Hayes a *lairic* configuration so I can Dreamweave with him from the other side. Now, she's brewing *nafini*—a potion that should, hopefully, unlink Hayes's and Ikenna's souls from the barrier.

It's the plan that feels the most stable, but it's still so frail it could easily crumble to dust. Drina is a powerful witch, but that kind of magic—the magic of souls—has long since gone out of practice. She's never brewed *nafini*. She knows the general process, but there's no guarantee it will work.

That's not even getting into the other potential obstacles. It requires a full lune to brew, and since she only started about a week ago, we have another three weeks before it's usable. Another issue is the Resistance on the other side. Supposedly, they have a massive, vicious army out to spill Keirdren blood. We can't risk bringing down the barrier if it means everyone in Keirdre, including my family and Hayes, gets killed in the process.

These are all problems I don't have the capacity to solve. So many cracks that could easily lead to ruin.

"Did Spektryl tell you where the doorway is?" asks Hayes.

"He says he doesn't know."

Hayes groans. Another dead end.

Four days ago, Hayes spoke with my former training instructor, Pierce Flynn, to see if he knew anything about the other side. All he could tell us was that the doorway was somewhere in Kurr Valley.

Translation: nothing useful.

The barrier wraps around Keirdre on all sides. Kurr Valley, one of two sectors for earth fae and home to most of Keirdre's farmland, is the largest sector. *By a lot.* It does little—scratch that, *nothing*—to narrow down our search area.

Our next step was the King's—*former* King's—office. Nothing. A word I'm growing weary of. The only thing we found was a freya candle I'm certain is the same one Larster used to pass letters to Reyshka.

Unfortunately, my hunch is just that, because Hayes couldn't get the damned thing to light. We think it needs his father's hand to work, but there's no way to prove it. Larster is dead.

Our *next* step was Carrik. He gave us an answer, but not the one we need.

Which means our next step . . .

"Your Majesty," I say gently.

Hayes's head is still flopped against the carriage seat. "I know what you're going to say."

Ikenna.

Queen of Keirdre. Hayes's mother.

That freya candle in Hayes's office might not work for the new King, but maybe it'll work for the former Queen. That's my theory, anyway, but Hayes has been reluctant to bring his mother into this.

"Can you arrange a meeting with Ikenna?" I ask, keeping my voice as gentle as possible.

"Yes," he drags out the word with obvious loathing. "I doubt she knows anything. My parents weren't close. They had separate bedrooms and separate lives."

I open my mouth, ready for a spat, but he cuts me off. "Fine. We've exhausted all other options. I'll arrange a meeting with her tomorrow. Did Spektryl say anything else?"

"I don't know if there are sirens on the other side."

Crushing words but ultimately meaningless to our mission.

There was a time when Hayes would've asked for some kind of insight into what I was feeling. Just like there was a time when *I* might've asked why he's so against talking to his mother. It wasn't that long ago, but it was a completely different world.

Hayes said he forgave me for all the secrets and lies. He meant it. He hasn't been angry with me—he's been cold. Which is worse. I want him to glare. Yell. Punish me so we can move forward. Instead, we live in a weird, cold space where we fake smiles and avoid eye contact like strangers.

"Saoirse?" Hayes prods when I take too long to answer.

I shake my head. "No. He didn't say anything else."

Hayes nods, accepting this. We lapse into chilling silence for the rest of the ride.

CHAPTER THREE

OVERSIZED THRONE

Hayes still looks out of place in his father's office. Scratch that—it's *Hayes's* office now. No matter how many times I remind myself of his new role, it doesn't feel right.

His desk is on a raised platform and the office walls are drab and gray, as is the stone basin of water behind him. The only splash of color in the room is the massive navy chair behind his desk. It's wider than it needs to be, with a curved spine that stretches up and up, almost to the ceiling. The combination of the elevated desk and foreboding chair is clearly designed to make the King look commanding.

For Larster, maybe it worked. But Hayes just looks small sitting in the oversized chair. Like a child trying on their father's shirt and drowning in excess fabric.

I sit in a cushioned gray chair across from him. His legs are hidden by the desk, but I can tell they're bouncing with nerves as we wait for Ikenna. I want to say something to put him at ease, but I no longer feel qualified.

Hayes's guards have dwindled over the past few weeks. Erasmus is dead, Laa'el is imprisoned, Devlyn resigned shortly after Hayes's disastrous birthday celebration, and I'm a fugitive.

Leaving Hayes with only Zensen and Jeune until he hires new guards to add to the rotation.

Jeune stands over my shoulder near the office door. In the few minutes we've been here, she's yawned three times. With such a small pool of guards, she gets less time to sleep than ever. A sharp knock on the door.

Hayes clears his throat. "Who is it?"

"You summoned me." I've only heard Ikenna speak a handful of times, but I recognize her voice instantly. She sounds calm, cool, and bored.

Hayes nods to Jeune. She unlocks the door and moves aside for the Queen and two of her guards to enter before locking it again.

The shorter of Ikenna's guards is staring at me, eyes widened in awe. He quickly looks away when he sees he's been caught, but the stale-bread flavor of his apprehension mingles with the heated flare of his desire.

Queen Ikenna is regal. Tall with an unyielding posture and stiff shoulders. Subtle lines frame her mouth and the corners of her eyes. Aside from that, she's ageless. Her hair is dark and thick, styled into a pouf that floats around her head like a crown, dotted with pearl beads that look like stars. She shares an eye color with her son, but her ocean gaze is harder. Crueler. She's dressed in yellow today. A rich, golden color that perfectly complements her dark skin. Plain from the waist up, patterned from the waist down. She's unmistakably powerful and undeniably beautiful.

Ikenna's eyes flit around the room before lighting on me. Her expression, detached up until this point, sours. I taste her acrid disdain, colored by something peppery. *Anger.* "I didn't realize you were inviting her," she says coldly.

A scathing response comes to mind, but Hayes speaks before I can voice it. "Remember, you're not to breathe a word of her presence in the Palace. To anyone."

"I already swore I wouldn't," Ikenna mutters. She eyes me expectantly. "Well?"

I gift her with a slow blink. "Well, what?"

"Are you not going to offer me your seat?"

I can't contain my incredulous laugh. "You're joking."

Her eyes narrow. "Have I said something funny? There are only two chairs. Your King has one. The other, clearly, is mine."

"And yet, here I sit."

Her mouth flattens into an unamused line. She glares at Hayes. "I've heard the rumors of your . . . *relationship* with this creature. Are you truly not going to command she give me my seat?"

Hayes lifts his brows. "I can't imagine what she'd do to me if I tried to 'command' anything of her."

Jeune chuckles but stops when the Queen glares at her. "Fine," says Ikenna. "I'll stand. Why am I here?"

Hayes procures a pale blue freya candle from a desk drawer. "Do you recognize this?"

Ikenna's face remains still. "It's your father's." Clears her throat. "*Was* your father's."

My tongue detects an emotion that's cold like ice and sharp like ginger. Heartbreak.

Interesting. I know little about Larster and Ikenna's relationship. I hadn't thought either of them capable of genuine affection for each other, but apparently, I was mistaken. I file this information away.

"I can't get it to work," says Hayes.

Ikenna stares at the candle for another two ticks before

looking at Hayes again. "It was spelled to work only for your father. I suppose it's useless now."

"It won't even work for you?"

"No."

It's convincing, but my gut tells me she's lying. "Do you know what it's for, at least?" I ask.

A muscle tics in her jaw, and my tongue bathes in her briny irritation. "I don't answer to monsters."

My hands fist in my lap. Ikenna sat idly by as her husband slaughtered thousands. Orphaned hundreds. Including me. And somehow, *I'm* the only monster in the room?

The water in the basin behind Hayes gurgles at me to punish her.

Hayes must glimpse my barely bridled anger because he quickly says, "Do you know what it's for?"

Ikenna nods stiffly. "For your father's communications with Reyshka. I assume you know about her?"

"I do. No thanks to you. Were you ever going to tell me?"

"Eventually." Her words are clipped.

It's clear from the hurt that dances swiftly over Hayes's expression that he believes her about as much as I do. "Had you told Finnean?"

She flinches at his name, and the gingery sorrow is back. She misses her late son as much as her husband. "Your brother—"

"That's a yes." Hayes is bitter. It settles on his face like dregs of tea sinking to the bottom of a cup. "Do you know where the doorway to the other side of the barrier is?"

Ikenna glances at me. "Why do you want to know?"

"I'm a King now. How do you expect me to lead without knowing what's happening in my own kingdom?"

"Your father was a private person. He didn't tell me every-thing. I have no idea where the doorway is."

She's lying. I'm certain of it, but the flavor of her emotions gives nothing away. Oddly enough, I detect a strong taste of sour grapes and stale biscuits—guilt and fear—only it's not coming from Ikenna, it's coming from one of her guards. The one who stared at me when he entered.

I didn't pay him any mind before, but I study him now. His build is scrawny—he's so small, he almost looks human. His skin is rough and light like sandstone. He has bright topaz-colored eyes and shorn hair. He doesn't stand still like Ikenna's second guard. He shifts in place, oozing anxiety.

"Are you sure?" Hayes, still questioning Ikenna, pulls my attention.

"Certain. I'm sorry I don't have anything more useful for you."

I don't believe she's sorry for a tick. Everything about her—from the steel in her voice to the ice of her gaze—makes it clear she's never uttered a sincere apology in her life.

Hayes looks at me with a raised brow: *Anything else?*

I have more questions, but we can't compel Ikenna to answer any of them. I shake my head.

Hayes sighs. "You're free to go, Mother."

Ikenna's lips twitch into a thin smile, and she turns to leave. Pauses. "Guard yourself. She's even more beautiful than I remember." She's looking at me but talking to Hayes. Before I can digest her words, she and her guards sweep from the room.

Hayes groans as soon as Jeune locks the door behind them. "She's hiding something. Could you sing to her? Make her tell us the truth?"

"My songs have limits."

"They don't work on women?"

"It's not about gender." A common misconception. "Siren Songs only work on people who are attracted to me."

Hayes's eyes rake slowly over my body, lingering on my face and again on my hips. His brow knits in confusion. "Is that not everyone?" Said differently, it might sound coy, but Hayes's confusion is earnest—he can't fathom anyone not wanting me.

"Not everyone," I say. "Definitely not Ikenna. But I think we have another option. Her guard—the smaller one—he got nervous when she said she didn't know where the doorway is."

Hayes frowns. "How do you know?"

"Sirens can taste emotions. He was nervous. And guilty. Like he was hiding something."

"I noticed it too." Jeune comes to stand alongside my chair. "He started fidgeting when Her Majesty said she didn't know where the doorway is."

Hayes's eyes are on me. "Can you get him to talk?"

Ikenna is a Queen. A powerful and cruel woman. We can ask her all the questions we want, but if she doesn't want to answer, she won't. *This* guard, on the other hand . . . I have lots of experience bending men exactly like him to my will. "Yes. Do you know if he's working tonight?"

"I can find out," Jeune offers.

"Thank you." I smile at her. "If he's not on rotation, I'll pay him a visit at midnight."

"Come find me after," says Hayes. "We'll meet in my room to debrief. And Saoirse, remember—"

"I know, I know," I say. "Don't let anyone see me."

CHAPTER FOUR

SHIFTING TIDES

Hayes mentioned the former King and Queen slept in different rooms. He failed to mention they have separate *wings* of the Palace. Larster had the eastern side of the third floor, and Ikenna the western side. It's a waste of space and resources, but having met them, I can't say I blame them for going to extremes to avoid each other.

Midnight is nearing as I slink through the corridors. Like Hayes, Ikenna keeps her guards close to her quarters. Their rooms are in her wing of the Palace, near her chambers.

It's late enough that the halls are empty, but I still wear a low-hanging hood and keep to the shadows to avoid being seen. I haven't passed anyone yet, but my heart hammers louder with each creaking floorboard I hear, no matter how distant.

Chaeliss lights in the halls are dimmed after sunset, but there's still enough light to make out the portraits on the walls of the Queen's corridors. They're all of Larster, Ikenna, and a man with brilliant eyes like the sea. Finnean. Hayes's brother, dead well before Hayes was born.

I examine more portraits as I pass. None of them feature Hayes.

My stomach turns in distaste.

I stop at the door eight down on the right. According to Jeune, this is my mark's room. She also told me his name—Thannen—but I don't intend to use it. He's a mark and I have a rule about that.

When I knock, there's shuffling on the other side before it cracks open.

Ikenna's guard peers through the gap between the door and jamb, eyes wary. "What—"

I wedge a foot into the room, stopping him before he's finished. One hand slams against the door, pushing it open, the other shoves his chest, moving him back as I enter. My face is still hidden, and I can't reveal myself until we're in his room, where there's no chance of discovery.

My mark was caught off guard by my sudden attack, but now that he's had a moment to process, he's alert. He tenses, preparing to try and fight me off. I kick the door shut behind me and shake off my hood.

His hostility extinguishes as his jaw tumbles to the floor.

"Hello." I smile. "Do you know who I am?"

He nods. Doesn't speak.

He seems still enough now, so I drop my hand from his chest. Disappointment darts over his face at the loss of contact. In response, I sing a hauntingly alluring melody.

My mark's body slackens and his topaz eyes go blank.

"You lied to me." My eyes glow silver and I step toward him.

He moves closer, his motion a longing echo of my own. "I would never lie to you."

"You did." I lean forward. My face lingers, a few shaking breaths away from his. "Queen Ikenna said she doesn't know where the doorway to the barrier is. That was a lie, wasn't it?"

His lips part to answer me—then his eyes go wide in horror

and he clamps a hand over his mouth to rein in the words. "*No. I—I can't—*"

I can hardly hear him through the hand over his mouth.

He's loyal to his Queen. Not surprising, but irritating. Gently, I reach for his arm. Draw his hand away from his face. "You can." My silver eyes capture his. Hold them captive to my whim. "For *me*, you can." I sing another few notes.

The soft tune draws a shudder from my mark. The song washes away his inhibitions, shifting the tides of his loyalty from the former Queen to a new one. *Me.*

I watch it happen. *Taste* the moment the burning sweetness of his lust for me becomes overwhelming. The moment he's no longer a Keirdren soldier, but a toy for me to play with.

"Ikenna lied, didn't she?" I say again.

"Yes." There's no hesitation in his answer now.

"Thank you for your honesty," I say encouragingly. "I need you to keep being honest. You can do that, can't you?" I lay a hand on his arm. Rub it soothingly up and down. "*For me?*"

He doesn't waver. His eyes are completely glazed with desire. "Yes."

"Good. Does she know where the doorway is?"

"Yes."

I duck my head. My lips skim his cheek as I speak. "Do *you?*"

"Yes." He's so eager—so enraptured by me—he nearly falls over. I hold his arms, steadying him. The contact sets his heart careening faster. "It's where the Jeune River meets the barrier," he says. "The doorway was made with water magic. Only water fae can get through. Or," he amends, "a siren."

"How?"

"The barrier was created by a warlock. When he sealed it, he left a tear. It's too small to pass through. You have to use water to push it open large enough to enter. But it's unstable. Once it's open, you only have seconds to cross before it closes again."

Carrik's words from last night ring in my mind. "How do you get back?"

My mark shakes his head. "You can't. The gap in the barrier is only on the Keirdren side. It closes as soon as there's no more water holding it open."

Lune above, I wanted Carrik's words to be a lie. My brain spins with this new information, so I pace, half forgetting my mark is still here, with greedy eyes that follow my every move. "Is that all?" I ask.

"Er . . ."

A faint hint of old bread intertwines with the taste of my mark's desire for me. *Nerves.*

In an instant, I'm in front of him again. "What? There's something else Ikenna is hiding?"

"Her Majesty . . ." He hesitates. "Despises you."

I almost roll my eyes. I already know that. There's more he's holding back. I soften my gaze and sing again, louder this time.

His fragile resistance crumbles. "Her Majesty has a private audience with a warlock tonight," he blurts. "To discuss you."

"*Me?* What about me?"

"She plans to use magic to force you out of Keirdre. Permanently."

Is that even possible?

A few weeks ago, I'd have said no. Now . . . I don't know what to think.

Is Ikenna capable of using magic to get rid of me? Maybe. But why bother? She must know—or at least suspect—that Hayes is already planning on sending me to the other side. She doesn't need a warlock to send me away. The fastest way to get rid of me would have been to tell me where the doorway is instead of playing coy.

Before Larster's death, I never thought much of Ikenna. Never saw her as anything other than her husband's wife. It's clear now that while she didn't share her late husband's bed, she shared his dark and twisted soul. And, apparently, his hatred of sirens.

"You said this meeting is happening tonight?" I say. "When?"

"Midnight. At the pier."

I'm reeling. It's midnight *now*. Ikenna is speaking to a warlock about how to remove me from Keirdre right now. "Which pier?"

"The one used for His Highness's birthday celebration."

Of course. The *Sea Queen* is docked there. Freshly abandoned and perfect for clandestine conversations.

My mark watches me. "Please don't tell Her Majesty I told you."

"I won't. But I need you to promise me something in return."

"Anything."

"Don't tell anyone we spoke." Having one of Ikenna's guards at my disposal could be useful in the future. Especially if she's planning something.

My first instinct is to drop everything and race to the pier to eavesdrop on the rest of Ikenna's meeting. Except, if I do, Hayes will worry something's happened. For all the times I've lied to him, I feel I owe him this.

I give my mark a stern stare. "Promise me." My hand trails up the side of his arm. "You won't tell a soul we spoke."

His head bobs earnestly. "I won't tell anyone. I promise."

CHAPTER FIVE

BLOOD ON HER HANDS

The corridor outside Hayes's room is chaos. I'm around the corner, back against the wall, trying to stay hidden. Just barely, I peek my head around to peer down the hall. Dozens of fae soldiers dart around in a panic; human servants scuttle about, looking equally frantic.

A soldier's head pivots in my direction.

My hood is up, so he can't see my face, but I swiftly duck back around the corner anyway. Out of sight, perfectly still. My breathing is unsteady as I wait . . .

Seconds tick away. Nothing.

It's a minor relief. Why are there soldiers here? Hayes wouldn't have summoned them—he knows I'm meant to meet him in his chambers.

Something must've happened. My mark said Ikenna is meeting someone right now. Maybe whatever she's planning is tied to whatever has soldiers swarming Hayes's room like locusts.

Meeting Hayes is out of the question now. There's no way for me to get to him without being seen.

I have two options: go to the pier myself and intercept Ikenna's meeting, or return to my room. Patiently sit on my hands and wait for Hayes to fetch me.

Mind made, I push off from the wall and head down the corridor.

I duck into my room. Lock the door behind me. And, as I've done countless times before, climb out the window and scramble down the side of the Palace.

My feet know the route to the pier by heart. Memories of my last time here—delivering Hayes and a vial of luneweed to Laa'el and Spektryl, my heart shattering with Carrik's betrayal, watching him pitch Rain into the sea—slink to mind. I shove them aside.

Focus.

I crouch in the greenery about a dozen paces from the dock. I look around, searching for anything out of place. The *Sea Queen* is instantly recognizable, with its navy exterior and gold-scripted lettering that glimmers in the starlight. The ship sways in the gentle waves. The shadows it casts over the pier elongate and shrink as it rocks. The movement is calming. The water whispers to me. It's not an urge to kill—there's no one around *to* kill—just the ever-present desire to submerge myself in the waves.

I take a breath.

Focus.

The night is still. There's no sign of Ikenna or a warlock anywhere.

Suspicion wraps around me like a scratchy wool blanket. It's enough to quiet the water's singing. Was my mark lying? Or misinformed?

I'm about to give up and return to the Palace when a piercing scream splits the night.

My head jerks up, seeking the source.

I can't hear anything over my roaring heartbeat. My chest heaves as I look around, scanning . . .

All is quiet.

The pounding drums of my heart start to settle—

Another scream. Loud enough for me to identify where it's coming from—the *Sea Queen*.

I take half a tick to check my hood is still up before charging from the shrubbery, over the ship's gangplank, and onto the deck.

Wind whistles, water splashes, and the wood of the ship creaks. But no more screams. Once again, the night is deceptively calm.

Fear has my pulse sprinting and eyes glowing silver. There's no one on deck. There must be someone beneath me.

Water rankles my senses as I move across the deck, headed for the doorway that leads below.

A voice—scratch that, a moan—catches me off guard. It's low, pained, and getting louder as an unseen person approaches.

I stop. A figure stumbles through the doorway. It's too dark to see their features, but I see enough of their silhouette to know that one hand is pressed to their side.

They lurch for me, free hand outstretched, before collapsing with another groan.

Are they—?

The deck whines as I close the distance between us. My stomach is twisted into a knot so tight and heavy, I fear it'll sink through the ship and drown.

I'm close enough now to make out his face and—*lune above.*

My mark.

Thannen. Jeune told me his name and I brushed it off. At the time, it didn't matter.

He's alive, but barely. The hand against his side is painted red with his own blood. Beneath the hand, the fabric of his navy shirt is cut open. His eyes meet mine, wild and frantic. He tries to speak, but he only manages a gurgling sound.

Panic clamps my heart. I know that sound. He's been stabbed. His lungs are slowly pooling with blood. He can't breathe, and in a matter of minutes, he'll be dead. It's an excruciatingly painful way to die.

I know this—because I've killed men this way before.

Get out of here.

My instincts—common sense—hiss at me. I should listen. Run off the ship, retreat to the safety of my room in the Palace. Someone did this to Thannen, and judging by the freshness of the wound and recency of his screams, they're still here. But if I leave now, he'll die.

Maybe I'm selfish, but if he dies, the odds of getting answers grow slimmer.

I kneel beside him. "What happened?"

Again, he tries to speak, but the words are too garbled for me to understand.

He seizes my arm. The blood on his palm streaks my sleeve. He stares at me, eyes intense with some meaning I don't understand.

I tug up his shirt to get a better look at his wound.

I inhale sharply, horrified.

His flesh is torn apart. The bloody gashes stretch up his side, from his abdomen to his chest. My hands flutter uselessly. I try and press his shirt over his injuries to put pressure on the wounds, but there are so many. Too many.

Blood soaks through the shirt, staining my hands until they're coated. "Hang on." My voice trembles. "I'll find who did this—" I try to rise, but again, he grabs me. His grip is weak but his meaning is clear: *don't go.*

There's nothing I can do for him here other than sit at his side and wait for him to die, but I comply.

His eyes get more frantic. The hand on my arm pulls my palm to his chest. Lays it there, against his heart.

"I won't leave," I assure him, voice shaking.

Thannen grunts. The expression in his eyes is urgent. He's trying to tell me something, but I have no idea what. Still, I nod as though I understand. Stay crouched by his side as his grip—already loose—slackens. As the expression drains from his face until there's nothing left.

His head falls against the deck.

My bloodstained hands shake as I shove them against his neck. Nothing. No pulse.

With my hand on his neck, I sense something sloshing in his lungs.

I expected there would be blood in his lungs. But this is *water.*

I wipe my hands, slick with blood, on my dark pants as my mind spins. Thannen is dead. It was the stab wounds that killed him, but the water in his lungs means that *before* he was stabbed, someone tried to drown him.

Why? And how the hell did someone have time to kill Thannen two different ways since I last saw him?

Orange light floods the deck before I've come up with an answer.

I jerk to my feet, blinking rapidly as my eyes adjust. Chaeliss lanterns float over the ship, now lit.

I twist around when I hear a shrill shriek from my right.

A woman stands on the pier, hands over her mouth as she stares at me with wide, horrified eyes. When she sees my face, she shrieks again, longer and louder.

Dammit.

I pull up my hood, but it's too late. More people spill onto the docks.

I hear scattered shouts of, "That's her!" and, "Isn't that the siren?"

Above them all, here I am, standing over a dead body with the victim's blood on my hands, and, complicating everything, *there's water in his lungs.*

I look like a murderer.

Worse—I *am* a murderer—just not his.

There are only two ways off the ship. The gangplank, which leads to the hordes of screaming people on the pier, or over the side.

I don't fully trust myself to be submerged in the ocean with my nerves so jangled and so many people nearby, but I don't see another option.

The sea goads me to leap off the ship. It doesn't want me to flee. The water wants me to take hold of it and silence the voices of the crowd. Permanently.

I back away from the front of the ship. More bodies piling up is the last thing I need. I'll jump into the water—I have no other choice—but I will *not* give in. I'm going to swim away. No one else is going to die tonight.

The water snarls at me, and I back up farther. Leave Thannen lying in a pool of his own blood.

Every step is agonizing. I'm fighting my instincts and trying to ignore how desperate my body is for a kill. The water's soothing tune reminds me how easy it would be to lure the entire pier of onlookers convinced I'm a monster into the ocean and prove them right.

Hiss.

Something sails past me and embeds into the wood of the ship. A navy crossbow bolt with a solid gold tip.

I look behind me. Soldiers have joined the crowd on the docks, and they're charging at me.

I take swift inventory of the situation: the pins fastened to their chests indicate they work for the Palace. The crossbow bolt struck the ship a hairsbreadth away from me. These soldiers intend to take me captive—dead or alive.

The ocean is louder now. Its wrathful song demands I sing to the soldiers gaining on me. My head throbs as the sea churns violently, sending an angry, salty spray of dark water splashing onto the deck, drenching me.

Kill.

I raise myself on the ship's ledge, preparing to flee.

Another bolt sails at me, nicking my leg.

I tumble off the side of the ship, splashing into the water on the deck. I steady myself against the railing and hold my other hand to my leg. Warm blood drips down my thigh.

My eyes flash silver.

I'm soaked, furious, and *terrified*.

A deadly combination.

The ocean chants. Using the boiling kettle of my emotions to fuel my need to sate our mutual desires.

Kill.

I take a breath, hoping to steady myself. Instead, I taste cloves and cinnamon and *desire* sweet enough to burn. I'm surrounded by potential marks, and they all want me. The knowledge—the *taste*—is intoxicating.

Kill.

The water calls and I'm lost.

I spin, facing the oncoming soldiers. The closest one runs

over the gangplank. My lips part and the water's rage flows into a song of beautiful devastation.

The crowd gathered onshore goes still. Despite my Siren Song, the soldiers keep running.

I squint, wondering how . . .

Something white pokes out from their ears—cotton. To tune me out.

Panicked, I dart forward, take hold of the nearest soldier by the front of his shirt, and rip out the tuft of cotton. My song flows directly into his ear. It's more of a scream than a melody, but he melts all the same.

His hold on his crossbow loosens. I snatch it, along with the blade holstered around his hips. Meet his enchanted gaze. Jerk my head to the side of the ship. "Jump," I snarl. "Don't hold your breath."

He doesn't hesitate.

My blood boils. I'm impatient and so is the water. My actions are hardly my own as I don't wait for him to comply. I shove him overboard myself.

He splashes into the sea.

I lick my lips, tasting the last remnants of his want for me along with the salt of the ocean. My last tenuous grasp on sanity slips.

A more in-control Saoirse would follow him. Leave the ship before the others reach me. But my restraint has snapped and I feel alive for the first time in weeks.

I don't care that the soldiers can't hear me. I open my mouth and a song screeches out. The stolen crossbow and blade clatter to the deck. I ignore them in favor of another, more captivating weapon.

Holding out my hands, I *grab* seawater and *pull* it, drenching the remaining soldiers.

Someone staggers to my right.

Water coils, wrapping around him, squeezing him. With a screech dark as night, I clench the watery fist around him and *hurl* him over the side of the ship.

There's another soldier to my left.

A blast of water slams into him, pitching him into the sea as well.

The ocean roars in response, pleased.

A third soldier makes his way to me. Water surges into his face, right at his mouth and nose.

He chokes on it. Staggers away, trying to escape as water pours relentlessly down his throat and floods his lungs.

I'm too focused on drowning him. I don't notice the fourth soldier until he's upon me.

Arms encircle my waist and tackle me. My back thuds against the wood of the deck and my head slams after it. My head spins, so dizzily I don't react as he ties something around my wrists, ceasing my fight. Then he shoves something into my mouth, silencing my song, and wraps something around my eyes, obscuring my vision.

Water seeps into my clothes, soaking my skin, leaving my instincts feral. I writhe in his grasp as I try to get away. Other hands grab at me, hauling me to my feet.

My legs kick out. My bound hands keep me from lashing my attackers with more water. Despite my kicking, grunting, and shaking, I'm dragged away by unknown soldiers, completely powerless.

CHAPTER SIX

THE COST OF WAR

I keep track of every twist and turn my captors make. Mentally, I construct a map of where I'm being taken.

Ocean sounds fade as they drag me up the pier. We're greeted by Palace guards as we enter. Down the entry corridor, around a corner . . . I can't see where we are, but I take note of the shifting brilliance of the lights. Bright when we first entered, dimmer where we are now.

Up a flight of stairs. Then another.

My pulse thrums in my ears as my suspicions grow. I have a hunch where we are. With this revelation, tonight's events gain clarity.

Questioning Thannen, Hayes's room being surrounded by soldiers, finding Thannen on the deck, the water in his lungs . . .

Hinges squeal as a door opens, and I'm pulled through.

"You're late," a voice murmurs.

I stiffen. Not in surprise, but resignation—my hunch was correct.

"Apologies, Your Majesty. There was an incident at the pier," one of the soldiers holding me says.

"Untie the blindfold, arm yourselves, and remove the gag. Then leave us," says Ikenna.

Pause. Nobody moves.

The soldiers holding me reek of stale trepidation and throat-burning fear. They don't want to leave me alone with their Queen. Fair, considering all I want right now is to sing a song sweet enough to compel them to strike her down.

Ikenna sighs. "My personal guards are here. If she tries anything, they'll protect me. Leave us. We have private matters to discuss."

The blindfold is removed. It takes a few moments for my eyes to adjust to the light and focus on Ikenna.

She sits on a sofa, looking far too comfortable, wearing a wide, smug grin. "Nice to see you again."

The soldiers leave my hands bound but remove the gag before exiting.

"Don't bother singing," she says. "My guards are protected against your voice. One move from me and they'll kill you."

I figured as much. Ikenna is a thorn in my side, but she's not a fool. I take a moment to gather my bearings. I assume these are Ikenna's bedchambers. They're excessively large, just like Hayes's. Everything in here—the walls, the bedcovers, the furniture—is the same shade of cream and gold. A gold-framed portrait hangs over her bed depicting Ikenna, Larster, and Finnean, all smiles. As with the walls of her corridors, Hayes is nowhere to be found.

Ikenna lounges on a cream sofa dotted with gold pillows, watching me. Two guards stand behind her. Their ears are stuffed so they can't hear me, but their hands hover over their blades, ready to attack at a moment's notice.

I meet Ikenna's gaze and tip up my chin in defiance. I refuse to give her the satisfaction of seeing my fear. "You orchestrated this," I say. Thannen was in on it—part of it anyway. Ikenna must have conveniently left out the part where she planned to frame me for killing him.

"I did," she agrees. "But I mean you no harm."

I almost laugh. "Really? You can say that with a straight face after tonight?" Ikenna must've fabricated a disturbance to occupy Hayes. So I'd rush to the pier to apprehend her. So I'd find Thannen. So her guards could arrest me. I made every choice she predicted I would.

Hayes's words ring in my ears: *"Think of the last possible thing I'd want you to do—the most reckless thing you could possibly do."*

Apparently, my recklessness is so predictable, even Ikenna picked up on it.

She's still studying me. "I do not like you."

I scoff. "The feeling is mutual."

"But," she adds sharply, "I don't want you dead. I wouldn't mind—but it's not what I want. All I want is for you to leave Keirdre. Permanently."

If my arms were free, I'd cross them now. "Why?"

Ikenna quirks an eyebrow. "Haven't you guessed? My son is in love with you."

My heart stops—breath catches so suddenly I'm sure she notices.

Breathe.

Inhale through my nose, exhale from my mouth. Try and regain composure.

There was a time Hayes's feelings for me were obvious. Maybe not *love*, but he wanted me. He looked at me like I compelled the moon to glow. He tasted like cinnamon on fire— *lust*—whenever he looked at me. For anyone else, I had to show them my true face and sing to get that reaction. For Hayes, I did neither.

Now, he barely holds my gaze for more than a few ticks at a time, and all I taste when he looks at me is cold grief and bitter disappointment.

It's justified. I lied to him, over and over. Killed his best friend. Unwittingly assisted in a plot to have him assassinated. His distance is warranted, but it *aches*. He doesn't hate me. He chose not to, and I find myself wondering if it would be better if he did. Because hatred is at least *heat*. His coldness now hurts more than anything else.

Ikenna examines my reaction. I practically see her take out a pen and make a mental note. "You're surprised?"

Yes. But I'll never confess that to her. "Why am I here?"

"My son would bring down the barrier for you." She ignores my question just as I ignored hers. "Put the kingdom in jeopardy. Burn down everything his father and I worked to build. All for you." Her face is still, but the rapid rise and fall of her chest gives away her anger. "Would you do the same? Give up everything for my son?" She doesn't wait for an answer. "You wouldn't. Your ambivalence hasn't gone unnoticed."

Ambivalence. It's almost funny she believes that. I fought like hell to feel ambivalence for Hayes. Turns out, he's stubborn like a sodding ox and managed to tunnel his way into my heart. None of that is any of Ikenna's business. "For that, I deserve to die?"

"I already told you I have no intention of killing you."

"Maybe not personally, but in case you've forgotten, death is the penalty for my crimes."

She rolls her eyes. "Hayes isn't going to order your execution. As soon as he learns you've been arrested, he'll send you over the barrier to protect you."

I scramble to follow her logic. "You went through all this

just to send me over the barrier? I was already going to do that. You *know* that."

"Not forever. As I said, he'd bring down the barrier for you without thinking, regardless of the dangers on the other side. Because he's not willing to let you go. I'm offering you a way to protect yourself and your human."

Rain. It irks me that she refuses to use my sister's name. I hold it in.

"When you go to the other side," says Ikenna, "all you have to do is tell Hayes it's too dangerous to bring down the barrier. He'll listen."

"Why would I do that? Bringing down the barrier is my only way back."

"Yes. But if you do as I say, I'll make sure your human and parents join you." She crosses the room to her bedside table and pulls out a freya candle. "This is for you. A gift. I had it enchanted to work only for you. And you can *only* use it to communicate with me. When you're on the other side, after you've told Hayes he can't bring down the barrier, tell me. As a reward, I'll send over your family. The barrier stays up, you get your family. Everyone wins."

"Except I'd never see Hayes again."

"Don't pretend to care about my son."

I bristle with anger. Picture ripping her hair from her scalp as I say, "I'm not using your candle. But I'm happy to tell you where you can put it."

She ignores me and hands it to one of her guards. My hands are still bound, so I have no way to fend him off as he puts it into my pocket.

I glare at Ikenna. "I won't use it."

"Don't be difficult. You and I want the same thing."

"No, we don't."

"We want to prevent war between Keirdre and what lies beyond the barrier. I want to keep other creatures from invading my home, you want to protect your human. If there's war, make no mistake, she'll be caught in the fighting. I'll make sure of it."

I tense. "Are you threatening her?"

"Yes. But think about what happens if you're foolish. There's a war, Keirdre wins, and then what? The world knows about your family. They'll never live freely again. Your family will either die in the fight or die in the aftermath. I saw what happened the last time Keirdre fought the outside world—we won. If there's war, history will repeat itself."

"Keirdre didn't *win*," I say. "You just stole what you wanted, hid away, and shut everyone out so they couldn't fight back. If you're so confident Keirdre would win, why are you fighting so hard to prevent war?"

"All war has a cost. Even for the winners."

"*If* Keirdre won, Hayes would be King this time, not Larster. Hayes wouldn't let history repeat itself—he wants the same thing I do."

"What he wants is to be a good King. But he cares too much about you to do that effectively."

"Being a good King *is* what I want for him. You just think that means killing anyone you don't like. You're wrong."

"And *you* are a fool. Being King means making difficult choices. My son will never willingly make the choice to leave you—even if it's in the best interest of himself and this kingdom. So, you must make that choice for him. If not for him, then for your family. You can't protect them in this war. You know I'm right."

It's true that what I want more than anything is a better life for Rain. I have no idea if that's on the other side of the barrier, but if it is, I would absolutely fight like hell to get her there safely.

Even if it meant betraying Hayes again?

I've been pushing the question off for the past week. I think about Rain. The sweetest person I know. She's everything I'm not, and she deserves the world—just not this one. She deserves a world where she's happy, free, and doesn't have to hide. What wouldn't I do to give her that world?

Anything for you, Rain.

"Let's say I do as you ask—which I won't," I say slowly. "Am I supposed to trust you're going to keep your word?"

"You don't have to trust me. Trust that I despise you and want you out of Hayes's life. Trust that I know if I don't send your family to you, you'll retaliate. We don't like each other, but at the very least, we understand each other."

She's wrong. I don't understand. I don't understand why she's so intent on getting rid of me. Why she's suddenly acting protective of a son she doesn't even have a damned portrait of in her room. I meet her cold ocean eyes. "I don't trust or understand you. And I want nothing to do with you."

"Regardless." She smirks. "When you're on the other side, there will come a time when you'll see what your life could be, you'll realize you can't have that here, and you'll know I'm right. Then you'll use that candle and do as I say. Of that, I'm certain."

She motions to her guards and they open the door to allow the soldiers to swarm back into the room. She's still smirking as the blindfold and gag are tied around me once more and I'm dragged away.

CHAPTER SEVEN

LEASHED FREEDOM

My feet are as slow as my foggy mind as I'm dragged to our next destination. I don't bother struggling. I'm outnumbered, my hands are bound, and I can't sing. Fighting is futile.

Still, I'm listening for anything to give an indication of where they're taking me next. I'd assumed we were going straight to the dungeons in Haraya, but they're not leading me outside.

I hear two bangs in rapid succession—double doors thudding open.

I'm yanked through. Dragged farther.

A soft rap—one of my captors is knocking.

A muffled voice I can't quite hear through the door mumbles a response.

Squeal—hinges long overdue for a greasing.

I'm shoved forward. The hands holding me release me, but I still feel the soldiers behind me—hear their heavy breaths, taste their anticipation.

Then, my mouth floods with the rotting, curdled taste of horror. It's not coming from the soldiers who brought me here, but from whoever is in front of me.

The taste is so strong, it eviscerates everything else. As I'm drowning in this feeling, another emotion rises to the surface.

I run my tongue over the roof of my mouth to identify it. It's ice-cold but somehow burns the back of my throat—like accidentally taking a too-long swig of a cold, stiff drink. Like fear, but stronger. *Panic.*

With those conflicting emotions sitting on my tongue, I know exactly where I am, and I know who else is here even before he says, "What's this?" Hayes's voice is deceptively calm. There's an undercurrent of urgency, so faint you might miss it.

"The fugitive siren, Your Highness," says one of the soldiers. His tone is proud. I imagine him in my mind's eye, standing just behind me, chest puffed out, eagerly awaiting his King's approval.

"Majesty," Hayes says. Normally, when he makes this correction, his voice is stern. Now, he sounds distracted.

"Yes, of course," the soldier rushes to say. "Your Majesty, my apologies."

The silence is so thick, I feel it on my skin.

Through the tension, a different voice speaks. "What—what would you like us to do with her, Your Majesty?"

The panicked taste of Hayes's emotions swells. "Where did you find her?"

"The pier, sir. She killed one of the Queen's guards. As well as a group of Palace soldiers."

Pause. "You're sure?"

"Yes, sir. We saw it. We were too late to intervene."

Hayes's disappointment is familiar to me—pungent, like rotting fruit. Tasting it now hurts worse than the bloody wound on my thigh from the soldier's crossbow.

Hayes doesn't say anything for several seconds. The soldiers are dripping with discomfort, clearly wondering why Hayes isn't showering them in praise for their capture of the monstrous siren fugitive.

Finally, Hayes clears his throat. "Good. Well done. Take her to the dungeons. Cell 333."

I want him to say something else. Some hint to me as to what he's thinking. Instead, he says, "You're dismissed."

The soldiers pull me from the room and down more halls.

Cool night air nips at me as I'm taken out of the Palace and into a carriage. I'm still as the carriage rocks into motion.

I feel eyes on me. There's burning lust and smoky curiosity. "Can we at least take off the blindfold?" one of the soldiers asks. "I want to see her face clearly."

"Don't. I've heard stories about monsters like her."

"Oh, hush. She can't sing. And look at her—she can't be too dangerous, with a face like that."

"The blindfold stays, you lightbrain. You can see her just fine like this. I'm not risking losing her just to see a bit more of her face."

No one speaks again for the rest of the ride. They lead me into Haraya, down the stairs. The cell door whines as it's opened. They shove me inside and slam it shut.

"Hold out your arms."

I thrust my arms forward, maneuvering them around the metal bars in front of me. The pressure around my wrists loosens as the ropes slacken and fall away. I use my now-freed hands to remove the blindfold and gag.

After their conversation in the carriage, I'm unsurprised to see the soldiers watching me intently through the bars. "Don't even think about singing." The soldier nearest me gestures to his ears, as though I might've missed that they're stuffed with cotton. "We've prepared for you."

He can't expect me to answer—he wouldn't be able to hear—so I say nothing.

They're mesmerized, staring at me as though in a trance, but there's something else lacing the emotion—fear. They're as enchanted as they are afraid of what I'm capable of.

The soldier in front is the first to shake off his reverie and leave.

The second one gives me one last longing look before following suit.

I take a breath, relieved—

"You missed me that much, Sorkova?"

I'm startled by the instantly recognizable voice. In the cell diagonally across from me, looking smug enough to churn my insides like butter, is Carrik Solwey.

Of course. I hadn't questioned it, but Hayes knew *exactly* what cell to put me in. He chose the one across from Carrik.

Maybe this is his way of punishing me.

Carrik grins. "I take it your Prince was the one who locked you up?"

I roll my eyes and move away from the bars.

Carrik chuckles. "Fine. Your *King.* Happy? Will you tell me what you're doing here?" When I still don't answer, he sighs. "At least tell me what this is about. Are they going to execute you?"

"No. Hayes wouldn't let them kill me." My words are almost convincing enough to fool myself.

"Really?" Carrik's voice raises with anger. "And yet here you sit, in prison. *He* put you here."

At the sound of approaching footsteps and taste of peppery anger, my reply dies. I know who's approaching before he stands in front of my cell.

"What the hell were you thinking?" Hayes's eyes flash dangerously. My tongue catches the taste of his anger, fear, and—again—that bitter disappointment I've grown to hate. "You were supposed to talk to Thannen and come to me. The next thing I know, you're arrested."

He's never yelled at me before, and I'm mad at myself for fixating on that instead of his words. "The plan was to meet in your room," I say. "But there were soldiers everywhere."

"Your next logical step was to go to the pier alone?"

"Thannen told me the doorway's where the Jeune River meets the barrier in Kurr Valley. I thought that was it—but then he told me Ikenna was having a meeting with a warlock. He said she was planning some way to remove me from Keirdre permanently. I went to find you. There were soldiers in the corridor and I couldn't get to you without being seen. I didn't want to miss what she was up to, so I went alone."

Hayes frowns. "My mother was at the pier?"

"No. She set me up. When I got there, Thannen was dead."

"That doesn't make sense. Why would my mother set you up?"

"She hates me. Wants me out of Keirdre." The candle she gave me feels heavy in my pocket. Ikenna thinks I don't care about Hayes. That I would willingly betray him all over again by crossing the barrier and never coming back. Now is the moment to prove her wrong and tell him. I'm about to say it, but—

Anything for you, Rain.

I *despise* Ikenna, but she was right about one thing: Rain will always come first.

If I had to, for Rain, would I really abandon Hayes?

I want to be the kind of person who wouldn't. The kind of person who isn't capable of destroying the only boy I've ever wanted for my own selfish ends.

But I'm not that person. And I don't have an answer.

So, the candle stays in my pocket, and I stay quiet.

I'm not sure what Hayes sees in my face, but the harshness fades from his expression and he sighs. "I'm sorry. I shouldn't have raised my voice." He looks me over, brow creasing with concern. "How are you? Did they hurt you?"

"I'm fine." His concern is a salve to my bruised heart. "I'm sorry too. I was being reckless again."

"Don't apologize to him," Carrik grumbles.

Hayes rolls his eyes. "I don't remember asking for your input, Spektryl."

"Maybe not," Carrik says back. "But you're about to ask for my help."

I expect Hayes to correct him, but his face tightens and I'm left with the sinking feeling everyone here knows something I don't. "Your Majesty, what is he talking about?"

"He put you in a cell right across from me." I wasn't asking Carrik, but he answers anyway. "He must want something."

I look accusingly at Hayes. "What is he talking about?"

"I can't exactly unlock the cell and walk you out of here myself," says Hayes. "I'm going to help you break out so it can't be traced back to me. Spektryl's going to help."

I wait for him to crack a smile and confess this is all some unfunny jest.

He looks deadly serious.

"You want me to break out of Haraya with *Carrik*? And go where? Hide in the Palace?"

"Saoirse." Hayes shifts, looking uncomfortable. "You can't come back to the Palace. The kingdom's in an uproar. Once you escape, they're going to tear that place apart searching for you. They think you've finally been captured. They're expecting an execution. If you're in the Palace, I can't protect you."

Ikenna's words resurface. *"He'll send you over the barrier to protect you."*

She's a terrible mother and an even worse person, but apparently, she's better at anticipating Hayes's next moves than I am.

"You need to leave. Get out of Keirdre. As soon as possible." Hayes's voice cracks, and he squares his shoulders to disguise the slip. "This is what we planned. I'm just moving up the time line."

Sure, but there was a reason we established a time frame. For one thing, I still know next to nothing about the other side of the barrier. For another thing, there's still no way for me to come back. Drina is preparing the *nafini* to unlink lives from the barrier, but there's another few weeks before it's finished. Which means, for at least that long, I'll be stranded.

All of that isn't even the biggest issue. The scenario neither Hayes nor I have been brave enough to mention: *What if the other side isn't safe? What if I can't advise he bring down the barrier?*

Too many concerns to discuss now. I pick one: "Carrik wasn't part of the original plan."

Hayes's eyes flicker.

I raise my brows. "Or . . . was he?"

"He was part of *my* plan."

I'm teetering on the edge of franticness. His words give me an excuse to be angry, so I cling to that instead. It grounds me. Keeps me from falling into panic. "You didn't tell me?"

"I knew you'd react like this."

"Because I *hate* him."

"Maybe. But he doesn't hate you. Look, I have no affection for Spektryl, but I would protect you with my life, and I know he'll do the same."

I fold my arms, annoyed. "I can take care of myself."

"Bold words for someone who just got arrested."

"You think if Carrik was there, he would've stopped me?"

"This isn't a debate, Saoirse."

I scowl. "Someone's gotten used to his new role very quickly."

He sucks his teeth in exasperation. "Spektryl knows more about the other side than either of us. I have no idea how dangerous this is. If you're angry, fine. I can handle that. But I *can't* handle—" He breaks off, and the steel of his eyes is back. "I don't want to fight with you on this, but I will if I have to."

He's not going to back down. My fingers dig into my biceps hard enough to bruise. "*Fine.* How are we getting out of here?"

Hayes holds up something silver. It winks at me in the orange torchlight. A key.

I reach for it—he jerks it away.

My hand falls, jaw clenching in irritation. "You're being childish. What, you won't give me the key unless I swear I'll play nice with Carrik?"

"I'm not asking you to swear anything. You and Spektryl have different locks," he says. "*This* key will unlock Spektryl's cell." As he speaks, he slips the key through the bars and hands it to me. He procures another from his pocket. "And *this* one will unlock yours." He moves to Carrik's cell and hands him my key.

Hayes gives me a look. "Before you think about singing to him, consider that the moment he so much as hears a note, he'll slide that key away from you so neither of you can escape. I know you're stubborn, but please don't be foolish. Once you've taken care of the guards upstairs, there's a carriage waiting for you outside. Good luck."

I expect him to say goodbye and take his leave. Instead, he moves to Carrik's cell.

Carrik's expression grows wary as Hayes approaches. Warier still as Hayes grabs something from his pocket.

I don't see what it is right away. Just watch Carrik's jaw slacken as shock sets across his features.

Hayes moves his hand, and I see what it is. A dagger. As familiar to me as my own name. It belonged to Carrik's mother. The only thing he has left of her. He's kept it on him—tucked into a sheath on the side of his boot—for as long as I've known him.

My breath catches as Hayes holds it out through the bars. "I believe this belongs to you."

At first, Carrik doesn't move. Just stares, eyes misting. After a pause, his hand slides forward, slowly, as though waiting for Hayes to yank it back and laugh.

He doesn't.

Carrik's fingers wrap around the dagger, and I'm unprepared for the explosion of orange on my tongue. *Joy.* He snatches the dagger, eyes shooting from the weapon to Hayes and back in awed disbelief. Back and forth, so quick it's dizzying. "I— Your Majesty—"

"Please. Call me Hayes."

What the hell is going on? Since when does Hayes *like* Carrik?

Carrik tucks his dagger into the sheath on his boot. When he straightens, his expression has neutralized, but I still taste the brightness of the orange. "I—I don't know how to thank you."

"Don't." For a fractured moment, Hayes half turns to me, eyes softer than they were when we spoke. "Just keep her safe for me." He looks back to Carrik. "For *both* of us."

"You have my word. Hayes."

Hayes gives a single, firm nod. Turns and strides away without looking back at either of us.

Carrik's frozen. It takes him a moment to collect himself. When he does, his eyes shoot to me with a teasing grin. "Looks like we'll be seeing a lot more of each other." His tone doesn't match his eyes. He's tearing up, but he masks it well.

I glare. It's easier to be angry and irritated than scared over what's to come. "Give me the key."

He tuts at me. "C'mon, Sorkova. You don't really think I'm that lightbrained. You want this key, give me mine."

When my glare doesn't lessen, he sighs. His expression turns pleading. "Tell me what to do. What can I say to make this better? I can't apologize any more than I already have."

"I don't want you to apologize. You won't mean it."

"So, that's it?" I hate how my traitorous heart twinges at the sight of his crestfallen expression. "You're going to hate me forever?"

He says it as if he's the only one hurting. It's not like I *want* to hate him. Repelling someone from your heart is hard when they're a part of you. Hating Carrik hurts—but not as much as seeing the blood dotted on Rain's throat as he held a dagger against it. That's all I see whenever I so much as think of my former friend. "What did you expect? You went after my sister."

"I knew you wouldn't—"

"You know *nothing*." I'm angrier now. Angry at Carrik and this situation and *myself* for, even now, briefly caring that he's hurt.

Not hurt enough, a cruel part of me whispers. *Hurt him more.*

Rain's muffled shrieks as Carrik shoved her off that pier echo in my mind. Maybe it's vicious, but I don't care. I want to plunge a knife into his heart the way he did to my back, and twist and twist and twist until I don't despise us both.

"Understand this: I *hate* you. I want nothing to do with you. If I had my way, you'd rot in that cell. Apparently, I don't get a say. We're leaving here and crossing the barrier together. Fine. I accept that. But we aren't friends. You can't fix us. There aren't enough pieces left for you to put back together."

I've never seen the great Carrik Solwey look so small.

I thought it would make me feel better.

"I really am sorry," he says softly.

"And I really don't care. On the count of three, we'll slide our keys to each other. All right?"

He's radiating sadness so intense I have to grit my teeth against the urge to chatter. *"All right?"* I repeat, louder and more forcefully this time.

"Fine." He holds up his key. "One . . . two . . ."

"Three." I make as if to slide my key but don't release it.

Neither does Carrik.

I give him a look. "You didn't toss it."

He chuckles. "Neither did you." The chill from his sadness lingers, and his green eyes don't reflect the mirth of the laugh. "You might hate me, Sorkova, but I know you. I told you— you're not getting this key before I get mine. For real this time, on three."

I'm irritated but unsurprised. He *does* know me, and I didn't expect such a childish trick to work anyway. This time, when we count to three, I actually slide his key under the cell door and he does the same with mine.

I snag the flash of silver and insert the key into my lock, twisting it open as Carrik mirrors me on the other side.

Now we just have to find a way past the guards upstairs. The easy solution is singing. With a Siren Song, they'll move aside and let us exit—but then we'll only have a few minutes

before the spell wears off. Using water to render them unconscious is out of the question as well. We need more than a few
minutes to escape Haraya; we need enough time that they can't
easily follow after us.

Carrik waves his key in my face. "You can make a man follow you into the ocean. Think you could make them follow you
into a prison cell?"

Do I loathe him? Yes. That doesn't mean he's completely
void of good ideas. I toss him my key. "You'll wait here?"

He catches it. "Ready when you are."

I slink down the corridor and head up the stairs. I place my
hands on the door at the top and knock.

"Who's there?" a voice calls through the wood.

Good. If I can hear them, they can hear me. I start to sing.
Low and smooth, soft and sweet. I can't see them through the
door, but I taste the combined spice of their desire for me. "Let
me in?"

When the door is hastily yanked open, I resume my song.

There are two guards, both staring at me. My mouth stretches
into a wide smile as I keep singing. They taste like smoke, cloves,
and brown sugar. I lick my lips, savoring it. Hold out my hands.
"Come with me?"

They seize my hands eagerly as I guide them down the
stairs. I don't speak, just sing. They happily and clumsily trail
after me.

"Where are we going?" one of them asks when we reach the
base of the stairs.

I flash him a secret, sly smile. "Somewhere private."

His breathing picks up as his mind floods with possibilities.
Prisoners rush to the front of their cells to watch me as I

sing, just as enthralled as the guards. As we near Carrik waiting outside our former cells, I drop their hands.

Both guards' shoulders drop in disappointment. I reach for one. Loop my arms around his neck and sway. We dance in tune to the crests and swells of my song.

His disappointment flits away. He drowns in the swirling silver of my eyes and melodious hum of my voice. As we move together, I back him up until he's in my former cell. He doesn't react as I unwind my arms from his neck and close and lock the door. All he does is watch me with longing sweet enough to rot my teeth.

I turn to the next guard. Place my hands on his chest. Meet his eyes with my own. "You know what would make me happy?"

"Anything," he says immediately. "I'll do anything."

I lean up on my toes and hover my lips over his ear. "Walk back." My voice drops to a soothing whisper that rasps against the sensitive skin of his neck, eliciting a shudder. Hands still against his chest, I push. He's taller than me, bulkier too. But I don't need to push hard. He doesn't resist as we walk back and back until he's in Carrik's former cell.

Still doesn't resist as Carrik locks the cell door behind him as well.

I can't help a smirk. It's my second time escaping prison in two days, and I didn't even kill anyone.

CHAPTER EIGHT

BREAK ME A PROMISE

The carriage waiting for us is black. Usually, Royal carriages tout navy and gold—Keirdren colors—but ours is designed to meld with the night. It sits beneath a large tree, with dark curtains drawn over the windows. Its driver is Jeune, also decked in black.

Her eyes are dull from boredom, but they sharpen when she sees me and Carrik approach. Briefly, we make eye contact, and an unspoken greeting passes between us. I'm glad to see her, but we need to be silent and invisible—now isn't the time to speak.

I climb into the carriage, Carrik takes the bench across from me, and Jeune takes off the instant the door is closed. The carriage rattles as we move along. I feel Carrik's stare on my face so intensely, I'm tempted to peel open the curtains to avoid him. But I'm not a fool. My anger isn't enough to blot out common sense and risk being seen.

My solution: face forward in stony silence, staring at nothing.

He allows it for a few hoofbeats. Then groans as though it's been hours. "Are you truly going to pretend I'm not here?"

"I'm not pretending. I'm wishing."

"This wasn't *my* idea. Your Prince is the one who arranged it."

The reminder is as unnecessary as it is painful. Hayes planned for Carrik to accompany me all along and didn't tell me. I'm not being fair—I've lied to Hayes more times than either of us can count—but it's another thing between us that's changed, and I hate it. I ignore the twinge in my chest and keep quiet.

Carrik sighs dramatically. "Fine. We won't talk about your Prince. Do you have any idea where we're going?"

I shrug. I'm not sure where the carriage is taking us, but I have a dark inkling it's headed directly for the barrier. Hayes was furious with me earlier—was he furious enough to send me away without a proper goodbye? Without letting me see my family one last time?

A few weeks ago, I'd have immediately dismissed the thought. Now, I'm not sure. That uncertainty fills me with dread, heavy like sand.

I keep my face carefully impassive, but Carrik knows me well enough to sense the ebb and flow of my emotions. He must take pity on me, because he sighs again, looks away, and allows us to travel in peace.

Time passes like mist—it drifts by and I can feel it, but it's not tangible enough to grasp. By the time the carriage slows, it could've been hours or only a couple dozen minutes. One thing I'm certain of: we haven't traveled nearly far enough to have reached the barrier. My fear of Hayes casting me aside without a word lessens. Slightly.

The door opens just a smidge, and Jeune shoves two navy cloaks inside. Carrik and I tug them on and pull up our hoods before exiting the carriage.

We're somewhere near the border of Vanihail and Serington, stopped outside a small stone cottage with a thatched roof. The shutters are closed and there aren't any other houses around, just grass and spindly trees that cast our surroundings in dancing shadows.

Jeune leads us to the front door. "I'll be waiting outside." She keeps her voice low, as though we might be overheard by the wind. "We'll leave when you're ready." She draws a key from her pocket and holds the door for us to enter.

I'm the first inside and the first to be attacked.

"Pinecone!"

Rain's coarse pouf of hair is shoved into my eyes and mouth. Her arms tangle around me, and her shoulders shake—she's crying.

"Beansprout." Instinctively, I hug her even closer as I stagger into the house. She smells like tree sap and oranges. Like Rain. Like *home*.

My heart warms at the familiarity of my sister. For a moment, it's like nothing's changed. I close my eyes and we're back at the mill. I've just come home from the Barracks for a visit, and she's *safe*.

Tension unfurls from around my heart like a ribbon. Hayes let me say goodbye.

Gently, I set Rain on the floor. Her head is tilted back to look at me, tears trailing down her cheeks.

"Hey . . ." I squat and swipe at the tears under her eyes. "None of that crying. How are you? Are you all right?"

She sniffs. "I should be asking you that."

I'm fine. I open my mouth to feed her the familiar lie. Pause. I've spent my life hiding my problems from Rain. Forcing her to rely on me while refusing to do the same. I do it almost without thinking. But I'm leaving—possibly forever—and I want to be better. "I'm . . . tired. And frustrated. And scared. It's been a long night," I admit. "But I'm going to be fine."

"What happened?" Mom comes behind Rain and pulls me

close. I taste the cold ginger of her sorrow and feel her tears on my shoulder.

"Mom . . ." I sag against her.

"It isn't fair." Her voice is thick with tears. "You shouldn't have to go. You should stay here—"

"It's dangerous."

"Don't leave." Her hold tightens, as if she means to force me to stay with brute strength.

"What happened tonight?" My dad's voice is gruff, but I taste his anxiety and near-petrifying fear for me.

I release Mom and wring my hands together, unsure how to explain. "One of the Queen's guards was killed." I decide to tell them the truth for once. I'm leaving, and I want our parting to be honest. "They think I killed him."

Long silence.

"I didn't," I rush to add. "Someone framed me. I was ambushed by soldiers. They attacked and . . . I retaliated." I don't need to explain further. I can tell from their expressions they know I killed the soldiers who attacked me.

Part of me expects them to cower away, but my dad just moves in closer and hugs me. "Good."

I'm rigid with surprise. "You're not mad?"

"You're about to leave. It's a relief to know you can take care of yourself." He squeezes tighter. Lowers his voice so only I can hear. "Stay safe. Whatever it takes. I don't care what you have to do, just so long as you come home, Pinecone."

I bury my face in his shoulder. "I will."

Rain tugs on the back of my shirt to snag my attention. "You're coming back, right?"

"Yes. I just have to figure out what's on the other side of the barrier. Once I know it's safe, I'll see you again. You won't have to hide in a safe house. You won't have to hide at all."

"What if it's not safe?"

There it is. The question I don't know how to answer. "Then . . ." I look into her brown eyes. "I'll *make* it safe."

Or lie.

I want to be honest with my family, but that's one truth I keep to myself. If it comes down to a choice between lying to Hayes or never seeing my family again . . .

Anything for you, Rain.

I don't say that.

"Saoirse," says a different voice behind me.

The hairs on the back of my neck stand to attention. *Hayes.*

I half turn. He's near the door. I hadn't noticed him enter, but I'm relieved to see him. Relieved he wanted to say goodbye.

"Your Majesty," I say.

"Can I speak with you?" His tone is soft, but his words immediately set me on edge.

My throat is dry as I follow Hayes from the main room. It branches off into a narrow hall with two doors on either side. He leads me into the room on the right. It clearly hasn't been used in years. It's dusty and forgotten, with one curtained window. There's a sputtering hiss as a chaeliss light ignites above us. At the sudden brightness, I have to back up a step. Hayes is standing closer than I anticipated.

We're separated by a pace and a half and I feel every lick of distance. The light casts shadows over his perfect face. Draws attention to the sharpness of his cheekbones and jawline cut like glass. His emotions taste murky. I try and sift through them, sensing what he wants to discuss, but there are too

many—burning fear, stale anxiety, cold grief, metallic pain—
for me to pick out his intentions.

He's the one who requested a private word, but now he just
stares at me, not speaking and feeling so many things, he may as
well feel nothing at all.

Fine. If Hayes won't breach this silence, I will. "Why didn't
you tell me about Carrik?"

He looks startled, like he hadn't expected me to speak, before
his face goes blank again. "I didn't want to fight with you."

"Why send him at all?"

"To protect you." I hate how calm and matter-of-fact his
voice is.

"I can protect myself. And I *hate* him. So do you."

"I know. But he cares about you."

I cross my arms to give them something to do other than
strangle Hayes and his irritating, impassive face. "You barely
know him."

"I did some research. His father was arrested. Spektryl
used to write him letters in prison. I read them to see if he
mentioned anything useful about the Resistance or the other
side of the barrier—but he didn't talk to his father about that.
Would you like to guess what he wrote about?"

I don't trust myself to speak, so I settle for a shrug.

"You."

I'm surprised and I don't know what to do with my face.
"That doesn't mean I can trust him."

"You don't have to trust him with information, but he wasn't
pretending to care about you. And he knows more about the
other side than either of us. Use him as a resource. Nothing
more, nothing less."

I want to argue further. Still, as much as I despise Carrik, I can admit he likely knows more about the other side than he's let on. Having someone with a connection across the barrier could be useful. Begrudgingly, I nod. "Fine."

"Good. Take this." Hayes's face is still infuriatingly dispassionate as he hands me a scrap of parchment. I unfurl it. It's a series of runes—the *lairic* configuration Drina gave him so we can stay in contact while I'm on the other side.

"I already have it memorized." I try and hand it back to him.

"Keep it anyway. Just in case." He thrusts a bag into my hands. "And take this."

Only now do I realize that his hands aren't as steady as the rest of him. I don't comment as I peer inside the bag. Dried meats and fruit, a canteen of water, my *lairic* bracelet, and a stack of letters bound with cord. "You packed this for me?"

"Yes."

"Thank—"

"Don't thank me," he says. "I'm not finished. Remember, Y'ddrina still needs another three weeks to brew the *nafini* to unlink me and my mother from the barrier. You'll have to stay on the other side for at least that long."

He says this as though it's new information. As though we haven't gone over this already, time and time again. "I know."

"I've included the letters my father received from Reyshka," Hayes continues like he hasn't heard me. "Including the instructions for how to find her."

I nod. Something else I already know.

He lapses into silence again, staring at me. There's urgency in his eyes now, like he's waiting for *me* to do something. I try and guess what he wants from me. "I'll be careful."

A corner of his mouth lifts wryly. "No, you won't. You don't even know what 'careful' means." His teasing tone doesn't match his expression. Or the myriad of emotions battling for dominance on my tongue.

"Was that all, Your Majesty?" It seems ridiculous that this is possibly the last time we'll see each other and this is all we have to say. I was honest with my family. More so than I usually am. With Hayes, it's different. Honesty can't fix what's broken with us. I'm not sure anything can.

"Yes." He pauses. Shakes his head and starts to pace. "No. I—" The taste of his fear and worry build, overpowering the fury and grief.

Abruptly, he stops pacing. His eyes fix on a point over my shoulder. His back is rigid and his hands are fists at his sides. "I need you to be all right."

"I will be."

"Safe." Slowly, he drags his feet closer to me. "I need you to be safe."

"I will be," I say again, willing him to believe me. Willing myself to believe it.

He looks at my chin. More direct than before, but he still won't meet my eyes. He inhales. "You're reckless," he says softly. Moves closer. The air between us crackles, charged with a devastating energy that makes my palms sweat. "You take unnecessary risks. You're too headstrong for your own good. You have no regard for your own life. I'm *terrified* of you."

The admission sends a painful jolt through my already unsteady heart. He presses on. "More than that, I'm terrified *for* you. My biggest fear is that you'll—" Pause. "I shouldn't be this worried about you." His eyes are now trained on my nose, still refusing to meet my tremulous gaze. "I *can't* be this worried about you. I'm a King. I'm trying to ensure a peaceful transition of power.

Prove myself. I have an infinite number of things to be afraid of. But the only thing occupying my mind is— What if—"

"Nothing is going to happen." My arms encircle his waist, pleading for him to finally *look* at me. "I'm going to come back. I promise."

He steps out of my embrace. "You've broken promises to me before."

Slap. That's what it feels like. A strike across my face, hard enough to leave a Hayes-shaped mark.

I stagger back, reeling. He's right and I deserve it, but that doesn't mean I want it thrown in my face. Not now, when I'm preparing to leave and possibly never come back.

I curl my arms around myself, trying to restore the warmth he took. Trying to hold myself together. I built up what I thought were impenetrable defenses. But with Hayes . . . I let him slither behind them.

"I'm sorry." I sound small. "For everything."

"I know you are."

I expect him to relent. Wrap me up and whisper that despite everything, he's still Hayes. That he still wants me.

He doesn't.

Silence has never been this agonizing.

I blink rapidly, holding in tears. "We should go. Your Majesty." I turn for the door. Twist the handle, crack it open—

"Dammit."

I'm spun around. The door *slams* shut. Hayes's hands burn my waist, there's a door thrust into my back, and his lips are on mine.

There's nothing cold about this kiss. His lips are firm and demanding—like a King—but his hands at my sides are gentle and warm. Like Hayes. His lips part my own and his tongue dives into my mouth, seeking more from me. I gladly give it to him.

I've kissed before—my marks—and I've tasted emotions my entire life. I hadn't realized until now how subtle the rest of the world is in comparison to this. How muted and dull everything was before *Hayes*.

Everything about him—from the scintillating sensation of his lips on mine, to the spicy-sweet intensity of his desire for me, to the rapid pace of his heart I feel where his chest presses against mine—is a whirlwind and I can't get enough.

Faintly, I'm aware there's a door handle shoved into my spine, but it doesn't faze me. My senses are consumed by Hayes. My arms twist around his neck and tighten. His hands trail up my waist, caress my sides, trace a path over my shoulders, ghost the sensitive skin of my neck.

They stop at the juncture where my neck meets my jaw. His thumbs slip under my chin and tip my face up, bringing me even closer as he nips teasingly at my bottom lip—once, again, a third time—before his tongue glides back into my mouth.

We're breathing in tune with each other. The pressure on my chest is gone now, replaced with a burning that's sweet, savory, and intense all at once. I'm no stranger to desire, but in this moment, I'm drowning in it. Hayes's. My own. I can't tell them apart. I've never wanted anything as badly as I want him right now. To lose myself in his arms, his wandering hands, his *lips*. Our desire is an ocean and I'm happy to let myself be dragged under.

When he pulls back, too soon, he rests his forehead against mine. Our shallow breaths intertwine in the single gasp of air that separates us. His ocean eyes are wide open, drinking me in with that familiar longing I've missed. My tongue is on fire, both from the kiss that's left me scorched all over and the cinnamon-infused heat of his want for me.

My eyes dip to his lips again. *More.* I want more of him.

Before I can act on my impulses, he tucks a finger beneath my chin and tilts my head up. I'm forced to drag my gaze over his perfect face and meet those heady eyes.

"Come back to me." His words are an urgent whisper—a command.

I'm powerless to do anything but nod.

"Promise me."

"I—I promise."

He stares for a few ticks longer.

"You've broken promises to me before."

The words taunt me with their truth. I imagine he's thinking them now, remembering all my lies. Imagine him counting all the reasons he can't trust me, no matter how badly he wants me.

I expect him to say something else—maybe even kiss me again—but it's his turn to disappoint me. With a final nod, he's gone. Out the door, headed back to the main room like he didn't just shove me into a door and kiss me senseless.

My breathing is still ragged, my thoughts so scrambled I take a moment—*several*—to collect myself: feel my hair, braided around the crown of my head, to ensure it doesn't look out of place; smooth my rumpled shirt; press my palms to my face to cool my burning cheeks.

I still feel like a wreck when I finally exit the room to say my last goodbyes to my family.

CHAPTER NINE

JEUNE

The carriage rumbles away from the safe house, from my family, from Hayes, and from everything I've ever known. Carrik and I sit in silence. For once, it's not because I hate him but because I'm too busy holding in tears to try for conversation.

I think he senses how thin the thread holding me together is because, for once, he doesn't push.

The journey to the barrier is about a week—but only if you make good time. Our trail leads briefly through Serington and Phydan, but the bulk of our travels will be through Kurr Valley, the largest sector in Keirdre. Serington and Phydan are more densely packed and residential, so the first leg of our journey will be only by cover of night, to avoid being seen. Once we get to Kurr Valley, a wide, open sector of mostly farmland, we'll be free to ride during the day. Since Jeune is the only one of us who isn't a wanted criminal, she's the only one steering the carriage.

Which all means that the trip will be around ten days of travel with only Carrik Solwey for company.

The first day passes without a word. I use the time to collect my thoughts and take inventory of the carriage. It's stocked with the essentials: food to last the journey, canteens of water, the bag Hayes packed for me, and two freshly sharpened blades in case of emergency.

By the second day, I've gotten a firmer grasp on my sanity. Without looking at Carrik, I say, "Tell me about the other side. I'm assuming you left things out before?"

After a full day of zero interactions between us, he's clearly startled to hear me speak. "How are you? I know this must be difficult—"

"I'm fine," I say sharply. "I'll be better once you tell me if you've kept anything from me. Have you?"

"A bit." He looks sheepish. "Only because I didn't want to risk you finding some way to cross over and abandon me."

I'm completely unsurprised he lied. Again. "Well? What did you leave out?"

"I've been talking to a friend in the Resistance on the other side for years. They run a safe house—like the one you grew up in."

My heartbeat quickens. I try not to let myself get too excited. "Safe house for who?"

"For people fleeing Keirdre and seeking refuge on the other side. They have a lot of safe houses for creatures unwanted in Keirdre."

Unwanted creatures. The ones from the paintings in Larster's secret tower. I wonder how many creatures have successfully left Keirdre. How many of them are still on the other side?

The loudest question ringing in my mind like a tolling bell: *How many of them are sirens?*

I keep that one for myself. "How many of them are there?"

"I'm not sure. From what I've heard, it's a network that's been passed down for centuries. Generations of creatures making safe spaces for others. There could be hundreds." He answers the question I refuse to ask. "I don't know how many sirens. I didn't lie about that."

My hopes sink, but only a little. Just because he doesn't know doesn't mean they're not there. Hundreds of creatures thought to be extinct fled from Keirdre—odds are at least *one* of them is like me.

My tongue toys with the gap behind my false tooth as I temper my feelings. "What about the army?"

"I know it exists. And that it's ready. Standing by and waiting for the barrier to come down. Unfortunately, I have no idea how large it is."

I don't believe he's telling me the full truth, but he doesn't taste guilty like I'd expect if he was hiding something, nor does he taste anxious like he's worried I'll catch him in a lie. I guess it doesn't prove anything. Carrik spent years lying to my face, not feeling guilty at all. "Do they know Larster is dead?"

"I'm not sure. I didn't tell them—I've been locked up since it happened—but someone else in the Resistance probably did." He pauses to crook an expectant eyebrow. "Your turn."

"My turn to what?"

"Your Prince told me there are Keirdren soldiers on the other side and you're going to find them. Why are they there?"

I frown. "When did you talk to Hayes?"

"While you were saying goodbye to your family. Don't change the subject—tell me about the Keirdrens."

I consider not answering until he adds, "We can either talk about this *or* I can speculate about the state of your clothes after you spoke to your Prince in private at the safe house."

My face burns and I scowl to hide it. "I don't know anything about the other side. Larster never told Hayes. I have to figure it out when we get there."

"Perfect. I can help you," says Carrik.

He can't be serious. "I'll manage on my own."

"Your Prince wanted me to help, remember?"

My eyes roll. "First, he's not *my* Prince. Second, he's a King, not a Prince. Third, I don't take orders from him. Fourth, he only sent you to make sure I don't die. And fifth, I *hate* you—I don't need or want your help, Spektryl."

Carrik flinches but, to his credit, doesn't argue with me for the rest of the day.

Days pass slowly when you're trapped in a too-small carriage with a travel companion you detest. Carrik often tries sparking up conversation to pass the time, but I ignore him. There's nothing to say that hasn't already been said.

I take the time to review the letters Larster received from Reyshka. *Again.* At this point, I could probably recite them word for word, with every sodding comma in the right place. Still, it's a better pastime than talking to Carrik.

While rereading, I devise a strategy. It's clear from the dates on the letters Reyshka was used to talking to Larster fairly often. Since Larster is her primary contact with Keirdre, she probably doesn't know he's dead. I see no reason to tell her. When I find her, I'll need a plausible explanation for Larster's silence for the past few weeks and a way to earn her trust so I can pry information from her to feed to Hayes.

I have a plan. Tentative and flawed, but I'm going to make it work.

By the end of the ninth day of travel, I'm so bored, my eyes are drooping. I inhale, taking in the scents of harvest season outside. My favorite time of year. At the Barracks, I'd sit next to Carrik at his gate post and we'd watch the trees change colors. At home, Rain and I would gather leaves into a giant pile and jump into it. We got leaves and dirt and tiny twigs stuck in our hair and clothes, and my mom would pretend to be angry but she was always smiling.

Harvest reminds me of home, but I can't stare out the window to watch because we can't risk being seen.

My head rests aimlessly against the seat. We're in one of those rare moments when Carrik is sleeping and not trying to capture my attention. His head bobs against the carriage door, unbothered by the way it rattles as we move.

When he's like this, expression empty and vulnerable with sleep, it's easy to pretend nothing's changed. Remember him as it used to be. When we'd battle sleep in the early mornings for *one* more minute of meaningless conversation that felt really important at the time; *one* more round of sparring, not because we needed the practice, but because we enjoyed each other's company. Because he was worth the exhaustion. Because even though I was lying to him (and apparently, he was lying to me as well), he always managed to make me feel like myself.

I try not to dwell on those memories. They're clear as polished glass but covered in tiny fractures—dotted with the cracks of what I know now. Forever altered, forever fractured. There's no getting them back to what they used to be.

The carriage comes to a sudden halt, jostling me from my thoughts.

Carrik's eyes fly open as he sits up, immediately on alert. "What—"

A shrill, startled whinny from the horse pulling our carriage.

Carrik and I freeze as we listen to what's happening outside.

Crunching leaves, getting louder with someone's approach.

My hand slips under my bench, grabbing hold of a blade. Carrik reaches for the dagger strapped to his boot.

The door is wrenched open.

I raise my sword—but stop when I see it's Jeune. My relief dies when I note how frazzled she looks. Blue eyes frantic, breaths heavy.

I tense. "What's wrong?"

"Grab your stuff. You need to get out of here." She speaks so quickly, her words trip over each other. "Follow the river— you'll get to the barrier in a day's travel if you hurry—but right now, you just need to *run*. Avoid the fields, hide in the trees. It's getting dark, they won't see you there."

I'm trying to understand the reason behind her frenzied words as I follow her instructions and snatch the bag Hayes packed from beneath the seat. "Why—"

"Get out of the carriage!" a gruff voice yells.

Jeune scowls. "Soldiers," she mutters to me. "There's a barricade in the road up ahead. It's getting dark, so I didn't see it until now. They're inspecting carriages. You need to leave. Quickly."

Inspecting carriages? What are they looking for?

My first thought: *me*. I'm a fugitive, I recently fled prison, and I'm a siren—all punishable offenses.

"I said *get out!*" the voice roars again.

I pull up my hood and tumble out of the carriage, hands raised, palms out. Behind me, I hear Carrik do the same.

"Don't sing." Jeune is still speaking quickly, voice low. She's facing the soldiers and not looking at me, but the direction of her words is clear. "No one can know you're here. If anyone discovers a King's guard helped a siren escape, this'll end badly for Hayes."

I count the soldiers up ahead—three. They're on horseback, spread out to block the road. They each have pins fastened to their chests, marking them as soldiers who work for Enforcers. Except Enforcers are supposed to answer to the King. They can't authorize searches and raids without his permission, and there's no way Hayes approved a search of this scale knowing we're trying to escape Keirdre—so who the hell are these soldiers working for?

"Is there a problem?" Jeune raises her voice to address the soldiers.

"Identify yourselves." The lead soldier ignores Jeune and looks between me and Carrik. "Lower your hoods. And step away from the carriage."

I glance around, taking notes on my surroundings. As Jeune said, the sun is slowly setting over the horizon. There's still fading sunlight, but not much. We're on a dirt road, dotted with overgrown browning grass and fallen leaves. To our right, the fields stretch as far as my eyes can detect. To my left, densely packed trees. Over it all, I hear the rush of crashing water coming from the tree line—the river is nearby.

The soldiers carry blades, not crossbows or any other weapons of distance. With a brief distraction and a sprint, Carrik and I can make it to the trees before they attack.

"Have we done something wrong?" asks Jeune calmly.

"We're searching all passing carriages," the soldier in the

center of the barricade says. "We are authorized by the Enforcer of Kurr Valley—"

As the soldier speaks, Jeune grabs her blade and slashes forward, feinting an attack.

They startle. At the sudden assault, the three soldiers shift their attention to fending off Jeune. It's only for a moment, but it's all I need to snag Carrik's sleeve and run. We race to the left, veering into the trees.

I hear a shout as a soldier calls after us, but it's cut short by the clang of steel—Jeune.

Trees, clouds, and the darkening sky make the ground impossible to see, so I stumble against the brambles underfoot, but I don't fall.

Behind us, I hear metal striking metal and a furious screech. Is it Jeune? One of the soldiers? The uncertainty twists me up with panic. Jeune is a skilled warrior, and I have every confidence in her abilities—but she's one person against three.

My instincts want me to turn back for her, but Jeune was right. No one can know that a King's guard aided the escape of two of Keirdre's most wanted. Revealing ourselves would jeopardize Hayes and his already unsteady ascent to power.

"Do you know where we're going?" asks Carrik.

"Right now, our destination is *away*," I say. "But if we follow the river, we'll reach the edge."

"What about your friend?"

"She'll be fine." I speak with more confidence than I feel. Even skilled soldiers would break a sweat fighting off three assailants. Even if Jeune manages, she still has a long journey back to Vanihail ahead of her. I'll have no idea if she's made it back safely for at least a week. Add that to the fact that she has a family—a wife who's no doubt out of her mind with worry.

I don't reveal any of my fears to Carrik. I swallow them, tune out my thoughts, and move faster.

Even though I turn off my churning thoughts, I can't ignore the feeling of guilt gnawing at me from the inside out that we left her behind.

CHAPTER TEN

DEADLY ECHO

Years of training have crafted me into a near-perfect soldier. I can run for hours without becoming winded, navigate forests in the dark without getting lost, and kill a man with a smile and a song—but lune above, I hate hills.

The terrain around this part of the Jeune River isn't designed for trekking. The weeds and tree roots are skinny and numerous. They gather underfoot into clumps at *just* the right height to be aggravating. But all of that is fine. The *real* challenge is this damned incline. I've always hated hills, but this one is ridiculously steep and hasn't let up for hours.

We trudge along the marshy riverbank, exhausted. The flowing river is as much an asset as it is a curse. On one hand, the light spray of water that occasionally splashes me keeps up my energy. On the other, I'm irritable from the hill, furious with Carrik, and anxious about Jeune. The combination has my instincts desperate to lash out. A problem, considering the only nearby target is Carrik.

Normally, I'd jump at the chance to kill him, especially here, away from witnesses and Hayes's disappointment. But he's my only connection to the safe house on the other side. My hope for more of me—more sirens—is tantalizing enough that even I have to admit killing him is a bad idea.

"Any idea how long we've been walking?" asks Carrik.

It's not a ridiculous question, but I'm tired and I've grown to hate the sound of his voice, so I scowl. "No."

"Your Prince didn't include a timepiece in that bag?"

The only thing close to a timepiece I have is that freya candle Ikenna gave me, but there's no chance I'm showing that to Carrik. "We'll get there soon enough." Still annoyed, I say, "And I caught that."

"Caught what?" I can tell from his tone that he knows what I'm talking about.

"You called him a Prince again. He's a King."

"Not mine."

The harvest air is chilly, but I pull off my navy cloak and shove it into my bag. I'm generating enough warmth from hiking that I don't need the extra heat, and we're so far away from a walkable path and other people, I'm no longer afraid of being seen. "I don't understand why you hate him. He's the reason you're not in prison facing execution. And he returned your mother's dagger."

"That wasn't kindness. He did it so I could better protect *you*."

I roll my eyes. "You're childish."

"For what? Hating him? Until a few weeks ago, you hated him too, remember? And don't forget—he hates me as well."

I bite my tongue against the urge to point out that Carrik essentially saying "but he started it" doesn't make him any less of a child. "In his defense, you spent the last several years plotting to have him killed. Meanwhile, you only hate him because you hated his father. They're different people."

"Are they? He hasn't proved that. What has he done as King that's different from his father? The barrier is still here."

"Because *you* told him about the army on the other side waiting to kill him and the rest of Keirdre."

"Keirdre *should* die. It's corrupted from the inside out. A good King would see that. If you were honest with yourself, so would you."

There's no point having this same foolish argument again. I glare and keep marching, no longer engaging.

I'm closer to the other side of the barrier than I've ever been. With each step, the terror and exhilaration build.

Terror: I don't know what to expect. No idea if I can return home. No idea if whatever is on the other side wants me dead.

Exhilaration: I've got a chance at a world better than the only one I've ever known. A chance to *finally* learn about where I come from. A home for me and Rain. A safe haven for those hunted since Larster's creature culling.

I'm lost in thought, moving mindlessly, when suddenly, my foot *stops*.

I can see the river winding ahead of us, but my foot can't move forward.

"What's wrong?" I taste a wave of concern as Carrik rushes to my side, wondering why I've stopped.

I don't answer. Just slowly reach a hand forward. Like my foot, it *stops* in front of me. There's something here. I can't see it, but it *feels* solid—like a wall. "I think we're here."

It's like a veil lifts from Carrik's face. He lights up with boyish excitement, a wide smile splitting his face open. He shoves out his hands and runs them over the barrier. They move back and forth, his expression getting brighter each time. "We're standing at the edge of a new world, Saoirse." His voice is hushed, and he looks at me with the widest smile I've ever seen, green eyes alight with eagerness.

His enthusiasm is infectious. It coats the back of my throat, sweet like the berry wine the fae drink, sharp like lemon zest, and laced with orange-flavored happiness. *Feeling* his joy like this, I can't help it—I grin back at him, despite myself.

I pictured the barrier as something dark. Maybe gray like smoke or pitch-black like Larster's heart. It's not. It's more like a large painting. I see the same river, the same trees, the same marshy grass ahead of me in an illusion that melds so seamlessly with the rest of Keirdre, I only see it now because I physically can't move past it.

Carrik steps away from the barrier and looks to me, still buzzing. "How do we get over?"

My stomach is twisted like gnarled tree roots. For two weeks I've known I'm leaving Keirdre, but actually standing here, at the barrier, it feels real. Endless and permanent and terrifying.

"There's a gap where the river meets the barrier." Somehow, my voice is steady. "It's really small. We have to feed water through and open it up."

Carrik hums in acknowledgment, and our eyes skirt along the barrier, searching, searching, searching . . .

I'm not sure what we're looking for until I see it. It's a speck. A minuscule blemish that's not like the rest of the wall. It's blank. Not black, not gray, just . . . empty. It's half a pace to the right of the river, at knee height.

"There." I tug Carrik to stand next to me, pointing to the blank space.

He squints. "It's small."

"I told you it was going to be small."

"Well, it's smaller than I expected."

It's smaller than I expected too. Only slightly bigger than my thumbnail. Still, I can't help goading him. "Are you saying the great Carrik Solwey can't manage?"

"Oh, I can manage."

"Prove it." I set my feet hip-width apart and hold out my arms. A trick to help me focus my affinity.

Carrik mimics my stance. His emotions are still zesty and sweet—*eager*.

Together, we *pull* water from the rushing river and slam it against the barrier. I feel each drop of water. Feel how much of it uselessly hits the invisible wall to slide down, back into Keirdre. Feel the thin trickle that actually slips through.

I take another breath. *Focus.* This time, I channel the water faster and harsher to make my aim more precise.

More water makes it through the barrier the second time.

Good.

The satisfaction evaporates almost instantly. More water moved through the barrier, but the opening is still just as small as it was before.

Attempt number three: as the water glides through the opening, I *shove* it, pushing outward so it presses against the doorway, opening it wider. I feel the gap expanding. The change is meager at best, but enough that I feel the difference.

We push harder, shoving water more forcefully against the barrier.

It takes several minutes of this for me to realize what's taking so long—and why weariness is starting to sneak in: the barrier is pushing back. For every smidge of width we steal, the doorway fights us, robbing us of our minimal progress.

Sweat beads on my brow. Using my affinity doesn't usually drain me, but the barrier is a worthy opponent. From the corner of my eyes, I see Carrik looks as exhausted as I feel. As though he senses my gaze on him, his eyes shift to me.

In that brief instant of slipped focus, the gap shrivels up again. We're back to where we started.

"Dammit." My arms fall.

Carrik is out of breath. "We need more force. It's like the barrier doesn't want us to get out."

Considering the barrier is a manifestation of King Larster, Carrik's probably not too far off. Even from beyond the grave, Larster is a nuisance.

I hold up my hands. "Let's try again."

Carrik doesn't move. Just studies me through narrowed eyes.

My arms lower. "What?"

"You're holding back. Right now, you're matching me. But you're stronger than me. You're a siren, and I know what you managed on the pier."

I'm hot from exertion, but his words douse me in sobering, icy water. The pier was different. It was a release of years of pent-up rage and fear. And I *sang*. Which, for me, is always dangerous. I was a single strand away from losing control.

Still, Carrik is half-right: When I sing, the water doesn't just do as I command, it wants to move with me. But there's a drawback. When I sing, it's not just *my* song—it's a deadly echo. I sing, the water bends, yes, but it sings back. We fall under mutual spells of manipulation, and when our wills intertwine, I can't foresee which of us is more compelling.

"You don't want me to sing," I say. "I could kill you. Anger and hatred are a deadly combination."

"You have more control than you think."

"You know that from what? Reading a few books about sirens? Asking your friends in the Resistance?" I'm tense, and the water feels it. It likes the challenge, and we're both twitching to prove Carrik's confidence in me wrong.

"Not from books, from *you*. You're a top-ranked Delta from the Vanihailian Barracks. That takes discipline. You spent eight years in control."

"I wasn't." I shake my head. "You have no idea how many times I let my instincts win."

"What about the pier? You were in control then."

Just barely. And even still, less than two weeks ago, the night Thannen died, I was back at that same pier, on that same ship, out of control once again. "The pier was an anomaly."

Carrik rolls his eyes in exasperation. "Your entire existence is an anomaly."

I hesitate.

"Saoirse." He softens. "I *need* to see the other side. I need to know there's something more than this. I need to see that someone who grew up unwanted, told they aren't meant to exist, can have better. This world is cruel and unforgiving, and it took *everything* from me. You're worried you might accidentally kill me, but I don't care. I've already lost you—what else do I have to lose?"

I give him a look. "Carrik—"

"Just once, I want to be somewhere I'm wanted. I'm willing to risk my life for that. What are you willing to risk?"

Anything. For Rain to have better—for *me* to have better— it's worth anything.

My hands are shaking. "All right . . ." I keep my voice still despite how rattled I feel. "Plug your ears, just in case. If I try and kill you, don't let me."

"Saoirse." Carrik puts a hand over his heart with a smirk. "Your concern is touching."

"The only thing 'touching' is how mad you're going to be that you risked everything to get over the barrier only to die right before," I snap. "Plug your damn ears, Spektryl. If you hear me, you'll do what I want. And what *I* want is for you to go headfirst into the river and never resurface."

Carrik tugs at the bottom of his shirt and tears off a strip. He yanks it in two, shoving one end in each ear.

"Can you hear me?"

He doesn't react. Good.

With a steadying breath, I step into the flow of the river. Stop as the water rushes around my ankles. A tightness I hadn't realized I was carrying floats away with the feeling of bliss that comes from the water on my skin.

The sweetness of Carrik's excitement lingers, now joined by the rank taste of nerves. For all his talk of welcoming death for a glimpse of the other side, he's anxious.

The water starts a thrum in the back of my head. Wanting me to act on my impulses. Carrik stands close. Eyes closed, not even looking at me. I could grab him. Wrap my arms around him. Drag him under the stream . . .

I dunk the thought underwater and hold it there to drown.

Raising my arms, I *pull* the river and my lips part. A song rushes out. The release fills me with warmth and newfound energy. I *shove* the water into the barrier.

My song raises. The water isn't fighting me, it's moving with me, rushing up, faster than before. This song is *to* the water, *to* the river, and it listens to me.

I'm aware of Carrik standing just a few paces away. The water whispers, it wants me to—

No.

Like on the pier, this is enough. The euphoria of moving

with the water. It has its own kind of beauty. Killing Carrik won't make it any sweeter.

There's a safe house on the other side. Carrik knows where it is. There's an army on the other side. Carrik has a connection. As long as he's useful, I'm going to keep him alive.

I give the order to expand. The water obeys. I tell the water to *fight* the barrier as it tries to close again. It obeys.

My song grows louder, and the gap grows with it until it's so tall, it's big enough for a person to fit through.

I tear my gaze from the barrier and look at Carrik. His eyes are open now, wide as he stares at me.

"*Go!*" I motion for him to move.

Carrik shudders as he rips his gaze from me and tumbles through the open doorway.

I keep forcing water through the gap as I hurtle toward the opening. My hold loosens with each step I take. I feel the doorway closing, getting steadily smaller.

With a final screech, the water lashes outward and the gap parts, one last time, as I dive forward.

The opening seals itself the instant I'm through.

I tumble to the forest ground on the other side just as the doorway closes, leaving me and Carrik alone in a new world with no way to return home.

CHAPTER ELEVEN

THE WORLD WE LEFT BEHIND

I try not to be disappointed that, at first glance, the other side of the barrier looks exactly like the world we left behind. Same clusters of trees shrouding us in shades of green, red, and orange. Same sky, pale yellow streaked with the soft pink hues of dawn. Same river flowing alongside me.

I rise, brushing dirt from my wet clothes as I do. Carrik is already standing, neck craned as he peers around, taking everything in. "It smells better over here," he says.

I inhale before I can stop myself. "Liar. It smells exactly the same."

"But for a moment, I fooled you, didn't I?" He grins, looking so eager, he's bouncing on the soles of his feet. "I can't believe we're *here*. I wished over and over I'd get here, but I never actually thought I would." He holds out his hands. The water coating us flings away, leaving us dry. "I was told the safe house is in a city. I don't know how to get there from here."

We're surrounded by forest on all sides. All I hear is the river, no sounds of civilization. I pull my navy cloak from my bag and sling it around my shoulders, tugging up my hood. I don't see people yet, but I don't know how secluded we are. If we run into someone, I'm not sure what their reaction will be to

seeing my face. "Well. The barrier is behind us. Let's go forward. See if we find anything."

"Works for me."

The forest is eerily quiet. Just trees as far as my eye can see.
Carrik and I walk without speaking for a few minutes before I
feel pressure on my hip. Glancing down, I see a branch extend-
ing from a nearby tree, twisting into my bag.

Moving swiftly, I snatch the branch.

Magic.

My head twists around, searching for a witch, or some other
kind of magic-wielding creature, as my hand prepares to snap
the branch in half—

"Wait!"

I freeze, startled by the sudden voice. I keep looking around,
but I don't see anything except for Carrik, a bunch of trees, and—

I shriek.

A *face* emerges from the bark of the tree to my right. A girl's
face, younger than me. Her skin is the exact same shade as the
wood, with the same grooves and ridges as the bark carved into
her skin. As I watch, her face moves forward farther until she
has a full head with a neck that stretches out, connecting her to
the trunk. Her hair sticks out from her head at the same angles
as the branches, darker than the tree's leaves but with the same
undertones. The result is a pouf of hair with varying shades of
orange and red so muted, they're almost brown.

My racing heart calms as I recognize what she must be: a
dryad.

For a tick I'm excited—my first dryad. Rain will be thrilled
when I tell her.

The moment dulls when I remember she's currently trying
to steal from me.

The branch that tried to reach into my bag—still in my grasp—has shifted into an elongated arm with twiglike fingers.

The girl's wide forest-green eyes snap from me to the branch—arm—I'm holding, and back. "Please don't break it. It'll take forever to grow back."

If she were a bit older, I'd snap it anyway, but her age gives me pause. "I'll consider it . . . ," I say slowly. "First, tell me what the hell you were doing."

"I'm sorry!" Her voice is a squeak. "I didn't think you'd fight back. You looked lost."

An odd defense. She only tried to steal from me because she thought I was an easy target. "There's nothing for you in here." I gesture to my bag. "How often do you steal from strangers in the forest?"

"We don't get too many visitors." She looks at her hand. "Please. Let me go? You have a firm grip."

"You were half-right." I ignore her request for now. "We're a bit turned around. We're trying to get back to the city."

"Pennex?"

I have no idea what the city is called, but I figure if she suggested it, it must be the closest one. "Yes."

"Sure, sure, it's no problem. I can take you to Pennex—and you'll let go of my arm?"

"I might. But I'm warning you—try to steal from me again and I'll snap both of them off."

"I won't," she says quickly. "Promise. I didn't think you'd miss anything. That cloak . . . it looks like fine quality." Her eyes widen. "Where'd you get it?"

Something in her tone has me on edge. The way she widened her eyes . . . I recognize that look. Rain makes the same one to make herself seem innocent when she's about to do something I won't like.

"You couldn't afford it."

She steps away from the tree, into a full person. Away from the tree, she's smaller—she comes up to my shoulders. I motion her forward. "Lead the way."

"Of course." She casts a wary look at the blade around my waist. "Where did you say you come from?" she asks as she leads us through the trees.

I glance around, wondering how many of the trees we pass are dryads and how many of them are listening to us. "We didn't."

"Is this your first time in Pennex? Where'd you come from, Calamid? Wystmeren? We don't really get too many people in the forest."

"Why not?" asks Carrik.

She looks surprised. "Because of the barricade, of course. Nobody wants to get too close. They say Keirdrens sneak over and filch your stuff when you're not looking." Her tone is light, like she's teasing.

"You sure they're not talking about you?" I ask wryly.

She pouts. "I hardly ever steal anything. I just figured you looked wealthy and clueless."

"Who's 'they'?" asks Carrik. "You said 'they' say Keirdrens come over the barrier?"

"Why? You worried?" She giggles. "It's just a myth. I think they say it to keep people away from the barricade."

Like the stories they tell back in Keirdre about Reyshka Harker. That she was too curious about the barrier and it consumed her. It seems the stories here are somewhat based in truth as well.

We reach the end of the tree line. We stand at the edge of a grassy valley. Sitting in the mouth of the valley is a city. Small buildings cramped together, with one larger structure in the middle. It's bigger than any of the other buildings I can see from here, but in Keirdre it would be the size of a typical manor house a wealthy Vanihailian water fae might live in.

The dryad gestures forward. "Here you are. Next time you wander out of the city, I recommend you bring a map." She looks pointedly at my hand, still gripping her branch-like arm. "Can you let me go now?"

Finally, I release her. The branch immediately shrinks into an arm. She sighs, looking relieved. "Welcome to Pennex, travelers." With a flash of a smile, the dryad disappears back into the woods without another word to us.

CHAPTER TWELVE

QUEEN OF HIS HEART

People are staring. My face is hidden by my hood, but still Carrik and I attract attention as we weave through the streets of the city. Pennex, the dryad in the woods called it.

Unlike the tall, imposing buildings of Vanihail, with cobblestoned streets, everything here is small. Each building looks domestic, like a house, and they're all neatly arranged in tight rows. The only exception is that stone manor in the heart of the city.

Most of the buildings are made of plain gray stone with thatched roofs—not much color. But nearly every window we pass is a lovely stained glass, making the whole city feel vibrant.

It's early morning, the sun is still rising, and there's a scattering of people out doing morning chores. We pass a street where a group of witches stand on either side of the road, using magic to do laundry. A line of wet clothes floats in the air, lightly steaming as the witches use magic for drying.

Down another street, the houses are split. A set of what look like storm doors opens down into a cellar, and a front door leads into the main house. Small creatures—waist height—roll wooden logs down the street and into the storm cellars.

I study them all as I walk, looking for a face like mine.

Another siren. In the walk from the forest to the safe house, I see none.

We keep to the sides of the streets, trying to stay hidden. It's not an easy feat. The streets are cramped and narrow. As people rise for their chores—dumping out bathwater, clearing out hearths, hanging clothes to dry—they clog the streets. Fortunately, it's early enough that not everyone has risen yet.

Carrik guides me through the streets looking so confident, you'd think he grew up here. I have no idea how long we've been walking before we finally stop in front of a house. Like all the homes I've seen in this world, it's small and made of gray stone. There are four windows facing the road, each of them stained a beautiful light purple. The house is crowded against the surrounding buildings so tight, there's no space to slip between them. The only thing that distinguishes this house from the others is the pine tree painted on the front door.

Carrik practically runs up the stoop and knocks.

After a few moments, a man opens the door. He looks older—a few years more aged than my father—and his eyes are kind and brown. In Keirdre, those eyes would mean he's human. Here, I guess it doesn't mean anything.

He doesn't speak. Just stares at Carrik. He tastes *shocked*. Like an explosion of ginger and lemon. I try and guess what kind of creature he is. He's too broad to be human. He's not tall—mostly legs, with a short torso—but his build is sturdy. His hair is dark, curly, and wispy. His nose and chin are long and sharp.

"Er—hello?" Carrik says when the silence stretches long enough to be uncomfortable. "Maybe I have the wrong—"

"No, no!" The man scrambles to move aside. "You're *exactly* where you're supposed to be. You're Carrik, aren't you?"

"Yes." Carrik looks relieved and moves past him into the house.

I try to trail after him, but the man moves to block the doorway with a frown. "Did you bring a—" His sentence falters as I raise my head enough for him to see my face. His lemony shock is back, stronger now. He's frozen for so long, Carrik has to put a hand on his shoulder and guide him aside, letting me in. Even still, the stranger continues to stare, not speaking.

Carrik clears his throat, dragging the man's attention away from me. "Hello?"

"Hmm? Yes, sorry. I'm Zaire. And *she*—" He's still looking at me. "She must be Saoirse. The siren."

"How do you know who we are? Were you expecting us?" Carrik asks.

Zaire chuckles. "I had no idea you were coming, but it wasn't hard to guess who you were. I mean, look at you—" He motions between us. "You look like Keirdrens. And *she* is the most beautiful person I've ever seen." His gaze snaps back to me. "I assumed she was the siren I've been hearing so much about."

I don't like how he refers to me like I'm not standing right here.

"Did anyone see you?" Zaire finally peels his gaze from me to address Carrik directly. "On your way here?"

"We had to walk through the city. We got some looks. But that's to be expected with this one." Carrik gives me a lighthearted grin.

Zaire doesn't smile. "Was she wearing that hood the whole time?"

"Yes."

"They weren't staring at her face."

Carrik and I exchange looks. "Then what were they—"

"Your clothes." Someone else speaks. "You can't walk around looking like that."

My eyes seek the owner of this new voice. I hadn't noticed another person in the house, but they enter the room now, flitting about, hastily drawing the curtains closed.

Zaire smiles. "This is my partner, Lex. I believe they're who you've been communicating with, Carrik."

Carrik's eyes brighten with recognition. "Nice to meet you in the flesh. What's wrong with our clothes?"

Finished with the curtains, Lex comes to stand next to Zaire. They're tall, with skin dark and textured like tree bark, eyes glassy and green, and hair a deep forest green and spiky, like each strand is a pine needle. Another dryad.

"Keirdren clothes are all so . . . *dark*." Lex's nose wrinkles. "You're wearing black, your cloaks are navy—a Keirdren color— and you look violent." They point at the blade around my waist. "I mean, look at you—you're walking around with a sword like you're going off to war."

"I'm a soldier. Do you not have soldiers here?"

"We do, but our Nightmen dress just like everyone else, and they don't flaunt weapons for anyone to see."

"Nightmen?"

"Soldiers around Alkara who maintain the peace and reprimand lawbreakers."

Alkara. It must be the name of this new kingdom. I tuck that information away.

"Don't worry, we'll get you new clothes," says Lex. "It's *such* an honor to meet you. I've heard stories about both of you, but to see you in person . . ." They smile widely. "Can we get you anything? We've already discussed clothes, but what about food? Are you hungry? Or maybe you're tired." They jump between subjects. "You *must* be tired. We have a spare room for you. What would you like to do first?"

I probably should be tired—I haven't slept in over a day—but the thrill of being *here*, so close to what I've longed for, invigorates me. "I'd like to meet the others first."

Lex's smile smudges at the corners. They exchange a long, loaded look with Zaire.

My eyes narrow. "What?"

"Nothing," says Lex quickly. "How about you get some rest—"

"No," I speak over them, tensing. They're keeping something from me. My hand creeps toward my waist, readying to snatch my blade and pair it with a song. "You asked what we wanted to do first. What *I* want to do first is see the others. This is a safe house, right?"

"Yes," Zaire drags out the word, clearly reluctant. "However, you two are—er—well, you're the first we've ever had."

I taste a wave of sharp and lemony shock. Carrik. "You—you mean the first ones in this specific safe house?"

"Er—" Zaire looks uncomfortable. "No. We're the only safe house. And you two are the first of the Resistance to escape Keirdre."

My heart stills. The fantasies I'd built up in my mind—of arriving here and finding other creatures like me—flickers out of existence like the cruel jest it was.

Carrik's expression is shattered. "You—" His shock warps into peppercorn-infused anger, disappointment like rotting fruit and curdling milk. "You said there have been illegal creatures crossing over from Keirdre for centuries."

"The invitation has always been open, but no one knew how to cross the barrier," says Lex. "We wanted the Keirdren Resistance to have *hope*. If we told the truth—that our numbers have been dwindling for years and no one here takes us seriously— Keirdre would give up. We need the Resistance on *both* sides."

I need to stop being surprised when people lie. It would spare me a lot of disappointment. "What does that mean about the army? The Keirdren Resistance said you have an army to invade Keirdre once the barrier comes down."

Silence.

Carrik stares between Lex and Zaire with wide, hopeful eyes.

They both taste like wine gone rancid. *Guilt.* "I'm sorry," says Zaire. "There's no army."

"*Yet*," Lex hurries to add, like that means anything.

"You're a bunch of liars," I snarl.

"No!" Lex shakes their head. "We're working on it. Alkara doesn't see Keirdre as a threat anymore. We've been trying to get Alkara's leadership to take us seriously so they'll agree to send their army to fight with us when the barrier comes down. They've always refused. The truth is, the Keirdren Resistance is larger and better equipped than ours."

The Keirdren Resistance is a scruffy group so small, most Keirdrens assumed they'd died out until recently. If *that* group is more equipped than the Resistance here, there's no way they'll be able to take on Keirdre's military.

I'm furious, and the exhaustion I've been putting off creeps in.

The one bright spot through all the lies: if there truly is no Resistance army, there's no threat. Which means after I find Reyshka and figure out what she's been doing over here, Hayes can bring down the barrier with no risk of war. "You don't need an army," I say. "Larster is dead."

"We know. We have informants in Keirdre," says Zaire.

"Good to know *something* you said was true," I mutter. "With Hayes on the throne, you don't need to destroy Keirdre. He wants to change things and bring down the barrier."

Lex's hand snatches Zaire's arm with obvious excitement. Zaire looks cautiously optimistic, while Lex is . . . *intense*. Their stare is probing and unsettling. Like they can see right through me—like they'd slice me open and pluck out my insides just to see what I'm made of. "Does this mean the rumors about you are true?"

"What rumors?"

"That you hold the ear and heart of the new King of Keirdre."

My breath stops.

I was prepared for allegations of people I've killed. I hadn't thought to arm myself against questions about my relationship with Hayes. I scramble for a snappy response, but I'm too sluggish to think clearly.

"It's true," says Carrik when it becomes clear I won't answer.

Lex looks so excited, I think they might jump at me. Zaire elbows them in the side, silently telling them to calm down. "If the Prince truly wanted to bring down the barrier, why hasn't he? Larster's been dead for weeks."

He sounds like Carrik. "Because *you* told us there's an army waiting to kill everyone. If that's not true, maybe we can safely bring down the barrier sooner than we thought. Without casualties. I'll have to corroborate what you've said first."

"That's not a problem," says Zaire. "We'll show you where and how the Resistance operates. Everything you want to know."

He speaks confidently, but I'm unconvinced. After they've been lying to the Keirdren Resistance for years, nothing he or Lex says is very convincing.

"In the meantime, Zaire will show you where you're staying," says Lex. "I have to go to work, but I'll be back tonight to show you the Festival of Reds."

"What's that?"

"You'll have to wait and see." They grin. "Please, make yourselves at home. And welcome to Alkara. I know you're disappointed, but this place is better than where you came from. I promise."

CHAPTER THIRTEEN

EVEN HUMANS

I can't blot out the taste of Carrik's disappointment. It sits stubbornly on my tongue, refusing to leave. He's angry too, but the disappointment is more potent. He barely even looks at Zaire as he leads us to the second story of the "safe house." It feels wrong to call it that now that I know how much of what the Resistance told Carrik wasn't true.

It doesn't mean there aren't sirens here. That Rain can't be happy here.

I cling to those thoughts. Just because creatures from Keirdre haven't fled here before doesn't mean this isn't a world worth fleeing to.

There are two doors on the second story. Zaire holds one open for us to enter. "This is our spare room. You can rest here. I'm sure you're exhausted after the day you've had. There are extra clothes in the wardrobe . . ."

He keeps talking, but I tune him out to assess the room. It's small, around the same size as my former chambers in my family's mill house, and there's only one damned bed. If *this* is their only spare room, this place was never going to be a safe house.

Has there seriously never been a *single* culled creature that successfully fled Keirdre? Does that mean . . .

"I have a question." I blurt out the words, cutting off whatever Zaire was saying. Maybe it's rude, but if I don't ask now, I'll lose my nerve. I don't *want* to ask—from Zaire's reaction to seeing me for the first time, I suspect I won't like the answer—but I need to hear it confirmed. "Are there any sirens here?"

Zaire pauses for a few moments. "Er—no. I thought you knew. All sirens are in Keirdre." He winces. "*Were* in Keirdre. They lived near the coast, and most of the coastline is inside the barrier. You're the first siren I've ever seen."

I'm crumbling. Or maybe everything around me is. I can't tell because it all feels the same.

My first instinct is to cry.

I know better than to give in to my first instinct.

Second instinct: Skip the tears and just *scream*. Call Zaire a liar and any other name I can think of, because being angry is better than feeling devastated.

I've known I was the last of my kind since I was a sprig. I never exactly made my peace with it, but I accepted it. It wasn't enough, but it was manageable.

And then, I climbed into a hidden tower and found a painting of someone like *me*. Discovered there was once an entire sector devoted to people like *me*. Whatever acceptance I'd built up burst into flames, and I'd foolishly let myself hope that maybe here, in another world, there were others.

I was wrong. Alkara may be better than Keirdre—that remains to be seen—but at the end of it all, no matter what happens between these two kingdoms, I will be just as alone as I've always been.

I'm battling tears but don't let them fall. Can't let this stranger see through me.

So, I give in to my third instinct: Swallow my feelings. Choke on them. Force my lips into a thin, unbothered smile. "Oh." I sound hollow. I need a distraction—something else to focus on so he can't see how much his words have broken my heart. "What are you?" I ask. "What kind of creature?"

"I'm an impundulu."

I remember reading about impundulu in the storybooks I read with Rain. Shapeshifters who transform into massive birds. Knowing they exist would make Rain happy. Yesterday, it would've made *me* happy. But yesterday, I still hoped this violent call that lives in me would be joined by another. Yesterday was a lifetime ago.

I nod to show I've heard him. What I really want is for him to leave. I want to be left alone to curl into a ball and cry myself an ocean to sink into.

Carrik comes to stand beside me. He doesn't say anything, but I feel the heat of his hand on my back, comforting me. He knows. Without me saying a word, he knows what I'm feeling, and as much as I hate him, right now his hand on my back is the only thing holding me together. "We're in the city of Pennex, right?" he asks Zaire. "What other kinds of creatures live here?" His tone is casual, but I know what he's doing. He's volunteering to ask all the questions I would if my throat wasn't too dry to form words.

"Whoever wants to," says Zaire. "In Alkara, we don't make distinctions between creatures. At least, not in a way that matters."

"Really? We didn't pass any giants or ogres on the way here."

"There are no laws saying they *can't* live here, but we tend to settle in places that make sense for us. Creatures that take up or require more space mostly live out of the cities. We're surrounded by forests here, so there are a lot of dryads and earth fae. In cities with rivers and lakes, there are more water fae, naiads, and sprites. If you're looking for giants, they mostly live in the open plains and mountains out in Uryefell. Ogres prefer marshy areas, like in Moerus or Niri. We go where we fit."

"Is Pennex the biggest city?"

"It's the most heavily populated. And the capital of Alkara, where our Queen lives. In Keirdre, you have a fae King who prioritizes fae. Here, we have a rotating monarchy to ensure the voices of all creatures are heard. Every five years, the crown changes heads. And creatures."

Carrik raises his brows. "That sounds impossible to manage."

"It's not. We have a council with four of each kind of creature. Every five years, a member of a different set of creatures serves as the monarch, and the rest of the council ensures that whoever reigns has a duty to the other species. They can't only serve their own."

I think of my sister. Thoughts of her help me find my voice. They also remind me to hate Carrik. "Even humans?" I subtly step forward, moving away from Carrik's hand. It falls to his side. He doesn't comment, but I taste his hurt.

"Even humans," Zaire confirms.

There's nothing to indicate he's lying, but I find it hard to believe.

I must wear my mistrust plainly on my face, because he says, "You don't believe me now, but you'll see. This world is better than yours. For everyone."

"You said there's a rotating monarchy. Who's on the throne right now?" says Carrik.

Zaire wavers. His eyes are still kind, but they tighten in the corners. "Her name is Queen I'llyaris. A witch. She's been on the throne for almost five years now."

Which means at the end of the year, the witches' reign will end. "Who's next in the rotation?"

"Sprites."

I've never seen a sprite, and I'm immediately curious. In the stories we used to read, they're small, winged creatures. Part of me wonders how true that is. The rest of me is too weary to be curious. I'm relieved when Zaire tells us he'll be downstairs if we need him and turns to leave.

"Wait," I say quickly before he's gone. "Where would I go if I needed two freya candles?"

Zaire's eyes narrow. He looks me over, trying to guess my motive. After a moment, his expression clears. "We'll help you get some from the Festival tonight. There will probably be a few witches selling them." With a final smile, he leaves.

Carrik has the sense to wait until Zaire's footsteps retreat to grin smugly at me. "Well," he says cheerily. "This room is cozy."

Right. During our conversation with Zaire, I'd let myself forget we're sharing a room. The look I give him is sharp enough to splinter glass. "You're taking the floor."

His grin stretches wider. "I know. Trust me, I know." He leans against a wall, watching me. "So, how do you want to do this?"

"Like I just said—you, floor."

"I mean *this*." He motions around him. "We're here. We have to figure out what Reyshka's doing and if the Resistance is telling the truth. I'm assuming the candles you just asked for have something to do with your mission, so how do you want me to help?"

"I don't know how many times I have to tell you I don't want your help." I can tell he means to object, so I hold up a hand. "No. Whatever you're about to say, the answer is no. I'm tired, I'm going to sleep. You can do whatever the hell you want, just so long as it doesn't involve talking to me."

CHAPTER FOURTEEN

RED

Scarlet. I've always preferred wearing dark colors, but tonight, I'm dressed in brilliant red. It's my own fault for letting Lex choose my outfit. In my defense, I only agreed because I assumed they'd find something plain to call as little attention to me as possible. They did the opposite.

In Keirdre, harvest season means leaves rustling underfoot, windy days, and a brief surplus of food where everyone—even lowly millers—has a bounty for a few days.

In Alkara, harvest means the Festival of Reds. According to Lex and Zaire, it's a celebration and a plea: a celebration of increased crop yields, and a plea for the prosperity to continue.

"Each night of the first lune of harvest is dedicated to celebrating a different crop," Lex explained when they returned from work. "I don't remember what tonight is, but it's always something fun and there's always plenty of food."

The dress they picked for me is long, with a heavy skirt and draped sleeves that hang from my wrists like elongated bells. It's laced around the waist and neckline, with gold thread that makes me feel even more like a flaming target than I already do.

To combat the attention-seeking brilliance of this damned dress, I braid my hair around the crown of my head. I prefer my hair free and loose, but I'm trying to give people fewer reasons to stare.

There's a knock on the bedroom door.

"What?" I assume it's Carrik, so I don't bother with politeness.

Sure enough, I see him poke his head through the doorway in the mirror. Lex picked out his clothes too. Soft green pants and a loose-fitting, slightly wrinkled tan shirt. When he sees me, his expression slackens.

After a few moments, I pointedly clear my throat. "Something wrong?"

"Sorry." His green gaze sweeps over me a few more times. "I'm not above staring. You do know you're beautiful to the point of distraction, don't you?"

"I'm trying not to be."

"Wearing *that*?" He laughs. "Not likely."

"Blame Lex. *I* wanted to wear black. They insisted." I turn from the mirror to raise a brow at him. "Did you want something?"

"Yes." He flashes an easy grin. "You ready? Lex and Zaire are waiting."

By way of answer, I motion him out of the room and down the stairs.

Zaire and Lex smile at Carrik as he descends.

They stop breathing when they see me.

Silence.

At least ten ticks pass before Zaire rips his stare from me and turns it to Lex. "*This* is how you dressed her?"

"Everyone wears red at the festival," Lex defends. "She'll stand out less like this."

I want to point out that no one made Carrik wear red, but I say nothing and let them keep arguing.

Zaire is still frowning. "Is there anything you can do about"—he waves a hand at me—"*that?*"

"You mean my face?" I say dryly. "Not unless you have a *keil* bead. But I'm happy to change. Maybe into something black?"

"We don't have *keil* beads," Zaire grumbles. "Thanks to Keirdre, they're nearly impossible to find here."

"And you definitely can't wear black," Lex adds. "It'll make you look Keirdren."

They bicker for a bit longer before Lex wins and we finally leave. Zaire is still muttering to himself, but we ignore him.

My steps falter on the front stoop. When Lex returned from work, a mere hour ago, the streets outside were calm and quiet, the way they were when we arrived. From then to now, Pennex has transformed. The sun is nowhere to be seen, and the ink-black night is studded with twinkling stars and the winking firelight of hundreds of chaeliss lanterns made from colored glass. Some are deep violet, some bright silver, and a scattered few are red like blood—like this damned dress I'm wearing—draping the city in a multicolored haze.

The streets are crowded now. There are carts and stalls every few paces, each decorated with something red—red wood, swatches of red fabric, red flags—and manned by a creature trying to entice passersby to their stand. We pass a man loudly proclaiming his tarts taste delicious *and* relieve joint pain. A witch offers to tell patrons their future in exchange for a few coins. A creature I've never seen before—tall, wide, skin dark like pitch—has some kind of game involving bird feathers dyed red. His cart is already surrounded by sprigs shrieking with laughter.

It takes about a half tick's perusal to see what crop tonight's celebration honors: apples. They're everywhere. Stalls with apple pies and pastries and sweets. Games of throwing darts at plush apples. People wandering the streets drinking from hollowed-out apples (judging from the glazed looks on their faces, the drink inside is stronger than cider).

"How did this get set up so quickly?" I'm in awe as we walk through the Festival.

Lex chuckles. "The reigning monarch is responsible for the Festival. Whenever the witches are in power, they show off their magic."

We stop at a booth and Lex hands a few silver coins to the vendor in exchange for a loaf of bread bundled in parchment and a small metal container. He's short with a heavy build. His face is round and youthful, but his hands are withered and wrinkled, like those of an old man. His eyes are black all around, with no white area, and he's bald.

I wait until we're a safe distance away to ask, "What kind of creature was he?"

"A goblin." Zaire rips off a chunk of bread, dunks it into the metal dish, and shoves it into his mouth. "Goblins make the *best* loaves."

"Goblins don't look like that in Keirdre," says Carrik.

Lex laughs as they also eat a hunk from the bread. "Let me guess: in the stories, goblins are ugly and evil? That sounds like something your King would do. Goblins can withstand intense heat, and they like to work with their hands, so they do a lot of metalwork. They're not ugly, and they're certainly not evil. Here, try this."

They thrust the bread toward me and Carrik.

I dip the warm bread into the container—butter, I now see—and try it. It melts on my tongue. The bread tastes like apple, but there are no lumps of fruit. It's perfectly sweet and light and delicious. The butter is warm and tastes like cinnamon. The perfect blend of sweet and spice.

"It's delicious." I speak with my mouth full.

"Could something evil make something *that* good?" Lex laughs. "We have a dozen more stalls to visit. We're going to show you *all* the best food at the Festival."

As we walk, my head twists to take in everything. Lex was right, most people are dressed in shades of red. Zaire was also right: I'm attracting lingering stares. At least five people stop so suddenly when they see me, they trip.

I'm used to people watching me, but never out in the open like this. In the past, I've only revealed my true face to my family or my marks. Being so exposed, just wandering around the streets looking like *me*, is new. And oddly refreshing.

As a sprig, I loved my face. Until I learned to fear it. As I walk through this new world, there's no fear—not mine or anyone who passes. No one fears what I'm capable of or resents my existence. The realization makes me feel lighter. Like I've been living my whole life with heavy stones tied to my back and they've finally fallen away. My tongue fiddles in the space where my *keil* bead used to go, and I revel in its absence.

After our third stall, Lex snags Zaire by the sleeve and whispers in his ear. Zaire nods and guides us to another stand. It looks like all the others. Made of wood and decorated with rich red fabric. Nothing special. Two people stand behind it, selling slices of pie with a thick-looking crust, layered with apples and dripping with sticky caramel. My mouth waters just looking at it.

"Here." Zaire hands me a few coins. "Buy some for all of us."

I don't take the money, immediately suspicious. "Why?"

"Your sister's human, isn't she?"

My eyes narrow. I'm not surprised he knows about Rain, but it puts me on edge just the same. "Yes . . ."

"So is she." He inclines his head to one of the vendors.

I examine them. A man and a woman. The man has green eyes like Lex and bark-like skin. A dryad. The woman is short— the top of her head would barely come to my chest—and scrawny. Her skin is dark like wet sand, lashes full and dark, hair full of thick, coarse curls, and eyes brown like my sister's. She's beautiful. And she's human.

Her face lights up as she laughs at something the man next to her says. One glance and I know that he loves her and she loves him. They're out in the open, smiling and loving each other like it's normal.

My feet float over to them. "Four slices, please." I don't recognize my voice. I'm just staring at her and imagining my sister. Picturing Rain *here*. Happy and smiling because she's not a secret.

The human woman takes my coins. She counts out six and hands the rest back to me while the dryad packages up the pie. He's tall, like Lex, with dark hair that reminds me of bay leaves.

"Here you go." The human's expression stills when she sees me. "You—" She's staring. "You gave me a bit extra."

I take them from her. "Do you mind me asking if you're from here?"

"No. I'm from Bellehave. Moved because of *this* one." She hasn't taken her eyes away from me, but she waves a hand in the dryad's direction with a playful grin. "He's a very important man. So, here I am."

All I see as I look at her is Rain. More than anything, I want this life for her.

Anything for you.

I promise myself, right here and now, I'm going to get this for her. No matter what it takes.

"Thank you." I'm dazed as I take the pie and make my way back to Carrik, Lex, and Zaire.

Lex and Zaire taste pleased. They planned this. Wanted me to see the human woman and think of my sister. I'm torn between irritation at the obvious manipulation and satisfaction because I wanted to know what life was like for humans here. Now I have my answer.

Lex waves at the couple. "Thanks, Isren."

"Lex." The dryad sounds surprised. "Glad to see you made it to the Festival."

I didn't realize Lex knew the owners of this stall, but I guess it makes sense for them to know other dryads in the city.

"Wanted to show my new friends around." Lex drops a casual hand on my shoulder.

Isren's eyes track the motion and stop on me. He must not have seen me while I was buying the pie, because he stares now. "Er . . ." It takes him a moment to remember his words. "How nice. Hope you enjoy the Festival." He keeps looking as Lex guides us away.

For the next few hours, we wander, eating apple-themed foods at every stand Zaire and Lex drag us to. Keirdre doesn't have festivals like this and, if we did, certainly not with so many different creatures together. I'm told goblins make the best loaves, fae the best spirits, sprites the best drinks, elves the best sweets, and they keep going but I lose track the longer the night stretches.

I'm stuffed near to bursting by the time we stop at a stall owned by a witch for the freya candles. Zaire mentioned how expensive they are, so I'm surprised when the witch hands Zaire two of them without asking for payment. According to Lex, the witch is a member of the Resistance and happy to help.

Armed with weary eyes and two freya candles, I'm drained. Lex and Zaire are muttering to each other about where to take us next, but Carrik gives a very clearly fake yawn. "Actually . . ." He stretches his arms over his head to sell the feigned exhaustion. "I'm getting tired. I think I'm going to head back to the house."

"You sure?" Despite Carrik's obvious lie, Zaire seems convinced. "There are still a few more—"

"Maybe tomorrow. But please, don't let me ruin your night. I'll find my way back from here." Carrik raises an eyebrow at me. "Saoirse? Want to join me?"

Join *him*? No. But I was looking for an excuse to leave and he's offering it, so I nod, and together we wind through the streets headed back to the house.

We're only a few streets away when we pass a stall hosting a game for children. Three troughs of water sit behind the booth. Children are lined up behind the stall, each holding a flat stone painted with a bright red apple. It's a competition to see who can get the highest number of skips from their rock.

Carrik says something to me, but my eyes are fixed on the troughs of water. They're entrancing, and as I stare, the water starts to hum, urging me to—

One of the girls skipping rocks glares at a boy next to her. "You cheated!"

"Did not!" the boy shoots back.

The girl has dark skin hued blue, with black hair twisted into tight braids and eyes a crystal blue like the Jeune River in summertime. A naiad—a river nymph. I recognize her from storybooks. Her face scrunches with anger at the boy next to her. "Then where did my other rock go?"

The boy laughs. "I dunno. Maybe a Keirdren took it," he says mockingly.

The naiad looks furious. "You're a *liar*. You stole it." She holds out her hands, and water from the trough *slams* against the boy.

A few stray drops sail past him and land on me.

I stop moving.

It sits on my skin, radiating heat and comfort. Starts a longing in me for *more*. The water wants to kill, and as I stand here, tired, surrounded by unsuspecting potential marks, the idea becomes more and more enticing.

Carrik latches on to my arm and yanks me away.

The feel of his hand combined with the water on my skin is too much for my nagging instincts.

Kill.

The water's song is a whisper. It grows, getting steadily louder until it's screaming at me.

Carrik moves to stand in front of me. "Saoirse." He waves a hand in my face. "Saoirse? Are you all right?"

I scramble away from him, not wanting to be closer than I need to. Physical contact always makes the water's call more enchanting. I swipe a hand over my arm. The water *sails* off me, leaving my skin dry and brain clear. "I'm fine." I shake my head to sweep it clean of my bloodlust. "Totally fine."

CHAPTER FIFTEEN

ACROSS THE WORLD FROM YOU

I lie on my back. Staring, listening, waiting.

Staring: at the ceiling. Listening: to Carrik's breathing. Waiting: for it to taper out with sleep.

The room is dark and the drawn curtains block outside light. I can't see Carrik, but his normal breathing tells me he's awake, lying on the floor, listening and waiting for something as well.

"Saoirse." His soft voice pierces the darkness.

I purse my lips. Maybe if I'm silent, he'll take the hint and go to sleep.

"Saoirse," he says again, louder this time. I hear rustling as he turns to face me—pointless considering the darkness of the room. "I know you're awake."

"I'm trying not to be." A lie. Despite how much I'm itching to bury my face in my pillow and shut off the world, I still need to dig out my *lairic* beads and update Hayes tonight. Something I can't do until Carrik is asleep.

Carrik acts as though I haven't spoken. "Today at the Festival—"

"I don't want to talk about it." *I don't want to talk at all.*

"Hear me out. Please?" It's phrased as a question, but he presses on before I can refuse or agree. "I know you've struggled with your . . . instincts in the past. I've heard the stories King Larster liked to tell. About how sirens are bloodthirsty monsters. He made people afraid of sirens by saying they *had* to kill. But that was a lie. Just like everything else he ever said. For centuries, sirens existed peacefully alongside other creatures."

"I know. They protected the coasts."

"It's more than that. They were *never* bloodthirsty. Most sirens went lunes—sometimes even years—without killing an invading force. If they're ingrained with the need to kill, how is that possible?"

I don't have an answer, so I say nothing.

"Larster rewrote your history to make it sound more grim. To make *you* sound more grim. I think you can have more control than you think. If you'd let me, I can help you. You deserve better than the lies you've been told."

I stay still. Try and keep my breaths even. He and I are alike. I know he's listening to my breathing. Trying to guess what I'm thinking from the sounds I make in the dark. "No."

"Why not?"

"I don't trust you."

"We're sleeping in the same damned room, Saoirse. You're going to have to trust me eventually."

"I fully intend to fall asleep after you."

He chuckles, but he sounds more exasperated than amused. "I'm sorry, by the way. I don't think I said it before."

"You've said it dozens of times."

"I mean for what Zaire said," he says gently. "I really hoped there'd be other sirens over here."

My heart rate picks up. I was trying *not* to think about it. Thinking about it means I'll have to accept it, and I'm nowhere near ready to do that. "It's fine." I sound stiff, even to myself.

"Saoirse—"

"Just drop it, all right?"

Long pause. Finally, "Yeah. Fine. Good night, Saoirse."

I don't say it back and he doesn't speak again.

I listen to his breathing until it evens out. Keep waiting until I'm sure he's in a deep sleep.

Slowly, my hand slips under my mattress, where I've stored my *lairic* bracelet. Ideally, I'd want to be out of the room when I Dreamweave, but Carrik is a trained soldier. I'm not arrogant enough to think he wouldn't wake if I snuck out.

I bring my wrist to my face and squint at the runes, twisting the beads into the correct configuration before slipping my wrist under the blanket to hide it from view in case Carrik wakes while I'm gone.

My eyes slide closed as I press the bloodstone in the center of the bracelet. The familiar whir starts up as the world around me melts away.

I keep my eyes closed until the spinning stops. When I open them, I'm in an office I recognize.

King Hayes Finnean Vanihail sits behind his father's desk— *his* desk—head ducked over something. He still looks out of place in the massive desk chair. Zensen is over his shoulder, murmuring intensely in his ear.

Hayes hasn't seen me yet, so I let myself stare. It's been almost two weeks since I saw him, and it's easy to lose myself in memories of our last encounter. He had me backed against a door, mouth open on mine. If I close my eyes, I still feel the heat of him surrounding me. Feel his hands on my hips, those arms . . .

I clear my throat to interrupt my own thoughts.

Hayes's head jerks up and his gaze finds me instantly. He

holds me captive with his intense ocean eyes. My tongue bathes in the flavors of his feelings. Surprise, like lemon juice; happiness, like biting into a fresh orange; mingled with concern, like oversalted stew.

Zensen frowns, looking from Hayes's face to where I'm standing—except he can't see me. "Hayes?"

Hayes shakes himself. "Could you give me a minute, Zen?"

I'm inexplicably nervous. The last time I saw Hayes, he kissed me. Before that, all of our encounters were encased in ice. I have no idea which Hayes I'm going to get tonight: the Hayes who wants me, or the one still processing my betrayal.

"Of course." Zen still sounds confused, but he's stoic as always as he leaves Hayes's office.

As soon as the door is closed, Hayes is on his feet. My anxiety builds as the distance between us shrinks—

Suddenly, I'm swept into a tight hug and lifted until just my toes graze the floor.

My fears melt away as I melt into his embrace. I don't think about the history hanging between us, just hug him back because I've missed this.

"I'm glad you're all right." His voice is muffled from my hair. He sets me down. "You *are* all right, aren't you? You arrived safely?"

I can't help smiling. "Yes, Your Majesty."

At the reminder of his title, his eyes dim and he releases me. "Sorry. I didn't—" He steps back, looking embarrassed. "Glad to see you're all right."

Pause.

The kiss hovers, unspoken, daring either of us to mention it.

A braver me would question what it means. The coward in me fears what he'd say: he kissed me because I was leaving and he might not ever see me again. It didn't change *us*. Change that he's a King and I'm his former guard on a mission across the world. Change that he's still grieving the loss of his best friend, and I'm the reason he's gone.

I clear my throat. "We ran into some trouble. We were separated from Jeune right before we reached the barrier. There were soldiers blocking the road in Kurr Valley, searching carriages. Jeune got me and Carrik out before they saw us, but she had to stay and fight. I don't know what happened after that."

His forehead creases. "What soldiers?"

My suspicions are confirmed. The soldiers weren't acting on Hayes's orders. "They had Enforcers' pins. I assume you didn't authorize it."

"No." Hayes's expression darkens. "I've heard reports of this. Some Enforcers are ordering unauthorized raids and illegal searches all over the kingdom."

"You can't stop them?"

He blearily rubs his eyes. "They aren't listening. The Enforcers are angry with me given . . . recent events."

I hear what he doesn't say. "You mean me."

"Yes. They suspect I helped you escape Haraya. Rumors are flying that you've seduced me," he says wryly. "The fact that everyone thinks you killed Thannen doesn't help. Apparently, he comes from a powerful family of Vanihailian water fae."

I'm almost afraid to ask. "How powerful?"

"Remember the Rusters?" Hayes's tone is even, but his eyes turn sharp—he knows I'm all too familiar with that family. It wasn't that long ago that I killed Trellis Ruster.

Neither of us mentions it. Like the kiss, we let it sit between us, unspoken.

"Thannen's family is related to them," he says.

Of course they are.

"And now, his family has gotten all the powerful Vanihailians riled up. They blame you for my father's and Thannen's deaths, and me for being the lightbrain who let you escape. They're convinced I've got you stashed away somewhere, so the Enforcers are having their soldiers conduct raids until you're brought to justice."

"I'm sorry," I say. "This is my fault."

"This is *my* mess. You have your own things to sort on the other side." He gives me a fake smile. "I can handle this. I'll get the Enforcers under control. And Jeune . . ." He wavers. "Well, it'll take her at least a week to make it back here."

If she's alive.

Neither of us says that.

"Enough about me, how are you?" asks Hayes.

"Fine. We made it to Alkara in one piece."

"Alkara?" Hayes perks with interest. "That's the name of the other side?"

"The kingdom is Alkara. I'm in a city called Pennex."

There are bags under his eyes; he's clearly weary from a long few days of dealing with angry Enforcers and Vanihailians, but he comes alive with curiosity. "Tell me everything." He leans against the front of his desk. "Don't leave anything out."

His eagerness thaws my fatigue. So, I tell him everything. About our journey over the barrier, the dryads in the forest, Lex and Zaire, the Festival of Reds . . .

"I met a human there," I tell him.

At this, he raises his brows. "At the Festival?"

I nod. "She was married to a dryad."

He hums noncommittally. "That's nice." He's been excited

since I started talking about Alkara, listening intently and nodding along, but at this, his tone turns subdued.

"What's wrong?"

Hayes purses his lips, thinking for a moment before answering. "You mentioned a lot of creatures—but you didn't say anything about sirens. Does this mean . . . ?"

My heart stills. I wasn't planning to talk about this. "No. They're all dead." I thought if I said it bluntly and dispassionately, it wouldn't hurt as much. I was wrong. Saying it out loud hurts *everywhere*.

"I'm sorry." Hayes moves closer. "It's awful. Do you want to talk about it?"

The wound is fresh, and I haven't decided yet if thinking about it makes me want to cry, scream, or hit something.

Hayes means well, but I don't know what we'd talk about. If I let myself think about the devastating loneliness I feel—let alone *talk* about it—I might give in to the tears I've been battling all day. "I don't want to talk about it."

"Let me know if you change your mind."

He means that. He truly wants to ease my pain, despite all the hurt I've caused him. I have a bad habit of being unfair to him. He has a bad habit of being kinder than I deserve.

"It's late." Hayes's voice cuts into my thoughts. "You should get some sleep. You look like you've had a long day."

"You look like you've had a long *year*." I force a teasing grin. "Are you sure you've only been King for a few weeks?"

He grins at that. His eyes are still tired, but his smile is genuine all the same. "It *feels* like it's been years. There's no time for sleep now. Zen and I still have a few things to work out."

"Before I go, would you write a letter to Rain for me?"

"Of course." He circles around his desk and grabs a sheet of parchment and a pen. "What do you want me to write?"

Beansprout,

I miss you. I made it safely to the other side. You will never believe this, but I met a real dryad today. Did you know they are really tall? I don't think our books mentioned that. And goblins aren't anything like what we thought. I want to show it all to you one day. But for now, just know that I'm safe and I love you.

Love,

Pinecone

CHAPTER SIXTEEN
TEMPORARY TRUCE

My eyes mist over as I stare at yet another scrap of parchment. The longer I stare, the more the shapes of the letters on the page lose all meaning. By the end of the night, I fear I'll have lost the ability to read altogether.

The second room in the upper story of Lex and Zaire's house is an office. I was told I have free rein, so I take advantage of the desk, pens, and parchment.

Except all I'm doing is wasting office supplies because it's been hours and I haven't actually accomplished anything. Lex and Zaire have taken Carrik to the Festival of Reds for the third night in a row, leaving me here alone with my spiraling thoughts, a growing pile of crumpled parchment, and a plan that seems more futile by the minute.

I sit behind Lex's desk. To my right is the only letter from Larster to Reyshka I have. In front of me, there's yet another sheet of parchment where I've penned:

Reyshka,
By now, I am sure

My hand slashes across the page, crossing everything out. *Again.*

I can't get Larster's handwriting right.

I spent the journey to the barrier plotting how to convince Reyshka to trust me so I can learn what the Keirdrens are plotting in Alkara. Tomorrow, I intend for my plan to be realized.

That is, *if* I can pull this off.

My tentative strategy: find Reyshka (since I have the letters from her to Larster, this is the easiest part of my plan) and earn her trust. If I can convince her I was sent by Larster, I can use the freya candles to make Reyshka think she's talking to Larster—except I'll be on the receiving end of her letters, prying whatever I can from her.

I've practiced my cover story. I've obtained two freya candles—one for me and one for Reyshka. All I need now is a letter from "Larster" convincing enough to fool her. But no matter how much parchment I burn through, I can't replicate his penmanship.

Again. Try again.

I snatch another sheet. Stare at the sample of Larster's letter. Slowly drag my hand over the page, trying to copy his looping pen strokes—

I scratch it out again, holding in a scream of irritation.

Two knocks on the office door before Carrik enters.

I don't know what face I'm making, but I wasn't expecting company so I haven't hidden my frustration yet.

He raises his eyebrows. "Whoa. Who died and killed *your* spirits?"

"My spirits were never high to begin with," I grumble.

He comes around Lex's desk to look over my shoulder. "What are you—"

"Nothing." I jerk the parchment out of his sight.

Carrik is undeterred. "Was that a letter? One of the ones Larster used to write to Reyshka?"

"You mind backing up and giving me some space?"

He humors me and takes an exaggerated step backward. "There. I'm distanced. What's got you so worked up?"

"Nothing," I say. But as soon as the word is out, I question myself. Think about the blackmail notes he penned to Rain and me. He mimicked a completely different handwriting, convincing enough that I didn't recognize it.

He can read the shifting thoughts on my face. "What?"

"You were really good at convincing me your handwriting wasn't your own . . . ," I say. "Is this a skill of yours? If I gave you a letter in someone else's hand, could you replicate the penmanship?"

"Probably."

I tamp down the giddiness that rises at this. Best not to get excited until he's followed through. "If I gave you this"—I hold up Larster's letter—"and asked you to write—"

"I can do it." He studies the letter for a moment before snagging a pen. Eyes narrowed in focus, he starts to scrawl. Every few moments, he glances at Larster's letter for reference. When he's done, he hands it to me.

Saoirse,

Remember that time I bet you I could climb a tree faster than you and then lost on purpose to boost your ego?

My jaw unhinges. It's a near-identical imitation of Larster's penmanship. "This is perfect."

"I'll take that as a thank-you."

"The day I thank *you* is—"

"Today?" he guesses with a smirk.

"Shut up." My lips twitch, almost betraying me with a laugh. I stifle it, but I know he sees it anyway. "This letter is a total lie, by the way. You wanted to win. You lost because I was better than you."

"No. I wanted *you* to win."

"You're such a liar!" I can't help laughing this time. "If you remember, you were so desperate, you fell out of the tree."

"All part of my ruse."

"Let's play pretend that I believe you—what would you have to gain from falling from a tree *on purpose?*"

"Easy. It made you smile."

I don't have a good retort for that, so I shove more parchment at him. "Get to work. I'll dictate, you write."

"You're not going to say please?"

He's still teasing me. I give him a sugary-sweet smile. "Careful, Solwey. There's a window *just* over there, and I know the perfect song that'll make you want to jump."

Carrik scoops up the pen again. "Sounded like a 'please' to me. What do you want me to write?"

Reyshka,
By now, I am sure you are wondering why I have fallen out of contact. The Palace has been under attack by enemies of the crown. My office was destroyed, and the candle I used previously to communicate with you was stolen. I have sent a messenger with this letter and a new freya candle. With it, I will be in touch.
—King Larster Vanihail

I study the letter he's written, *floored.* "You're a bit too good at this."

"It's all practice." Carrik smiles, this time without humor. "I used to write my father in prison. Before he died."

Died?

I go still, listening. I knew his father was in prison. I knew Carrik wrote him letters—Hayes told me before we left. I had no idea his father died. Briefly, I wonder why Hayes didn't tell me, until I realize he likely assumed I already knew. Carrik was my closest friend, after all.

Carrik studies the letter, not looking at me. "We weren't allowed to have contact, so I disguised my penmanship. I copied an Enforcer's hand and addressed the envelopes as if the letters were from him and not me. Of course, my dad couldn't write back, but I like to think he read them. That they . . . I don't know. Made him happy. Before the end."

I can count on one hand the number of times Carrik has mentioned his family. I never asked. Didn't want to push him into a conversation he didn't want to have. "I didn't know your father died."

I've seen Carrik feel a lot of things. Happy, amused, curious, angry . . . but right now, his sorrow is deep enough to drown me, cold enough to make my teeth chatter, salty enough to dry my throat, and bitter enough to make my lips curl. It's as if I'm seeing him for the first time. Seeing the fury and grief that was lurking under the surface of my carefree and cheery former friend.

"He lasted two years in prison," says Carrik. "I got a letter when he died. They didn't even spell his name right."

Two years . . .

That means Carrik and I were friends when his father died. He never mentioned it.

"I'm sorry." It doesn't feel like enough. Even after everything,

I feel guilty. He was my best friend and I didn't notice when his father died.

I can't find it in me to be angry with Carrik right now, not when I feel like I owe him a shoulder to cry on, three years too late. "What's his name? Can you spell it for me?"

"It was Mykah." Carrik grabs a pen and writes it out. "My mother was Aylix." He writes it too. Stares at their names on the page. "Mykah and Aylix Solwey."

"Tell me about them."

He opens his mouth to answer but shakes himself with a shudder. "I'm sorry. I shouldn't have brought them up. You don't have to do this, Saoirse."

"Do what?"

"Pretend to care."

"I'm not." I mean it. Maybe I'll never be able to look at him without thinking about what he did to me. Maybe we'll never be friends again. But for a time, we were. "We can have a truce. For a few minutes."

His face is full of shadows. "I can't talk about them. Not to you. You're only looking at me like that because you think I'm sad. You're wrong. Talking about my parents doesn't make me sad. It makes me *angry*. So angry, I want to break something. Maybe everything.

"I hate that they're gone. I hate that taking them away left me all alone and no one cared. I hate that they loved me and I don't have that anymore. The more I think about it, the more I hate Keirdre and the King and your Prince and the Enforcers and the fae, and I want them all to *burn*." His breaths are uneven. His hands shake, so he folds his arms together, hiding them from view. "But when I say things like that, you look at me like I'm a stranger. You're all I have now. Please don't ask me to talk about them. Don't ask me to make you hate me more than you already do."

I've never tasted anger so intense. Scratch that—what he's feeling is too potent to be anger. It's *rage*. Peppercorn and chili peppers on fire. It's so heated, I have to gasp, sucking in air to cool my burning tongue. I don't know what to say. I don't know that there's anything left to do but give him what he wants. "All right." My voice sounds small. "Let's not talk about them." I force a smile to lighten the heaviness. "Can you teach me how to alter my handwriting?"

"Absolutely not." The intensity melts from his tone and he's back to smiling, as though his overwhelming rage doesn't still linger on my tongue. "If I do, you might try to get away with writing letters without me."

"Might?" I pretend to be offended. "There's nothing *might* about it."

"Exactly why I'm keeping my infinite wisdom to myself." He hands me the finished letter. "What's your plan?"

Minutes ago, I wouldn't have considered telling him. I can't imagine cutting him out now. Not when he's wearing his shattered heart bare on his sleeve. Besides, he wrote the letter, so I'm sure he's worked most of it out on his own. "I'm going to steal Reyshka's trust. Then, I'm going to use her to figure out why Larster sent her here in the first place."

"I imagine you'll need more letters?"

I see where his questions are headed. "Probably."

"Can I help you with those?" His angry green eyes fill with hope.

I want to say no. I still don't trust him—*but* I can't write these letters without him. Reluctantly, I nod. "Fine."

He grins. "Excellent. While you're with Reyshka, I'll be with

Lex and Zaire, learning about the Resistance. I'll report everything I find out back to you."

I cross my arms doubtfully. "I'm supposed to trust you're
telling me everything?"

"If you want to spend time learning about the Resistance
with me, you're welcome to. But since you'll be busy with
Reyshka, let's split information. I'll keep track of everything
Lex and Zaire do. You do the same for Reyshka. At the end of
each day, we'll trade. I'll tell you what I've learned, then you do
the same. If you think I'm leaving something out, you don't
have to tell me anything."

It's a good plan. If he were someone else—or if he were still
the Carrik I knew before I learned he was Spektryl—I'd agree
without hesitation.

Except I still don't trust him, and I'm petrified of what he
and his anger are capable of. Still, even if he's a liar, I'd be a fool
to outright reject insight on the Resistance while I'm with
Reyshka. I keep my expression blank. "I'll think about it."

CHAPTER SEVENTEEN

LEGENDS OF FLESH
AND BLOOD

Pennex sits in a valley surrounded by a dense forest. Most of the city is in the pit of the valley, but there are a few homes on the incline between the heart of the city and the woods where Carrik and I came through the barrier.

From the instructions Reyshka gave Larster, I know she lives on that perimeter. Unlike the crowded houses around Lex and Zaire's, the homes here have sprawling green lawns and plenty of space.

A blend of terror and excitement twists my stomach. I adjust the strap of my bag to settle my nerves. I have everything I need: two freya candles, a letter from "King Larster," and a cover story I can only hope is enough to fool Reyshka.

Her house is made from brown bricks and gray mortar. The door is plain, the windows are purple stained glass, and the silver curtains are drawn shut. Wrapped around the property is a fence made of pale, dense-looking wood.

It's eerily quiet. Chill wind whistles, blowing a few crinkling leaves through the air. Birds chirp with the rise of the sun, and faintly, I hear the bustle of morning chores from the city behind me. Aside from that, nothing. Heart stuttering, tongue toying with the gap behind my false tooth, I rap my knuckles against the door.

There's a pause long enough to send my pulse racing before a man opens the door. He's kind of tall, kind of muscular, and kind of has a stoop. His cheekbones are sharp and his eyes are bright blue—a fae. Likely a water fae, knowing Larster. There's nothing about him that immediately identifies him as Keirdren. He wears a loose-fitting white shirt and plain tan pants.

My stomach is still knotted, but I ignore it. "I'm here for Reyshka." I keep it simple. The less I say, the less he has to dissect and work out that I'm lying.

He doesn't react to my words. Just stares, immobile.

Right.

Lost in my tangled maze of dread, I forgot I no longer have a *keil* bead.

My fear dissolves. This is familiar territory. This man isn't a threat—he's a mark. My lips curl into an easy, beautiful smile. "Can you take me to Reyshka?"

He nods jerkily. Moves aside and guides me through the small house. The front door opens into a wide room. Sofa on one side, staircase that leads up, and a dining table. I'm led forward into a kitchen. There's a pantry door to my right, back door ahead, and a closed door to my left.

The soldier stops suddenly in the middle of the room. "What am I doing?" he mutters under his breath. "I shouldn't—"

I breeze past him out the back door into the yard behind the house. Doesn't matter that he's come to his senses, he's taken me where I need to go.

There are *dozens* of soldiers here. All dressed like Alkarans— bright colors, loose-fitting clothes—and all fighting like Keirdrens.

For a tick, it's like I'm back at the Barracks, watching my fellow Deltas train. I'm struck stunned, for a few reasons.

One: the sheer number of soldiers. Just how long has Larster been sending Deltas here? As far as I know, there's only one soldier sent over at a time, at most once a year. Clearly, this has been happening for *decades*.

Two: None of the soldiers are quiet. From the front of the house, I couldn't see or hear them. Which means there must be some kind of magic at play, keeping them hidden.

The backyard stretches out over the incline of the valley. The pale wood fence extends around the yard. My roving gaze comes to a halt—a woman prowls through the soldiers, eyes watchful and piercing, missing nothing.

"Wait—" The man I followed here hurries out the back door. "You can't be here." He looks past me, sounding petrified. "Enforcer Harker!"

The woman casts those sharp eyes in our direction.

She's tall. So tall, she towers above everyone. Her dark hair is twisted into locs that fall to her waist, pulled back to leave her face clear. Her eyes are a glittering olive color and keen. Frown lines encircle her mouth, so deep they could be runes on a *keil* bead. Otherwise, her face is so smooth, she looks younger than my mother. She's the only one dressed in dark colors: black pants with a black chain mail vest draped over a long-sleeved brown shirt.

Even if she hadn't just been identified, I'd have known she was the leader. Everything about her—from her presence, to her stance, to the authoritative quality of her eyes—makes it clear she's in charge.

I grew up hearing stories about Reyshka Harker, the woman consumed by the barrier. Now she's in front of me, a legend brought to life. Foreboding and terrifying and real.

Her olive eyes glide past the soldier who brought me here, expressionless, then over to me.

There's a shift. The blankness fills with curiosity and a flicker of recognition as she soaks in my perfect features. I hold in a shiver. There's something unsettling about the sensation of her eyes on me that puts me on edge.

Reyshka's scrutiny doesn't waver as she raises a hand. "*Stop.*" Her stare: aimed at me. Her words: clearly targeted at the soldiers around us.

Instantly, the soldier on her right, caught mid-spar, stops.

His opponent isn't as quick to heed Reyshka's order. Her blade, still moving, slices across her opponent's arm, drawing blood and Reyshka's ire.

The soldier looks horrified. "Verin! I-I didn't—"

"Silence." Reyshka's brows crease. "Verin, why didn't you block the attack? It was sloppy."

"I—" The bleeding solider—Verin—looks stunned. "You told everyone to stop—"

"I told you to stop fighting. Not to let your guard down. *Never* lower your defenses. If your opponent is slow-witted and doesn't halt her attack, my yelling 'stop' does *not* give you leave to be careless. Five laps. Now."

Verin doesn't argue. Just turns and starts to jog around the perimeter of the yard.

As the others stand still, awaiting another order, she comes toward me. "You're a siren." It's not a question, nor an accusation. It's a statement. One I can hardly deny.

Gasps ring out from those surrounding us. I don't flinch. Don't move. Don't react at all. "Yes." I tip up my chin. "My name is Saoirse, ma'am. I was sent by His Majesty." Part of me wonders how she immediately recognized me. Does she usually assume all beautiful creatures are sirens?

But she's already moved on. "His Majesty did not tell me—"

"There was an attack on the Palace," I interrupt her. "It's why you haven't heard from His Majesty. The freya candle he used to communicate with you was destroyed."

The corners of her eyes narrow in suspicion. "How convenient."

"Hardly," I say. "It was incredibly *inconvenient*. I have a letter from His Majesty confirming what I've told you." I will my hand not to shake as I pass her the letter Carrik penned.

She looks doubtful but unfurls the parchment regardless. As she reads, I pull out a stack of letters—the ones she wrote to Larster. "He also wanted me to show you these. As evidence that I speak the truth."

Reyshka flips through the stack. "His Majesty sent these?"

"Yes. He wants to reestablish communication with you. Which is why I have this." My last gift for Reyshka. I hand her one of the freya candles Lex and Zaire got for me at the Festival. "His Majesty sends his regards."

I've laid everything before her. My tongue toys with the gap behind my tooth as I wait. Hoping she believes me.

Slowly, Reyshka turns the candle over, examining it. She looks at me again. "There haven't been sirens in centuries. Why did His Majesty send *you* to me?"

I inhale, taking that brief moment to ready the story I've prepared. "Because I'm a powerful weapon. As I'm sure you're aware, I possess abilities fae do not. His Majesty has been training me in secret for years for the purpose of assisting you on your mission. I'm the last of my kind. And a recent graduate of the Vanihailian Barracks. I placed first in my year's Ranking. I assure you, His Majesty sent his best."

Her eyes narrow. "How recent?"

"This past year."

"Truly?" She raises a hand. "Kasselton!"

My stomach drops. I recognize this name.

A girl emerges from the crowd, as familiar as she is unwelcome. Her dark, kinky hair is short and her eyes are bright blue. Rienna Kasselton. My would-be rival from the Barracks. She despised me, but I never thought her enough of a challenge to hate her.

I hadn't realized she was one of the water fae sent to Alkara, but it makes sense. I was told that only the top Deltas of their years were sent over the barrier. In our Ranking, I was first and given an assignment in the Palace. Rienna was second and, apparently, was sent here.

There's no recognition in her expression as she comes to Reyshka's side. Clearly, she didn't hear me introduce myself. She looks me over with a blend of curiosity and interest.

"Do you know this soldier?" asks Reyshka.

Rienna blinks in surprise. "I've never seen her before."

I fight the urge to roll my eyes. Drina's *keil* beads are powerful magic. I saw firsthand how someone could look at an image of me without them and see me in person, right next to it, but not realize we were one and the same. "You don't recognize me, Kasselton? And here I thought we were such good friends."

At the sound of my voice, she goes rigid.

"I see." Reyshka's sharp eyes study her reaction. "You *do* know her?"

"I—" Rienna is still staring at me. "Sorkova?"

"Pleasure to see you again, Kasselton," I say wryly.

"Who is she?" asks Reyshka.

"She is—was—" Rienna grapples to find the words, still stunned by my new appearance. "She was a Delta in my year. An ikatus. She couldn't go near water without getting ill."

"That was a lie," I say quickly. "Kasselton didn't recognize me because I used to wear *keil* beads. I'm not an ikatus. I'm a siren."

If Rienna was stunned before, it's nothing compared to her expression now. "Impossible."

"She *is* a siren," says Reyshka. "Look at her, she's certainly not fae."

"Enforcer Harker." Rienna's voice is firm. "The Saoirse I knew couldn't go near water without getting ill."

"I'm happy to demonstrate my skills," I say. "You never could beat me in a sparring match, Kasselton. How about I show you?"

Rienna glares. "I hardly think—"

"An excellent idea." Reyshka looks pleased. "No weapons. Just sparring. The siren has agreed. Kasselton?"

She grits her teeth, but she clearly won't deny an order from her instructor. "Of course."

Without a word of warning, she draws near and swings a fist at me. She clearly means to catch me off guard, but I see it coming. It's been a few weeks since I last sparred, but some things are instinctive. Fighting is one of them.

My arm raises, blocking her.

Rienna scowls.

Fighting Rienna feels natural. We fall into the pattern I've missed. I'll admit, either she's better than I remember or my skills have rusted a bit from underuse—likely a combination of both.

Rienna pulls up her knee, intending to draw it into my gut and wind me.

One of my hands shoots forward, catching her knee and shoving it down while she attempts to drive her elbow into my face.

Fortunately, it leaves her chest exposed, leaving me free to jab her rib cage. Once, twice, a third time. She jerks with each hit.

Taking advantage, I swipe out my leg, knocking hers from under her. Rienna crash-lands on her back, out of breath. I stay standing, press a foot on her chest, and apply pressure. Not enough to crush her, just enough to hold her in place. Remind her I'm there. And alert her that, as always, I've won.

Rienna's face is flushed from exertion and fury—but I don't care about her. All that matters is that I taste Reyshka's surprise and satisfaction. She's pleased with me.

Reyshka instructs the soldiers to carry on without her and motions for me to follow her. I give Rienna a parting smirk as I follow after Reyshka, leaving my opponent lying on her back, panting and furious.

Reyshka guides me into the house and up the stairs. The rickety wood creaks the entire way up.

My nails dig into my palms, mind spinning with questions. I *need* to learn why Reyshka is in Alkara. But I can't just ask. Can't tip her off that Larster didn't really send me. To obtain more information, I'll need to pretend I already have it.

There are three doors at the top of the stairs. Two are plain, and the third is the same pale, dense wood that makes up the fence surrounding her yard.

Reyshka gestures to one of the plain doors. "I have an extra room. The other soldiers live in houses nearby, but seeing as you're a special guest of His Majesty, you're welcome to stay here."

"His Majesty has made other arrangements for me." I can't stay here. For one, I need to keep as close an eye on the Resistance as possible. And for another—perhaps more important—I don't want any more eyes on me than necessary. Staying here, under Reyshka's watchful gaze and Rienna's probing hatred, is just asking for one of them to work out what I'm truly doing here.

Reyshka doesn't pry further. She presses a hand against the door made of pale wood. She holds it there for a tick or two. There's a soft *click* and the door opens.

I enter behind her. Reyshka used some kind of magic to enter this room—clearly, secrets are kept here.

"No one can hear us in here." Reyshka closes the door.

The pale wood must do something to block sound—maybe even block sight. It would explain why I couldn't see or hear the soldiers from the front of the house.

I soak in my surroundings. The room is small. A desk with a basin of water sitting on top and two chairs across from it. A decorative blade hanging on the wall is the room's only adornment.

"I won't insult your intelligence," Reyshka speaks over my thoughts, "so long as you don't insult mine."

My pulse races.

She knows.

Somehow, she's worked out that Larster's dead and she knows I'm a fraud. Mentally, I plot my escape. Use the water to disorient her. Grab the blade from the wall, slice at her before she can—

"I know His Majesty must have sent you here for a specific reason you cannot fully disclose," Reyshka continues. "Whatever I can do to assist you, please let me know."

My tongue darts around my mouth. I don't taste any suspicion or anger. Nothing to suggest she doesn't believe me.

My hands—clenched at my sides—slowly unfurl. I'm still cautious, but less panicked. "You're correct. I have a private assignment from His Majesty I'm not allowed to discuss. What I can tell you is that I've been instructed to train with your soldiers. I ask that you treat me the same as them."

I hold my breath, waiting to see if my story is believable . . .

Reyshka nods. "Understood. I should caution you—I will *not* go easy on you. You must succeed or fail by your own merits. I expect you to arrive at training on time every morning. There is a gap in the fence's magic you may use to enter the premises. We cover a variety of subjects here. Sparring and combat, speed and agility, and Alkaran customs, to name a few. I cannot stress enough how important it is that the Alkarans remain unaware that Keirdrens live among them. If you have conflicting orders from His Majesty that take you away from training, I expect forewarning. Is that understood?"

I'm still in shock she actually believes me. "Seems fair."

"I wish you luck on your mission, siren. I assume His Majesty has explained the importance of blending in here, but I'll reiterate. You cannot, under *any* circumstances, wear navy, gold, or dark clothing. No one here can know you're Keirdren. If you ever need more clothing of appropriate colors, I have a stash of suitable Alkaran attire to better allow you to fit in here."

"Thank you, ma'am."

She holds out a hand to me.

I keep the relief from my face as I shake it.

"Welcome to Alkara, siren."

CHAPTER EIGHTEEN

CINNAMON

My world dissolves like raindrops sliding down a windowpane. I squeeze my eyes shut to keep the dizziness at bay until it all stops spinning. When I open my eyes, I'm in a familiar bedchamber.

I turn, searching for—

Lune above.

A dark, toned, and altogether-too-beautiful-for-his-own-damned-good man stands in front of me. And he's not wearing a shirt.

I must make a startled noise, because I hear him whip around to face me. Hear—not see—because I've already twisted the other way so I'm no longer drooling over his muscular back.

Normally, I'd resist such an obvious retreat. Hide the effect he has on me. Mask my weakness behind a scowl and a quip. But I acted on pure instinct. I've tried to get used to how beautiful Hayes is. When I'm prepared, I erect walls sky-high to keep him out. When I'm prepared, I can stare into those eyes, heart pounding, gaze deceptively calm.

When he surprises me, I'm a mouse in a freshly tilled field and he's a cat with razor-sharp focus. There's nothing to hide behind.

I'm still not looking at him. I made the impulse decision to turn around. Facing him again would be even more mortifying. So, I don't move.

Hayes hasn't said anything, but I taste the zest of his surprise and, even more potent, his amusement.

Dammit.

I clear my throat. "Sorry." My voice sounds too high. I try again. "I didn't realize you were—that you weren't dressed." I'm acting as if I've never seen a half-dressed man before. I have. But with someone as otherworldly beautiful as Hayes, it's different. Everything is different with Hayes.

Hayes chuckles, and lune above, it's *unfair* how smooth that sound is. "It's fine. I suppose you can't knock with a—what's it called, again?" His voice is amused and getting louder.

My heart shudders—he's moving closer. "This is called a *lairic* bracelet." I hold up my wrist, still not turning. "What I'm doing right now is called Dreamweaving."

"Right. Dreamweaving." His breath hits the back of my neck, and the sweetness of his mirth at my expense coats the back of my throat. "You can look now."

I take a breath. Steadying myself and shaking my mind of the image of him shirtless, I face him. I saw him last night, but now I can't look at him without also envisioning him bare from the waist up. It's a distracting mental image. "Good to see you, Your Majesty."

"You as well, Pinecone."

I frown. Pinecone is my family's name for me.

He grins at my confusion and hands me a sheet of parchment. "Sorry. Couldn't resist. That was my way of saying Rain wrote back. Don't worry, I didn't read it. And I won't make a habit of calling you Pinecone."

I snatch the letter eagerly. "If you bring me messages from my sister, you can call me whatever you want," I say as I unfold it.

Pinecone,
Finally. Mom and Dad were worried you'd been killed, but I told them you're too stubborn to die. Which means you have to prove me right and live forever.
   The King came to visit us. He told us we can call him by his first name! He said he's going to give you this letter, so make sure he doesn't read this, but I think he's really pretty.
   I'm mad you saw your first dryad without me. My life is boring compared to you. Mom and I started an indoor garden because we're hardly ever allowed outside.
I can't believe I actually miss school.
   Write me back and stay safe.
I love you!
Beansprout

I feel like I can breathe again. Rain is safe. The worst thing she's experiencing is boredom. I can live with that.

I hand the note back to Hayes. He looks surprised. "You don't want to keep it?"

"I do, but I can't take anything with me in a Dreamweave."

"Oh. Right." He tucks it away in his desk. "I'll keep these for you. For when you get back."

If I come back.

Neither of us says it.

"Thank you," I say. "Can you write me another one?"

"Of course."

I dictate a response, taking care not to mention how Rain

thinks he's "pretty." Given my reaction to seeing him without a shirt, I don't think his ego needs any more inflating today. When he's finished, he puts the letter away, promising to deliver it.

"I had another question for you," I say. "About letters."

He closes his desk drawer. "I was wondering when you were going to mention Spektryl."

"You said you read all the letters Carrik wrote to his father. Do you—" I hesitate. Carrik didn't want to talk about it, but I can't fight my curiosity. "Do you know if his father ever got them?"

Hayes's expression doesn't change, but my mouth fills with something cold and dry, like icy sawdust. Sadness. "They were still sealed when I found them."

Which means no. Mykah Solwey never opened his son's letters. Probably never knew they existed.

I didn't know him personally, but there's something gut-wrenching about the fact that he spent years in prison, completely alone. That Carrik wasted years writing letters to a man who would never read them. All for the crime of loving a human. "Why didn't you tell me before?"

Hayes's lips twitch into a small, sad smile. "I didn't think it mattered. It's not like you're going to tell him."

Why wouldn't I?

I almost ask, but it's useless—I already know the answer: *because it would break his heart.*

It shouldn't bother me. Carrik deserves it. He stopped my heart with that first blackmail note to Rain. He manipulated me. *Used* me. Kidnapped and threatened my sister. Even now, I can't think about her without seeing that blip of red on her throat when he dug a knife's blade against it. He threw her into the ocean and left her to die, knowing it would shatter me.

I want him dead. At the Palace, after Larster died, I *would* have killed him if Hayes hadn't stopped me.

So then why does the thought of telling him his father never read any of his letters seem so much crueler?

Hayes is watching me, eyes soft with knowledge I struggle to admit to myself: I'm not going to tell Carrik. Despite my rage, I'd sooner snap his neck than break his heart.

I refuse to acknowledge this out loud, so I shake my head. "How are you?"

Hayes arches an eyebrow but moves on, letting me drop it. "Same as yesterday. The water fae hate me. I've had to fortify security in the Palace in case anyone tries to attack."

"You think they would?"

"They're powerful people who've just experienced massive change. I have no idea what they're capable of. Today, I officially assigned a team to hunt for you. I'm hoping it will calm the water fae for a bit. It's only a temporary fix though because, obviously, they won't find you. Right now, I'm shifting my focus to finding who actually killed Thannen."

"I told you who it was—Ikenna. She had Thannen killed to frame me and force you to send me away."

"I thought so too. Until today." He looks weary as he thuds into a cushioned armchair. "A group of Vanihailian water fae held a demonstration calling for my removal from the throne."

"*What*? That's treason."

"They don't seem to care." He groans and buries his face in his hands.

He's struggling under the weight of frustration and helplessness. I can't resist. I stand behind him and run a hand between his shoulder blades, trying to relieve the tension.

It doesn't completely work, but I taste a citrusy tang of

happiness—it's sinking in desperation and sadness, but it's there all the same. "I'm sorry."

He twists to give me a feeble smile. "I'm going to work it out. I believe my mother is capable of a lot of things, but she wouldn't do anything that would have people calling for my removal from the throne. She wants the crown to stay in the family, no matter what."

"Maybe she didn't realize this was going to happen."

"Maybe . . ." But he sounds doubtful.

"Why don't you ask her?"

"She's hardly going to tell me the truth."

"She might if you ask the right questions. You can interrogate her without her knowing it's an interrogation. Make it seem like you just want to talk, and then poke around and get her to tell you what you want to know."

Slowly, Hayes straightens, and my hand on his back falls away. His expression doesn't change, but there's a chill in his gaze that wasn't there a moment ago. "Is that how you'd do it?" His tone is even, but there's a question hidden in his words: *how many times did you use this trick on me?*

My stomach churns with guilt. I ignore the feeling. Try to. I clear my suddenly dry throat. Cross my arms to keep my hands still. "I can help you. If you arrange a meeting with Ikenna, I'll Dreamweave and tell you what to say. She'll never know."

Hayes mulls it over. "She wouldn't have killed Thannen herself. She'd have ordered someone else to do it. Or hired someone. If we get her to admit it, we can find out who that person is. We present that person to the public . . ."

"The water fae will stop blaming me for killing him and punishing you for my escape."

"Well, there are a lot of other things they want you executed for."

True. But eliminating this most immediate infraction seems like a good step. "What do you think?"

Hayes yawns. "It's worth a try."

I lean against the back of his chair. I don't try to touch him again, but for the next long stretch of time, we talk. I tell him about Reyshka and he listens. Chimes in with questions or anecdotes, wholly attentive. He tells me about the new soldiers he's been recruiting and interviews he's conducting. About all the new responsibilities he's still adjusting to. His fears for the future. I've lost track of time when he yawns for the fifth time.

"It's getting late. I should go," I say. "I'll see you tomorrow?"

"Yes." He stands and I expect him to make his way to his bed, but instead he nears his bedroom doorway.

"Where are you going?"

"I have a few more things I need to take care of in my office."

I examine the dark circles under his eyes. "Your Majesty, when was the last time you slept?"

"Last night."

"How long?"

"At least a few hours," he says evasively.

"*Sir.*"

"There's no time," he defends. "I have too much to do."

"I promise you, you'll have too much tomorrow as well. And likely, the day after that. That doesn't mean you give up sleep. You're no use to anyone exhausted."

"You're one to talk. Remind me, how much sleep did you get in the Barracks? As my guard? Do you think you're getting *more* sleep over the barrier than you did before?" He doesn't give me time to answer. "I know you. You're prone to neglecting sleep as well."

He's right. But we're not the same. I've been discarding sleep in favor of training since I was a sprig. Hayes is new to this. He'll wear himself out in less than a lune if he keeps on like this. "This isn't about me."

Hayes yawns—*again*—but doesn't relent. "Maybe it should be. Let's make a deal: I'll sleep when you do." Despite his fatigue, his eyes are bright. He's challenging me. He means for me to accept that neither of us sleeps and leave it at that.

For someone who claims to know me, he apparently doesn't realize that I *never* back down from a challenge.

"Really?" I crook a coy eyebrow. "Promise?"

"Sure, Saoirse. You get a decent night of rest, and so will I."

He's teasing and I know it, but I decide to accept his challenge. Without breaking eye contact, I kick off my old boots, one by one. Walk to the side of his bed. Fold back his bedcovers . . .

Hayes tracks my movements in disbelief. "What are you—"

"What does it look like?" I slip into his bed, resting my back against the headboard. "I'm taking you up on your offer. I sleep, you sleep, right? Do we have a deal, or was that just talk?"

For several moments, he stares at me, jaw hovering somewhere near his feet. All at once, it seems to hit him that I'm not kidding.

Slowly, he unlaces his shoes while holding my gaze—as if he's afraid I'll change my mind and bolt if he looks away. Which isn't an unfounded fear.

He peels back the covers on the other side and crawls into the bed, eyeing me warily all the while. He's still fully dressed, and I'm relieved he doesn't challenge me further and actually ready himself for bed. The longer this moment drags out, the more likely I am to change my mind and sprint away like the coward I am.

My heart thumps so swiftly, I struggle to maintain even breaths. I didn't think this through. It's hard enough being near Hayes when we're both standing upright in daylight. Now— sharing a bed in the middle of the night . . .

He adjusts his position. The bed is massive enough there's a chasm between us, but his body heat travels the distance and wraps around me like an embrace.

"Just until you fall asleep," I blurt. "Then I'll leave."

Hayes doesn't answer. Just reaches for the chaeliss stone on his bedside table. He presses the rune in the center and the lights wink out, casting the room into darkness.

Rustling as he situates himself more comfortably in the bed.

My confidence—fleeting to begin with—is completely gone. I want to flee, but I can't. That would be a retreat. I settle on a compromise. Turn over on my side, facing away from him.

I feel his breath on the back of my neck. "How are you going to tell if I fall asleep first if you're facing away?" His voice is deep, husky, and sensuous.

I shudder at the sound of it. The feel of it down my spine. "I'll listen for your breathing."

How is it that he sounds totally in control? He's calm and alluring. Meanwhile, my throat is so dry, I'm raspy.

"*I want you.*"

He said that. On the deck of the *Sea Queen*, once a lifetime ago. He hasn't said it since.

He kissed me. Almost two weeks ago. He hasn't brought it up since.

And now, we're sharing a bed. I don't know what any of it

means. This was a mistake. Lying here, knowing he's so close and staring at me—it's overwhelming.

"Saoirse?" The huskiness of his voice sends my body wracking with more shivers.

"Yes?" I fake a yawn. I was exhausted at the start of this night, but his nearness and my hyperawareness of it have me wide awake. "Sir?"

"Good night."

Cinnamon. My tongue is on fire from the taste. It's more than that. His presence cocoons me in desire hot enough to send a trickle of sweat down my back. For a tick, the flavor swells and the heat grows from burning to sweltering. I wonder if he's going to close the space between us. Snake an arm over me. Twist me around the way he did in the safe house—

The bed shifts, and the warmth of his breath on my skin flees.

He, too, has rolled over to face away from me.

I should be relieved. Instead, I'm flooded with disappointment, like rainwater in a bloated river after a storm.

"Good night," I say softly, "Your Majesty."

CHAPTER NINETEEN

IRON FIST

I didn't want to fall asleep here.

Liar.

I *told* myself I didn't want to fall asleep here. I didn't *plan* to fall asleep here. But the truth—the full truth: I was hoping that *if* I fell asleep here, in Hayes's bed, I'd wake up tangled with him.

It was wishful thinking. When I wake with the early rays of morning, I'm huddled under the thick bedcovers, freezing cold. Night passed and I'm still over here and Hayes is still over there. He's rolled over to face me, but he's just where I left him, oceans away on the other side of the bed.

His eyes are closed, breathing even—still sleeping. I take a few ticks to study him. He looks peaceful like this. The crease in his brow that's formed since ascending to the throne is gone. The weariness of his new title is wiped away like smudge marks on a glass. Sleeping, he looks as carefree as he did when we first met.

Hesitantly, my hand reaches for him—to press against his face, tap him awake to say goodbye, I'm not sure—but halfway there, I think better of it.

Waking him means acknowledging I spent the night. It

means looking into his ocean eyes while questioning why he didn't reach for me in his sleep. It means dealing with my disappointment at the distance between us.

I press the bloodstone to return to Alkara without a word to the sleeping King.

When my eyes open back in my own bed, Carrik stands over me, smirking without humor.

I sit upright. "What the hell? Trying to restart my heart, Solwey?" To emphasize my words, I place my left hand over my heart, leaving my right wrist with my *lairic* bracelet hidden beneath the blanket.

Carrik raises a knowing brow. "I've been trying to rouse you for a few minutes. Everything all right?"

He knows exactly where I was and who I was with. I pretend I don't realize. "I'm just tired. What do you want?"

"The Saoirse I know would wake if a leaf blew against her window. Why did it suddenly take so much effort?"

"Maybe something to do with being in a new world."

Carrik scoffs and sits on the corner of the bed. "There's no need to play coy. I know you were with him. Figured you must have some way to contact him. Didn't realize you had *lairic* beads, though. They're expensive."

"Drina runed them for me."

"Expensive present just so you can talk to your Prince."

His tone grates my nerves. "It's none of your business, but I've had these since before I met Hayes. And, yes. Talking to Hayes is a necessity. In case you forgot, you need me to be in contact with him so I can tell him when to take down the barrier, remember?"

"You're right." He holds up his hands in surrender, but I still taste something bitter.

"What's your problem?"

"Nothing. Just wondering why your conversation with your Prince lasted till morning. He doesn't strike me as such a witty conversationalist he could keep you up all night."

My face gets hot and I roll my eyes to disguise the embarrassment. "None of your business. You woke me for a reason? What do you want?"

"What do you think about rekindling our tradition of a morning run? Maybe a bit of sparring?"

"Can't," I say, swinging my legs out of bed. "I have to meet Reyshka and the Keirdrens. I'm starting training."

"Oh." He looks disappointed. "Maybe some other time?"

He helped me with writing letters in Larster's hand, but that doesn't mean things between us are back to what they were. "I don't think so." I tuck my *lairic* beads under my mattress. No use hiding them—Carrik already knows I have them.

My hand brushes something hard and smooth. I'm confused until I realize it's the freya candle from Ikenna. In the shuffle of everything, I'd forgotten about it.

The thought of throwing it out tiptoes into my mind, but it's swiftly joined by thoughts of that human at the Festival. The one with the pies and the wide, happy smile. My hand tightens around the candle.

I don't want to use it. Doing so would mean condemning Keirdre to stay trapped inside the barrier, possibly forever. It would mean breaking Hayes's trust again and losing him—permanently.

I should destroy this candle before it has a chance to burn me, but am I really willing to lose a potential contingency plan? If all else fails, I need something to ensure that Rain has a chance at better.

Anything for you, Rain.

"Saoirse?" Carrik sounds concerned. "Everything all right?"

"Fine." I leave the candle buried beneath my mattress as I stand and ready myself for training.

Just in case.

My first day of training under Reyshka focuses on form. It's not as fun as sparring, but I fake enthusiasm anyway. We're standing in rows in Reyshka's backyard. Each soldier has a training figure—large, misshapen sacks filled with stuffing to represent a flesh-and-blood opponent. Reyshka trails between rows, watching us with her hawklike gaze, overanalyzing our every move, assessing our flaws.

The drill is simple in nature but difficult in execution. Reyshka calls out a strike, and we respond as though we were attacked the way she describes.

The aim is to react quickly—if you're too slow to draw your weapon, you're reprimanded ("a real opponent isn't going to stop just because you're a lightbrain")—and react *correctly*—countering a punch to the left side with a jab isn't effective ("your opponent won't attack where you *want* them to—they'll attack where it hurts").

"Remember," Reyshka drawls as she saunters behind me, "more fights are won at close quarters than people realize."

In the few hours I've been here, I've noticed she does this often. Chats with us as she strolls around before suddenly barking out a command to catch us off guard.

A swift intake of breath alerts me she's about to shout out an attack. My hand tightens on my knife's hilt, waiting.

"Your opponent swings a blade at you from the right side—*react!*"

I take in this information: my opponent has a blade and I, a knife. I duck, allowing the imaginary blade to slice overhead. As I do, I jab the knife out, ripping into the sackcloth currently standing in for my assailant's knees.

"Good." Reyshka nods her approval. "Odion!" Her voice sharpens. "That was slow. What are you waiting for—your opponent to take your head off? Five laps. When you're back, try again—but do it well."

A boy a few rows over immediately drops his weapon and dashes from the rest of the group to run around the perimeter of the yard. One of Reyshka's favorite punishments.

Next to me, Rienna snickers. "Lune above," she mutters to the girl on her other side. "I swear he *wants* to be ranked last."

With that, she's snagged my attention. "Ranked?"

Rienna scowls, and I know she's not going to answer me.

In Keirdre, rankings mattered. We trained for years, worked grueling hours to be on top, and it all culminated in the Ranking—the event that determined our assignment after graduation. The fixation on rankings made sense back home.

Why should it matter *here*? This *is* an assignment, in and of itself. These soldiers already placed highly in their Rankings and were sent here. What do they have to gain from additional rankings?

Rienna won't answer me. She's hated me since the Barracks. Besides, I don't want to ask too many questions outright and raise her suspicions that it wasn't King Larster who sent me.

Reyshka barks out another attack and I react automatically. My body moves while my mind is far away, thinking. I need someone willing to divulge information about the ranking system without being pushed.

I glance at the soldier jogging laps who was just singled out—Odion.

When interrogating someone while looking like me, my best strategy has always been singing. That's out of the question now. Which leaves the *next* best way to convince someone to open up: mutual commiseration.

Odion has no reason to despise me, and even better, he's just been publicly shamed, meaning he likely wants to vent his frustrations.

I look around for Reyshka. She's still roaming through the rows, shrewdly watching us. She's far from me right now . . .

I wait. Reyshka calls an attack and I react. Over and over, patiently.

"*Very* good, Jarek," she says loudly. "Everyone, take note at how sharp his movements are. He never wastes motion."

I'm flooded with the intense, acrid flavor of irritation from just about everyone. Rienna grumbles something under her breath.

Reyshka has heaped more praise on Jarek than anyone else. Clearly, he's the favorite.

Not my problem right now. I need to get Odion alone before he's finished running his laps. I wait, listening for Reyshka's steps until she's closer behind me.

The next time she announces an attack—this one an attempted stabbing with a curved dagger—I fumble.

I haven't dropped a knife in *years*, but I send mine clattering to the ground and give an exaggerated gasp of horror.

Reyshka's sharp gaze snaps to me.

Beside me, Rienna snickers. I ignore her.

Reyshka looks unamused. "If you can't keep up, siren, tell me now."

"I can," I say. "I'm sorry. It won't happen again."

"Five laps. We don't allow incompetence here."

I try and look dejected as I jog across the yard to trace the same path as Odion. I fall into step beside him.

He glances over. At first, it's a passing look, but when he sees me, his eyes widen and his running slows.

I flash a thin-lipped, self-deprecating grimace. "I got called out by Reyshka too."

He hums in response. Either because he's out of breath or because he's still recovering from my appearance. Likely a combination of both.

Regardless, silence won't work for me. I need him to talk. "Is she always like this?"

His head flaps in a frazzled nod.

Still no words. I shift tactics. "She's a bit of an ass, isn't she?"

It works. He's startled into a laugh. As soon as the outburst releases, guilt flits over his face and creeps across my tongue.

Interesting. He feels guilty for making fun of Reyshka, even in jest when she can't overhear. In the Barracks, it was typical to poke fun at our training instructor. Other Deltas—the ones who played nice and made friends with each other, while ignoring me—vented about him endlessly. They never felt bad about it. Or bothered to include me.

All Odion did was *laugh* at an insult directed at Reyshka, and he feels bad about it. Which means he respects her. *Very* interesting.

"Sorry," I say. "I'm just trying to find my footing here."

"Don't worry." He smiles. Still looks nervous, but the smile appears genuine. "One mistake won't throw you off. You were doing really well, from what I saw."

I don't comment on the fact that he's confessed to watching me. "Yeah? So, this won't make me bottom-ranked?"

He shrugs. "Maybe for today, but as long as you improve, you won't stay there." He sighs. "Not like me. Reyshka *hates* me. She'll never give me an assignment."

Assignment? What kind of assignment?

I can't ask. Not directly. "What kind of assignment are you hoping for?"

He shrugs, looking despondent. "You heard me. I'm always at the bottom. I have no idea what kind of prizes winners get— you'll have to let me know, if you make it to the top." For a moment, he grins, but it fades into bitterness. "Well, I guess you won't be able to."

"Why not?"

He looks surprised. "You're not allowed to talk about your assignments. If you come back, that is."

If I come back? My interest is piqued.

Don't react.

I force an unbothered laugh. "I know that. But you're my first friend here." I give him a smile that's sweet with just a dash of flirtation. "If I ever get an assignment, keep being nice to me and maybe I'll tell you about it."

He perks. "We're friends?"

"Sure." The grin I give him now could blot out the sun. As expected, he melts under its force.

We continue our run with casual conversation—he's easy enough to entertain—but I'm not focused. Reyshka is ranking us, and whoever's on top gets a clandestine assignment no one can talk about. This is exactly the information I'm after.

If I want to know what Larster and Reyshka are planning, I need an assignment. I can't afford any repeats of today. I need *more* than to gain Reyshka's trust—I need to do what I mastered in the Barracks: win.

CHAPTER TWENTY
SHATTERED ILLUSIONS

Carrik and I are dressed as Alkarans. This time, I refused to let Lex choose my outfit. I'm wearing a plain soft-yellow dress with a white kerchief around my hair. Carrik wears a dove-gray shirt and light pants.

It's midmorning, so the streets are crowded as Lex walks ahead of us, chattering away. "Your sister is of school age, isn't she?" They keep talking, giving me no chance to answer. "We have excellent schools here. You don't even need to be fae to enjoy them."

Lex has already informed us that when they're not working for the Resistance, they're a teacher at Courliss—a schoolhouse in the city.

Over the past few days, while I've been with Reyshka, Carrik's been accompanying Lex to Courliss. He's told me a bit about it. The building itself is a schoolhouse, and the cellar is the base of all Resistance activities, complete with a library and archives.

"You'll like the archives," says Lex. "Carrik said you like history, is that true?" Once again, even though they asked a question, they don't pause for the answer. "We've got all kinds of history books. You'll really like— Oh, here we are."

We stop in front of a short building—all buildings in Alkara are short—made of gray bricks and decorated with wreaths of ivy and multicolored flowers. It's surrounded by a pale wood fence—the same thing that surrounds Reyshka's house.

"What is this?" I ask.

"Isi wood. I wouldn't—"

My hand grazes the fence.

Sharp pain shoots up my arm. *"Ah."* I yank my hand back, but the sensation lingers, working its way through my body. For the next fifteen seconds, I feel as though liquid fire is flowing through my veins.

I'm still shaking as the pain finally subsides.

"Dammit, I'm sorry, Saoirse." Lex grabs my hand, inspecting it. There's no mark. "I should've warned you. Isi wood is enchanted to only let certain people pass. It's for protection. Here." They touch the wood and unlatch a gate to push it open. "You can walk through now. You just need someone who's allowed in to open it for you. I'm sorry."

I cradle my hand against my chest, making a mental note to never touch isi wood again.

Lex guides us around the schoolhouse. At the back, there are cellar doors built into the ground. Lex pulls out a key from their pocket and unlocks the doors to reveal a set of wooden stairs that lead into darkness. Lex starts to walk down, and Carrik and I follow.

As we descend, we enter a wide room dotted with tables and a handful of creatures—some recognizable, others a complete mystery to me. The floor is stone tile, and the walls are covered in tapestries: some are beautiful patterns, others have stories woven into the fabric—depictions of scenes with characters and creatures.

Two archways lead out of this central room, one on either side. At the table closest to us sits a woman with skin that glitters in torchlight. When I look closer, I see they're *scales*. Her eyes are narrow and brown. When she smiles at Lex, her teeth are sharp—fangs. I try not to stare.

"Hey, Fatima," says Lex as they casually usher Carrik and I farther into the room.

The creature, Fatima, dissolves into smoke. I'm startled, until smoke billows in front of me, solidifying as she materializes less than a pace away from me.

I jump, stunned.

Her eyes look me over, unblinking. "This is the siren?"

"Yes." Lex puts a hand on my shoulder, pulling me back to create distance between me and Fatima. "Maybe give her some space."

It's too late. At the word "siren," the room comes alive.

There were only a handful of people in this room, but more spill in from neighboring rooms, and suddenly, I'm surrounded. There are a dozen of them. A few with sharp features and bright eyes—fae; some with weathered hands and youthful faces—goblins; others with bark-like skin and hair like leaves—dryads; one with dark skin that shimmers when she moves who I can't identify; and a tiny creature I decide must be either a sprite or an elf.

I'm in awe, but my shock is nothing compared to theirs. They stare, clamoring to see me, shouting out questions eagerly. They all speak at the same time, so I can't answer any of them, but I'm too absorbed in studying them to care anyway.

The tiny creature is stuck at the back of the crowd. They huff in irritation and *rise*. Float into the air and come around to me, hovering at my side. I'd narrowed it down to sprite or elf—seeing this, I settle on sprite.

The sprite examines every inch of my face curiously.

Lex shoves them aside. "Kindra, please, give her space."

"Is it true you're going to help us take down the barrier?" the sprite, Kindra, asks eagerly.

The snakelike creature appears in a cloud of smoke right next to me again. "Can you sing for us, siren?"

Something curls around my waist. I glance down to see a long, thin branch wrapped around me. With a sharp tug, I'm pulled to stand in front of a dryad. "You are even more beautiful up close."

"*Stop.*" Lex's arms extend into branches that grab me and pull me back to them. "Saoirse didn't come here to be bombarded. We're leaving until you learn to *behave.*" They yank me away, Carrik trailing behind us, through the arched doorway on the right.

We're in a library. Wall-to-wall, floor-to-ceiling bookshelves on three walls, all full of heavy-looking books, and spanning the fourth wall is a massive map.

My eyes slip over the map. "Is that . . ."

"Everything," says Lex excitedly. "Keirdre, Alkara, the other lands."

"*Other* lands?"

Lex laughs. "Alkara is one kingdom. Keirdre is another. Did you think the entire world was just two kingdoms?"

I've spent my life trapped in one world. The thought of two was revolutionary. I don't know how to handle the fact that there are more. "Have you ever been to faraway kingdoms?"

"I've never ventured outside of Alkara. But we trade with other nations, make treaties, and some people travel."

I like the way they say it. *Travel*. Like it's a hobby as casual as reading a book.

Carrik taps my arm. "Look up."

Curious, I tip my head up. The ceiling here is high—we're pretty far underground—and painted with a massive, slightly peeling mural. There are trees with faces, figures made of water rising from a river, creatures with wings and tails. Some small, some large. Some with skin light like sandstone, others with skin so dark it's pitch.

"Creatures," says Lex excitedly. "All kinds. It was painted in the early years of the Resistance."

I want to lie on my back and stare at the ceiling for hours, but Lex moves us into an office off the library with a desk and sofa. Carrik and I sit on the sofa as Lex closes the office door, looking embarrassed. "I'm so sorry about that."

It takes me a moment to realize they're apologizing for the Resistance swarming me. Honestly, I'd already forgotten them. "It's fine. I was curious to see them too."

Lex sits at their desk. "I told them you were coming, but I guess all that did was make everyone want to be here today."

My brows shoot up. "That was everyone?"

"It was most of us."

If the dozen or so creatures I saw out there is *most* of the Resistance, they're smaller than I thought. "You said the Resistance isn't taken seriously here," I say. "Why?"

Lex scowls. "Larster is cleverer than we gave him credit for. When the barrier was first created, we learned Larster planned to send Keirdrens over the barrier. We informed the council of the impending attack. But nothing happened. This happened over and over, and each time there was no attack, the council lost more faith in us." They sigh. "Eventually, we realized Larster *was* sending over soldiers, but they were in disguise. He was *preparing* for war, not starting one. But now, of course, no one believes us."

I frown. "How long has he been sending over soldiers?"

"Since the barrier."

That doesn't make sense. The barrier has been in place for centuries. That would be countless soldiers. Surely, they'd die out over time? "The council doesn't trust you?"

"Not yet. We've been trying to get them to accept that Keirdre is a threat, but they're convinced the barrier's never coming down and no one can leave Keirdre. They won't even fortify security along the barrier."

I think about the dryads in the forest, living casually near the barrier. Not paying attention to whether anyone crosses over from Keirdre. "You're saying . . . the only people over here who want to see Keirdre destroyed are you?"

"No. Alkarans hate Keirdre as much as we do. *But* they see them as obsolete," they say bitterly. I taste the burning spice of their anger. "They think we're just a group of rebels clinging to the past."

"They spent years trying to destroy the barrier from this side," Carrik chimes in. "All unsuccessful."

"How have you tried?" I ask.

"Everything. We know there has to be some way over—all magic has its counter, after all. But nothing we tried worked. Brute force. Going over it. Tunneling under it. Magic . . . We lost many witches to soul magic."

"People *died*?"

"Soul magic is dangerous. And permanently binding. Many

witches studied it so we could bring down the barrier. They all failed, and some died in the process. It doesn't matter now. Soul magic was outlawed, and now there's almost no one left who knows it."

"*Almost* no one?" Carrik picks out the word.

"The Queen—Queen I'llyaris—is incredibly powerful. The last witch who knows soul magic. Not that it's done us any good. She's just like the other monarchs before her. Refusing to invest an army in our cause."

I'm still skeptical of Lex. They manipulated the Keirdren Resistance. United them under the belief that if the barrier came down, there'd be an army on the other side, ready to wipe out Keirdre and start over. It was a lie.

If they're telling the truth about Alkara, then there's room for peaceful resolution. If I can prove to the Resistance that Hayes is a good King and Keirdre has changed for the better, they won't *need* an army. Except I still don't trust the Resistance. Lex *claims* there's no army, but that could still be a lie.

Lex is watching my reaction to their words. "You're wondering if you should believe me."

"You lied to the Keirdren Resistance for years. Why should I believe you're telling the truth now?"

"I can't make you trust me. But I want to show you something." They rise from behind their desk and search the rows of bookshelves lining their office walls. They pull out two thick books. *Thunk* them both on the desk in front of me.

I look at the books, then at Lex. "What's this?"

Lex's eyes gleam. "See for yourself." They flip the first book open to a specific page and slide it toward me. "Here."

I skim the page they've flipped to.

After the creation of the barrier, sirens bathed the streets of Keirdre in blood. At first, they hunted only at night. King Larster attempted to enact a curfew to keep Keirdrens safe. Unfortunately, the sirens grew restless. They began to hunt and kill at all hours of the day. They hunted for fun and without conscience. Sirens have an insatiable bloodlust, only satisfied by death and destruction. Hundreds of innocent Keirdrens were slaughtered. His Majesty had no choice but to

I slam the book shut, not wanting to read any more. "Why the hell would you show me this?"

"That's from a Keirdren history book. Children read that in your schools."

Is this what they had Rain read about me? I once asked her what kinds of things she was taught about sirens. If *this* is the history she read of me, it's no wonder she was so evasive.

She told me she didn't believe it, but is that true? Even if she doesn't believe it, do *I*?

"How do you have this if it's Keirdren?" I ask Lex, mostly to distract myself from my thoughts.

"We're in contact with many Keirdrens. As I said, we've spent years collecting information, including information in schoolbooks."

"Using *lairic* beads?"

They scowl. "We don't have any over here. We communicate with letters and freya candles."

My jaw drops. "You copy entire history books through written letters?"

"You see now why it's taken years. Here, read this." They push the second book to me.

Sirens lived alongside other Keirdrens in the sector of Szeiryna. Keirdre was rich with resources, from their plentiful forests of samsam trees to the rich deposits of umbian clay in the rivers. They were the target of many invasions by ship. Sirens protected the waterways, singing to invaders and plunderers, protecting Keirdre's coasts.

After the creation of the barrier, sirens were no longer needed for protection. They coexisted peacefully within the kingdom of Keirdre for many years. With their ability to breathe underwater, many were divers, assisting with fishing and collecting umbian clay in the riverbeds.

When I look up, Lex is grinning at me. "This is *our* history. Real history. Larster twisted the truth into something dark and ugly to justify his massacres. I understand why you don't trust us yet. But stay with us and you'll see. Larster was a liar. He lied about your history. Here, we value the truth. Let me prove it to you. Prove that our history is real and that we mean what we say."

CHAPTER TWENTY-ONE

DESTRUCTIVE PRETTY THINGS

Hayes is slumped over his father's desk—*his* desk—head resting on his hand, eyelids drooping with exhaustion. He hasn't noticed me yet.

I look around. His office is empty, meaning whatever guard is on duty is waiting in the hall and won't be confused by Hayes talking to himself.

I clear my throat.

His head snaps up. When he sees it's me, his body eases. It does nothing to shallow the deep crease on his forehead. "Saoirse."

"Sir," I say back.

He drags a hand down his face. "Please tell me your day was better than mine?"

"Depends." I sidle around the desk to peek at the pages strewn about the surface. "How was your day?"

"Good. Then awful. Then good again. This morning was good—Jeune returned to the Palace. In one piece."

A massive weight lifts from my shoulders. "She's all right?"

"Aside from a few minor scratches, she wasn't injured. Just tired and missing her wife. I gave her the rest of the week to stay home with Sherri."

Good. I'm so relieved at Jeune's safe return, I almost forget to ask about the rest of Hayes's day. "What made everything else awful?"

"I met with the Enforcers." He hands me a sheet of parchment from his desk. "I had the meeting transcribed if you want to read it. It was brutal. They refused to stop the unauthorized raids until you're found and executed."

I've never heard of Enforcers being so blatantly disrespectful. "Can they do that?"

"No. I'm going to strip them of their titles. But I can't do that without sufficient reinforcements. The thing about making laws is you need people to *enforce* said laws. And those responsible for doing so on my behalf hate me. I've been recruiting new and loyal soldiers, trying to find new Enforcers."

"Maybe tonight's a bad night to talk to your mother." We've already put it off for a few days, but I don't want to add to Hayes's stress any more than I have to. "I can come back—"

"No." He abruptly stands. "The sooner I prove my mother is the reason Thannen is dead and not you, the sooner I can get the Vanihailians under control. Besides, today wasn't completely horrible."

"Really?"

"Since all the Enforcers were too busy arguing with me, they didn't notice there was a mass pardoning at Haraya until it was too late. I released all prisoners whose only crime was having a relationship with another species."

It takes me a moment for his words to sink in. My heart jolts with surprise. "You're serious?"

"I wouldn't jest about that. I assumed this meeting would go poorly. So, I had some of my new soldiers escort the released prisoners home. It's not much, but it's a start."

My arms don't belong to me. Without my consent, they're thrown around him in a hug so tight, neither of us can breathe.

For a few ticks, I feel lighter and this all feels possible.

This is going to work. We're going to play this game right. Fix Keirdre. Bring the barrier down. Reverse Larster's damage . . .

When I pull back, Hayes is looking at me like he used to. "What was that for?"

"I wanted to thank you."

He looks bemused but pleased. "I didn't do it for you."

"I know." He did it because he's Hayes. He's nothing like his father, and that knowledge eases my fears. I don't say any of that. "Are you ready to talk to Ikenna?"

"As I'll ever be." He makes as if to leave his office, but I block his path. "Whoa. Slow down. You've never interrogated someone before. We need a plan."

"All right." He crosses his arms. "What should I do?"

"Whatever I tell you to."

"Should be easy enough." His words are laced with good humor. "Following your orders is practically second nature. Although, given my title, I think it's supposed to be the other way around."

There's affection in his tone that makes me smile. "If you'd like to take a stab at interrogation by yourself, be my guest."

"That wasn't a complaint. Just an observation."

"Remember, only you can see or hear me. You can't talk to me or look at me once we leave this room."

His eyes dance with mischief. For a pause, they rove over me, spending extra time on my hips. I frown. "What?"

"Nothing. Just taking in my fill of you before I can't look anymore."

My face feels hot. I've missed him flirting with me. I try and act unbothered, but I think he sees through me. "Have her guards leave the room so she feels comfortable being open. And remember, you don't want to accuse her of anything."

He nods. "What should I ask her about?"

"What do you usually talk about?"

He scoffs. "We don't talk. Ever. We don't even eat together—or at the same time. She takes her meals alone in her room at seven, midday, and six after midday, every day. I eat if I get the time."

I shouldn't be surprised. She didn't have a single portrait of Hayes or any indication that she even has another son in her chambers. Still, I figured she must care *somewhat*. Why else would she go through such lengths to have me exiled away from Hayes?

Hayes needs to appeal to what she values. If not Hayes, what does Ikenna care about?

I think about the portraits in her chambers. Larster and Finnean. I think of the way she tasted genuinely devastated when Hayes mentioned Larster. How she snapped when I blithely mentioned Finnean.

That's what she cares about—not Hayes, but the family she lost. "Tell her what you told me. How difficult things have been since your father passed. That you need the kingdom to accept you the way they did Larster."

"You want me to tell her the truth?"

"Half-truths are the best lies. And don't worry. I'll be right there. If you need me, clench your hand. I'll tell you what to say."

He inhales, holds it for a few ticks, then exhales. "Let's get this over with."

A guard I don't recognize stands outside his office. "Sir." He immediately stands to attention. He looks young—barely older than me—and disgustingly earnest.

Hayes looks even more exhausted than he did in his office. "Again, Kalen, you can just call me Hayes."

Kalen follows as Hayes starts down the hall. "Where are we going, sir?"

"To visit my mother." It's clear from Hayes's expression that he noticed Kalen once again refused to use his name, but he doesn't comment.

When we reach Ikenna's wing of the Palace, I eye Hayes to see his reaction. As before, all the portraits on the walls are of Ikenna, Larster, and Finnean. Nothing with Hayes. He can't have missed his absence, but judging from the way he walks so assuredly, he's been here before.

He's already seen the portraits and noted that his mother didn't care enough to include him. I don't even taste bitter resentment or sense the heat of unresolved anger. He's used to it. Which is sadder than if he were tense and irritable.

Hayes leads us to a samsam wood door with a polished erstwyn handle. Two stone-faced guards stand outside. They bow. "Your Majesty." The shorter of the two guards speaks. Like Kalen, he looks fresh-faced and new. I figure he's Thannen's replacement. "I wasn't aware Her Majesty was expecting you."

"She isn't. Is she available?"

"Of course, sir." They move aside.

Hayes's hand hovers over the door, and I taste a glimmer of his nerves before he squares his shoulders and knocks.

"Yes?" Ikenna calls.

"It's Hayes."

Shuffled footsteps. Ikenna opens the door, surprise evident in the arch of her brows. She looks different. Less regal. Instead of her usual drapings of Royalty, she wears a floor-length blue silk robe tied with a pink sash. She's washed her face of makeup for the night. Her dark hair is tucked away, wrapped in rose petals sewn into a cap. It reminds me of my mother, but she wraps her hair in olive leaves.

It's jarring to see her look . . . mundane. Beautiful, yes, but so ordinary it seems absurd that she's capable of all the things I know she is. "Hayes? What are you doing here?"

"We need to talk."

"Now? It's late." She looks past him, scanning the hall. When her gaze sweeps over me, I tense, but her quick look doesn't waver.

"Yes, now," says Hayes. "Are you busy?" A pointless question. She's clearly not doing anything.

Ikenna forces a smile. I know it's forced because she has the same pinched look as Hayes when he's faking a smile. "Of course not. Come in."

We enter her room. Ikenna's guards and Kalen stay in the hall as she closes the door. "What did you want to talk about, Hayes?" Ikenna sits on the gold-and-cream armchair and gestures for Hayes to take the sofa.

"I need advice." Hayes sits, and I take the space next to him. "These past few weeks haven't been easy. With Dad gone, I feel like I'm drowning. Letting him down."

The fireplace isn't lit, but with a touch of Ikenna's finger to a runed stone, flames leap to life. "Well, that's natural when you step into a role you aren't prepared for."

Hayes bristles. "You *expected* me to fail?"

"You haven't failed, Hayes."

"Yet. You meant to say I haven't failed *yet*."

"Don't put words in my mouth. You're going to be a great King. Greatness takes time."

Hayes's expression tightens. "What if I don't get that chance? Dad was a natural. He ruled with an iron fist and everyone respected him. I just want a *sliver* of the respect he commanded."

"Your father had years to learn. You've only had a few weeks."

"How am I supposed to earn Keirdre's trust if they won't listen? The Enforcers want stability—but I need their support to run a stable kingdom. And the Vanihailians want justice for Thannen—but I can't do that without the stability to properly investigate."

"You have to do right by them," says Ikenna.

I almost laugh. It's an absurd response coming from the wife of the man who elevated fae above all, made witches outcasts, and kept humans as little more than slaves. Not to mention the creature cullings, which slaughtered *thousands*. I bite my tongue.

Hayes's hand, resting on his thigh, tightens into a fist—our signal.

Manipulation is my element. Loosening tongues to get what I want. Ikenna is just another mark. I think about what makes her tick—her interests, goals, and what will make her crack to pieces. "Ask her how to do that if the Enforcers still blame you for Thannen's death?"

"How am I supposed to do that without the Enforcers' support?" says Hayes. "They've hated me since your guard was killed. They blame me for his death."

"No. They blame the siren." Ikenna scowls at the mention of me.

"Saoirse didn't kill Thannen."

"Of course she killed him. They found water in his lungs."

Yes. Because you *told whoever you paid to kill him to drown him first.*

"And a stab wound," says Hayes. "Why would Saoirse drown *and* stab him?"

Ikenna frowns. "Stab wound? What are you talking about?"

Hayes's eyes flicker, and for a moment I think he's going to look at me and give us away, but he doesn't. "Thannen was stabbed. You didn't know?"

"No . . ."

I search her face for a sign of deception. Find none. Root my tongue around my mouth, seeking a glimmer of guilt or nerves or anything I usually associate with dishonesty. All I taste is something cloudy, like oversalted stew. Confusion.

If she was the one who ordered Thannen's death, why would she be *confused* about his stab wounds? Why would she pretend not to know he was stabbed?

Unless she genuinely didn't know about it.

What the hell is going on?

"Thannen was stabbed, Mom," says Hayes. "Why would a siren do that?"

For a moment, Ikenna's confusion hovers, but she shakes it off. "Sirens do more than drown. *Your* siren certainly does."

"Usually not at the same time," says Hayes. "Saoirse didn't do this. Someone else killed Thannen. The water in his lungs was an attempt to frame her."

"If she didn't kill him, then who did?"

Until a few moments ago, I would have said Ikenna. But now, I'm not sure.

"That's what I'm trying to figure out," says Hayes. "You don't know anything?"

Her eyes narrow. "Are you accusing me of something?"

"Not unless there's something you'd like to confess?"

I tense. Bold move on Hayes's part.

Ikenna and Hayes stare at each other. Years of unspoken resentment reverberates in the space between them. After a few terse ticks, Ikenna glances away. "I admit I wanted her gone. But I didn't want Thannen to die."

"What are you saying?"

"I *may* have slipped Thannen some incorrect information about my whereabouts that night so he would mislead your siren. I *may* have tipped off some soldiers that the fugitive siren was going to be at the pier. But Thannen was only supposed to tell her where to go. I don't know what he was doing at the pier. He wasn't supposed to be there—and he certainly wasn't supposed to die."

I'm stunned. I'd assumed that whoever wanted me at the pier—Ikenna—was the same person who'd had Thannen killed. She's claiming she was only responsible for the first part. Despite myself, I believe her.

There's no time to dissect this, Ikenna's still talking. "It doesn't matter if she killed him or not. You'd have to convince all of Keirdre she isn't responsible. I don't think you can do that."

"There's no other way to ensure the Enforcers' trust?"

"You have two options: one, hold the siren accountable for her actions."

"She didn't *do* it. Regardless, you know I can't do that. She's not in Keirdre anymore."

"Yes." Ikenna's lips curl into a sneer. "I'm well aware you sent her over the barrier. As I said, you have *two* options. If you can't execute the siren, your only other option is to make an example of the Enforcers."

My blood runs cold.

Hayes stills. "What?"

"It's what your father did. Show the Enforcers and anyone who follows them what happens when they step out of line. If you can't make them respect you, make them fear you. It's just as effective. More so, in fact."

"You want me to—" Hayes is already shaking his head. "You're talking about dozens of soldiers."

"No. I'm talking about *hundreds*. Anyone who supports the Enforcers. Anyone who disobeys you. They must be punished."

"I'm not going to kill anybody."

Ikenna's expression shifts, so subtly it's easy to miss. Before, her eyes were cold. Now they're *hard*. "There are consequences for actions, Hayes. Your siren has killed many. There are consequences for that. Someone killed Thannen. If not your siren, then who? Whoever it was needs to pay the price. That's why people are upset—because they understand that actions have consequences. If you can't punish Thannen's killer, you need to punish those who step out of line. They'll never take you seriously if there are no repercussions."

Hayes is on his feet, hands clenched at his sides, jaw tight with disbelief. "That's not how I want to rule."

"I was under the impression you were asking for advice. I've given it."

"That's not the kind of advice I wanted."

She tilts her head to one side, looking almost bemused. Like she truly can't fathom why Hayes would be resistant to her suggestion. "You asked me how your father earned the obedience of the Enforcers. I've told you. I'm sorry you don't like the answer."

"That's not a solution!" His voice rises as he moves closer to the armchair, towering over Ikenna, who remains seated and irritatingly calm. "You think I can kill hundreds of people and expect them to trust me?"

She chuckles without humor. "You misunderstand me. It's not about *their* trust in you. It's about *your* trust in them." Slowly, she rises. She's still shorter than him, but the tilt of her chin and cruelty of her eyes make her look more powerful. "*You* are a King, why should you have to prove yourself to anyone? You make an example of anyone who opposes you and elevate those you trust. Enforcers should be desperate to prove themselves to you. Not the other way around."

"I want to be someone they respect."

Ikenna's expression doesn't change, but I taste her disappointment like a rotten apple. "Then you want to be weak."

For several long beats, Hayes stares at her. Then, he turns on his heel, apparently done. "Have a good night, Mother."

Ikenna remains still and calm as he moves for the door. "You're just like him. Your brother."

Hayes stops, paces from the door. Slowly, he turns to face her. "What do you mean?"

Something deep and sad brews in Ikenna's eyes. Flavors of pain, loss, and longing lodge on my tongue. "He loved his monster too. Just like you, it clouded his judgment."

"Monster? You mean the siren who . . ." Hayes casts a swift glance at me before looking away.

A sick feeling settles in my stomach. Finnean was lured to

his death by a siren. Drowned in the bay. I didn't realize he had
a relationship with the siren who killed him.

Hayes's hands shudder. "Saoirse wouldn't—"

Ikenna chuckles darkly. "He said the same thing. I think I'm
cursed. Cursed to bear children drawn to their own ruin. She
doesn't love you. She can't. All she can do is kill. You'll spend
the rest of your short life sacrificing everything for a pretty
monster who will *destroy* you. To be King is to make sacrifices
and examples. Finnean could only do one, and he was never
King. You want to be great? Do both."

They hold each other's stares.

Finally, Hayes shakes his head. "You're wrong about her.
And about me. Good night, Mother."

The journey to Hayes's chambers is silent.

He doesn't speak as he leaves Kalen in the hall and sits on
the corner of his bed, staring at the floor. After a long pause, he
says, "They never told me." His gaze doesn't leave the floor.
"Eighteen years his memory has hung over me, and they never
mentioned."

It explains why Ikenna hates me. Why she'd risk killing
her own guard to have me exiled. At least, it would, if not for
the fact—

"I think she was telling the truth about Thannen," I say.

Hayes's expression is heavy. "I thought the same."

It raises more questions. Ikenna planned for me to go to the
pier to be captured and for Hayes to send me over the barrier to
protect me. But there's someone else pulling strings in Keirdre.
Someone who didn't just want me gone—they wanted me
blamed for Thannen's murder.

"Why would someone want to frame me?"

"Considering everything that's happened, I'm guessing they want me off the throne," says Hayes. "Kill Thannen, make the Vanihailian water fae hate me, undermine my authority."

The pieces fit, but it does little to identify the person at the helm of this plot. "*If* Ikenna is telling the truth, then whoever had Thannen killed must've known what she was planning. Who would your mother trust with something like that?"

"I don't know. She doesn't talk to anyone. She's mostly alone . . ." He straightens as a new thought hits him. "Aside from her guards. They know her every move. One of her guards has been around for as long as I can remember."

"Can you look into him?"

"I'll see what I can find." He rubs his eyes. Nerves and fatigue surround him like fog. "I still don't know what I'm going to do about the Enforcers. I was hoping after tonight, I'd know who killed Thannen and be able to appease them."

"Your mother is wrong about a lot of things, but she was right when she said it's not going to happen overnight. Give it time. You freed prisoners today. Gave people their lives back. That's a major victory."

Hayes bends over, unlacing his boots. "It's late. I think I'm going to bed." He looks at me, unspoken question in his eyes—wondering if I'll be joining him. We've developed a ritual. I've slept in his bed just about every night since I arrived in Alkara. And yet, every night, he gives me that same questioning look.

"I should probably head back . . ." As always, I feign reluctance. But I don't leave.

He grins. "I'm sure my bed is more comfortable than whatever you're sleeping on in Alkara." He slides into his bed and pulls back the covers on the other side—*my* side. His grin slips away, turning more serious. "Besides . . ." He glances away, expression almost embarrassed. "I sleep better when you're here."

His honesty crumbles my thin resolve. I can fend off cruelty and attacks with sharp tongues and sharper blades—but I have no defenses against Hayes's vulnerability.

I climb onto the other side of the bed, slowly, to disguise my eagerness.

Without looking at me, Hayes pulls off his shirt. I watch his back muscles flex, comforted by the knowledge that he's facing away and can't see me stare. It's impossible for my eyes not to trail over his body. For a brief few ticks, I let them.

"Good night, Saoirse."

He looks at me and I remember myself. My head jerks away to stare at the ceiling instead. "Good night, sir."

He extinguishes the chaeliss lights. Sheets rustle as he lies down, still not touching me.

We're silent, listening to each other breathe.

Finally, "Why do you think my parents never told me? About Finnean?"

I swallow. It doesn't sit well with me that Finnean was killed by a siren he loved. I never knew him, but it's easy to picture him as Hayes. Handsome, spoiled, and too trusting. Easy to see Finnean, like Hayes, putting his faith in the wrong person. A monster. *Me.*

Is that my true nature? Betraying Hayes over and over until he breaks?

I've already hurt him. Broken his trust so many times it should be shattered beyond repair. And now there's that candle Ikenna gave me, burning a hole through my mattress. I can't tell Hayes about it.

"They probably didn't want to acknowledge it," I say. "It's easier to deal with things when they're left unspoken."

The bed shifts and I know he's facing me. "Do you believe that?"

So much hangs unsaid between us: When he told me he wanted me. When I almost kissed him and he pulled away. When he *actually* kissed me before I left. The distance between us in this bed right now.

Do I believe it's easier to leave things unspoken?

No. Yes. Maybe.

None of it feels right, but the silence is dragging long enough it feels loaded, so all I say is, "I think your parents are lightbrains."

It's the truth. But, as always, only half.

CHAPTER TWENTY-TWO

SLOWLY SINKING

As time passes, I keep an eye on Reyshka. I need to know what she thinks of me. At the Barracks, I wanted Flynn's approval, but here, I *need* Reyshka to see me as the best if I'm going to get an assignment and uncover what she and Larster are planning.

Which is another reason I watch her. To see what secret things she does on Larster's behalf.

The problem is, she doesn't *do* anything. Oh, sure, she watches and criticizes and makes comments, but other than that, nothing. If she's not training us, she's in her office. Sometimes, when she doesn't think anyone's watching, she slips into the cellar through the door in the kitchen.

That's it. She never leaves to go on missions, never leaves at all. The other soldiers come and go, but Reyshka never moves past the isi wood fence surrounding her house.

She's also the only one who doesn't follow Alkaran customs. At least once a week, we have lessons about how to act like an Alkaran. How to dress, how to talk, their holidays and traditions, and so on.

We're taught to wear bright clothing, to refer to their soldiers in plainclothes as "Nightmen," to stay indoors on the first day of spring and plead for heavy rainfall. Despite our lessons,

Reyshka wears almost exclusively dark clothing. The rest of us aren't allowed.

Today, I'm watching Jarek as well as Reyshka. Reyshka *adores* him. She rarely gives out praise, but she showers Jarek in it daily. We're having a sparring tournament, and so far, he's won every single one of his matches.

The order of the sparring rounds was random, but Jarek's first match was early on and he's been winning ever since. I've lost track of how many opponents he's bested.

I'm going to be the one to break his winning streak.

I stand next to Odion, who's so nervous, he's already sweating in the chill harvest air. Neither of us has fought yet, but it's becoming increasingly clear that when it's our turn, our opponent will be Jarek.

After he defeats his next opponent, Reyshka swoops in to crow about how great he is. My mouth floods with acrid jealousy from the other soldiers.

At the Barracks, I was used to that jealousy being directed at me. At first I resented it, but once I accepted I'd never be friends with my fellow Deltas, I learned to relish that feeling. Seeing these new soldiers jealous of Jarek, I miss it.

Odion sighs. "Hardly seems fair," he murmurs lowly to me. "Not that I'd ever question Reyshka, but how is someone freshly back from assignment supposed to defend themselves against someone who's been training nonstop?"

Freshly *back* from assignment?

My eyes follow the soldier Jarek just beat. He was sent out on assignment? Doing what? Why did he come back?

"How long ago was he sent away?" I ask as casually as I can.

"Before I got here."

Odion has been here for four years, meaning this soldier

who returned was sent away *years* ago, and now, just as I've arrived, he comes back?

I don't believe in coincidences.

"I'm still getting used to all the new faces," I say. "How many others are back from assignment?"

"About a dozen so far."

"Siren!" Reyshka calls before I can question him further. "You're next."

Why are soldiers suddenly returning? I have no idea and no time to think about it as I take my stance across from Jarek. His eyes are bright and gray and blank—until he sees me and they darken with desire.

I smirk.

He wants me. His desire will be his downfall.

I flash him a sickly sweet smile and raise my blade—

Too late. Jarek moves suddenly, faster than I was expecting. He swoops upon me with effortless grace.

I manage to block his first swipe, but just barely.

I feel off-kilter. I expected his lust to distract him, but he's just as fast as he was in previous matches.

As I raise my sword, he's kicking at me and, somehow at the same time, pulling water from the morning dew toward me, tangling it between my legs, trying to trip me.

I grab hold of it. I want to push it back at him, but it's whispering to me.

Kill.

I *shove* the water aside and don't use it to fight Jarek. I don't trust I won't do something I can't take back.

That moment's hesitation slows me down. Jarek doesn't need to think when he fights, he just *acts*. He flows seamlessly from one motion to the next. All my energy goes to fending him off—I don't think I've gotten a single offensive attack in.

He slams his elbow against my wrist, knocking my blade to the ground.

I'm shocked. I haven't been disarmed in *years*.

In my surprise, Jarek curls a hand around my throat and slams me into the ground. He lies atop me, using his body to pin me down.

He smirks, just a bit, and I get the feeling he's liking this position a bit too much.

"Jarek wins again," Reyshka says.

I'm dazed as I stand and pat dirt from my clothes. We were only sparring for a few minutes. He doesn't even look out of breath.

It's not until I'm standing next to Odion again and he offers me a few comforting words of encouragement that it sinks in: I just *lost*.

At the Barracks, mediocrity was an impossibility. For some, being solidly in the middle was an acceptable goal. Not me. I was an ikatus. If I wasn't the best, I was nothing. The only way for anyone to think *anything* of me was to be formidable.

Fighting Jarek just now, I didn't feel formidable. I didn't even feel mediocre. I felt weak.

CHAPTER TWENTY-THREE

ONE HAND TIED

Once again, I've woken up next to Hayes and he remains stubbornly on his side of the bed.

It doesn't matter.

I figure if I say it enough times, I'll start to believe it.

I'm still pretending not to be disappointed when I leave the Dreamweave. Carrik is just beginning to stir from his makeshift bed on the floor.

He grins as he sits up, stretching. "Morning. It's early, so I know you don't have training yet—want to kick my ass at sparring?" He asks every day. We're too used to rising early to sleep past dawn, so we always wake around the same time.

Usually, I go for a run alone. I have no idea what he does before it's time to accompany Lex or Zaire to Courliss. I never ask.

He expects me to refuse, the way I always do. Except yesterday, I lost my first sparring match in years. More than lost—Jarek defeated me like it was *easy.*

If I'm ever going to get an assignment, I *need* to be the best.

Unfortunately, I was always at my best when I trained with Carrik.

I glower at him. "Fine."

He stills. "What?"

"Want me to change my mind?"

He scrambles to his feet, expression still disbelieving. "Absolutely not."

"We have enough time for a run and a bit of sparring. If you can't keep up, I'm leaving you behind."

His eagerness is sweet and annoyingly refreshing—like freshly squeezed orange juice. "Sounds good to me."

An hour later, I slam Carrik on his back—again. He groans—*again*.

Either he's gotten rusty in the time we've been here (or from his brief stint in prison) *or* he's letting me vent my anger with him through sparring.

"Up." I position my feet hip-width apart and ready my fists for another round.

Carrik groans and stays on his back on the forest floor. "Give me a minute." He closes his eyes. "Or five."

We're in the forest surrounding Pennex. Here, away from the city, it feels private. I suspect some of the trees around our clearing are dryads, but for now, they stay hidden.

I wait a few ticks, hoping Carrik will spring up, ready to continue. But he keeps lying there, staring at the canopy of trees.

With an exaggerated sigh, I flop on the ground next to him, watching the sky flush muted orange with sunrise. Now that I'm here, I can admit to myself that I'm sore and semi-pleased to take a break. I won't admit it to Carrik, though.

After a few minutes, leaves crinkle as he turns to look at me. "I want to spar some more."

"Great." I sit up, waiting for him to do the same.

He doesn't move. "I think we should try it with nothing held back this time."

"Is that not what we were doing? Or are you giving me permission to try and kill you?"

"I mean with our affinities." He sits up, bringing a few dead leaves stuck to his hair with him. He drags his fingers over the forest floor. "There's morning dew on the leaves. Enough for us to use. And we can try sparring closer to the river. This isn't Keirdre. You don't have to hide."

I take a moment to close my eyes, *feeling* the water on the leaves around me. My instincts prickle with the familiar reminder of how easy it would be to kill him. I open my eyes. "That's not a good idea with you."

"Because you hate me."

"Because me and water and anger are a dangerous combination."

"Didn't you hear what Lex said? Larster lied to you. You don't have to be dangerous."

"I have seventeen years of evidence that says otherwise."

Carrik doesn't say anything for a few moments. "Why'd you finally agree to spar with me? I'm guessing something happened in training. Did someone beat you?"

I don't answer, but my silence says it all.

"It's like when we came over the barrier. You're holding back. When you fight your instincts, you're fighting two people at once—your opponent and yourself. Your opponents are only battling half of you. Half of you is better than most people. Definitely better than me. But apparently, whoever beat you yesterday is better than half of you. I doubt they're better than *all* of you."

"When I'm all of me, I kill people."

"Do you like using your affinity? The water?"

"Yes." I don't hesitate.

"What about when you go too far?"

My eyes snap to his. "You mean when I kill someone?"

"Yes."

I can't look at him when I confess, ". . . *Yes.*" I dig my fingers into the dirt around me so I don't have to see his reaction. "Larster was a liar about a lot of things, but he was right about me. I *am* a monster."

"Do you know how my mother died?"

It feels so completely off topic, I'm not sure how to react. "Yes. When they discovered you were part human—"

"That's the why. I asked *how?*"

"She was executed." I remember the display I saw in Keirdre. Of the human man—barely more than a boy—in Haraya. The way the crowd of fae roared as Enforcer Anarin Arkin slashed a dagger across his throat. The horrible spectacle of it all. "Publicly, I assume."

He nods. "They wanted her to suffer. *Both* of us to suffer." I've never heard Carrik speak so softly. "To make an example of her. Did you know that the Enforcer of Sinu is a water fae? She rules over an entire race of people and she despises them. She ordered for me to be transported to Sinu with my mother. We rode in the same carriage from Vanihail to Sinu, but we weren't allowed to speak. She tried. Once. They gagged her for the next two days and refused to give her anything to eat or drink. She didn't make that mistake again.

"We cried the whole way there. There's no building like Haraya in Sinu—why waste money on humans? It's just a stage in the town center. Humans are forced to attend, so the square was full. I was in the front row when they brought my mother up to the stage. The Enforcer announced her crimes and stabbed her in the stomach. She died slowly and painfully, and I sat there and watched and there was *nothing* I could do.

"They brought me back to Vanihail. Put me on nursemaid's duty. The only time I had to grieve was the journey back from Sinu." His hands are clenched where they rest on his lap as he glares at nothing. "You're not a monster, Saoirse. The people who did that—the King who decided *that* was justice—they're the monsters. Not you."

Gently, I put a hand on his back. When he doesn't move, I wrap my arms around him. He said talking about his parents doesn't make him sad. That it only makes him angry. He's right in that I can taste the fury, fiery enough to burn the world down.

Right now, I taste the grief too. It's cold and sharp and hurts my teeth. My head rests on his shoulder as I hug him like I used to. "I'm sorry," I murmur into his chest. "She didn't deserve that. Neither did you."

He's still and unyielding. "You don't deserve this either, Saoirse."

"Carrik," I say softly as I pull away from him. "I appreciate the sentiment, but you're wrong. I *like* killing people. I'm the same. Worse, maybe."

His eyes are aimed at the forest but empty in a way that tells me he's not really looking at anything. "My mother was the best person I ever knew. She couldn't cook. She was dangerously clumsy. She loved to sing, but she was *awful* at it." The corners of his mouth twitch as though he's holding in a laugh, even as his eyes pool with unshed tears. "She was selfless. Kind. Had a smile that made everything better. She had great intuition, and she would have *loved* you. She wouldn't have thought you were a monster—because you're not."

"Carrik—"

"Listen to me. Do you know how they figured out I was half human? It was *my* fault. My father was a blacksmith. Did I ever tell you that?" He doesn't pause or give me a chance to answer him. "I never wanted that life. I dreamed of glory. I wanted to be a soldier. So *I* joined the Ranks. *I* risked my parents' lives because I couldn't stop being selfish and just follow in his footsteps. If I had sucked it up—been a damned blacksmith—my parents would still be here. My mom wouldn't have had her stomach slashed open on a stage. My father wouldn't have died alone in prison.

"I was reckless. I thought being a blacksmith was beneath me, and it cost me everything. I put my happiness over their lives. They *died* for it. You're not a monster. Not any more than I am."

My heart aches for him. "You were just a kid."

"So are *you*. I know you think everything is your responsibility, but it's not. You're still figuring out what it means to be *you*, let alone what it means to be a siren. You think you're a monster because Larster told you so. He rewrote your history because he was afraid of you. He wanted everyone else to be afraid too. He wanted you to fear yourself more than he did. Let's prove that bastard is a fool."

"I—" I'm out of arguments. "If you're doing this because you think we're going to be friends again, you're wasting your time."

"If it's time with you, then it's not wasted." He jumps to his feet and holds out a hand to me. "Come on. Spar with me the way sirens do. You exist. I'm glad you do. No more apologizing for it."

I study his hand for several long moments before I reach out and take it.

CHAPTER TWENTY-FOUR

SILVER AND HONEY

I met Carrik Solwey every day for six weeks before we finally spoke.

I'd joined the Barracks with dreams of grandeur. I wanted to secure a high-paying job after graduation to protect Rain, yes, but I also wanted one place where I wasn't seen as weak.

Those dreams were foolish. No one in the Barracks took me seriously as an ikatus. So, I decided to be the best.

I rose every morning, well before training began, and went to the training rooms. I practiced handling weapons so I didn't struggle under their weight, dodging blows so I was attuned to my surroundings, footwork so I was quick on my feet . . .

After the legendary fall of Carrik Solwey, he snuck into the training rooms early as well. Guards weren't allowed to use the facilities, but there was no one else there to catch him, so he didn't care.

For six weeks, the two of us trained side by side—but completely separate. I focused on my training, he focused on his.

He approached me first. I was content to stubbornly ignore him for the rest of eternity, but he flashed a charming smile, made some lightbrained joke that wasn't funny, and asked if I wanted to spar with him.

I thought about refusing. But his smile was sincere, he didn't mind when I told him I was an ikatus, and—though I'd never admit it—I was lonely.

Falling into a pattern with him was as easy as breathing in and out. He cracked jokes endlessly. None of them were funny, but he kept at it anyway. Five weeks in, he finally told an unfunny joke that was so ridiculous it made me laugh. He crooned about it for *days*.

It was the moment I first considered him a friend. Not that I ever told him, but he knew. Early-morning trainings turned into late-night conversations. His abysmal sense of humor turned into shared jokes between the two of us. And a stranger I'd ignored for weeks turned into my best friend.

Former best friend.

I stand ankle-deep in the flow of the river, hands raised, preparing to spar.

It's my first day training in Alkara with, as Carrik calls it, both my hands freed.

Carrik's face is calm, but I taste his fear—he's terrified of me but willing to practice with me anyway. "Anytime you find yourself wanting to kill me, think about something that grounds you instead. You ready?"

Neither of us waits for the other to agree—we just start. It's the same way we've started sparring countless times before. Both of us standing still until one of us springs suddenly at the other to catch them off guard.

We're not using weapons, just our bodies and the water. Our limbs move swiftly in tune with each other. I swing, he blocks. He kicks, I dodge.

For a few moments, we fall into a rhythm.

Kill.

The water's chant starts soft.

I scramble for something to ground me. My first thought is Rain.

I duck under his arm as he swings it at me. Quickly, I move around so I'm behind him. My foot kicks the back of his knee, buckling it and making him fall forward into the river, splashing more water against me.

Thinking of Rain was a bad idea. Because now all I can think about is how close Carrik is, how easy it would be to kill him, and how close my sister was to death by his hand.

Kill.

Rain usually tethers me to reality—except for when I'm with Carrik. With him, she reminds me of how much he's hurt me.

Killing him now would be easy—but if I do, I'll be just as out of control of my instincts as I was before, and I still won't get an assignment.

Carrik straightens and spins around. He swings again and I block him. At the same time, I pull water from the river to snatch the hand not coming at me, wrapping it in its watery grip.

It leaves his chest exposed. I jab him right in the middle—knocking the breath out of him.

In response, he feints left, then gets me from the right. He hurls water against my knees, trying to knock me over.

I lurch, but remain upright. Carrik and I trade blows, blocking and dodging, easily anticipating our next moves.

I manage to snatch his wrist with one hand. At my bidding, the river rises to wrap around his waist and drag him back, deeper into the water.

He's knee-deep in the river, slightly off-balance. He's a bit taller than me, so as I approach, the water comes up to my thighs. I love this feeling. Of water rushing around me, soothing me.

Kill.

The river rushes faster, growing more insistent. It knows how much I despise him. It wants me to drag him downstream. Punish him.

It taunts me, reminding me of everything he's done. Every tear I've spilled over him.

The knot inside me coils tighter with my mounting rage.

I raise my hand, bringing a sphere of water with it. My arm shoots forward, hurling it at Carrik. Then another. And another. Until I'm launching water at him so quickly, so forcefully, he can't move.

But I can.

I think about those damned silver envelopes threatening to expose Rain. The shadowy figure outside Haraya who forced me to reveal how to bring down the barrier. Spektryl holding Rain captive, dangling her life over my head, making me dance like a puppet on his string . . .

Focus.

I can't think about Rain around Carrik. I force myself to think about the water itself. Its coolness against my skin. I remember stolen, happy moments from my childhood. Before the water turned against me. Before my first kill. When it offered solace and nothing more. Before I learned to fear the water as I fear myself.

I focus on *that*. Relish the sensation of my control over the water, not its control over me.

The water is just another mark, I tell myself. Not my enemy. It *wants* to do as I say.

Do I want to kill Carrik? Most days. But right now, he's my path to improving, defeating Jarek, earning an assignment from Reyshka, and foiling her plot.

I can't get petty revenge on Carrik because of what he did to Rain. I need to control myself *for* her. For her chance at a better future.

I feel my eyes fade back to honey. I stop hurling spheres of water at him.

Control. I'm in control. Close enough, anyway.

Still, I don't want to drag out this fight any longer and tempt fate—or my instincts. With a snarl, I lunge forward. My hands curl around Carrik's throat. Water rises on either side of him, wrapping around his wrists like manacles as I tackle him.

I land on his chest, hands around his neck, pinning him against the floor of the river, holding his head underwater as the river courses around us.

I smirk. I've got him pinned. I won.

I rise to my feet and pull him up into a seated position.

He's soaking wet and sputtering for breath. I very nearly killed him. I *could* have killed him.

But I didn't.

CHAPTER TWENTY-FIVE

FROM THE ASHES

I've always liked the rhythm of a routine. Carrik and I fall into familiar patterns. We wake before dawn, run for a bit, then spar in the forest before I go to meet Reyshka to train with the Keirdrens.

Training with Carrik makes me think of what used to be. Sometimes, it's easy to pretend we're back in Keirdre, in the times before he broke us.

I feel myself improving. I haven't had to spar Jarek again yet, but my skills are sharpening. I feel myself getting lighter on my feet, my reflexes quickening, and, most important, myself becoming more comfortable with the water.

Progress in Keirdre is slower. Hayes spoke with Ikenna's oldest guard, but he didn't know anything, and we still have no idea who Ikenna told about her plans to get rid of me and no idea who had Thannen killed.

Carrik spends his days with the Resistance. He's yet to see any indication that they're lying about not having an army. As far as he can tell, their numbers really are as dwindling as Lex and Zaire said.

I'm not sure if I believe him. Even if I *did* believe him, that doesn't mean I trust Lex or Zaire. Which is why today, I told

Reyshka I have a private assignment from Larster so I can shadow Zaire to learn more about Alkara and the Resistance.

So far, all I've learned is that Zaire walks really fast and has a tendency to forget to check if Carrik and I are keeping up. He has a bag slung over his shoulder and a pen in his hand, which he taps against his thigh as he walks. His brown eyes move as quickly as his feet as they sweep over our surroundings, taking everything in.

"Are you looking for something?" I have to trot to keep up with him.

"Nothing in particular." Zaire's rapid pace doesn't slow. "Sorry. I walk fast. And I feel especially slow right now, so I'm trying to make up for it."

"*This* is slow?" says Carrik.

Zaire turns to face us. He walks backward, eyes still darting around to observe everything as he addresses us. "I'm used to working from the air. I'm faster with wings."

Right. He's an impundulu. He can transform into a lightning bird. "What exactly is your job?"

"The city is divided into zones." Somehow, even walking backward, Zaire's pace barely slows. "Every day, I review my zone and report back on anything out of place. The city then assigns specific tasks to whoever is best suited to fixing them." Zaire points. "For example, those cobblestones are coming loose and need to be replaced. I take note of that here"—he pulls a notebook from his bag—"and report it to the city. Most likely, an earth fae will be assigned the task of fixing it."

"You can see something like *that* from the air?"

"Impundulu have excellent vision." Apparently satisfied he's sated our curiosity for now, Zaire faces forward again and keeps walking. Every few moments, he jots something down.

"There's someone like you doing this everywhere?" says Carrik.

"Yes." Zaire's tone is absent. He's very invested in his task. "In smaller places like Wystmeren, there's just one person assigned to the entire town. Pennex is a densely populated city, so there are more of us here."

"Even poorer areas?" I ask.

Zaire gives me a confused frown. "Why should wealth determine quality of life?"

I don't have a good answer. Not because I think wealth *should* determine quality of life, but because I can't fathom a world where it doesn't. "Are they always impundulu?"

"If there's a lot of ground to cover, yes. We tend to live in areas where we best fit. A lot of impundulu live in Pennex. We're mostly left over from the early days. After Keirdre erected the barrier." I can *hear* the scowl in his voice. "Alkara spent the next several decades trying to find a way to bring it down. Many of my kind spent years trying to fly over, but it was impossible. Even after we gave up, many impundulu settled here."

"What about dryads?" asks Carrik. "We met some in the forest when we first arrived."

"Dryads used roots to try and tunnel beneath the barrier. They were also unsuccessful. Many of them still live in the forest near the barrier. They *used* to be our first line of defense." The anger in his voice grows more pronounced. "But many Alkarans have decided Keirdre is no longer a threat. If and when they decide to attack, we'll be all but defenseless."

We fall silent as Zaire continues to complete his responsibilities and I mull over his words. We pass a short stone structure surrounded by an isi wood fence. Zaire scribbles something in his notes.

"Is there something wrong with the isi wood?" I ask.

"See the banding here?" Zaire gestures to a few light streaks of gray on a piece of wood. "It means the enchantment's fading and the wood needs to be replaced."

"What *is* it exactly? Is it like samsam?"

"We don't have samsam trees here. Your King took them all." I taste his peppery anger. "He made a point to take all resources that could benefit him and anything he thought would make it easier for us to fight back. He sent soldiers around Alkara to burn all samsam trees that wouldn't fall within the Keirdren borders right before the barrier was created."

Larster only ever had one trick. Steal and burn. Over and over.

"Isi wood comes from the trees we planted in the ashes. It can't be runed, but it can be enchanted. Unfortunately, the enchantments are difficult—not all witches can manage. They fade quickly and they're easy to counter."

"How?"

"All magic has its counter. The enchantment of isi wood can be undone by samsam trees. We don't have samsam here, so it's mostly impenetrable. But we are not Keirdre. We don't encourage people shutting off the world to escape responsibility for their actions. Which is why isi wood isn't available for individual use. Only public spaces."

That can't be true. Reyshka has it. "Are there exceptions?"

"The only way to obtain isi wood is to receive a license from a member of the Royal council. They only approve requests for public use, like the schoolhouse where Courliss is located. There are no exceptions."

For a tick, I wonder how Reyshka obtained it for herself— but the answer is obvious. She stole it. I don't know how or from where, but I'm confident she copied her King and took what she wanted for herself.

Samsam is so common in Keirdre, I can't imagine life without it. My *lairic* beads are made from samsam, and it's how I've maintained contact with my aunties over the years. "If samsam can counteract isi wood, would a *lairic* bracelet be able to?"

"Probably." Zaire looks at me sharply. "Why? Do you have *lairic* beads?"

I know better than to tell him the truth. "No." I pair the lie with a convincing scoff. "*Lairic* beads are still expensive and very rare in Keirdre. They're like *keil* beads, we're running low." A half-truth.

Zaire's face darkens. "Because your King is a fool and your people are foolish. Do you know why your King constructed the barrier in the first place? Resources. Keirdre was flowing with umbian clay and samsam trees, and it's right on the coast. It wasn't enough for your King. He picked a fight with Alkara to steal what few resources we had. We fought back. When it was clear he was going to lose, do you know what he did?"

I've never heard this version of the story, but it's not hard to guess how it ends. "He built the barrier?"

"Not yet. First, he arranged a meeting to talk about a peace treaty. Then he gathered Alkara's leaders in one place to discuss peace—and he slaughtered them. *Then* he built his barrier. And now, you squander the things he killed for and run yourself dry of everything that made you plentiful to begin with. Using *keil* beads to solve all your problems. Runing whatever you like . . ."

"We're not all like that."

"Did you not use *keil* beads every day?"

My face heats in anger. "I *had* to."

"Yes." He waves me off like a fly. "*That's* the problem.

Larster's created a world where excessive use of limited resources is necessary for survival. Keirdre is a poison to everyone, even itself. Designed to leech itself dry of everything it needs to flourish."

I see where Carrik gets his anger. I can picture Carrik and Zaire exchanging letters over the years, Carrik venting about all the things he hates in Keirdre, Zaire fanning his flames. "You speak as if Alkara is without flaws."

"No world is perfect. A *good* one corrects itself. A world willing to seek out its flaws and *change* is the only kind that's sustaining. How long do you think your kingdom can last under dictatorship of the fae?"

"We have a new King. He's not his father."

Zaire rolls his eyes. "Maybe you're right. Maybe your boy King is different. Or maybe it doesn't matter. Larster ruled for centuries. Following the death of someone so powerful, you need a firm hand and a clear plan. Or all you have is lawlessness."

He keeps walking. "Alkara takes pains to constantly improve itself and hear the concerns of its people. Tomorrow, there's a Town Hall. A meeting at Faraday House every lune where the Queen addresses the people and answers their questions."

I assume Faraday House is the stone manor in the heart of the city. "Your Queen just lets anyone into her home?"

"Town Halls take place in the courtyard. And Queen I'llyaris likely won't be in attendance anyway, after . . . recent events." His sentence trails suggestively.

My eyes narrow. "Are you going to make me ask? What happened?"

"There was an assassination attempt a few lunes ago. She barely survived. Have your Keirdren friends mentioned it?"

His voice is casual, but I know what he's hinting at. "You think they're behind it?"

"Who else would want her dead?"

"I have no idea, but why would Keirdre try and kill her? The monarchy rotates. If she dies, next on the throne are the sprites, right?"

"The rotation is only for *natural* transitions of power. If there's a death, it changes—to discourage foul play. In the event of the unforeseeable death of a reigning monarch, the crown passes to a predetermined council member."

"Who?" asks Carrik.

"It's a secret. Only the council member knows. For security."

"You think whoever tried to kill the Queen is going to try again?"

"I think assassination attempts, when gone unpunished, are rarely isolated events. Whoever tried to kill the Queen failed. Whoever wanted her dead before—Keirdren or otherwise—likely still wants her dead. If your Keirdrens were responsible—"

"They're not *my* anything."

"If *the* Keirdrens were responsible," he corrects, "they'll likely try again."

The entire time I've been here, I've wondered *why* Larster sent Reyshka over. If Zaire is right—as I suspect he is—and Reyshka's purpose here is to kill the Alkaran Queen, we'll have no chance of peace.

I need to know for certain that the Keirdrens tried to kill the Queen. If they did, I need to stop them from trying again—and succeeding.

CHAPTER TWENTY-SIX
A VIOLENT NATURE

The thing about sharing a room with a skilled and well-trained soldier is that sneaking out is impossible. I don't *want* to involve Carrik in my plans, but considering I have to do this at night, keeping him out isn't an option.

Still, I try. I keep quiet, wait until I hear his breaths slow with sleep, and creep out of bed. I take about two steps before his hand snags me by the ankle. "Going somewhere?" He sounds amused and drowsy at the same time.

I hold in a groan. I didn't actually expect it to work, but I'm still annoyed. I tug my foot out from his grasp. "Any chance I can convince you to go back to sleep and leave me alone?"

I don't need to see him to know he's smirking. "Not a chance. So, where are we going? If you don't tell me, I'll just follow you." I turn on the chaeliss lights so we can see each other. His expression is light, teasing, and curious. "You knew I was going to wake up."

"And hoping you wouldn't."

"Where are we going?"

"Courliss."

He frowns. "You're welcome there anytime. I go just about every day."

"I'm welcome when Lex, Zaire, and the rest of the Resistance are there, watching over my shoulder. I want to go when no one can direct me away from anything. If they have nothing to hide, why should it matter if I go in at night?"

"There's an isi wood fence around it, remember? It's enchanted to only allow select people to pass. I'm not one of them. After last time . . ."

"That's fine." I slip my hand beneath my mattress and pull out my *lairic* beads. "I can get past that."

Carrik reaches for his boots. "Let's go, then."

"You're still not invited."

"Neither are you," he points out.

I'm annoyed but he's not wrong, so with a scowl, I tiptoe downstairs, Carrik right behind me. As we approach the door, he pauses to grab a ring of keys from a hook near the front door. My eyebrows shoot up. "They just leave that out in the open like that?"

He shrugs. "They're trusting. You should try it sometime."

My eyes narrow. "I did. Ended up with a dagger to the back. Yours, if I remember correctly."

The teasing light fades from his eyes. He sighs as we leave Lex and Zaire's and start weaving through the streets. The Festival of Reds has ended, leaving the city quiet and empty.

When we reach the isi wood fence that surrounds Courliss, I pull my *lairic* beads from my pocket. Hesitantly, I run them against the fence.

Carrik alternates between glancing around to make sure no one's coming and watching my hands. "You sure it's going to work?"

"Not until I try it." The memory of the last time I touched enchanted isi wood—of the searing pain that engulfed my body—comes to mind. I bat the thought away. Breath bated, I reach for the fence—

Carrik knocks my hand aside, shoves himself in between me and the fence, and throws a hand against the wood. He's tense, preparing for pain, but after a pause, he sighs in relief and drops his hand. "It worked."

I whack his arm. "Why the hell did you do that?"

He shrugs as he pushes the gate open and holds it out for me. "It hurt you last time. I didn't want it to do that again."

I almost say thank you. Until I remember that it's Carrik and he's already hurt me more than this damned fence ever could. I don't say anything as we walk inside.

We circle around to the back of Courliss. The double doors of the storm cellar are locked. I half expect the keys not to fit and to have to pick the lock anyway—but with a click, the doors unlock, and my shoulders ease.

We descend the stairs in complete darkness. When we reach the bottom, Carrik fumbles around until he finds a chaeliss stone and bathes the chamber in torchlight.

It looks as it did in daylight. Except now, I'm not being attacked by overeager strangers. Last time I was here, I didn't spend much time in the main room, just followed Lex into the library and their office. I won't make that mistake this time.

My legs start a slow circle of the perimeter of the main room. Tension rolls off Carrik as he follows. "What is it you're looking for?"

"I'm not sure." I examine the tapestries on the wall. Each is a woven story depicting a different creature. They remind me of Larster's hidden portrait room, but instead of showing a single creature frozen in time, they weave stories. History.

We enter the library next. I walk around the room, examining the books, looking to see if anything appears hidden. When I reach the wall entirely spanned by a map, I slow. My fingers glide over the surface of the map and my eyes follow their trail, taking it all in. I'm fascinated by the idea of faraway lands . . .

My perusal stops.

Szeiryna.

It's marked within the borders of Alkara, outlined in faint gray. From the looks of this map, it's near Pennex.

I feel Carrik behind me. Taste a burst of lemon—he's surprised. "I didn't realize it was so close to here. Do you want to go? We could get there in—"

I'm shaking my head before he's finished. "No." My hand falls away from the map. I'm curious—more so than I care to admit—but I'm not sure I can handle seeing the ruins of a life I'll never have. I move away from the map, continuing my perusal of the library, but my thoughts are jangled and I'm not really seeing anything.

Carrik follows me at a slight distance, giving me space. "They have a myth here. About a Prince and a siren. According to legend, the Prince's family told him he had to choose between the siren and the throne. He told them he picked the crown, but he continued to see her in secret. Can you guess how this story ends?"

He loved his monster too.

This sounds like the story Ikenna told Hayes—about what happened to Finnean. "She killed him?" I guess.

"No. The Prince's family killed *her*. In retaliation, the siren's family killed the Prince."

My feet echo my thoughts and trip over themselves. All legends are based in truth. Is this legend a more faithful retelling of what happened to Finnean?

I prefer this version. Where the siren isn't a monster, chained to her instincts, cursed to kill the boy she loved.

Unfortunately, wanting something to be real doesn't make it so.

Lex showed me two versions of the same history—history taught in Alkara and a completely different account told in Keirdre. I admit, I like me better through the lens of Alkaran history. But again, just because I *want* that to be my truth doesn't mean it is.

"Why are you telling me this?"

"I thought you wanted to know about the history of sirens. This legend is part of that. So is Szeiryna."

I allowed myself to hope before coming to Alkara—hope for more sirens, hope for some clue about my nature. My hopes were shattered, as was my heart. Am I curious about where I come from? Of course. Is it enticing to know that Szeiryna is *here*, close enough to visit? Absolutely.

Part of me—a large part—wants to see it. But then there's also the part of me that's terrified it'll break me all over again. "I don't want to see Szeiryna."

"Why not?"

I don't know if I can handle seeing irrefutable proof of how completely alone I am. I hold my tongue. "Leave it alone. I don't want to go. End of story."

He wants to keep pushing, but I shove past him into the office that branches from the library. Lex sat behind the desk the last time we were here, and I didn't look through anything aside from the books they put in front of me. It felt invasive to rummage through someone's desk in the daytime. At night, away from the curious eyes of the Resistance, nothing is off-limits.

I stride over to the desk as Carrik comes into the room. I feel him watching me, but he wisely decides to keep his mouth shut.

I yank on the first desk drawer. It rattles uselessly and doesn't open—locked. I grin to myself. *Finally*. Something they don't want me to find.

I procure my lock picking equipment from my pocket. I'd brought it in case we didn't have keys for the padlocked storm doors.

In less than a minute, the drawer's open and I'm feeling around, searching. I find a pamphlet of membership rules for the Resistance. Useless. Next, a leather-bound journal. A ledger. Curious, I flip to the final entries to see how many members of the Resistance there are.

Twenty-one names. Not even two dozen. I can see why this drawer is locked—Lex and Zaire have been cagey about how many members they have. They said numbers were low, but I had no idea they were *this* low.

An envelope is shoved into the back corner of the drawer, crumpled, like someone wanted to get rid of it but then thought better of it. Zaire's name is on the front.

I pull out the scrap of parchment inside. The creases are worn from constant folding and refolding. This letter has been read repeatedly. But judging by how rumpled the exterior is, the reader didn't like its contents.

Zaire Aimes,

Once again, your request for a private audience with Her Majesty Queen I'llyaris is denied. The Kingdom of Alkara will not provide you or your group access to an army on a whim. We have heeded your warnings in the past. Enough is enough. Kindly cease sending pointless letters with absurd requests.

Any more letters will result in your protective license being revoked and heavy fines.

I read that letter at least seven times, heart leaping with each reread. Lex and Zaire told me no one in Alkara took them seriously, but I hesitated to believe them. *This* is my confirmation. As of right now, the Resistance doesn't have an army. When the barrier comes down, they'll have no way to attack. My family will be safe.

I think of the human woman at the Festival. The way she laughed with her partner. I'm one step closer to securing that kind of happiness for Rain.

The *only* threat facing Keirdre if the barrier comes down is Reyshka. As soon as I foil what she and Larster had planned, I can finally, finally tell Hayes to bring down the barrier.

CHAPTER TWENTY-SEVEN

HIS MAJESTY

The last time I was in the King's war room, Hayes told Vanihail's elite that I was a fugitive and that he intended to continue his father's putrid legacy.

I'm here in a Dreamweave, but it's just as tense now as it was then. Maybe even more so.

Hayes sits at the head of the long table. His advisers stand around him, as they once did for his father. With a few key differences. For one, Hayes has much fewer people loyal to him, so his group of advisers is slimmer. For another, Hayes's advisers aren't all water fae. A welcome change if not for the tangible tension that threatens to engulf me.

". . . building more numbers, Your Majesty," one of his advisers—a water fae—is saying.

The grooves of anxiety in Hayes's face have deepened since I last saw him. "I need to speak with Enforcer Arkin. Now."

I stand off to the side, watching. He hasn't noticed me yet.

"She's refusing, sir," says the adviser.

"I beg your pardon? She's refusing to speak to her King?"

"She and the other Enforcers are unhappy given your most recent enactment, sir." The adviser's tone is carefully blank, but I taste rancid disgust. Whatever Hayes has done, this adviser disapproves. "We've received word that the Enforcers have joined with the Vanihailians calling for your removal from the throne."

Hayes looks seconds away from burying his head in his hands and screaming. Instead, he sits in stony silence, thinking. Or maybe he's quietly panicking. It's impossible to tell which.

What have I just walked into? I knew the Enforcers were refusing to listen to Hayes. I knew the water fae wanted him to step down from the throne. *This* sounds like the Enforcers have shifted their allegiance entirely. The Enforcers are no longer merely bad listeners—they're planning to mutiny.

After an excruciating pause, Hayes says, "Where are they stationed now?"

"Kurr Valley. Near Ketzal."

"How bad is it?"

"They're conducting unauthorized raids every day. Dozens of people have been imprisoned or had their homes burned."

Hayes says nothing for a few moments, thinking. "How many soldiers can we send to go and fight?"

"Not enough. We need to fortify the Palace."

Hayes's emotions are dry and acrid, like burned bread. "We'll have to spare soldiers at the Palace, then."

His words draw heated reactions from three advisers. They begin talking over each other.

"Sir, we can't—"

"That would be dangerous—"

"I can't advise that, Your Highness—"

At that, Hayes's eyes flash darkly. "*What* did you just call me?"

The adviser flinches, recognizing his mistake. "M-my apologies, Your Majesty. I meant no disrespect."

Hayes glowers at him, long enough to make him squirm. "We're sending soldiers to protect people. I can spare guards here."

"Sir," one of them objects further. "It will open us up to attacks—"

A wave of water crashes over the room, dousing everyone. It tightens into a rope and slithers around the adviser like a necklace. It doesn't squeeze, just hangs around his neck in an obvious threat. Hayes glares. "I was not *asking*. Our options are either allow well-trained soldiers to sit here and play nursemaid to me *or* send them to defend those unlucky enough to *not* have an army at their disposal." Hayes's voice is a steel blade—sharp and swift. "This is not up for debate. We'll send soldiers to Kurr Valley tomorrow. Understood?"

The adviser looks like he's bitten directly into a rancid lemon, but he nods. "Understood, sir."

"Good." The chain of water drops away from the offending adviser's throat. "We'll reconvene tomorrow at midday. For now, you're all dismissed."

"Yes, sir."

The room clears, leaving Hayes with Jeune.

He buries his head in his hands. Doesn't speak.

"Hayes?" says Jeune hesitantly.

"Can you give me a moment, please?"

"Of course." She brushes a hand over his shoulder comfortingly and slips out.

He hasn't noticed me yet and I'm not sure what to do. Should I leave? Or—

"How much of that did you hear?" Hayes's voice is muffled from his hands.

"Enough," I say softly.

He pulls his head up and looks at me. *Really* looks at me,

with eyes that are blue and intense and impossibly sad. "Saoirse?"

"Yes?"

"Can I ask you a favor?"

In this moment, I'm not sure I could deny him anything. "Of course."

He pushes back his chair and approaches me with slow, cautious steps, as though afraid I'll dart away if he moves too suddenly. "Do you think I could . . . hold you? Just for a moment?"

It's embarrassing, the effect he has on me. I don't even think—just meet him halfway and wrap my arms around him.

We don't speak. He holds me, taking in my warmth. I hold him, wishing I could lift the weight of countless impossible choices.

When he pulls back, he keeps his arms loosely around my waist. "I'm not very good at this, am I?"

"What do you mean?" I know what he means. I only ask the question to give myself a few more moments to think of a good response.

"Being King."

"You just need time." I don't know if I believe that anymore.

"I don't *have* time."

"You care about people," I say. "That's important."

"Is it enough?"

I scramble for a lie—or a half-truth. I'm afraid he's right. Hayes is a good person and I love that about him, but there's so much to combat: the Enforcers fighting him in Keirdre, Reyshka fighting Alkara on the other side . . .

Hayes is one good person against centuries of evil. How could that ever be enough?

I can't say that. He's looking at me with desperation, and though he'd never say it, he *needs* me to lie to him.

I force a smile. "Of course it is."

He still looks unsure. His arms fall from my waist and he smiles, like my words of comfort were enough. I smile back like I don't taste his lingering doubt.

"I only caught the end of your conversation with your advisers," I say. "What happened today?"

"I officially changed the law so it's no longer illegal to be in a relationship with a different creature. And I replaced the Enforcer of Sinu with someone I trust to make sure it's actually carried out," he says. "I figured if they're going to hate me anyway, what am I waiting for? I want to make a difference."

Their reactions make sense now. Sickening, frustrating sense. Hayes stomped on one of Larster's most cherished traditions. In response, the Enforcers determined he's no longer fit to rule. It used to just be the Vanihailians who wanted Hayes removed from the throne—now they've been joined by the Enforcers and their army.

"Good. I'm glad." I smile weakly, hoping it masks my doubts.

Hayes did the right thing. He always does. But he's facing a mutiny because of it.

When I left Keirdre, I thought our biggest threat was the Resistance army. Now I know there *is* no army.

Yesterday, I figured our biggest threat was Reyshka. I was wrong about that too.

Our biggest threat is Keirdre itself—the Enforcers.

Yesterday, bringing down the barrier felt possible. Today I'm wondering, what's the point? If we bring down the barrier while the Enforcers are revolting against Hayes, will anything really change?

I take a breath. Force some life into my thin smile. Hayes doesn't need to hear my fears. Not now.

I don't know how he's going to get the Enforcers under control or when the barrier can come down—but I do know what I need to do tomorrow if I'm going to stop Reyshka.

CHAPTER TWENTY-EIGHT

GLEAMING SILVER

My hood is pulled low as I skulk around the side of Reyshka's house. I waver, just in front of the isi wood perimeter. Once I enter the yard through the gap in the fence—as I do every morning for training—I won't be able to hear what's happening at the front of the house.

I need to get into the cellar. The storm doors around back provide the best and most secluded point of entry. As long as Reyshka is otherwise occupied.

Thud. Thud.

Right on time, Carrik knocks on the front door.

Did I want to recruit him for this? Of course not. But even I could admit this is a job that requires at least two people, and he's all I've got.

I hold my breath until I hear the front door hinges squeal as Reyshka opens it.

Since she *never* leaves the house, I couldn't wait for her to leave or try to draw her out. Carrik will keep her distracted at the front door, giving me time to break into the cellar and find whatever secrets she's hiding.

I hear the low timbre of Carrik's voice as he speaks to Reyshka. Can't hear what he says, but when I hear the higher notes of her response, I know their conversation—and my countdown—has begun.

I dart through the gap in the fence.

Zaire said that isi wood is *only* available to those who get a special license from the Royal council. I figure if Carrik can convince her he's a Nightman—Alkara's version of Enforcers, who dress in plainclothes—he can question her about how she obtained her isi wood and steal me a few minutes to poke around.

The storm doors are set into the ground behind Reyshka's house. They're fitted with curved handles secured by a chain that's padlocked shut.

My pulse roars in my ears. With the isi wood fence, I can't hear what's happening out front—if Reyshka is still occupied—but I don't have time to worry about that. I dig out the thin metal rods used for lock picking and get to work. I maneuver them into the padlock's keyhole and twist, feeling for the tumblers shifting . . .

Click.

I exhale in relief.

A small victory, but thrilling nonetheless.

I slide the chain away and open the storm doors. Stone steps lead into a dark cellar. With one hand pressed to the slate wall beside me, I walk down. Faint morning light filters in, illuminating my surroundings as I reach the bottom step. The cellar walls are stone and jagged. The floor is gray slate, piled high with dozens of wooden crates.

My eyes flit over to the back wall. I don't see Carrik's signal yet, which is a good sign, but I still have no idea how long he'll be able to keep Reyshka occupied.

I drop to my knees and pry off the lid of the crate closest to me.

My breath catches. Heart leaps into my throat.

Blades.

This crate is full of them. They're brand-new, gleaming silver, and freshly sharpened with a violet hilt.

Dread rises in my throat like bile, threatening to choke me. I shove the feeling aside. I'll have time to panic later.

My palms are sweaty as I replace the crate's lid. Move on to the next.

More blades. Also gleaming silver and brand new.

What the hell were she and Larster planning?

The next crate has crossbow bolts. Silver with a violet tip, like the ones we use in training, except, like the swords, these have never been used.

I get through three more crates. Each full of weapons. Enough for hundreds of soldiers. Enough for war.

There are more weapons here than soldiers in Reyshka's camp. Which means she must have *more* soldiers scattered around Alkara. My first day of training, Odion said soldiers sent off on assignment didn't come back. Since then, dozens of soldiers have returned from their missions. Which makes me wonder: How many more soldiers are preparing to return to Pennex at Reyshka's command?

As I sift through the hundreds of hidden weapons, shards of information clink together, forming a clearer image. For the past several years, Reyshka's been building an army of Keirdren soldiers scattered around Alkara, hidden in plain sight. She taught us the art of blending in. Trained us to be warriors. All for a war against the unsuspecting Alkarans who were foolish enough to let their guard down.

Reyshka tried to kill the witch Queen. I'm sure of it. And she's going to try again. Zaire said that right before Larster created the barrier, he weakened Alkara by gathering their leaders in one place and slaughtering them. Reyshka's going to make history repeat itself. Kill the Queen, weaken Alkara, and use the chaos that ensues to lead her army to victory over this new kingdom.

CHAPTER TWENTY-NINE

GAME OF A THOUSAND MOVING PARTS

Reyshka,
Is everything in place?

Carrik pens the letter, I send it.

And wait. Tongue fiddling the space where my *keil* bead used to be. Barely resisting the urge to pace.

I'd only just opened another crate of crossbow bolts when Carrik gave me our signal: water trickling down the stone cellar walls.

Later, he apologized for not being able to steal me more time. Apparently, he did successfully convince Reyshka he was a Nightman. The issue was that she actually had a license for the isi wood. Since Carrik didn't know what the license was supposed to look like, he couldn't challenge it.

My tongue stops as the freya candle burns blue with Reyshka's response.

Your Majesty,
Almost, sir. Soldiers have been returning steadily to camp,
but time is running low. Shall I send out the next soldier on
assignment?

"What does she mean, 'time is running low'?" asks Carrik.

I have no idea, but I need whatever response he pens to sound like I do.

Reyshka,

Are you certain you are prepared for the next assignment?

Answering her question with another question. Vague enough, but hopefully it still gets her to reveal something useful.

Her response comes minutes later.

Your Majesty,

Yes, sir. Ezenniel assures me he is prepared for his role. We only await the next assignment and your signal. Once it's complete, we will be ready for the barrier to move.

My first thought: *Who the hell is Ezenniel?*

He's not one of the soldiers training under Reyshka. I assume that means he's out on assignment, but doing what? What role is he preparing for?

My next thought: she said the barrier is going to move.

In my mind's eye, I see everything play out like a board game of Larster's creation. Mentally, I set up the pieces. Plot my moves—*Larster's* moves. Try and figure out his end goal.

Only one conclusion makes sense.

Larster and Reyshka have been building an army. They're going to kill the witch Queen and send Alkara into disarray. In the wreckage, Keirdren soldiers will swoop in and take over as much of Alkara as they can.

I already figured that out. This letter reveals another piece I hadn't considered: Larster plans to move the barrier to extend Keirdre's borders.

Larster's only ever had one trick: steal what he wants and burn what's left. He's going to repeat history, and Alkara is all but defenseless. There's no security along the barrier, no one who sees Keirdre as a legitimate threat, and their soldiers are completely unaware of an impending war.

If I stop this plot—stop Reyshka from killing Queen I'llyaris—I can prevent war. The barrier can finally come down, and we'll have peace.

If Hayes gets the Enforcers under control . . .

A nagging thought that gets louder every day. I try and shake it loose, but it hovers in the corner of my mind, loud and persistent.

Carrik nudges me. "How should I respond?"

Knowing Reyshka plans to kill the Queen is meaningless unless I also know how and when so I can stop her. "Tell her to have another sparring tournament next week," I say. "Whoever wins gets the next assignment."

Carrik's pen wavers. "I thought you said there was another soldier who always wins?"

Jarek. He's beaten me once before. He won't again. I won't accept any other outcome. Over the past few weeks, I've been improving. I have more control over my bladework, footwork, and, most important, my instincts. If I'm going to win, no more fighting with one hand tied. No more ignoring the pull of the water. "I'm going to win. The next assignment is *mine*."

Still, Carrik doesn't write anything. "You're sure?"

The truth: No.

But I figure if I lie enough, I'll start to believe it. "Positive."

CHAPTER THIRTY

RANCID WINE

It takes me a moment to recognize my surroundings when I Dreamweave with Hayes tonight—I'm in the training room.

I'm still gathering my bearings when I hear a grunt behind me. I turn—just in time to catch *Hayes* swinging a blade. He's wearing a loose shirt with no sleeves, leaving his arms bare, muscles clenching as he tightens his grip . . .

I'm distracted. Maybe drooling. So much so, I don't immediately realize he's fighting Jeune until she moves toward him, also armed with a blade. She's moving slower than she normally does, giving Hayes time to block her strike with the steel of his blade.

Jeune grins. "Good job. Next time, try and—" She stops as Hayes glances to the side and catches sight of me. He freezes, body rigid, clearly no longer paying attention to her.

Frowning, Jeune twists to look at me. She can't see me, but her brows quirk knowingly. "You know what? I'm actually going to go stand outside for no reason." She winks vaguely in my direction. "Hope you're fine here *all by yourself*, Hayes. Yell if you need me." She smirks as she leaves the room.

I smile at Hayes, glad Jeune can't see the way I'm still struggling not to stare at his arms. "She's teaching you to fight?"

Hayes takes his time returning his blade to the weapons wall, his back to me. "Yeah." There's something different in his voice. When he turns to face me, he's not smiling. I'm hit with a wave of emotion. *Guilt.* Sour like rancid wine and pungent enough to make my eyes water.

It's sudden. When he was sparring with Jeune, there was nothing. When they paused for her to instruct him, still nothing. Now that he's looking at me, the guilt is overwhelming.

My smile fades. "Everything all right?"

"Yes." He gives me his usual easy grin. Except there's tension in the corners of his eyes and his fingers twitch at his sides with nerves. He's lying. "Well, as good as can be expected. I've had Jeune looking into Thannen. To see if he was close to anyone."

That's not what he's feeling guilty about. There's something he's not telling me. I'm not used to Hayes keeping secrets. It doesn't seem fair to call him out, given everything I keep from him, so I mask my suspicion and change the subject. "I didn't know Jeune was teaching you to fight."

He looks relieved that I believe him. "I asked her to teach me. She's also been teaching me strategy. You know, for war. The more I learn, the angrier I am my father never trained me. Or that I never tried to figure it out myself."

"You didn't know you'd have to."

"I should've known. I was a Crown Prince. Next in line for the throne. I wasted *so* much time. And now, I'm completely useless."

"You're not useless. There are other skills aside from combat. Like authority. I saw how you commanded your advisers in the war room. That's a skill too."

He smiles, grateful for my words, but I can tell I haven't actually made him feel any better. I sigh. "Come on." I grab his arm and pull him into the center of the training room. "Practice with me. We can talk and train at the same time."

"I'm not as skilled as you at multitasking."

I smirk. "I'll go *really* slow, just for you." I hold up my arms. "I'll even let you get the first hit."

After a pause, Hayes grins and jabs, striking me gently on the arm.

"You're going to need to hit harder than that."

"I don't want to hurt you."

It's adorable he thinks he could physically hurt me. I bite back a smile. "I promise you, I've had worse. Besides, I'm not really here, so you can't leave a mark." I stand still, waiting as he strikes again, slightly harder this time. He's still holding back, but I don't comment. "What did Jeune learn about Thannen?" As I speak, I punch him in the gut, softer than I normally would. I hold it there longer than I have to, giving him time to snag my arm and twist it away.

I'm pleased when he also takes the moment to hit at me again, though still not as hard as he should. "Apparently, he kept to himself. He was new and still missing home. Didn't have many friends."

I yank out of his hold and pause, letting Hayes land the next hit. "What about friends from the Barracks?"

"He didn't attract attention in the Barracks. Wasn't a top-ranking soldier."

I feint right, then strike with my left hand, slowly. Hayes's eyes light up as he blocks it, looking pleased with himself.

"Then how did he get a job as a Palace guard?" I ask. Thannen had a powerful family, but for something as important as a guard position, it's not enough.

"Anarin Arkin recommended him to my mother personally."

Hayes blocks another one of my slow hits—snatches my arm and twists me around, pinning me against him, his front against my back.

Anarin Arkin. I freeze. A theory spins together in my mind.

Hayes must feel my body tense, because he releases me and spins me around to look me over. "What's wrong?"

"Has someone else replaced Thannen yet?" I already know the answer. The last time I saw Ikenna, one of her guards was young. Like Thannen, he must have been new.

"Yes . . . Why do you ask?"

"You should go see your mother," I say, still ignoring his question. "Keep her guards in the room. Tell her you're planning an ambush against the Enforcers. That you're sending a wave of soldiers to set up camp in Krill to attack from the east, not the south like they're expecting. But don't actually do it."

"Why?"

"I think Thannen was a spy and your mom's new guard is as well." Thannen was small, timid, and easy to manipulate. Not desirable qualities for a Royal guard—but exactly the kind of person Anarin Arkin would recruit to do her bidding.

Anarin has been instrumental in the Enforcer uprising against Hayes. On the ship, right before Thannen died, he couldn't speak. He just tapped his heart. I thought he was being sentimental, but I realize now he was tapping the pin fastened to his chest—he was trying to tell me who killed him.

Gears turn in Hayes's mind as he follows my line of thinking. "You want me to feed false information to her new guard to confirm he's a spy. And you don't want to confront him because he might be useful in the future."

I grin. "I see strategy training with Jeune is going well."

He laughs. "Or maybe I'm more cunning than you think

I am." As soon as he says it, his smile fades and the rancid-wine taste of guilt is back. His expression wavers, and for a tick, I think he's going to confess what's weighing on his conscience. Instead, the moment passes and his face clears. "I'll talk to my mom tomorrow. If and when he feeds information to Anarin, I'll let you know."

He's still hiding something. "Anything else you want to talk about?"

Pause. Then he shakes his head. "No."

I really wish he wasn't lying.

CHAPTER THIRTY-ONE

UNMARKED GRAVES

Carrik and I travel on horseback. The farther we go, the denser the trees become and the more the knots in my belly tighten with unease. This was my idea, but I grow more reluctant and petrified with each stride.

At some point, the trees become so tightly packed, we have to tie up the horses and continue on foot. The roots are massive. Clustered together in thick gray knots, some ankle-height, some high enough we have to crawl over them.

The tree branches are also growing thicker and harder to see through, until they're so dense I can't even see Carrik up ahead, just the occasional flash of pale yellow—his shirt. The rest of him has been swallowed by gnarled branches.

We've been trekking on foot for around twenty minutes when I push a heavy branch aside and find my nose shoved into Carrik's back. He's stopped moving.

I back up half a pace. "What's wrong?"

"We're here."

My heart stutters.

There's a curtain of leaves ahead of him. Carrik raises a hand to push them aside but stops. "We don't have to do this. If it's too much, tell me and we'll go back," he says softly.

My nails dig into my palms. "I'm sure."

It's a complete lie—not even a half-truth—but he peels aside the last layer of leaves anyway.

My stomach plunges to the forest floor.

We stand at the top of a cliff. The drop-off isn't steep, and yet my feet are rooted in place.

The base of the cliff is an endless expanse of black. Charred remnants of what used to be.

The dense trees weren't here by accident, but by design. A shield meant to guard this graveyard from the rest of the world.

Szeiryna. What used to be Szeiryna, anyway.

I was reluctant to come here. Reluctant to see all that's left of what should have been my home. But proving myself to Reyshka means giving up the fight against myself. Recognizing the parts of me that I lost. The aspects of my life that were stolen and burned.

I think Carrik says something, but my mind crackles, too loud to hear him, and my feet act of their own accord. They stumble down the cliffside until I'm standing at the edge of the wreckage.

I stop here.

Soft wind blows ash through the air like gray fog.

There are no sirens in Alkara.

Lex told me that when I arrived and it *hurt.* But it never felt real.

Standing here, seeing the blackness of a kinship I'll never know, *shatters* me.

I'm close to falling over and my throat is clogged and I can't speak, but Carrik knows without me having to say a word, what

I need. His arms encircle my waist. He doesn't say anything, just holds me.

I knew they were gone in Keirdre. Knew they were gone in Alkara. Knew Larster burned their home—*my home*—to the ground and cast it aside without a second thought.

It's in front of me now. Inescapably real. Seeing it, I can almost picture what my life could've been. Surrounded by creatures who see me and know me and love me and struggle with their instincts like me.

I love my family more than anything, but what I want— what I've always wanted—is another monster like me.

There are no signs of life in this wreckage. The only monster left standing is me.

The pain starts in my chest. Works its way to my back. Up my spine. Through my clogged throat. I'm drowning in hopelessness and grief and anguish, leaving me submerged in the waves of all the feelings I tried to suppress.

I'm crying.

When the tears started, I have no idea. I'm standing in a field of ash that used to be the only creatures in the world who might understand me, and the tears won't stop flowing.

My mind flashes to that coin Hayes wears around his neck. The one he and Felix found in his father's office. It was a coin Larster kept from Szciryna—a trophy.

It feels even more twisted now. Somehow, Larster saw all this and decided he wanted a permanent reminder of what he destroyed.

Carrik's arms tighten. He turns me around in his hold. "I'm sorry."

Carrik broke my trust and my heart. He lied to me,

manipulated me, and used my sister against me. Right now, it feels foolish to be angry with him. Spektryl and I have always had the same enemy: the monster who set fire to an entire species and left me here, all alone.

Spektryl's anger scared me, not because it was foreign but because it was all too familiar. He and I are born of the same loss, the same rage.

The scream that's been building up inside me—since we reached Szeiryna, since I sang for the first time and realized what I am, since I dragged my first mark underwater and resurfaced to my father's disappointment—bursts out. A scream of heartbreak, pain, and overwhelming loneliness.

The sky darkens with my release. The ache inside me is a knot, wound so tight it hurts. It wants *out*. My screech gains volume. The tightness coils further, squeezing more painfully, until the scream reaches its crest. The knot releases and it's pouring rain. In a few ticks, we're drenched in the downpour, and still, all Carrik does is hold me.

Lightning flashes and I pull my face from his chest. "I'm sorry."

"Don't be. I like the rain." He doesn't flinch as water lashes his face. "Saoirse, I know what you're thinking, and you're wrong. You're not alone. You have me. Always will."

The water around us is cold but my chest burns. "It's not the same."

"I know. But my parents were buried in unmarked graves too. It makes me so angry, I want to scream with you."

Thunder rumbles in the distance. "Why don't you?"

"I don't like to show you my anger. I don't want you to hate me anymore."

I don't hate you.

But I don't say it.

I reach for Carrik's hand and give it a squeeze. "Scream with me. I'll hate you again tomorrow."

He hesitates only for a moment before opening his mouth and *screaming*. He's not a siren, so it's not the same powerful shrill, but there's pain in his cry. Raw, searing pain that makes my tears flow faster. I scream with him. It feels good to unleash my anger, my loneliness, my heartbreak.

I don't know how long we stand in the remains of Szeiryna, screaming our grief. It's not enough to make me feel better, but for the first time in a really long while, I feel understood.

This—the endless expanse of destruction—is what Larster wanted. What the Enforcers are fighting for.

And, I realize with a jolt that makes my stomach drop, if Hayes doesn't get the Enforcers in line, it's exactly where Keirdre is headed again.

CHAPTER THIRTY-TWO

BURST OF BLUE, BEAD OF RED

Jarek slams Rienna onto her back. She groans, but she looks more like she's annoyed than in pain. She'd been doing well in the tournament. Up until this point, she'd won all her matches. The moment Jarek stepped up, she knew—like we all did—she was going to lose.

Odds are, everyone he fights after Rienna will lose. Until he faces me, of course.

Two days ago, I was anxious. Not anymore. Not since I saw Szeiryna's remains. There's a lot about my history I don't know—a lot I'll never know. Still, one thing I'm certain of: I'm stronger than Jarek. Stronger and angrier and I have more to lose.

I have Rain and my parents and my aunties. Keirdre has already taken more from me than they had any right to—I won't let them take my family's chance at a future too. I won't let their home be reduced to ash.

Losing to Jarek again isn't an option.

Jarek makes quick work of his next few opponents, including Odion. With a few deft moves, Jarek knocks the blade from his hand and pins Odion to the damp ground.

Reyshka nods her approval, looking bored. "Excellent, Jarek. Odion, you're dismissed."

I don an expression of false condolences as Odion makes his way to me, his shoulders slumped. *Perfect.* The best time to get Odion to spill information is when he feels inept.

"Sorry." I pat his shoulder comfortingly.

He looked dejected just seconds ago, but my presence soothes him. "It's fine. I'll do better next time."

I nod placatingly. "Can I ask you something?"

He perks, glad to be of use. "Anything."

"Reyshka mentioned someone named Ezenniel to me the other day. I don't know anyone here by that name."

As always, he's excited by the prospect of making himself useful to me. "We've all heard of him, never met him. He's before our time—more of a legend than a person. He was given an assignment years ago. Apparently, before he left, he was Reyshka's favorite. Like Jarek."

Interesting.

"Siren!" Reyshka barks. "You're next."

No time to think about Ezenniel or shove my thoughts into order. First, I have to beat Jarek and earn this next assignment.

Armed with a blade, I stand before Jarek, ready.

He smirks. "I've been looking forward to having you beneath me again, siren."

There's no warning. One moment, Jarek is still and composed, the next, he's swinging his blade at me.

Mentally, I track its trajectory. I envision where the blade will end its arc and, more important, where my opponent's hand will be when he finishes the swing.

I duck the blade and throw up my hand, coiling my fist around Jarek's wrist and squeezing tight.

He wrenches out of my grasp. He draws up his blade swiftly,

meaning to take advantage of my disorientation, but my focus holds and I evade the swipe.

It rained last night and the air is thick with humidity. There was a time this would be a hindrance, but now, I use it. After weeks of training with Carrik—of *using* the water, rather than letting it control me—I don't fight it. The water sings to me and I let it. I don't have to use it to kill. I only have to use it to beat him.

I seize water from the air and *pull*. It forms a long, thin tendril. Winds itself around Jarek's hand gripping the blade.

The water loves to do my bidding, and right now, I need to win.

Today, losing isn't an option. Reyshka will decide who is sent on the next assignment, and above all, I need to ensure that the soldier she picks is *me*.

Jarek swings the blade, but the water grips him, freezing him in place.

His eyes narrow. I feel a tug in the back of my mind as he struggles to force the water to release him.

I smirk.

In terms of brute strength, Jarek has me beat, but the water is *mine*.

Jarek's hand gripping the blade is stuck. I swoop forward, slicing his legs. He jumps over my blade. Draws up his hand to snag the wrist connected to my sword—he means to disarm me.

More water flows with my will. Slams against his face. It courses into his mouth and nose, choking him.

He makes a strangled noise. I don't pause. Swing up my blade, pausing it to rest at his neck. I don't dig it in. The sharp end grazes the skin at the side of his throat and a tiny bead of red appears.

I know the moment he feels it and knows he's lost when I *taste* the sharp citrus of his shock.

Jarek stills.

A slow clap from behind. "Nice job, siren."

I release my hold on the water.

Jarek doubles over, drawing in deep, shuddering breaths, still tasting shocked that he lost. I turn to Reyshka. There's a gleam in her olive eyes. "Clearly, you've been practicing."

"Every day," I say.

I feel the familiar weight of jealous stares on me. I revel in the taste of their envy on my tongue and the way it feels wrapped around me like a scarf.

Lune above, I've missed this.

Reyshka raises her voice to address the other soldiers. "Everyone take note of Saoirse's technique. Every move has multiple purposes. A strong fighter can overpower. A smart one can outmaneuver." She inclines her head to me in a gesture of respect. "A skilled fighter can do both."

Everyone's staring at me, including Reyshka. It's the first time she's called me anything other than "siren" or "girl" since my arrival.

For all my achievements, I'm not used to receiving praise from superiors. Flynn was never one for compliments, no matter how hard I worked to earn them. Even though I was *always* first in my year, his praise was sparse. He made us work for his approval but rarely gave it out. And when he did, it was reserved for the soldiers who *weren't* ikatus like me.

Reyshka has a different approach. Get us to work hard for her approval and, once earned, dole it out accordingly. Nothing extravagant, but just enough that I feel the rush of her praise. Even though I know it's all a mind game, it works. She's successfully gotten me to crave her approval. Not just because I need an assignment—but because I want her to tell me I've earned it.

"Thank you," I say with a tight smile.

The rest of the day passes easily. I defeat the few remaining soldiers and am declared the victor of today's tournament.

I'm still floating with the weightlessness of victory when Reyshka announces the end of training for the day.

As I make to leave, Rienna's shoulder brushes—scratch that, *shoves*—against mine. It's too rough and lacking in apology to be anything but intentional.

Looks like she's back to resenting me for besting her. Unlike in the Barracks, her jealousy isn't accompanied by mocking nicknames. I've shed the title of ikatus, and she can no longer pretend to think I'm weak.

Her envy tastes like curdled milk. It should disgust me but it doesn't. I've earned it.

Reyshka steps in front of Rienna, glancing between the two of us. "Both of you." She jerks her head toward the house. "Come with me." She turns and marches inside.

Rienna shoots me a wide-eyed, panicked look. I keep my expression impassive. I have nothing to worry about. Reyshka's going to do as she's told and give me the next assignment.

Still, my tongue flicks the space behind my false tooth as we follow Reyshka up the stairs. She presses a hand to the isi wood office door and opens it.

Rienna and I stand rigidly in the middle of the room as Reyshka goes to stand behind her desk. "Both of you, please, sit."

I've never heard her say "please" before.

Hesitantly, Rienna and I take the seats across from her desk.

"You both have excelled recently," says Reyshka. "Sorkova,

you've steadily improved since you arrived. And you won the sparring tournament today. Kasselton, it seems the siren's presence has encouraged you to improve as well. You two push each other to be better."

I hold in a scoff. Rienna has never pushed me to do anything but trip after she's shoved me in the back.

Reyshka *is* right about one thing: my presence infuriates Rienna to try harder to best me.

"You've both risen far in a short amount of time," Reyshka continues. "I've decided to give you an assignment. Together."

I taste Rienna's fury and feel it myself. I intend to use this assignment to foil Reyshka's assassination attempt on the Queen. That's going to be a hell of a lot more difficult with Rienna strapped to my side.

Despite myself, I force a smile. Really, I just bare my teeth, but Reyshka wouldn't know a smile from a scowl, so she doesn't seem bothered. "Thank you. What kind of assignment?"

"I need you to test something for me at Faraday House."

Faraday. Where the witch Queen resides. Where, I'm assuming, Reyshka made her first attempt on the Queen's life. Where I'm certain she'll make her next.

"It's surrounded by an isi wood fence," says Reyshka. "We've had soldiers swapping out portions of the wood to disrupt the perimeter. This *should* mean there's a breach where we can enter. There's a council meeting next week. Your task is to see if the perimeter is now breachable. If it is, enter Faraday and report back to me what additional defenses we'll need to evade. If you are caught, you'll deny any and all connection to Keirdre or myself. Do you understand and accept your assignment?"

Rienna and I nod. "Of course," says Rienna, just as I say, "Thank you for this opportunity."

CHAPTER THIRTY-THREE

ONLY A PHANTOM

I'm still reeling from the thrill of my victory when I Dreamweave to see Hayes. He's in his chambers, sitting at his desk. When he sees me, his eyes narrow for a tick, before his expression clears and he grins. "Let me guess—you won and got an assignment."

I laugh. "How could you tell?"

"You're smiling." Hayes rises from his chair to stand in front of me, eyes traveling over my face, grin stretching wider. "You hardly ever smile. Plus, you're you. I never doubted you for a moment." He folds his arms. "You were nervous about beating that soldier Reyshka loves, weren't you? How'd you do it?"

The truth: *Seeing Szeiryna*. Realizing I'm willing to do anything to ensure history doesn't repeat itself.

The half-truth I tell Hayes: "Training with Carrik again."

"Ah." His amusement shrivels as his jaw tightens. "How *is* Spektryl?" The warmth in his tone is gone, replaced with frosty eyes and a stiff cadence.

"He's fine," I say warily.

Long, awkward pause.

"You seem . . ." Hayes wavers, thinking of the right word. "More comfortable talking about him now. Less angry."

"He's been useful. I'm a better soldier when we train together."

It's more than that. I'm still angry with him—I don't think that will ever go away—but Szeiryna solidified for me that Carrik isn't my enemy. Keirdre is.

Hayes is still watching me. "You've forgiven him." He says it like it's a fact.

"I didn't say that."

"Have you?"

I haven't. But there's more to my relationship with Carrik than forgiveness—or lack thereof. I don't need to forgive him to understand his rage. It's the same anger that's been festering in me for just about as long as I can remember.

Instead of saying any of that, I shrug. "I don't know." I'm getting defensive, even though Hayes hasn't accused me of anything and I haven't done anything wrong. "You're the one who sent him over here with me. Without asking."

"I know," he grumbles.

"Then why are you upset?"

"I'm not." He's lying. His emotions are sour like curdled milk and lemon juice. *Jealousy.* I can feel it. Tight and itchy like a too-small sweater in blistering heat. I could leave it alone—let the envy sit and rot, and pretend I don't notice—or . . .

"It's easier to deal with things when they're unspoken."

Do I believe that?

I *act* like I believe it. I've been biting my tongue with Hayes since we met. Even after he learned what I am, I've practically started a collection of all the things I refuse to speak about. The taste of his fear when I tried to kiss him and he jerked away like I was a creature from his nightmares come to life. The feel of his hands when he kissed me like we were both drowning right before I left . . .

There's so much we've left unspoken.

I could brush off this moment—the sourness of his jealousy and the questions burning in his eyes—like it never happened, like I always do. Tack it onto the growing list of things we pretend don't exist between us.

Or I could stop being a coward and tell him what I'm thinking for once.

I swallow. "Are you jealous of Carrik?"

Hayes's eyes widen with surprise. He didn't expect me to ask.

After a pause, his surprise hardens into steely determination. "I don't know. Should I be?"

For him to have reason to be jealous, we'd have to be more to each other than what we've said.

Hayes kissed me before I left Keirdre—we don't talk about it. I spend every night in his bed—we don't touch. It has to mean something. *I* have to mean something, but the thought of asking terrifies me.

We're in his room, between his desk and the sofa in the sitting area. My legs feel weak and I have the urge to take a seat and back away from Hayes's intensity.

I inhale, rein in my nerves. Men don't make me nervous. I craft strings from my voice and use them to manipulate marks like puppets. At least I did before Hayes. Before I realized that losing him would crush me. Before I tasted his fear of me and I realized that to him—someone who genuinely *knows* me, all of me—I might be more terrifying than I am alluring.

In through my nose. Out through my teeth. "We've never talked about what we are to each other, but I need to know—did you change your mind?" Finally, I ask the question that's been weighing on me for lunes.

His head falls to one side in confusion. "Change my mind about what?"

"About *me*? On the ship, you said—" *Inhale. Exhale.* "You said that you wanted me. But that was before. And now I can't tell if you—if you still—"

"Want you?" My anxiety builds as the distance between us shrinks until he's right in front of me, bending so our eyes are level, his expression so soft, my breath catches. "Are you serious?"

I falter, losing my nerve for a moment. My heartbeat is so fast it's a hum. "Yes."

Moving achingly slow, his hand glides up and rests against my cheek. "Saoirse," he breathes my name like an exasperated sigh. "There's not a world you could travel to where I wouldn't want you."

My eyes slip closed in sweet, cool relief.

His thumb grazes my bottom lip. "How do you not know that? Lune above, I ask you to sleep with me every night."

I flush. Open my eyes so I can see him. "You don't touch me." It sounds childish when I say it out loud.

Hayes's eyes darken. He leans forward, guiding me back until my spine rests on something soft—the sofa. He hovers over me, eyes boring into mine. He's so close, our breaths rasp together in the small space between us. "Do you want me to touch you, Saoirse?"

My mouth is on fire. The cinnamon of his desire for me *burns*. A good, rich kind of burn.

My brain shuts down. I see his lips move, hear the words, feel his breath on my face. Forming a response is an impossibility. My lips part—the only thing that comes out are heavy gasps.

Hayes seems amused by my silence. His mouth curves into a smirk, and the cinnamon joins with the citrusy tang of his mirth. He bends leisurely until his lips brush my collarbone in a kiss so soft it's like mist at dawn. "Do you?" His tone is more insistent as his mouth glides over my skin, trailing from one side of my neck, over the hollow in my throat, to the other side.

"W-what?"

I feel that damned smirk widen against my neck. He brings his head up, just by my ear. "Do you want me to touch you?"

His lips have traced a path over my skin, but they've refused to make full contact. He's teasing me. Something I've been doing since my first kill. I've never had it done to me before. Never been this on fire from someone not even touching me.

I push through the haze of desire he's stirred up. Force my brain to recall what I wanted when I started this conversation. "You kissed me," I finally manage shakily. "Before I left."

Hayes drags his nose down the column of my throat. "I remember."

I'm shuddering from the feel of him *everywhere*. His lips graze my shoulders and up my neck. Light enough to feel, but he still won't fully press them to my skin. It's just the lightest ghosting that's making me wild. "You haven't done it since," I say.

He chuckles. He's close enough to the sensitive skin on my neck that the low and sensual sound sends a pulse through me. "You're on the other side of the world."

My hands find either side of his head and pull his face to hover over mine. "I'm right here."

He stares at me for several torturous seconds. Then his face descends, nose brushes mine. "You want me to kiss you?"

"Yes." I sound breathless.

"Then ask."

I hate him.

I've never felt this out of control. "Hayes, I want you to kiss me."

His lips dive, closing the narrow distance between us—

—and press chastely against my cheek. "No."

He pulls away.

I feel as though I've been doused in ice water. *"No?"*

He's kneeling on the sofa, grinning as though pleased with himself, but his eyes are full of sweet longing. "No."

I sit up. "Why not?"

He doesn't answer right away. Instead, he traces a finger over my face. His eyes follow the motion with unmistakable yearning. Gently, his hand cups my cheek and he drags a thumb over my mouth, lingering on my bottom lip. "You feel so real." His voice is hushed. "But you're not really here. I want to kiss you, Saoirse. I want to kiss you to oblivion. I want to be so wrapped up in you I don't know where I end. I want to leave you with swollen lips. I want to wake up to sheets that smell like you. I told you before, I want you—*all* of you. I won't settle for a phantom."

I hate how badly I want him. Hate that he has this power over me—the power to make me crave him, the power to break my heart. And I *hate* him for being so beautiful I can't breathe.

"You didn't have to tease me like that," I grumble.

He throws his head back and laughs. "I said I wouldn't *kiss* you. If you want me to touch you . . ." Before I've had a moment to cool down, he scoops me into his arms.

I'm startled, but he's Hayes so I don't protest as he carries me across the room. He deposits me gently on what's become my side of the bed and walks around to his. For the first time, when he lies down, his arm snakes around my waist and drags me to him.

My head rests on his chest, under his chin. He presses a kiss to my hair.

He tastes happy. Happier than he's been in a while, but there's still something tinged with it. Fear.

I tilt my head to look at him. "What are you afraid of?"

"I'm not afraid of anything."

I roll my eyes. "I'm serious. Something's bothering you. I can taste it."

"I forgot about that trick of yours." He hesitates. "Can you taste *all* my emotions?"

"Just the strong ones."

"Really?" Another long pause. "What do I taste like right now?"

He stares at me, and the fear is still there, but as his eyes bore into mine, it's overpowered by desire.

My face flushes. "Cinnamon."

The arm curled around me tightens, bringing me in closer. "What does cinnamon mean?" His voice is husky, like he knows *exactly* what it means. It's almost enough to make me forget the question I asked that he's trying to evade.

Almost.

"You're trying to distract me."

"Hmm," he hums, trailing his hands lightly down my arms, drawing out goose bumps that chase his skirting fingers. "Is it working?"

Yes. "You're not playing fair." I push away from him, sitting up to clear my mind. "Answer my question—what are you afraid of?"

Instead of answering, he pats the space on his chest just above his heart, entreating me to lean back into him. "I'll answer you, I promise. As soon as you come back to me."

With a sigh, I curl back up into his side. His heart is beating so fast, it's a whir beneath my cheek, matching my own. It's comforting to know that as calm as he sounds, his heart and mine beat the same, frantic rhythm.

"You are my favorite part of every day." He laces our fingers together and holds our intertwined hands above us. "But you're not real." He squeezes my hand with a sad smile. "I'm terrified you won't come back. That I'll be stuck chasing a phantom for the rest of my life."

I wish that was it. I wish all I tasted was cinnamon and whiskey—lust and fear. But at his admission, I taste something else: sour grapes. *Guilt.* There's something else he's hiding from me. The same something he's been hiding from me since that moment in the training room with Jeune.

But I don't say that. "I'll come back." I tilt my head, touch my lips to his chin. "I promise."

"You've broken promises to me before."

Neither of us says it, and I'm left wondering if some things truly are better left unsaid.

CHAPTER THIRTY-FOUR

ROTTEN MONSTER

Rienna doesn't speak to me and I have no desire to speak to her, so we wind through the streets without exchanging a single word. Faraday House is in the heart of the city. The front of the house is framed by a gate of brambles. The back is a green yard surrounded by an isi wood fence that's just below waist height.

We don't go directly to the fence. First, we take a few laps. Circle the building. I keep an eye out for Nightmen. They're dressed just like everyone else, so I'm watching for anyone who looks like they're lingering. I don't see anyone who stands out. It doesn't mean there's no security—there could be soldiers standing just on the other side of the fence, hidden from sight by the isi wood—but it puts me more at ease.

According to Reyshka, we're looking for a mark. A small symbol burned into the underside of a plank of wood. The mark signals that the wood in that section has been swapped out with wood that is no longer enchanted.

Each time we circle Faraday, we inspect the wood, taking care not to *look* like we're inspecting it. The first time around, I don't see it. Or the second. By the third, I'm wondering if this mission is an elaborate jest and there *is* no breach in the fence.

The fourth time we walk around, I see it. A circular dark spot burned into the wood, so small I wouldn't have noticed it if I wasn't looking. My steps slow.

I dart out a hand, bracing myself for the sharp pain I felt when I touched the enchanted wood before I knew what it was. Nothing. Reyshka's soldiers were successful. The fence *looks* enchanted, but this section isn't.

Rienna follows my line of sight to the unenchanted section of the fence. We'll have to climb over quickly. Once we're on the other side, no one out here will be able to see us.

I take a swift look around. It's broad daylight and I feel exposed.

I don't think—if I overthink, I'll get caught—just throw myself over the fence and land on the other side. Seconds later, Rienna joins me.

We're in a flat green field. The yard between the perimeter fence and the back door to Faraday. Still, there are no guards here.

We sprint across the lawn to the back door. I try the handle—locked.

I press my ear against the wood, listening for anything on the other side. I hear nothing.

From my pocket, I procure metal rods—lock picking tools. Rienna and I don't need to speak. As I get to work picking the back lock, she pushes her ear against the wood of the door, listening for incoming voices or footsteps.

I push a narrow cylinder into the lock, move it around until I feel it resting against one of the lock tumblers. I reach for a second cylinder, when Rienna holds up a hand. "Wait—" Her stance tightens as she listens through the door. "Voices are coming this way . . . getting louder."

We're frozen. I don't dare manipulate the lock anymore. Not until—

"They've passed. Keep going."

I push the second cylinder into the lock and maneuver both around until I hear a faint *click* as the door unlocks.

Breath bated, I push open the door and creep inside. We're in a small room with walls coated in strands of ivy and wreaths of black-and-white flowers. Black curtains are draped over each window, making the room dark, contrasted by the flickering candles dotted around the perimeter. A portrait hangs on the back wall in a black frame. The woman in the portrait has russet-toned skin with bright silver hair. Her eyes are cobalt blue and flecked with olive green. A witch. Judging by the portrait of her in a crown, I'm guessing she's Queen I'llyaris.

Three doorways lead out of this room. On the left, a servant's kitchen; the door on the right leads into a closet; straight ahead, a corridor that leads into the rest of the house.

Voices come from the other side of the kitchen—someone's coming.

Without a word, Rienna and I rush into the closet. Rods run the length of the space with clothes draped over them. Uniforms, by the look of it. Plain white shirt with light brown pants.

I snag one of the uniforms and hold it out in front of me, raising a questioning brow at Rienna.

She wavers but ultimately nods, grabbing a uniform of her own. We shed the plain gray we're currently wearing in favor of these. If we want to look like we're meant to be here, we need to look like everyone else.

By the time we're dressed, the voices have faded. I start to leave, but Rienna grabs my arm, holding me back. "You need to cover your face. If people see you, they're going to know they've never seen you here before."

She's right, but Alkarans don't wear face coverings. "It'll only draw more attention to me."

Rienna's eyes skim my face. "Use your hair."

My hair is braided around the crown of my head, the way it always is when I'm a soldier. My fingers work through my braid, loosening it before I toss the thick coils a few times. When it's unfurled enough to obscure my face, we leave the closet.

We start for the doorway that leads down a corridor into the rest of the house.

"What are you doing?" A clipped voice from behind stops us as we're halfway down the hall.

Rienna and I freeze. Look at each other. Mentally calculate how hard it would be to dash back the way we came, shove whoever is behind us aside, and escape—

"If you're serving, you'll need a tray." The newcomer's tone is wry.

Relieved, we turn to face her. I keep my body behind Rienna and head down, so I don't see her face, but from the corners of my eyes, I see she's dressed the same as me and Rienna. Without a word, she heads for the kitchen, and we dutifully trail after her. "If you ever think there's nothing to do . . ." She chuckles. "Ask me or Elsie. I promise, we'll find something." She keeps speaking as we enter the kitchen.

My head is down, but I examine my surroundings from the periphery of my vision. Wide windows with lots of light streaming in against the white tiled floor. Wooden countertops polished to a shine and dotted with metal trays, each covered with glasses of wine, mugs of ale, and plates of food—fresh bread, bright fruit, and soft cheeses.

The woman who led us here gestures around. "You know the rules: Pick a tray, mind the back wall, don't speak."

"Yes, ma'am," says Rienna.

The woman barely glances at her as she moves around the kitchen. Clearly, we're dismissed.

Rienna and I each grab a tray laden with food. I raise mine to further block my face as we scurry down the corridor again. The hall opens into a wide chamber with a high ceiling that stretches as tall as Faraday is from the outside. The two floors above us, each framed by a railing, overlook the ground floor here. Rows of chairs filled with creatures are stretched out before a floating platform at the front of the room.

As Rienna and I take our places in the back of the room as instructed, my eyes skirt over the crowd. They're clustered together by species. Four creatures in each cluster. They converse among each other, not paying attention to the stage or their surroundings.

I taste the repugnant flavor of Rienna's disgust. I glance at her. Her expression is blank enough, but her nose is scrunched and she looks uncomfortable. Clearly, she's adopted Larster's view on creatures that aren't fae.

My eyes drift to the floating platform at the front of the room, and I see her. The Queen of Alkara. Her face is hidden by a slew of guards (I assume they're guards by their stances and demeanor, but I have no way to know for sure). She's around my height—maybe taller by a hair. Her brown skin is russet-toned and her hair nearly reaches her shoulders, bigger than it is long, with thick, silvery curls.

She's a Queen, but her clothing is plain—a long dress the color of grass. As I watch, one of the guards standing in front of her shifts, and I catch a clear look at her face. Her eyes are wide, blue, and flecked with green. There are no frown lines around her mouth or smile lines around her eyes. Odd. Witches tend to look young. Usually, lines around the face are the only indicators of a witch's age, but this woman is a blank canvas.

I'm so enraptured in watching the proceedings, I don't notice a figure approaching until they're directly in front of me. They don't speak, but their gaze sears the side of my face as they pick a snack from my tray—some sort of pastry, I'm not sure—and slink away.

One of the Queen's guards steps into the center of the stage and clears his throat. The sound echoes, although he doesn't speak into an asterval. My eyes narrow on his throat. There's a marble bead around his neck with a rune etched into it. "Let the council meeting commence."

The council falls silent. The remaining few creatures left standing immediately find their seats, giving the guard their undivided attention.

A wide-eyed creature with eyes dark like shadows and skin light like straw hurries onto the stage with a pad of parchment and a pen. A notetaker.

The Queen comes forward. As her foot passes from the periphery of the platform to the center, her outfit transforms. The plain attire melts away and she stands before the crowd in a shirt that slides off her shoulders and matching skirt printed with flowers of lavender, silver, and white. Her heavy curls are pulled back by pins shaped like crescent moons, leaving her face clear.

She doesn't smile, but her eyes sweep over the crowd. "I believe the dryads expressed an interest in speaking first." Her voice is smooth and her speckled eyes flick around the room. They land on me. For a half tick, they waver before passing on.

I imagined it. I must have. But I can't shake the feeling that she *saw* me. A terrifying thought.

"Councilman Calderman," she says. "The floor is yours."

A man stands. He has skin with deep amber undertones and hair the color and shape of bay leaves. A dryad. He sits with two others—their fourth member must be running late. "Thank you, Your Majesty." He doesn't bow. He looks familiar, but I can't place where I've seen him.

"Once again, I bring this council's attention to the southern border. We are Alkara's sole line of defense against invaders."

Meaning he's a dryad who lives in the forest near the barrier. I wonder if it's why he looks familiar—if we saw him when we first arrived.

My heartbeat picks up. Surely, he wouldn't recognize me here? It was several weeks ago, and we would've only seen each other for a few moments.

Except I'm a siren and people tend to remember my face. I raise my tray to block my face even more.

The Queen doesn't immediately respond to the dryad. Two of her guards lean to whisper in her ears. She doesn't say anything, just listens.

The dryad's brow scrunches in irritation. "It's not safe. We're all but exposed—"

"Exposed to what?" Finished listening to her guards, the Queen talks over him. "What threat are you so concerned about?"

"Keirdre," the dryad bursts angrily.

One of the Queen's guards chuckles. "You're worried Keirdre will suddenly decide to leave the safety of their barrier? They haven't for centuries. We've said it a thousand times—they never will."

The dryad looks at him disdainfully. "If I wanted the opinion of someone not on the council, I'd ask."

The Queen's nostrils flare. "You'll treat him with respect."

"Or what?" he challenges. "You'll banish me to the outskirts of Alkara to ward off invaders?"

"There *are* no invaders," the guard insists. "Only schoolchildren still believe Keirdrens can leave their fortress."

The air is charged as the two glare at each other.

There's something else, though. Through the crackling tension, there's a taste in the air—strong enough to stand out to me through everything and everyone else. *Fear*—mingled with nerves. It's coming from the platform. Someone at the front of the room is afraid and nervous, but I'm not sure what about this situation is fear-inducing.

While the dryad and guard bicker—with the Queen chiming in every once in a while—I search the crowd, hunting for . . .

My eyes stop roving when I see them. Humans. They sit in a group of four. They're part of this council just as much as any other species. They don't get looks of disgust thrown their way. The *only* person in this room whose disgust I taste is Rienna's.

It's fitting. Like Keirdre, she's rotten to the core, filled with unwarranted hatred. For Rienna, the concept of her own superiority is so ingrained in her soul, she believes it, even now. Even seeing firsthand that she's been misled does nothing to soothe her emotions. Doesn't smooth the disdain from her brow.

The front of the chamber drags my attention as the dryad finally takes his seat. The Queen's guard speaks again. "Are there any other concerns we need to address this meeting?"

He stands in the center of the stage, and the Queen stands to the side. Plainly visible, but silent. I study her guard. He's tall. Bald with weathering around his brown eyes, which means he could be human—or just about anything else. There's no way for me to tell. I've assumed he was a guard, but judging from the way he speaks on her behalf, he must be something more. An adviser, maybe? It's still weird, though. I've never known a Royal adviser to have the authority to command a room in the Queen's stead.

Maybe in Alkara, it's not strange. The Queen's role is much different than that of the King of Keirdre. She has power, yes, but she's still bound to the rest of the council's opinions. *Everyone's* opinions, not just the fae.

My eyes seek out creatures with sharp features and bright eyes—fae. I find them easily in the crowd. Not because they stand out, but because I've spent my life attuning myself to them. Avoiding them. Pretending to *be* one of them as needed.

I'm curious if there's a difference between Alkaran fae and Keirdren fae. Like the other creatures, there are four of them. Three women, one man. Two of the women are tall, the third is short. As for the man, he's medium height with a stocky build, short dark hair, skin deep like umbian clay, eyes bright and teal.

Rienna shakes my shoulder. She doesn't speak—best not to risk anyone overhearing us—but she nods her head back toward the door we came through. Her meaning is clear: time to go.

I want to keep watching, but we're not here to sate my curiosity. We've gotten the answers we need—we know how to break into Faraday—and it's best to leave now, in the middle of the meeting, so as not to get caught up at the end.

Reluctantly, I hoist up my tray, and we take our leave.

CHAPTER THIRTY-FIVE

WITHIN THE THUNDER

It's *way* too easy to get into Faraday House. If Reyshka wanted, she could send a few soldiers to assassinate the Queen right now. The only thing holding her back is Larster—well, me pretending to be Larster.

The last piece I need to stop her is Ezenniel. Once I know who he is and what role Larster and Reyshka have planned for him, I can end this.

It's early morning, ten minutes after the start of training. I'm across the street from Reyshka's house, waiting. She's punctual to a fault. Never starts training even a half second late.

This soon after training begins, everyone should be occupied. No one will—should—rush into the house to grab something. Meaning there shouldn't be anyone around to see me.

I cross the street purposefully and enter Reyshka's house. It's empty.

Slowly, I start up the stairs. My heart lodges in my throat. It's thumping so loud, I can barely hear myself think.

I told Reyshka I had an assignment from Larster that would take me away for the day. If she discovers me, all the trust I've built with her will be shattered.

Still, it's either take this risk or never know what role Ezenniel plays in the assassination of the Queen.

It has to be during the day. If I tried to sneak in at night,
Reyshka would hear the creaking steps and wake up, like any
half-decently trained soldier would.

Every few steps, I stop, listening for the back door opening
or any other sounds to indicate I'm no longer alone in the house.
When I reach the second story, I glide my *lairic* beads against
the isi wood door and push it open.

I duck inside, shutting the door behind me. My back rests
against it as I catch my breath and calm my heart. I only give
myself a few moments. My time is limited. With the isi wood
door, I won't be able to hear anyone approaching Reyshka's
office until it's too late.

I start with her desk. Open the first drawer: two freya candles, unused parchment, and a few pens. Nothing of interest.

Next drawer. A few opened letters shoved to the back and a
thin sheet of leather, folded over multiple times. I unfurl it over
her desk. It's a map of Alkara, printed on tan leather. There's no
mention of Keirdre or of the barrier at all. Cities and towns are
scrawled in dark ink. There are other names written in the
empty spaces of the map in deep blue. *People's* names.

In Pennex, there are names of soldiers I recognize, like
Rienna, Jarek, Odion . . .

There are names written outside of Pennex as well. Some
are crossed out, some underlined. I have no idea what it means.
If these are the names of soldiers who have died or soldiers who
have been sent somewhere else.

Just outside Pennex is a smaller town. Wystmeren. Written
in blue ink, right next to a small lake within the town's bound-
ary: *Ezenniel.*

My breath catches.

If this map is correct—if Ezenniel is truly in Wystmeren—then I know where he is. Which means I'm one step closer to stopping Reyshka. I'm still reeling as I refold the map and put it back in its drawer. There are more drawers, but I don't have time to search them. I slink across the office to the door. Crack it open—

Creak.

My heart stops. Someone's on the stairs.

Dammit.

I close the door. Panic boils in me, making me feel hot.

It has to be Reyshka. No one else can access this room. I have *seconds* before she finds me.

My hand reaches out—*snatches* water from the basin behind Reyshka's desk. *Pulls* it to submerge the door handle. I *clench*, freezing the water and encasing the doorknob in ice.

It buys me time, but not much.

My mind whirs, spinning through my limited options.

Can't hide behind the desk—it's the only place she sits in here. She'd find me immediately.

My only other option is to escape. Obviously, I can't leave through the door . . .

My frantic, roving eyes land on the window.

I hurry to the window and peek out. It overlooks the backyard, full of soldiers. If I climb out, I'll be plainly visible to all of them.

Unless . . .

I close my eyes.

I've made it storm before. When I was sad, angry, terrified . . .

It's always been in response to my emotions. I've never done it on purpose. If I make it storm hard enough, the rain will hide me from the soldiers training outside, and the thunder will mask the sounds of me leaving.

The tension of my power builds within me, tangling itself in a knot.

The doorknob rattles.

Dammit, dammit, dammit.

My panic eases some of the tension. The knot loosens, and light rain patters against the window.

I'm slightly relieved, but it's not enough.

I grit my teeth and reach *deeper*. Not for fear or panic but for *me*—control.

The water hears my cries and *pours*. The knot loosens and power surges out of me. My eyes are still closed but I hear water lashing against the windowpane in a heavy downpour.

My eyes shoot open. The rainfall is thick. Thick enough to obscure visibility outside. I pry open the window and scurry out.

The brick exterior is slick with rain. My fingers struggle to grip the sides of the house. I grit my teeth and pull myself out. One hand shoves the window closed behind me just as I hear the office door finally burst open.

I'm out.

My arms strain from the tension of supporting my weight. It's usually easy, but the side of the house is slippery. Lightning flashes, followed by a clap of thunder. Rain falls so hard, it's almost painful. I revel in this feeling.

Rain pelts me and thunder grumbles as I haul myself up. I tumble onto the roof of Reyshka's house with a splatter. For a moment, I lie on my back, letting the water wash over me and cool my body, flushed from the heat of my escape.

My heart is hammering and I feel *amazing*. Better than I've felt in years. I called, the water listened. Not because I was angry but because I told it to. I was in total control.

Finally, I move to the other side of the roof and climb down the front of the house, where no one can see me.

I think about stopping the rain as I make my way back to Lex and Zaire's. I decide against it. Instead, I savor the coolness of my victory against my skin.

CHAPTER THIRTY-SIX

TWO-FACED

Zaire and Lex are willing to lend me a cart and horse to travel to Wystmeren—so long as I take Carrik with me.

I don't bother fighting them. One, because I know they won't change their minds. And two, because I make Carrik steer while I sit in comfort inside the cart.

The journey to Wystmeren isn't far. We leave early in the morning and should arrive at night. The whole way there, my plan is to knock on doors around the lake until someone answers to the name Ezenniel.

When we arrive, my plans go up in smoke when I see a small house bordering the lake. Dark wood exterior, thatched roof, drawn curtains, and an isi wood fence. I don't need to knock to know this is where Ezenniel is.

Carrik and I approach the fence. It's splotchy all over—the way Zaire said it changes when the enchantment fades. Clearly, it hasn't been replaced in years. We walk past the fence, up the pathway to the front door.

I ignore the knots in my stomach and knock.

I mentally review my cover story. I plan to play the same role I do with Reyshka: a siren sent on behalf of King Larster with a hidden mission I can't reveal. I need to be consistent in case he reports anything back to Reyshka. Still, I shake off my hood—it'll be easier to convince him I'm telling the truth if he's already under my spell.

As the door swings open, I don a captivating smile.

And *freeze.*

The man on the other side is medium height with a wide build, short hair, deep skin, and teal eyes.

What startles me—shakes me to my core—is that I've *seen* him before. In Faraday House. He was one of the fae on the council.

For several long seconds, we stare at each other, neither speaking. Me in shock, him in awe.

Carrik clears his throat, shooting me a questioning look.

Right. I'm supposed to speak. My smile wilted when I first saw him, but I paint it back on, sweet enough to rot teeth. "Hello, *Ezenniel.*" I say his name with a hint of a lilt, making him shiver. "Can we come in?"

It takes Ezenniel another few moments to scoop up his jaw. "Y-yes. Of course. Please." He holds open the door. There's plenty of room for him to stand aside, but he gives me a slim berth, making it impossible for me not to brush against him as I enter.

He shudders as my shoulder grazes his. I pretend not to see.

"Er—please sit." Ezenniel guides me into a sitting room with an unnecessary hand on my lower back. He motions for me to sit on the sofa without so much as a cursory glance at Carrik.

It's only when I move away from him that he realizes he's led me into his home and has no idea who I am. "My apologies, but who are you?" His eyes slide to Carrik for a brief moment before shooting back to me. "And your friend."

"I'm Saoirse. His Majesty sent me." I wave a hand at Carrik, who hovers in the sitting room doorway. "He drove the cart."

"His—" Ezenniel's eyes widen. "King *Larster* sent you?"

"Yes. Can I have something to drink?"

"Lune above, where are my manners?" He looks appropriately frazzled. "Of course. I'll put on some tea." He hurries from the room, wringing his hands with fear. *Good.* I've disarmed him twice. First, with my appearance, and now, with the mention of Larster.

In his absence, I've stolen a few moments to *think.*

Odion told me Ezenniel was sent out on assignment years ago. It makes sense. He's spent that time masquerading as Alkaran. Gaining their trust. Obtaining a seat on their council, in close and frequent contact with their Queen.

Reyshka's been doing more than training soldiers—she's been crafting spies.

Ezenniel's space on the council is how Reyshka made the first attempt on the Queen's life. How she's perpetuated the myth that Keirdre is harmless. How she had obtained a license for isi wood when Carrik asked. All because of her spy on the council.

Ezenniel returns. His hands shake as he passes me a teacup.

I smile and raise it to my lips but don't drink. I don't trust him enough to drink anything he gives me.

His hands are still twisting nervously. "Have I done something wrong?"

He's rattled. Good. I can use that. If I play this game right, I can spark the response I want: fear.

With that, I can get what I'm really after: information.

"That remains to be seen," I say as calmly as I can.

"Is His Majesty displeased with me?"

I need to prey on his insecurities. "His Majesty is unhappy with your limited progress."

My throat burns with the taste of his fear. "I've done everything I've been told," Ezenniel objects. "I've gained the council's trust. I've convinced them to avoid the coasts and ignore the barrier. I'm doing the best I can."

He's still being too vague. "And yet here I am."

He gulps. "Please tell His Majesty there's only so much I can do while the witch is still alive. I swear on my life, as soon as Reyshka rids us of the witch, I'm ready to assume the throne. We only have one lune left before it's no longer an option."

It takes everything in me to remain still.

Assume the throne?

How is that possible? Sprites are next in the rotation. The only way for Ezenniel to take the throne . . .

Lune above. Zaire explained the rotation ages ago. The rotation order is set—unless a monarch dies while still on the throne. Then the crown passes to another council member. To avoid foul play. Except now, it's doing exactly the opposite.

Reyshka plans to kill the witch Queen before the end of her final year of reign. If she succeeds, Ezenniel will take the crown. As a proxy, I'm sure, to King Larster.

Carrik shifts behind me. I don't need to turn to face him to know he's rattled by this news.

I can't react. I have to act as though Ezenniel hasn't shared anything I didn't already know.

I keep smiling. "Prove it. Prove what you've done in your current position."

A gamble. But he must have documentation of *something* I can use. If I know where the weak points are, I can fix them.

"Of course." He nods quickly, eager to please. "I have records of every council meeting. You can see—I'm instrumental. I'm doing exactly as I've been told and no one suspects anything."

He doesn't move.

I roll my eyes. "Well, go and get them, then."

"Of course."

He rushes from the room. I hear him rifling around somewhere down the hall before he runs back and slams a heavy notebook on the table before me.

"Transcriptions," he says breathlessly. "They're all in order. Every council meeting I've ever attended. Is this—" He looks nervous. "Is this enough?"

Enough? This is everything I could've wanted and more.

I hide my enthusiasm and take hold of the book. Tuck it under my arm with a stiff nod, lips pursed to keep myself from smirking. "This is sufficient."

CHAPTER THIRTY-SEVEN

IF SHE'S WORTH IT

I thought Reyshka planned to move the barrier while Alkara was unstable. I was wrong. Larster and Reyshka planned to *own* Alkara.

Reyshka has an army of soldiers returning to Pennex to fight and hundreds of weapons to arm them with. Faraday House's defenses have been lowered. The witch Queen, I'llyaris, is an easy target. Once she's dead, the throne will pass to Ezenniel, a Keirdren in disguise. Giving Reyshka's soldiers the perfect chance to swoop in, take over as much of Alkara as they can. All paving the way for Larster to move the barrier and expand Keirdre. Probably kill any creature he hates. *Again.*

Larster might be dead now, but it doesn't matter. His influence has seeped into every area of this new world and my own. A poison. Just like Carrik's been telling me. A festering, slow-acting poison, killing us from within.

This whole time I've been searching for a cure, but what if there isn't one?

Within the next lune, Reyshka will kill Queen I'llyaris. When that happens, we'll have my worst nightmare: Keirdre on *both* sides of the barrier.

We're out of time. And I'm out of options. There's no chance of peace. Not anymore. The barrier has to come down.

When I Dreamweave to see Hayes, he smiles as he always does. He looks exhausted, as he always does. But he's genuine. As he always is.

I wish it were enough. I wish being good and genuine and heart-thumpingly sincere could counteract Larster's poison.

"Hey." His smile is tired. "It's good to see you."

I force myself to smile back. "You too." I inhale, preparing to tell him we need to talk, but he's turning away and speaking again before I can. "You were right about the guard. I just received word that the Enforcers have turned to the east."

I nod, unsurprised.

"I think we should speak to my mother again. Without her guards this time."

At this, I'm thrown off-balance. He *hates* talking to Ikenna. "Why? Do you think she knows something else?"

"I want her to know you didn't kill Thannen. Anarin did. I'm not going to mention her spy, but I think she should know who's responsible."

"Why?"

"My mother and I have no affection between us. Still, she's a Queen. With resources and knowledge that could be useful. The more she trusts me and doesn't hate you, the easier it'll be to obtain information from her."

Sharing just enough information with Ikenna to soften her up, but not enough to give her any leverage over us. Manipulative. I'm a little impressed.

Hayes frowns when I don't say anything. "You think it's a bad idea?"

I grin. "It's what I would do."

We're silent as we walk to Ikenna's chambers. Like last time, she's clearly surprised to see Hayes, but she clears the room when asked without questioning it.

"Hayes." She smiles thinly once we're alone. "To what do I owe this visit?"

"I know who killed Thannen." There's no buildup, no hesitation.

Ikenna sneers. "As do I. Your pet siren."

"She's not a pet. And it wasn't her."

"Honestly, Hayes, you've been on edge ever since that witch got herself killed in Ketzal, and now you expect me to trust the words of a siren who lies for a living?"

Witch? What witch?

I glance at Hayes in question. His throat bobs, and for a tick, his eyes shoot to me. I'm flooded with the now familiar flavor of sour grapes—guilt. *This* is what he's been keeping from me.

What witch was killed in Ketzal?

My first thought is Drina—but if it was my auntie, Hayes would've told me. I know he would've.

Hayes's eyes flicker back to Ikenna. "This has nothing to do with that. This is about Thannen. He was killed by Enforcer Anarin Arkin."

Ikenna's face doesn't change, but I taste a shift in her emotions. She's *smug.*

She knew. Ikenna already pieced together what happened the night Thannen died. I doubt she knew Thannen was a spy, but she knew Anarin orchestrated his murder and framed me.

I catch Hayes's arm. Gently, so he doesn't jump and alert Ikenna I'm here. "She already knew."

His eyes narrow. I taste a familiar emotion from him: disappointment. "You don't seem surprised. Did you already know?"

Ikenna shrugs carelessly. "What does it matter?"

"She killed your guard! She's trying to have me removed from the throne! I thought you wanted a Vanihail to rule?"

Ikenna bares her teeth into a cruel smile. "Of course I do. And you will. If anything, she's done me a favor, forcing you to finally *act*. As soon as you're willing to listen to my advice and do what needs to be done—"

"I'm not going to kill people to send a message."

"—then you will retain your role as King and earn their respect," she continues as if he hasn't spoken. "The Enforcers will be executed, including Anarin, and all will be well. I don't care what she did to make it happen. As long as it gets rid of your pet siren, I'm happy."

"She's *not*—" Hayes stops himself. Draws back and shakes his head. "You're not worth it. Have a good night, Mother." He starts for the door.

"You think *she's* worth it?" Ikenna challenges. "You think you can trust her? Tell me, did she mention the gift I gave her before she left?"

My heart stalls with panic.

No. That damned freya candle.

I snatch Hayes's arm and yank him toward the door before she can continue, but his feet have sprouted roots. He doesn't budge.

A slow smirk spreads over her face. "She didn't tell you?"

Hayes grits his teeth as he turns to stare at her. "What the hell are you talking about?"

"I gave her a freya candle. To contact me when she decides to stay on the other side. I told her I'd send her family over and she could stay there, with them." Ikenna's smirk widens. "*Without* you."

Hayes staggers back, a mix of hurt and disbelief crossing his face. Settling on my tongue. "She wouldn't—"

"And yet, she didn't tell you, did she?"

His silence is answer enough.

She swells from this minor victory. "You see? I tried to tell you. That girl will be the end of you. She's not loyal to anyone but herself. Deep down, you already know that."

Hayes opens his mouth to respond, but he must realize there's nothing more to say. Not even he can defend me against this.

CHAPTER THIRTY-EIGHT
SELFISHLY

Neither of us speaks for so long it hurts.

What dead witch was Ikenna talking about? Why didn't Hayes tell me? I'm a hypocrite and I know it, but for all the lies I spoon-feed him like porridge, I always assumed he'd be honest with me. I guess Kings don't have the luxury of honesty the way Princes do.

"What witch was she talking about?" I break the silence.

Hayes sits on the corner of his bed, face buried in his hands. When I speak, he brings his head up and looks at me. His guilt is back, but it's crowded now, with anger like pepper and disappointment like a rotten apple. "I wanted to tell you."

"Then tell me now." My hands are burning hot while the rest of me feels cold. I don't know what to do with them, so I leave them at my sides.

"There was a raid on a house in Ketzal. A safe house for humans, kind of like the one you and Rain grew up in. The witch who ran the home tried to protect them against the Enforcers' soldiers—she died fighting them."

A home like mine. Like Rain's. Like my aunties'. Human children as alone and terrified as my sister. A witch as kind-hearted and self-sacrificing as Drina and Aiya. Dead.

Desperation flashes over Hayes's face when I don't say anything. "I didn't authorize it."

I already know that. Of course he didn't. Honestly, that almost makes it worse. How little control he has. It's not his fault, but it's more proof of what I already know—it's not going to get better. "How long ago was this?"

"Two weeks." He hangs his head. "I was planning on telling you, I swear. I just—didn't know how. I know how important Rain is to you. I didn't want you to look at me like you are now."

I didn't realize I was making a face. I'm usually better at schooling my features. I do it now. "I'm looking at you like this because you lied."

"Don't. That's not the full truth and you know it. Yes, you're mad I didn't tell you, but don't think I can't see how disappointed you are in me. You don't think I can get the Enforcers under control."

I'm disappointed, yes, but not in Hayes. In the situation. In Keirdre. In *myself* for actually thinking all we needed was a good King to fix this. "I never said that."

"You're thinking it."

I can't refute him, because hadn't I come here tonight with the intention of telling him exactly that? He's never going to gain the Enforcers' support. It's a fool's errand to sit around waiting for them to change their minds.

He flinches at my silence as though I've physically struck him and I immediately regret not assuaging him with more lies. I've never shied away from lying to him before.

Hayes looks bitter and his eyes fix on the floor. "Was my mother lying?"

My turn to be honest now.

I sit on the other side of the bed—my side. I don't feel like we're any closer than we were before, but at least I'm sitting now and not standing shakily on my feet. "No. She wasn't."

He's so still I can't tell if he's breathing. "Why didn't you tell me?"

"I—" I scramble to think of the right response. How am I supposed to answer? That I was keeping my options open? "I don't know."

"Were you planning on using it?"

The truth: No. I wasn't *actively* planning on using it.

The *full* truth: I hadn't ruled it out. If something happened where I needed to use it, I . . . I don't know what I would've done.

"No," I say.

His shoulders sag and I know he doesn't believe me. I'm not sure I believe me either.

I take a heavy breath. "We need to bring the barrier down. I don't think Keirdre can be salvaged."

"You mean you don't think *I* can salvage it."

"No one could fix this. Your father made it his life's mission to ensure his putrid legacy would outlast him. You were right when you told me you couldn't change things all at once. Do you remember? When you first became King, you told me you needed support before you could change anything or they'd revolt. You were right. They would have. What we didn't realize was that it would've happened either way. Your father has designed this kingdom so you'll never get their approval. You tried waiting for the Enforcers to side with you. That didn't work. You tried making changes *without* their approval. That's not working either. It's not your fault, but there's nothing more we can do."

"Maybe . . . But the solution can't be to bring down the barrier and let an army from the other side kill everyone."

"I already told you they don't have an army."

"You also told me that Alkara hates Keirdre, and when the barrier comes down, Alkara will fight. People will die."

"Not everyone," I say. "But someone is going to have to take care of the Enforcers. And it's not going to be your soldiers. You've already said you don't have enough to fight them off. If we bring down the barrier, Alkara will mobilize their army and they can fight the Enforcers for you. Maybe with them gone, we'll have a chance of something close to peace with Alkara. Maybe you can actually change Keirdre the way you want to."

"You're asking me to intentionally cause a war I know I'm not prepared to fight."

"You're already in the middle of a war you can't fight!"

"It's not that simple and you know it. You make it sound like only the Enforcers and their soldiers are going to die. But civilians will die as well. And what if the Enforcers and Reyshka take over Alkara before they're prepared to fight back?"

"I can warn Alkara about what's coming. Give them a chance to prepare their army to fight the Enforcers when the barrier's down. In the meantime, we make preparations here to protect the rest of Keirdre," I say. "Gather soldiers loyal to you and not the Enforcers. Evacuate the sectors closest to the barrier." There will be war—it's inevitable at this point. But with Alkara, there's a chance of peace in the long term. Of Keirdre finally being a place where people are free, humans are treated fairly, and no one in my family has to hide.

"I don't have enough soldiers supporting me to fend off an army—let alone enough to fight off *two*. I can't bring down the barrier, knowingly start a war, and cause the death of who knows how many people."

"What exactly is *your* plan? Stay here, trapped in Keirdre, making laws no one follows? Giving commands to an army loyal to the Enforcers and not you? Peace is no longer an option. Within the next lune, Reyshka is going to assassinate the witch Queen. After that, Keirdre will control both sides of the barrier. You have to bring it down before that."

He studies me for several moments. Then, quietly, "How many lives are you willing to risk? How sure are you that the Enforcers won't win and we won't have another Keirdre all over again, *beyond* the barrier?"

"I don't know. But how many people are going to die if Keirdre continues as it is? The witch in Ketzal was the first of many. As long as the Enforcers are a threat, Keirdre isn't safe."

"I've already designated a new Enforcer of Sinu. If I appoint new Enforcers for the other sectors, we have the best chance of changing Keirdre for the better."

"Having new Enforcers doesn't fix the problem of the old ones. New Enforcers aren't going to make people suddenly start listening to you. If the barrier comes down, Alkara can fight off Anarin and the others."

"I'm not going to gamble the lives of innocent people! I already have blood on my hands. If I do this and more people die, that's my fault. Not everyone is like *you*."

Something in his tone makes the hairs on my arms prickle. I rise, putting distance between us. "What the hell does that mean?"

He's silent for so long I think he's going to refuse to answer. Then, "Not everyone is so cavalier about murder."

There's a ringing in my ears. It takes me a few ticks to

recognize it—hurt and rage, pulsing through me so loudly it's like a hum. "That's not fair." I mean it to sound angry, but instead, I sound wounded.

He chuckles darkly, but the taste of his emotions is anything but amused. "Nothing is *fair*, least of all you. You don't have thousands of lives dependent on you. You don't hold an entire kingdom in the palm of your hands. Except, I guess you do, because *I* hold this kingdom in my hands and you have *consumed* me. I haven't made a single decision since I met you without thinking of you. If there's war, it's on me. If there are deaths, it's on me. *Everything* is on me and you want me to spark a war?"

"War is inevitable. What you're doing now is sitting in a cage surrounded by hawks, waiting for them to stop being a threat."

He scowls at me. "You sound like Spektryl."

"Because he's *right*. At some point, you have to accept that this is beyond you and Keirdre can't be fixed."

"I can't accept that. Don't you trust me?"

Trust him with my life? Without question. Trust him as a King . . .

I'm not sure. Or maybe I am and I just don't want to admit it. "Do you trust *me*?"

"How can you ask me that? You lie to me constantly—"

I cross my arms. "If you don't trust me, how can you expect me to trust you? It goes both ways."

"*No, it doesn't.* Not when it comes to you and me. We are not the same."

I can't help scoffing. "Because you're a King?"

He laughs incredulously. "It has nothing to do with being King. Why should it matter if I trust you? I would light the world on fire for you. How is that not enough? We are *not* the same.

You make a reckless decision, it's for you or Rain. I make *any* decision, it's for you. It's always for you. You could do anything, say anything, break me time and time again, and the pieces left of me would crawl their way back to you. Don't ask me to choose between you and my kingdom, because I'll choose you—I always will—but I'll hate myself for it. We are not the same, Saoirse, because I am *selfishly* in love with you."

I'm upright but I might as well be lying on my back. I feel as though the air has been knocked from my lungs, the floor pulled out from beneath me. I've forgotten how to breathe—how to think. "Hayes." My speech sounds slurred. "I—"

"Don't." Those ocean eyes flash with devastation and he looks away from me. "You . . ." His words trail. The end of his sentence garbles like he's speaking to me from underwater.

I lean forward, straining to hear. "What?"

He tilts his head to one side. His mouth moves again. There's no sound. Not even muffled noise like before.

Frowning, I reach for him. My hand touches his—but I feel nothing. I might as well be touching air.

My breathing picks up. The edges of my vision start to fray like old thread in a worn tapestry. My heartbeat stutters with the frantic whir of my mind. "Hayes!" I call out his name. The sound of it echoes, slamming back to me, loud and painful.

Judging by Hayes's confused expression, he didn't hear me.

I try to call for him again, but the rest of my vision unravels. Colors blend together, swirling into a dizzying spiral so intense, I have to shut my eyes.

When they open, I'm no longer in Hayes's bedroom, but in the room I share with Carrik. It's black as pitch outside and the only sound I hear is the gentle breathing of Carrik's sleep.

My chest constricts with panic. I hold up my wrist to inspect my *lairic* beads. The runes have faded from gold to something fainter. There's no glow.

No . . .

My *lairic* beads have died.

Runes are powerful magic, but they're not permanent. Before I left Keirdre, I meant to ask Drina for fresh beads for my bracelet, but in the scramble to flee, I forgot.

I used my *keil* beads daily, so getting new runes was a routine. My *lairic* beads were less consistent. I used them far less often, so I rarely needed new runes.

Except—*lune above*—since coming to Alkara, I've spent hours lying in bed with Hayes, not thinking about how every moment of wasted time was draining the life from my only contact with home.

It's time I can't get back now. There's no way for me to tell Drina what's happened. Or Hayes.

Inhale, exhale.

But, I try and reason with myself, it's fine. Hayes will know something's happened when I stop checking in.

Instantly, I doubt myself. Ikenna just told him she gave me a way to bring my family here so I don't have to return. We just got into a spat over taking down the barrier. He *just*—

Deep breath in.

—told me he loves me.

Deep breath out.

In his mind, as soon as he said the words, I bolted.

He might think I left on purpose. I have no way of correcting him.

My gaze falls to Carrik, sleeping soundly on the floor. I can't tell him about the *lairic* beads dying. My leverage with the Resistance is that they think I can tell Hayes to bring down

the barrier. If they know I can't, any minor authority I might
have had is gone.

I force myself to stay calm. There has to be a solution. I can't
contact Hayes or Drina, but surely a witch here—

The thought fizzles as quickly as it formed. There's no samsam
in Alkara. So, no *lairic* beads. Which means I'm stranded, all
alone, with no way to communicate with the other side.

CHAPTER THIRTY-NINE

TWISTING THE KNIFE

I spend the next week pretending nothing has changed. Between keeping up practice with Carrik, keeping up training with Reyshka, and keeping up appearances, I don't have much spare time. The small bit I manage to steal I spend poring over the council meeting notes that Ezenniel gave me. I scour for anything he says, marking it with red ink. Ezenniel speaks on behalf of Larster and Reyshka, so anything he says is information I can use to foil their plot against the Queen. I'm the only one left to do it now.

Most council meetings are boring. I figured they'd resemble the Enforcer meeting I witnessed in Keirdre—endless bickering and conversations tinged with years of built-up resentment. But, no. For the most part, the Alkaran council gets along. They get into occasional spats, but there are no factions. No hostility between creatures. Their squabbles are about the issue at hand and not underlying, noxious hatred.

It bodes well for the future of Alkara (if I can keep the Queen alive), but it makes the transcripts a slog to get through. If they hated each other, there'd at least be something *interesting*.

Ezenniel has transcriptions going back for years. I start with the most recent meetings and work my way back. The council meets fairly regularly, but with whoever is available, not every-one. The large council meetings—what Rienna and I witnessed—happen once a lune.

Whoever takes notes has an inconsistent notation style. They label each line with the speaker, but the way names are written varies. Sometimes it's a full name, first and last; sometimes it's shorthanded with initials; sometimes it's written as just a first name.

There are too many names to keep straight in my head, but when I work my way back to one lune ago, I see a name I'm posi-tive I've never seen before: Lennex Aimes.

I start to read. Lennex speaks a lot—in the first two pages of this meeting's notes, they've spoken three times. As always, the name the notetaker writes varies. Sometimes Lennex Aimes, sometimes just Lennex, sometimes . . .

I stop reading when I see a name I didn't think to consider: Lex Aimes.

Lex?

It's a coincidence. Has to be. Lex isn't an uncommon name.

But I don't believe in coincidences.

Thoughts pile up and come tumbling down on top of each other. At the council meeting I attended, creatures sat together in groups of four—except for the dryads. There were only three.

It's not proof—just another coincidence I don't believe in.

I read through the rest of the transcript.

Lex Aimes: Your Majesty, my partner and I received an unexpected visitor today.

Today . . .

The day we arrived, Lex had to leave for "work," and Carrik

and I were in the house with Zaire until the Festival of Reds that night. I'd assumed they were at their teaching job. They weren't. They were at a council meeting.

I keep reading.

Her Majesty: A visitor?

Lennex: A siren.

Khan: Everyone settle down.

Her Majesty: That's impossible.

Aimes: She's a siren from Keirdre. I'm—quiet down, everyone—she found her way to us.

Her Majesty: Over the barrier? How is that possible?

Aimes: We've told you for years people from Keirdre can enter Alkara. She is one of them. And she confirmed there are other Keirdrens here. They have been coming for years. Living among us.

Khan: That's impossible.

Lennex: If a siren can come over the barrier, any-one can.

Khan: We're supposed to believe you? You have tried to convince us this is happening for years, and proof just falls into your lap?

Lennex: I can prove it. I'm bringing her to the Festival tonight. I'll take her to see other council members. When you see her, trust me, you'll know she's a siren.

Lex and Zaire dragged me to *dozens* of stalls at the Festival of Reds. I thought it was because they wanted to introduce me to Alkara. I thought it was because they wanted me to fall in love with their kingdom.

It was a ruse. They were showing me off to council members. Proving to them all that they'd found a Keirdren siren.

I feel sick.

Lennex Aimes: This siren is the key to bringing down the barrier, Your Majesty. She comes with a friend of our group, and he assures me King Larster's son, Prince Hayes, is in love with her.

Khan: What does that matter?

Lex Aimes: A girl with the heart of the Prince is invaluable. His life is joined with the barrier, so he can destroy it. If the siren thinks destroying the barrier is in her best interest, she'll command her Prince and he'll follow her lead.

Khan: You can't know he'll do it.

Lennex: I can. She's a siren and she's enchanted him to do as she wants. She's already told me the Prince wants to destroy the barrier as well. If I can convince the siren, she will order her Prince to bring down the barrier. I'm just asking for your support. If Alkara pledges the full force of its military to our cause, we can finally conquer the kingdom of Keirdre. Pay them back for all they've done to us. You have my solemn guarantee. I will convince the siren to tell her Prince to bring down the *barrier. Do we have your guarantee that when this happens, Alkaran soldiers will fight alongside us?*

Khan: If the barrier comes down, what are you asking us to do?

Lex Aimes: Exactly what they did. Kill their King, their Queen, and their Prince. Raze the rest of the kingdom to the ground. Make it ours. Do I have your word?

Khan: We'll have to hear it from the siren herself that the Prince plans to bring down the barrier.

Aimes: Absolutely. She'll tell you herself. Do I have your support?

Khan: Yes.

Lennex: Thank you, Your Majesty. With your per-mission, I'll excuse myself from council meetings until I've secured the siren's trust. It's best she doesn't know my role here.

Khan: Permission granted.

I'm not sure how long I sit staring at the notes before my brain churns to life again.

A few hours ago, I liked Lex. I'd even gotten over how they lied about the Resistance before we got here. Turns out, it was all a carefully crafted screen. All their talk about the Resistance being weak and having nothing to fight with? Lies.

From the moment I arrived, Lex and Zaire have had one goal: securing my trust to bring down the barrier and use me to destroy Keirdre.

The more I think about it, the deeper the knife twists. It wasn't just verbal lies. I *saw* with my own eyes the letter from the council rejecting Zaire's request for an army. Another lie. Zaire didn't send written requests for Alkara's army, Lex went to council meetings *in person* and requested it. They fabricated that letter knowing I'd go hunting for answers on my own.

Lies, lies, and more lies.

Apparently, they lied to everyone. Lex didn't even tell the council that Larster is dead—likely because they need Alkara to be angry and out for revenge. Revenge on a boy King following the death of his father is less enticing than revenge on the man responsible for all of this.

If Hayes had listened to me and taken down the barrier . . . He was right. Alkara's army wouldn't have just settled for killing the Enforcers. They'd have destroyed *everything*—including Hayes.

The whole time I've been here, I've been manipulated. By everyone.

No more. It's time for me to get smart. If they think they can use me, I'm going to use them right back.

Reyshka's Keirdrens want to kill Queen I'llyaris and take over the Alkaran throne. Alkara wants me to bat my eyes at Hayes so they can lay waste to Keirdre. The Enforcers want to overthrow Hayes and make sure Keirdre stays as broken as it's always been.

What do *I* want? Is there a way for me to get it? My *lairic* beads are dead, which means I can't speak to anyone on the other side of the barrier.

Well, that's not entirely true . . .

I still have that damn freya candle. The only person I can

talk to in Keirdre is Ikenna. Someone I hate more than anyone manipulating me on this side of the barrier.

There are no longer any good options. Which, again, leaves the question, what do I want?

For all of Alkara's faults, no matter what the council plans to do with Keirdre, I believe this is a better world for me and my family.

Anything for you, Rain.

I promised myself I'd do whatever it takes to get this life for her, and I meant it.

For the next half hour, I plot. By the time the door swings open with Carrik's return, I've tucked the transcripts beneath my mattress and come up with a plan. I'm going to get what I want.

Even if it breaks Hayes's heart. And mine.

Carrik flashes me his usual easygoing grin.

There was too much spinning through the dust storm of my thoughts to consider Carrik before, but seeing him now, I wonder what he knew about Lex and Zaire. He's known them for years. Am I supposed to believe he wasn't aware of their true motives? I don't. I can't.

"You should really learn to knock," I say as casually as I can manage.

I don't taste even a smidge of guilt. I should be used to it. After years of lying to me, I should know that Carrik Solwey has no guilty conscience.

My heart whines at me that I'm wrong—I must be—I ignore it.

"It's not like you're getting dressed," he says back.

"You didn't know that."

"Fine. I'll try and remember to knock to enter my *own* room from now on." He's smiling, but when he looks at me, *really* looks at me, his green eyes narrow. "What's wrong?"

I hate how well he knows me. "What do you mean?"

"You look . . . I don't know. Is something wrong?" His concern is genuine. But concern doesn't mean he's honest.

I still my features. He can't know that I've found out about Lex and the council. "I'm fine. I just need to talk to Zaire and Lex."

"All right . . ." He looks confused. "You can talk to them anytime. Seriously, is something wrong?"

"I had a spat with Hayes. And I think you're right. Keirdre is past saving."

I taste his surprise. Bright and zesty, like lemon juice. "What?"

"You heard me."

"What are you saying?" His voice is hushed, hardly daring to believe me.

I force a smile. "I'm siding with the Resistance. Keirdre is past saving, Hayes can't fix it, and the barrier needs to come down. I'm going to make sure it does. No matter the consequences."

CHAPTER FORTY

LET IT BURN

Hayes is going to hate me after this.

I try not to think about that as I sit at the dining room table with Lex, Zaire, and Carrik. Lex's unbridled enthusiasm is sweet enough to clog my throat. Knowing they're a liar has me fuming, but I smile as if I don't taste it.

"You're serious?" Zaire is more reserved than Lex. He's excited, but he doesn't fully believe me.

It's fair, considering just last week, I was adamant about Hayes being the solution to Keirdre's brokenness. Now, I can accept that he's a good person, not a good King.

"I am," I say.

"What changed your mind?" Suspicion lingers in his tone.

"I found out there was an unauthorized raid in a home like the one I grew up in," I say. "The witch who ran the house was killed, and the human children living there were sent away. They'll never have stability in Keirdre. Maybe no one will."

"Your Prince can't do anything?" Zaire is testing me. If I'm faking my change of heart, I might let the snub slide. Let him insult Hayes without defending him the way I have the entire time I've been here.

My eyes narrow. "He's a *King*. As you well know. Leave Hayes out of this."

"You're abandoning your attachment to him so easily? I thought *love* was enough to save your kingdom?"

"Zaire . . ." Lex puts a hand on his arm, but he pulls away, still testing me.

I glare. "I never said that. I said he's a good person. And he is. Better than you—*definitely* better than me. But good people can't compel evil. The Enforcers are steeped in it and they don't respect him. As long as they don't, people like my sister will always be in danger. I want better for her. I'm going to make sure she gets it. If you don't want to help me, that's fine—I promise you, I'm more than capable of doing it on my own."

Zaire leans back with a sort of smug satisfaction that makes me scowl. "Fine," he says. "If you're asking for our help, we're happy to give it."

"Maybe the council will finally hear us out," says Lex with an eager smile.

"The council?" I widen my eyes and feign ignorance.

"I told you, I've been pleading for the Alkaran council's support. They refused to give it. Now that you're willing to have the King bring down the barrier, they'll *have* to listen to us. Maybe we can get an audience with the Queen."

"I have a condition," I say. "Hayes and my family are spared."

Zaire and Lex exchange looks. Zaire speaks first. "You think your Prince will forgive you after this?"

No.

I keep that thought to myself. "I think that's none of your business. All I need to know is that his life will be spared when there's war."

"We'll discuss details with the Queen." Lex's smile is wide and sharp. It's unsettling.

Carrik frowns. "I thought the Queen has been in hiding since the assassination attempt?"

"Something tells me she'll be willing to come out of her shell for this meeting," says Lex. "Although, if we're able to speak with her, I think it's best to leave out the fact that King Larster was killed."

Carrik looks wary. "Why? They hate him. His death is good news."

"We want their support. Larster is a significant foe. If he's already dead, they might be less willing to assist us."

All eyes are on me, waiting to see what I think. I shrug. "Sounds good. If we manage to get an audience with the Queen, I won't tell her about Larster."

Carrik still looks wary, but Lex and Zaire are all smiles, pleased I've finally come around.

I've been spinning webs of half-truths my whole life. At this point, I'm an expert.

The truth: I want the barrier to come down.

The full truth: I *don't* want to see Keirdre burn. I'm going to meet with Queen I'llyaris and use her to learn exactly how big of an army we're dealing with. I'm going to use that information to make sure Alkara can't destroy Keirdre.

The Resistance used me. An unforgivable offense. I'm going to use them right back. To bring down the barrier, yes, but there's no way in hell I'm letting them destroy my home—or Hayes. Whether he forgives me for what I'm about to do or not.

CHAPTER FORTY-ONE

TRUE COLORS

When we enter Faraday House, I crane my head to look around, as though this is my first time here. An attendant leads us through the main chamber, where the council meeting was held, and into a dining room.

The walls are pale green and bare. There's a wooden table in the middle of the room surrounded by a dozen cushioned chairs, all empty. Queen I'llyaris stands stoically behind the head of the table. Up close, I'm even more startled by how smooth her face is. It's almost completely unlined.

Her guards—advisers, maybe—stand around her. In Keirdre, guards stand against the wall to give the Royals space. I'llyaris's guards hover right over her shoulder, crowding her. She looks small compared to them.

Carrik and I instinctively dip into bows when we see the Queen. Zaire and Lex quickly pull us upright.

Right. I remember how no one bowed to the Queen at the council meeting. It felt rude then and it feels rude now. I guess reverence is less of a priority here.

"Your Majesty," Lex murmurs. "A pleasure to meet you."

My teeth clamp down on a scoff at this performance. "An honor," I say with a small smile. Small because if it stretches any wider, my anger will knot it into a snarl, and I need to appear as unbothered as possible.

"The honor is mine." The Queen inclines her head toward me. "You're the first siren I've ever met. Likely the last. I imagine I'm far from the first witch you've ever met."

"You're the first I've met with a crown," I say.

That earns a smile from her. Strangely, it feels timid. "My name is I'llyaris."

"You may refer to her as Your Majesty." One of her guards speaks for her. I recognize him as the guard who did most of the talking at the council meeting.

Queen I'llyaris's expression flashes with irritation for a flutter of a moment before it's gone and she's impassive again. "Please. Take a seat. All of you." I'm motioned to the chair to the right hand of I'llyaris. Carrik sits next to me. Lex and Zaire are across from us. Zaire is calm, but Lex's excitement could sear a hole through my tongue.

There's a brief, stiff silence, and I wonder if I'm expected to speak first.

"I understand you hold the heart of Keirdre's Prince?" the Queen's guard finally says.

Lex tenses and shoots him a look I'm not meant to see. I pretend I don't. "The Prince and I have an understanding. If I tell him to bring down the barrier, he'll do it."

"You're confident of this?"

"I am. But before I agree to anything, I need some assurances."

The guard glowers. "Careful, Keirdren. You walk a narrow line. We've graciously allowed you into the home of our Queen. After all we've heard of your people and of *you*, siren, don't think—"

"My name is Saoirse," I correct him. "Not 'siren.' And certainly not 'Keirdren.'"

Something sparks in the Queen's eyes. "You denounce Keirdre?"

"I resent being referred to by a kingdom when I have a name."

"But *do* you denounce Keirdre?" Her speckled eyes are hard. "They are *vile*. The scourge of this world. Are you one of them or one of us? Who are you loyal to, siren?" She pauses, letting her blatant refusal to address me by name linger before adding, "Saoirse."

She did it on purpose. Wavered saying my name just to rile me. I don't react. "I'm loyal to myself."

The Queen raises a doubtful eyebrow. "That's cheating. Keirdrens are cheaters. Refusing to choose is the same as choosing the enemy."

I can't taste her emotions, but her anger is as plain to see as blood on fresh snow. Her brows are scrunched and there's fire in her eyes.

My first instinct is to answer her anger with my own. I temper that impulse. Take a long, steadying breath. "I want the barrier to be destroyed. I have no love of Keirdre—but there are people within it that I care for. When the barrier comes down, I need a few promises from you. First, you spare Prince Hayes. Second, you spare my family—I'll provide you a list of names." This is for Zaire's benefit. He's suspicious of me and I need him convinced I'm doing everything in my power to protect those I care about.

The Queen still looks furious. She opens her mouth to respond, but one of her guards—the main one—speaks in her stead. "How do we know you'll be successful in convincing the Prince of Keirdre to destroy the barrier?"

It annoys me how often these guards speak for or over their Queen. "You doubt me?"

"I question your claim that the Prince will do as you say."

I smirk. Slowly, I rise. Open my lips, start to sing.

Everyone in the room goes limp. My song is smooth and gentle. I sing him a song of safety and security. Like most things, it's a lie. My eyes glow silver as the song swells. The guard's eyes are fixed on me and glazed over. I crook a single finger, beckoning him toward me.

Immediately, his feet stumble the short distance to stand directly in front of me. I sing louder, staring into his eyes, ensnaring him in a beautiful, lyrical cage. "Tell me your name?"

"Khan," he says breathlessly.

I lean close to him. "Khan," I whisper into his ear, drawing a shudder, "I like to be happy. Do you?"

"Yes." His chin flaps up and down as he nods.

"What would you do to make me happy?"

He doesn't hesitate. "Anything."

I pull away and smirk, eyes fading back to honey. "I'd love to test that, but I'm hoping that's enough of a demonstration for you."

Still dazed, Khan blinks for several moments before he realizes what he's doing and shudders away from me as though I've thrown ice water over his head. "How dare you—"

"You asked me to prove to you the Prince will do as I say. Are you convinced?"

He stumbles back to his place behind the Queen without answering. I'llyaris's face is mostly still, but my demonstration has cooled a bit of her fury. The corners of her lips strain against a smile, and her eyes shine with amusement.

"I hope this allowed you to consider my position," I say. "I can give you a list of those I want spared. If harm comes to any of them, you'll have me to deal with. This is nonnegotiable."

"Your King slaughtered our kind," says Khan. He's addressing me but he locks his gaze on the dining room table to avoid being drawn under my spell a second time. "He attacked in the middle of the night like a coward. He set fire to our cities and torched good people and their homes to the ground. He stole our resources for himself and lives behind an impenetrable force with everything he took. And you ask for leniency."

"I don't ask for leniency for King Larster. You're free to torture and kill him as you please. You're free to kill Queen Ikenna as well. But you will *not* hurt Prince Hayes."

"All of your requests are reasonable—except for that," says the Queen. "You cannot expect us to spare any of the Royal family. Your kingdom stole from ours. Irreparable damage was done. Lives were carelessly taken. We cannot let atrocities lie. Your King must *suffer*. I will make him watch as I destroy his kingdom and his heir. And then I'll slaughter him too. It's what he deserves."

"Then how are you any better than they are?"

Lex flinches and reaches for me to calm me down, but I pull away before they make contact. "If you want the barrier down, you'll listen. I won't compromise on Hayes's life."

The Queen storms from the room.

Khan lurches after her. "Y-Your Majesty—"

She ignores him, and he's forced to chase after her as she leaves. She returns moments later holding a thin, gilded box. Her eyes are harsher than they were before, gleaming with something dark and terrifying. She slams the box on the table. "Do you know what this is?"

Khan glances from the box to the Queen, expression wary. "Your Majesty—"

She continues to ignore him and yanks the box open, revealing what's inside, sitting atop a sheet of rich purple velvet: a crossbow bolt. Navy with a gold tip. Keirdren colors.

"Your Keirdrens do not deserve mercy," the Queen snarls. "They massacred our people. They shot at our Queen. *This* is the bolt they used to try and kill me, and you ask that we spare the Royal family? It's an outrage. We *must* avenge those killed by their hand."

"I want Larster brought to justice just as badly as you," I say. "But I want Hayes—the Prince—to be spared. If you agree to that, we can discuss. If not, we have nothing more to say to each other."

The Queen looks ready to argue further, but Khan puts a hand on her shoulder, and the other guards close around her, heads bent as they whisper to each other.

Finally, Khan emerges from the cluster and nods. "If you are successful in convincing your Prince to bring down the barrier, you have our support. Your Prince will not be harmed."

I'llyaris stands stock-still, expression brimming with fury. Clearly, she didn't agree to this. Still, she holds her tongue. Bridles her anger.

"I have one more request," I say.

Lex groans.

"What?" says Khan, tone wary.

"It's nothing bad. If you want me to have the barrier brought down, I need to know what I'm dealing with. So I know if your army stands a chance against Keirdre. I want to see the army you're gathering. Can you make that happen?"

I'llyaris opens her mouth to speak, but again, Khan cuts her off. "Let us think it over."

I glance between the Queen and Khan. "What is there to think over?"

Khan looks as if he's about to answer for the Queen—again—so I raise a hand. "From Her Majesty, please."

I'llyaris's brows jump in surprise before resuming their previous position. "As he said, we need time to discuss and think it over." She speaks woodenly. "It was a pleasure to meet you, siren. Saoirse."

Quickly, Zaire and Lex push back their chairs to stand as well. As the Queen turns to leave, one of her guards reaches for the gilded box on the table. Once again, I see Keirdre's crossbow bolt before he snaps the lid shut, shielding it from view.

Something about it nags at me.

It's navy blue with a gold-plated tip. Keirdren colors. It makes sense. Keirdrens attempted to kill the Queen, they used a Keirdren crossbow.

My tongue fiddles with the space behind my false tooth as I think.

I've been training with Reyshka and her weapons since I arrived. In the cellar, I got a firsthand glimpse of her complete arsenal. None of her weapons had Keirdre's colors.

My tongue stops.

Reyshka's priority has been making sure no one in Alkara knows there are Keirdrens here. Why would she risk years of planning by firing a crossbow bolt immediately recognizable as Keirdren?

She wouldn't.

Which means whoever shot at Queen I'llyaris wasn't a Keirdren soldier.

It doesn't make sense. I already know Reyshka's plan: kill the Queen, get Ezenniel on the throne, and use Keirdre's army to take over Alkara. The pieces fit. Except—

Soldiers only *just* started returning to Reyshka's camp. Why would they have already made an attempt on I'llyaris's life if their full army wasn't here? Why did Rienna and I only recently test the isi wood exterior of Faraday House if they'd already tried to kill the Queen?

I was wrong. The pieces don't fit.

Which means—

Lune above.

Keirdre didn't try to kill Queen I'llyaris.

The Resistance did.

CHAPTER FORTY-TWO

WORTH THE RISK

Lex and Zaire are pleased with themselves. So pleased, they don't try to force conversation as we make our way back to their house.

Carrik walks alongside me, quiet. Quiet for the journey back to Lex and Zaire's. Quiet as we ascend the stairs to our room. The moment the door closes behind us, he rounds on me. "What's going on?"

I feign ignorance. "What do you mean?"

"Saoirse, I *know* you. What made you finally change your mind about Hayes? You've been fighting me the whole time we've been here. And now, you've what? Given up? You don't give up."

"If you don't think I'm capable of changing my mind, why have you been shoving your thoughts down my throat every chance you get?"

"I know you *can* change your mind, but not like this. Something happened. Tell me."

I want to refuse again, but I know it's pointless. My eyes skim his face, my tongue runs along the roof of my mouth, searching for an indication that he's lying.

Did he know Zaire and Lex planned to lie to me—*use* me—to get to Hayes?

I already know what lengths Spektryl would go to in order to convince me to side with the Resistance. He blackmailed me to uncover buried truths about Larster. He kidnapped my sister to force me to kill Hayes. Threatened her to make me tell him where the Royals were hiding.

He's a traitor. Not to be trusted.

But . . .

Carrik screamed with me at my ancestors' graves. Held me as I sobbed in the rain. Helped me fight *with* the water, not against it.

My instincts tell me to trust Carrik. My mind tells me Spektryl is never to be trusted again.

Carrik, *my* Carrik, is full of jests and laughter. Spektryl was born from fury and loss. How much of the boy standing in front of me is Carrik? How much of him is Spektryl?

I'm not sure.

He's an excellent liar. I can't trust my instincts around him. I have another trick—one last way to test whether he's betrayed me all over again.

"Carrik, did you notice anything strange about the crossbow bolt the Queen showed us?" I eye him, waiting to see and taste his reaction.

"I have no idea what you're talking about," he says. "Was there something wrong with it?"

"If I told you I don't think Keirdre fired that bolt, what would you say?"

"It was navy and gold. Keirdre's colors."

I taste oversalted stew and mushy peas. Confusion.

A weight lifts from my shoulders. A taloned hand of fear releases from around my heart. You can fake a lot of things, but not emotion. Which means he really, truly had no idea that Keirdre didn't shoot that crossbow.

My body sags in relief. Carrik and I might not be friends anymore, but I'm in need of an ally. Without speaking, I snatch his arm and pull him for the door.

He trots after me, startled. "What are you—"

"Shut up."

He shuts up.

So far, Lex and Zaire have tried every trick to manipulate me. I wouldn't put it past them to eavesdrop.

I stop dragging him when we're in the field just outside the city, near the forest where we first came to Alkara.

Carrik still looks confused. "Why are we here?"

I ignore the question. "Who do you want to help, Solwey? Me or the Resistance?"

"You." He doesn't waver. "If I have to choose, it's you."

The memory of the knife he plunged into my back—the one he held against my sister's throat—is still fresh. Still, I have two options: confide in him and have the slimmest fraction of a chance that this works out, or don't and stay stuck here while Reyshka kills the Queen and Ezenniel takes over.

It's an easy choice. Scratch that—not easy, but the right answer is obvious.

"Lex is on the council," I say.

"*What?*" I taste the spicy peppercorn of his anger. "No. That's impossible. I'd know."

"They hid it from you. It was in the council meeting notes Ezenniel gave me. Right after we arrived, Lex swore to the council they could convince me to side with the Resistance. They promised I'd get Hayes to bring down the barrier so the Alkaran army could destroy Keirdre. The council promised to send in their army to Keirdre if I told them in person that I agreed."

Carrik looks stunned, and the taste of surprise on my tongue can't be faked.

"They've been manipulating me since I got here," I say. "If they're successful, there's going to be war. On three sides. Reyshka wants war against Alkara to expand and move the barrier. The Resistance wants war against Keirdre. And the Enforcers want war against Hayes."

There are three possible outcomes, all of them deadly. If the Resistance gets what they want, the barrier comes down and they kill everyone in Keirdre—including Hayes.

If Reyshka gets what she wants, Keirdre will expand into Alkara. This world—the one I promised for my sister—will become a replica of the one I'm fighting to leave behind.

If the Enforcers get what they want, the barrier stays up, Hayes is dethroned, and Keirdre continues exactly as it is.

The only people who don't want any of those outcomes are Hayes (but without a larger army, he doesn't stand a chance against *anyone*, let alone his own people) and me.

"That crossbow bolt wasn't Keirdren," I say. "I've seen their weapons. They're not allowed to have Keirdren colors."

"If it wasn't Keirdre, then who?"

I fold my arms and give him a look. "Guess."

Shock and horror flash across his face. I taste it, like rotting fruit. "You think it's . . . the Resistance?"

"I can't think of anyone else it could be, can you?"

His mouth opens and closes a few times before he gives up and just stares at me, at a loss.

"Do you believe me?" I ask.

"Lune above, I do."

"Good. I have an idea. But it's . . . intense."

"I'm in," he says.

"You haven't heard the idea yet."

"You're my best friend. You need me, I'm there. No matter what. Maybe after this, you think about not hating me anymore. Maybe after *that*, you think about forgiving me."

"I—" *I don't hate you.* I don't say it. "Help me with this and I'll think about it. Deal?"

Sadness like watered-down, tepid tea soaks my senses. He smiles anyway. "Deal. What do you need?"

CHAPTER FORTY-THREE

FALLEN CROWN

*Y*ou *think your Prince will forgive you after this?"*

Zaire's words, as painful in my memory as they were in the moment. Because, no. I don't think he will.

My pen feels heavy as I hold it over the vellum. I didn't want to use this damned freya candle. I didn't want it when Ikenna gave it to me and I don't want it now, but there's no other option.

"I am selfishly in love with you."

Hayes already thinks I fled as soon as he told me. That I've been avoiding him ever since. With this, I'll confirm his fears: that I've given up on him. On us.

Breaking people is a skill. And I excel at breaking Hayes.

My hand shakes as I start to write.

Ikenna,
I agree to your terms. Uphold your end and send my family.
Saoirse

My stomach churns with guilt. I hold the vellum over the freya candle and waver.

"You could break me time and time again . . ."

I don't *want* to hurt him anymore. What I really want is to curl up and cry. Climb into a warm bed and spill everything I'm thinking to—

I stop. Blink faster to keep the tears at bay.

Hayes. I've fallen into the habit of ending my days with him. Talking about our lives. Exchanging jokes to lighten the weight of our responsibilities. When something happens, good or bad, I want to tell him about it. He's the best part of every day. When I send this letter, I'll lose him.

It's either lose Hayes or lose all of Keirdre—including my family.

Anything for you, Rain.

I drop the note into the awaiting flame.

Carrik stands over my shoulder. "You think she'll believe you?"

"Not at first." My foot bounces on the floor in restless anxiety for the next few minutes that tick by before the flame burns blue with her response.

I pass a hand over the flame to retrieve the letter.

Siren,

Why the change of heart? You claimed to care for my son. Are you admitting that was a lie? If you would like me to consent to this deal, I need to be certain of what you want. Tell me, in no uncertain terms, that you intend to abandon my son forever.

She addressed me as "Siren" and didn't sign it. She's mocking me. As infuriating as it is, her response isn't a surprise. I knew she'd be cruel enough to demand more. As soon as she has a letter in my own writing stating I want nothing to do with Hayes, she'll show him. It'll splinter whatever thin hopes he may have that my abrupt departure wasn't a permanent goodbye.

Carrik waits for me to respond for a few ticks before nudging my shoulder. "Are you all right?"

"I—" I pick up the pen but don't move it. "It's going to break his heart."

Carrik's eyes flash with sympathy. "He knows you. He'll forgive you."

"You've broken promises to me before."

I can't unhear those words any more than I can undo the damage I've already done.

"Saoirse," Carrik says gently. "The longer you wait, the more she's going to wonder why you're stalling."

I hate that he's right.

Ikenna,

If you swear to me you will provide for the safe passage of my mother, father, and sister to the barrier, I swear to never return to Keirdre or contact your son again.

I hesitate only a half tick longer before signing my name and pressing the vellum into the candle.

Ikenna responds almost instantly.

Excellent. My son will be delighted to hear this. I'll gather your family. Expect them in one week.

One week. One week before I see my family again. Except, if all goes according to plan—a significant *if*, at the moment—I won't actually get to see them yet.

But, *if* it all goes correctly, my family will be safe from this impending war.

I'm happy to spare them. Happy that, at the very least,

they'll be safe. Happy that the first phase of my plan is in place.

Still, it doesn't change the fact that, once again, Hayes's heart is collateral damage.

☼

It's dark as I circle around Faraday House, and the streets are as empty and calm as they were in Keirdre. I trace the path Rienna and I took when we infiltrated the council meeting—around the house, through the gap in the isi wood fence, to the back door. Pick the lock. Easy.

The door creaks as I enter. I hover in the room with the Queen's portrait, waiting and listening to see if I've roused anyone's attention.

Silence.

I keep my hood up as I creep through the halls into the dining room where I met with Queen I'llyaris. I saw where she and her guards left, so I retrace those steps.

At the end of the corridor is a spiraling stairwell. I climb to the top—the third story. I'll work my way down. Peruse each floor until I find the Queen's chambers.

My head pokes around the corner. Two guards stand outside a door halfway down the hall. Where there are guards, there is something—or some*one*—worth guarding.

I slip off my cloak and drag my fingers through my hair. It's loose and full of kinky curls, just the way I like it.

Hair free, I sidle from the stairwell and approach the guards. They stiffen at the sound of approaching footsteps, but their bodies loosen as I come into view.

The intense flavor of two men losing all reason at the mere

sight of me invades my senses. I inhale to make it linger. Soaking it in like a biscuit drenched in sweet butter.

My lips curl into a smile.

They stop breathing.

"Hello." My voice is husky. No song. Not yet.

They mumble something incoherent. My smile stretches wider.

One of them—the bolder of the two, I assume—moves forward, as though planning to speak. I smirk, and a song flows out of me. Low and sweet. It has a silky quality to it, and I watch as the feeling wraps around them and twists into a knot, binding them to my Siren Song.

Whatever he was about to say shrivels up. His mouth snaps shut and his expression melts into a puddle of longing.

I move closer, still singing.

Their eyes follow, trailing my every move ravenously.

A half pace away, I stop. The guard on the left swallows.

I lean, closer and closer, until I see each of his eyelashes. The sheen of nervous sweat beading on his forehead. The taste of his raw desire is intoxicating.

"H-hi." He stumbles clumsily over the word.

"Hi, yourself." My arms slide around his torso. "Is Her Majesty here?"

His eyes droop at our close proximity. "Yes."

"May I enter?"

"Er—"

I sing another few notes, and his protests fade away like background noise. "Let me in," I insist.

He smiles dreamily. "Will you come back?"

Instead of answering, I press my lips to the side of his neck, feel him tremble beneath me, and pull away. "Maybe."

I flit behind him and shove open the door. It doesn't make a sound as I enter the room and close it. The lights are snuffed, so it takes a few moments for my eyes to adjust. Compared to the opulence of the Keirdren Palace, where Hayes's and Ikenna's rooms are large enough to host lavish parties, Queen I'llyaris's room is tiny. There's a bed on the far side, just under the window. A figure is tucked under the bedcovers. Clearly, she hasn't heard me enter, because she's still sleeping away soundly.

I turn the lock on the door behind me. It won't keep the guards out once my spell wears off, but it should slow them down a bit.

I'llyaris snores softly as I tiptoe across the room to the side of her bed—and stop.

Queen I'llyaris isn't here.

In her place, lying in her bed, is a girl. The room is too dark to make out all her features, but I can see well enough to know that this girl *isn't* the Queen.

My first, panicked thought: I'm too late. I'llyaris is dead.

It's the first conclusion I come to—but then who the hell is this girl?

My hands reach for her bedside table, feeling for a chaeliss stone—something to light this room so I can see her. I don't feel anything.

With a start, the unknown girl in the Queen's bed sits up, eyes flying open with a gasp. She throws out her hands and the torches in the room spark to life, illuminating her face.

This girl is shorter than I'llyaris. Not by much, but enough for me to take notice, even as she's seated. Like the Queen, she has russet-toned skin. Her face is rounder, cheekbones less defined, the bridge of her nose dotted with dark freckles. This girl's hair is in thick twists for the night, but I can tell it's longer than I'llyaris's and pale like moonlight. She's beautiful like Queen I'llyaris, but younger. I can't guess by how much considering I never knew how old I'llyaris was and all witches look young, but I can read her youthfulness in her rounded cheeks and the agelessness of the corners of her eyes.

She blinks at me for a tick and a half before startling to attention. "What the— Siren—"

I think she's going to scream, so I clamp a hand over her mouth. To my surprise, she doesn't struggle, just stares at me with wide, panicked eyes. "Who are you?" I snarl.

She looks confused, still bleary from waking up, but then something dawns on her and she goes rigid. Her eyes shift. It's brief—so brief that if I wasn't staring her down, I'd have missed it—before her gaze snaps back to mine.

My eyes follow the trail of her own and land on her bedside table. I lurch toward it, keeping one hand over her mouth as my other yanks open the drawer.

Keil beads. Dozens of them. Sitting in her drawer like it's nothing.

Zaire told me they're rare here. Hardly any left. Was that yet another lie?

I look back to the unknown girl and see what I somehow missed before: her *eyes*. Cobalt blue and flecked with olive green. The same as Queen I'llyaris.

Jagged shards of information fit together in my mind. Breath flows out of me in a rush as my hand falls away from her mouth and I realize what's literally been staring me in the face.

The girl who's not I'llyaris inhales sharply. I expect her to call out—maybe fight back—but instead her eyes dart around frantically. Someone less well-versed in panic might assume she's searching for an escape, but I know better. She's scrambling for a lie to feed me. A story to explain her presence in the Queen's bedchambers.

"You're not Queen I'llyaris," I say. "But you're the one who's been sitting on her throne."

Her expression grows more frantic. "No! I—"

"Don't deny it." I gesture to her open bedside table drawer. "You've been using *keil* beads."

She pauses. Planning another falsehood.

"Now really isn't the time to lie to me. Where is the Queen? Who the hell are you?" I already know the answers to my questions, even as I watch those eyes flit around, racing to find something I'll believe.

I sigh and decide to give her the truth before she hurls a bold-faced lie that insults both of our intelligence. "She's dead, isn't she?"

Her face flashes with unmistakable fear. "No." She scrambles out of bed, and I realize just how small she really is in comparison to the Queen. "She's not—"

"Stop," I say as gently as I can. Somehow, I know she's not an enemy. She's *petrified*. Someone too young, saddled with too much responsibility. "You can tell me the truth. I'm not going to hurt you. Besides, I already know everything. I'llyaris is dead. She's been dead for a while, hasn't she?" I keep going, not giving her a chance to answer. "And you . . . you stepped in for her. Because you look like her." I look her over, fixating once again on those distinctive eyes. "You're her daughter?" I guess.

She's shivering. Her eyes well with some emotion—sadness, guilt, relief—I can't tell. After a pause heavy enough to sink in the waves of my nerves, her shoulders loosen. The admission is clear: she's giving up the ruse.

The bedroom door rattles.

"Your Majesty!" a frenzied guard shouts through the door. The force of my song has worn off.

The girl is stuck in place, looking from me to the door, wondering how to react.

"Tell them you're fine." I hold out my palms to show her I mean no harm. "I'm not here to hurt you. I just want to talk."

She licks her lips and raises her voice. "I'm fine. I asked the siren to come."

"Are you sure?"

Her hands quiver, but she grabs a *keil* bead fitted into a necklace from her bedside table and loops it over her neck. The change washes over her. Her body lengthens, her moonlight hair shrinks, and her face narrows. Head high, she crosses the room to open the door and address her guards directly. "I'm sure. I requested a private word. I ask that you leave us in peace."

She closes the door. "It's best they don't know you've seen my face," she says as she turns to face me. "Khan won't like it."

The guard who acts as her adviser and speaks on her behalf. "Was he your mother's adviser?"

She nods as she removes her *keil* bead and sits on the edge of her bed, eyeing me warily. "Yes. She trusted him more than anything."

Which is why he hovers and speaks over her. The Resistance's assassination attempt wasn't just an attempt—they successfully killed Queen I'llyaris, and her daughter has been pretending to be her ever since.

I assumed the Queen's thirst for revenge was born from her fury that Keirdre tried to kill her. The Queen's daughter is *more* than angry. She's grieving. Which is infinitely more dangerous.

"What's your name?" I ask.

"J'siiri." She gives a ghost of a smile. "I haven't said it out loud in a long time."

"J'siiri," I repeat. "It's pretty."

"Thank you." She sounds hollow.

"How old are you?"

"Sixteen."

Lune above. She's younger than me. And already she has the weight of the world on her shoulders.

"What are you doing here?" she asks tiredly. "If you wanted to kill me, you could've done it by now."

"I'm not here to kill you. I told you, I just want to talk without anyone else around. Especially not the people I'm staying with."

"Why not?"

"I know Lex is on the council."

J'siiri hesitates. "What are you—"

"Don't do that. Don't lie. I read the council transcripts. I know what they're doing. Maybe I could've accepted that lie, but when I was here last, I realized they lied about something else—to you. Keirdre didn't kill your mother."

At the mention of her mother, J'siiri's expression darkens. "What's your theory? She killed herself?"

"Someone else killed her and framed Keirdre."

She shakes her head. "You're lying."

"I'm not. Until you showed me the crossbow bolt, I believed it was them too. But the one you showed me was navy and gold."

"The colors of your kingdom."

"Yes. Except no one here is allowed to have Keirdren colors. I was sent to Alkara to find peace. I've been training under the Keirdrens since I arrived and I've *seen* their camp."

J'siiri's anger clears with her confusion. "Camp?"

"Keirdre's been sending over soldiers in secret. I'm not sure for how long, but they've been building up an army, right under your nose."

"And you expect me to believe your people didn't kill my mother?"

"*Listen.* Keirdre is awful and I have every intention of making them suffer for what they've done, but there are strict rules in the Keirdren camp about how to blend in. They're not allowed to have Keirdren colors."

"Maybe they made an exception."

"You think they broke their own rules just to make sure you knew they were the ones who tried to kill your mother? That doesn't make sense. They don't even have navy-and-gold weapons. I looked. Think about it. If they were so cavalier about using Keirdren colors, don't you think you'd have known they were here before now?"

J'siiri frowns. "If not them, then who—"

"The Resistance."

"*My* people? Why would they do that?"

"The same reason they didn't tell me they work on your council. They *want* war between Keirdre and Alkara. They want the force of Alkara's military to support them. What better way to make you hate Keirdre than assassinating your Queen?"

She still looks doubtful. "You're just saying that to make me doubt them."

"The Resistance hates how they've been treated and ignored by the council. They want vengeance against Keirdre, yes, but more than that, they want to be *right*. They lied to you. About a lot of things. Larster is dead."

"You're lying."

"I'm not. He was killed right before I came here. They didn't want you to know because they thought you'd refuse to go to war if you couldn't get revenge on Larster. He's dead and his son is on the throne. He's the one who sent me here."

"Your Prince."

I don't bother to correct her. "The Resistance is using your fears against you. When your mother died, why did you take her place?"

"Khan told me I had to. When we saw the Keirdren colors on the crossbow, he knew they were planning something. We didn't know what, but since whatever they had planned required my mother to be dead, we made it look like she wasn't. He said it would be easy. All I had to do was stay on the throne and stay alive until the crown passes peacefully." She hesitates. "Are you *sure* it wasn't Keirdre who killed her?"

"Positive."

"Why should I trust you?"

"Do you have siblings?"

"No."

"I do. A sister. She's twelve. She's smart and kind and curious and loves to laugh and she's the best person I know. But she's human. In Keirdre, that means she doesn't get to be any of those things. She's had to hide her entire life. We both have. You know what Larster did to my kind. I've been alone for as long as I can remember. I'm—" My voice breaks, but I press on. "I'm all that's left. I can accept being alone. But not her. I want a better life for my sister. *This* life, if it's possible. I want the barrier to come down. I want her to live somewhere she doesn't have to hide. Where people don't treat her like she's less than.

We have something in common, J'siiri: we both think this world is better than Keirdre. Which means you and I, we're on the same side. We want the same thing."

That anger I saw in the meeting flickers back to life. "We don't. I don't *want* peace. If you're telling the truth and Larster is dead, it doesn't matter. Keirdre has crimes to answer for. The Resistance may have killed her, but my mother's blood is still on your kingdom's hands."

"I agree. And I think only the people responsible should suffer. What if I told you I have a way for there to be war—but only for the people who deserve it?"

"I'd say . . . that's impossible." But the light of intrigue in her eyes gives her away.

"You want war, I'll give you one. But we can protect the innocent people in our kingdoms from bloodshed and make sure your army has the upper hand. I have a plan. In order for it to work, I need you. Well, your mother and her knowledge of soul magic."

"My mother is dead."

"I know. Did she ever teach you soul magic?"

Long pause. She still hasn't decided if she trusts me yet. Finally, she gives a slow nod. "Yes. But that doesn't mean I'm going to help you. Why should I?"

"You want revenge on those who killed your mother. I can give you that. My plan will take care of the Keirdrens who want you dead. It keeps your people—your mother's people—safe. *And* your mother wanted the barrier down, right? I can make that happen. We can both get what we want."

For several long moments, J'siiri stares at me. Her eyes are narrowed as if she's trying to search my mind for my intent. Finally, she says, "What would you need me to do?"

"Come to Keirdre with me."

"That's impossible. The barrier can only be crossed one way. Everyone knows that."

"All magic has its counter. I have another way over."

J'siiri stares at me. "Are you serious?"

"Deadly."

CHAPTER FORTY-FOUR

BEANSPROUT
AND PINECONE

Three letters. Three goodbyes.

Each envelope is individually addressed to a member of my family. I give them to Carrik. My hands are somehow steady, my pulse is anything but. If everything goes right, I won't see them before I cross back over. After that . . . There's no guarantee this plan will work. No guarantee I'll ever see them again at all.

I can't think about that, so I wrote them letters. Explaining what I'm doing. Telling them I love them. Most of all, making them swear that, no matter what, they're going to live their lives here. Safe and free and happy—with or without me.

I cried writing them. I didn't let anyone see.

With these letters, I fulfill my promise to my sister: to give her the life she deserves. No matter what.

Carrik takes the envelopes. "You want me to give these to your family?"

"Please. There's one for each of them."

He smiles sadly, watching the letters and not me. "You said please. You never say please."

"I want to make sure they're delivered."

"Of course. Whatever you need. Always." The slouch in his

shoulders tells me there's something else on his mind. He's silent as he tucks the letters away, giving me his back. "There's another solution," he says softly. "I already know what you're going to say, but—" He turns suddenly, meeting my eyes with an intensity that burns. "Don't go. Stay here. Your family comes over, we all—"

"No."

His brows draw together and his expression turns pleading. "*Please*. You said you came here for a better life for you and your family."

"I meant it."

"You can *have* that. Don't go."

"Have you forgotten so quickly that Keirdre's planning an attack on the Queen? They're going to turn this world into another Keirdre."

"We can stop that. We've been outsmarting Reyshka for weeks. Let's make it forever."

"What about everyone else in Keirdre? Creatures like us who aren't supposed to exist? What happens to them?"

He laughs bitterly. "You don't have to pretend you care about them—you're going back for your Prince."

"I'm not abandoning Keirdre. The people over there like me. My aunties." My hands curl into fists. "And yes, I'm not abandoning Hayes either."

He's quiet, studying me. "Do you love him?"

The question makes me flinch.

"I am selfishly in love with you."

"How the hell is that any of your business?"

"You're risking your life. You're putting yourself into the middle of a war—on three fronts. If something goes wrong—if you get hurt, if you *die*—I'll have no idea. You're gambling your life for some spoiled Prince we used to hate, and I know you.

You wouldn't risk never seeing Rain again unless he means something to you. I'm asking as a friend who would be devastated to lose you: Is he worth it?"

Hayes. The best and worst of me. He's *good*. Which may seem like a small, insignificant thing, but it's not. It's extraordinary. He's the product of two of the most rotten people to exist, in a world where evil is rewarded and goodness is a weakness, and he's *good*. He overcame his nature. I've been trying—and failing—to do that my whole life.

He's patient when I don't deserve it. Understanding when I'm rash. Kind when he doesn't have to be. Funny and charming and self-reflective and thoughtful and passionate and warm and *beautiful*, all around, and I would rather have an eternity of chaos with him by my side than peace without him. If he never forgives me after this, I won't blame him. But at least I'll know I saved his life.

"Yes," I say finally.

Carrik's head jerks up. He clearly wasn't expecting me to admit to it. "What?"

"He's worth it. You don't have to worry. I'm going to succeed."

"Or die."

"Carrik." I give him a lighthearted smile as I repeat Rain's words from a letter that feels ages old. "I think we both know I'm far too stubborn to die."

He laughs despite himself, but the taste of his fear doesn't fade. "You're not funny."

"You laughed, didn't you?"

"Because I laugh when lightbrains say lightbrained things."

I chuckle, but only because it feels better than crying, which is what I really want to do.

Without warning, Carrik stalks toward me and engulfs me in a tight hug. "Promise me you'll come back. If not for me, then for Rain."

"I promise."

His arms tighten. "I'm sorry. If you never come back, I need you to know that I'm sorry. For everything."

I don't hate you. But I don't forgive you either.

I don't say any of it.

My hands are trembling. I stand alongside the Jeune River, staring at the barrier that separates this world from Keirdre. It's different on this side. We've searched all over, but there's no empty space—no gap in the barrier in Alkara.

My stomach clenches.

Soon. My family will be here soon.

J'siiri is at my side, watching me. "Are you sure this is going to work?"

It's the thousandth time she's asked, and I'm just as uncertain now as I was the first time. I keep my answer short, sweet, and the same as every other time she's asked. "I hope so."

"If it doesn't, what's the contingency plan?"

I wish I could say I have one. All the things she's asking out loud are the questions racing loudly through my mind. I can't shut her up any more than I can turn off my sodding brain. We only have *one* chance. One chance to get back into Keirdre, and one chance at the closest thing to peace we can hope for.

I open my mouth to answer—not that I have one yet—but stop. Something flickers at the edge of my periphery. I squint my eyes at the barrier.

There's no gap on this side, but at a point about knee-height up from the ground, something blank flits into existence before disappearing.

J'siiri makes a noise of irritation. "Are you just going to ignore—"

"Look." I jab a finger at the barrier as the small space flickers again.

J'siiri's reprimand shrivels. "Is that—"

"Shh," I shush her. Not because I need silence to watch the space in the barrier widen, but because I want to know if I can hear my family as they come over.

The emptiness flickers again for a tick. Then stops. Then again, longer this time.

Tears well in my eyes. *They're here.*

I exchange looks with Carrik. Wordlessly, we widen our stances, hands out, preparing. The barrier is unstable and requires a *lot* of energy to break through. I was only able to do it last time through song. This time, we have the added bonus of having no idea if water can even pass through the barrier from this side.

All magic has its counter.

I have to believe that. What's done can be undone. If water can open the barrier on one side, surely, once that gap exists, water can flow through from the other?

The space in the barrier flashes again. This time, it's slightly wider than it was before. After a pause, it disappears again.

Movements in tune with each other, Carrik and I *seize* water from the river and *raise* it until it hovers near where the blank space glimmers in and out of existence.

We wait, breaths held, until—*there.*

It appears, wider than the last time. For the fleeting tick it's open, Carrik and I shove water through.

I feel the release as a trickle of water passes through the other side of the barrier.

Heated excitement swells within me, making me feel light. *It's working.*

I step into the river, feeling the coolness rush around my ankles. This is natural. The water sings to me, eager and ready. I open my mouth and echo the tune. There's no anger or fear in my voice. Just beauty. My eyes flash silver with the release of my power, and the water rises from the river *faster*, flows *faster* to the other side.

I feel the gap widening. It still needs *more.*

The barrier demands and I give. I pull more water from the river and feed it through. Faster. More. My song grows louder, bouncing off the surrounding trees and filling the air with my melody.

On either side of me, I feel Carrik and J'siiri staring, entranced. I'm not focused on them. The water only has one goal this time: *mine.*

As my song rises in volume, the doorway opens, more and more, until it's wide enough for a person to pass through. Still, I sing. Water surrounds me, soaking me to the bone. It's chilly, but when it comes into contact with my skin, it sizzles.

I'm singing too loudly to hear anything, but I feel arms wrap around my waist and a head shove itself against my chest. I inhale sharply. Smell the familiar scent of tree sap and oranges.

Rain.

I can't look at her. Can't even wrap an arm around her and risk breaking my concentration and the doorway sealing itself back up again. Still, she's *here.*

A presence approaches from my right. J'siiri. Just as we discussed; we need to be close.

Next is my mother. I feel her hands on my arm. Recognize the familiar calluses of her fingertips, smell the earthy scent of roses and thyme.

If Rain and my mother are here, that means my father is last, and we have to coordinate this. I need to switch places with my father, so he's here and I'm there, while both of us keep shoving water through the doorway from both sides, just long enough for J'siiri and I to get through. I can't be sure how all of this works, but since there's no space in the barrier on this side, I suspect if the water stops flowing from the Keirdren side, the doorway will close.

One chance. We get *one* chance at this.

"Beansprout, I need you to let me go." I speak quickly. My arms are still held out, eyes still silver. The water is loud, but I know she hears me because in the next moment, her arms reluctantly uncoil from around me.

"I love you, Pinecone." She has to shout to be heard, but I hear her.

My eyes are stinging. My hand twitches, yearning to reach for her, but I can't do that without losing my grip on the water. So, all I say is, "I love you more."

J'siiri grips my other arm. She hangs on to me as I step forward, still shoving water through the gap in the barrier.

I hear footsteps just in front of me. Through the water, I can't see it, but I know it's Dad, hovering just on the other side of the barrier.

With a final screech of a song, I shove another wave through, more forcefully than ever.

J'siiri and I sprint forward.

We pass my father and I whirl around just as my feet make it to the other side, hoping to catch a parting glimpse of my family before the doorway closes.

I'm too late. As I spin around, all I see is the reflection of the forest around me, bouncing off King Larster's impenetrable barrier. I'm in Keirdre again.

CHAPTER FORTY-FIVE

FIELD OF ASH

I don't have time to be devastated. Don't have time to feel anything, because there's a water fae standing behind me.

I hear him before I see him. Hear the metallic slice of someone drawing a blade. I spin around to face him.

A tall man with an overgrown beard, gray-blue eyes, and a Royal insignia pinned to his chest. Ikenna must've sent a water fae with my family.

He pauses when he sees me. His hand is on the hilt of his blade, halfway through pulling the weapon from the sheath at his belt. His eyes slide over my face, taking in my perfect features like a drowning man taking in air.

I push a few tendrils of wet hair from my face. Bare my teeth in a smile. "How did you get here?"

Silently, he motions behind him.

I look over his shoulder. There's nothing there, but then again, this part of the forest is densely packed. It would be difficult for something as large as a horse to maneuver the landscape. "Did you take a carriage?"

His head bobs in agreement.

"Which way?"

Again, he points.

I take a moment to assess him. He's not a threat yet. Each mark is different. This one is content with staring at me for now, but soon enough, he'll come to his senses and realize he shouldn't be freely giving me information. I sing a few notes, watching his eyes soften with obsessed affection. "Can you show us?"

Apparently, the sight of me has stolen his tongue, so without speaking, he leads me and J'siiri through the woods. I sing as we walk, keeping him enraptured until we reach a gray horse tied to a tree and a navy-and-gold carriage. Unmistakably Royal.

I disconnect the horse from the carriage. Looking like Royals will draw unwanted attention as we travel to Vanihail. My hands stop when I hear the slice of metal behind me.

I turn. The soldier is shaking, two bits of fabric stuffed into his ears, his blade pointed at me. "I—I shouldn't have brought you here. You're dangerous." His hands tremble, and I still taste his sweet longing for me.

I roll my eyes. *Lune above, I'm not in the mood for this.*

He looks like he means to use his blade on me but thinks better of it. Instead, he swipes at J'siiri.

My hands fly out. The water that drenches me flings away, condensing into a sphere that wraps around the soldier's head. At the same time, I shove J'siiri out of the way of his arcing sword.

The blade clatters to the ground. His hands curl around his throat—as though that will help him breathe.

I'm reminded of Trellis Ruster as I feel the faint tug of him attempting to force the water away from his face. Like Trellis, his efforts are futile.

I'm stronger than him.

In a few moments, the water wins. *I* win. The soldier crumples to the forest floor. Dead.

I feel that familiar rush that comes from killing a mark. He was a necessary death. He was about to kill J'siiri, and if he were allowed to roam free, he'd tell others I'm here.

I don't feel guilty for killing him. In the past, I killed because I wanted to and called it a need. I know the difference now. *This* was a kill of necessity and I don't feel bad for it. Maybe that makes me a monster. I think I'll always be just a little bit monstrous—vengeful and angry and violent. But, as I now know, I'm more than my instincts.

It's been years since I visited my aunties in Ketzal. The last time I was here in person, I was fourteen.

Returning after all this time, I feel even more out of place than I did before. It's no secret that the Royals have always valued Vanihail more than the other sectors, and the fae sectors more than the non-fae sectors. My memories of Ketzal are stained with disrepair. Dusty dirt roads instead of cobblestone. Small houses made of splintered wood, dark mud, and thatched roofs instead of something sturdier like stone or brick.

In my memories, Ketzal is messy and a little shoddy, but still full of life. Compared to what it looks like *now*, the Ketzal of my memory is a lush paradise. As J'siiri and I ride into the sector, it looks more like a wasteland than a place where people live. I remember the wood and mud homes as misshapen and feeble looking, but they were in one piece. I can no longer say that. There are a few houses still upright, but many of them are in tatters—knocked down and crumbling, or reduced to piles of ash.

The last time I was here, witches and warlocks flooded the dusty streets. Now, even though it's just after midday, the roads are deserted.

It's jarring. Especially given everything I know about Alkara. Zaire's entire job is to patrol the roads, searching for anything out of place. He may be a liar, but I can't forget the way he looked at me when I asked him if *all* areas of Alkara are well maintained. Like he couldn't fathom living in a world where some people don't matter.

J'siiri sits on the horse behind me. Her breathing picks up more with each burned house we pass. "This is our destination?"

"First destination." I keep my voice soft as we wind through the empty roads, tracing my spotty memory for the path to Drina and Aiya's.

"Is it . . . always like this?"

I hope not. "I don't know."

Dread pools in my stomach the deeper we get into Ketzal. The more devastation I see, the more terrified I am that my aunties have been harmed by rogue Enforcers.

My thoughts trip to a halt as I catch sight of a familiar home up ahead.

Short, with walls of thick wooden slats. Thatched roof. Sloping slightly from multiple cave-ins over the years that were patched over instead of fixed properly. A black door with a tiny blue handprint just under the doorknob. *Rain's.* She left it as a sprig. Drina was painting inside with a pretty blue pigment made from the kylith flowers Aiya grew in their massive garden. Rain got it *all* over her little hands. I was carrying her around the way I used to—never mind that I was too small and weak to fully support her weight. I'd circled around the house and tried to come in through the front door. I had Rain propped on my hip, other hand straining to open the sodding door. Rain was getting blue all over me. I didn't mind.

Just like I didn't mind when her hand slapped against the front door. At the time, the black paint job was glossy and new. I thought Auntie Drina would be furious. But when she found us—me still trying to get inside while holding a squirming Rain—she laughed and cleaned us up.

She never tried to get the handprint off the door. Years later, while the once-fresh coat of black is faded and peeling, the blue remains as bright as it always was.

My shoulders sigh with relief. The house is still here. Still in one piece.

I slide from the horse and tether him to a tree. I'm relieved, but just because their house is still here doesn't mean my aunties are.

Blood pulses in my ears as I knock on the front door.

Footsteps from inside, followed by soft whispers.

"We don't have any contraband," Drina's voice calls.

We. She said "we." My aunties are both here.

It's cold outside. Wind whispers against me, freezing in the late harvest season, but I'm warmed from the inside out.

I smile wider than I have in lunes. "It's me."

A gasp.

The door flies open, and the first two people I ever loved are on the other side, staring at me with rounded eyes.

We don't speak. Don't even move. Just stare at each other, taking in our mutual relief that we're all right. That we're *alive.*

And then I'm enveloped in the warmth of the family I haven't seen in person for three years. Drina smells like rosemary and something sweet like honey. Aiya smells like earth and metal and tea leaves. Home. A different kind of home I hadn't realized how much I've missed.

"It's really you," Aiya murmurs into my hair. "We hadn't heard— We thought—"

She's crying.

And, I realize, so am I.

I'm not sure who maneuvers us into the house, but at some point we're inside and the door is closed. J'siiri hovers slightly behind us, warily watching us greet each other. I realize I haven't introduced her or explained her presence to my aunties yet.

Reluctantly, I pull away to give them watery smiles. "I'm glad you're all right. I heard about what's been happening in Ketzal."

"It's going to take more than a couple of foolish soldiers to finish us," says Drina. Despite the levity of her words, her eyes are steely. Drina's gaze shifts to J'siiri. "Who's this?"

"Aunties, this is J'siiri. She's the Queen of Alkara—the other side of the barrier. Kind of."

"She looks a bit young to be Queen," says Aiya.

She's nearly the same age as Hayes. I hold my tongue. Mostly because I'm fairly certain her response would be, "Exactly," and I have no intention of spatting with her.

I'm spared having to respond by J'siiri. "My mother was Queen. She was killed."

Aiya and Drina exchange raised brows.

"Let me put on some tea, love," says Aiya. "Something tells me we're in for a long story."

An hour later, the four of us sit around the hearth. J'siiri and I are on the sofa, Drina and Aiya share an armchair. There's a second one, but from the way Aiya's hand grips Drina's arm, I've an inkling their seating arrangement is more for comfort than necessity.

"You're sure this plan of yours will work?" asks Aiya.

"Not even close to sure. But it's the best I've got."

"It sounds dangerous, love," says Drina.

I take a long sip of my now ice-cold tea to prepare my answer. "It is. But I'm going to be careful." *Lie.* "And no matter what happens to me, my parents and Rain will be safe." *Truth.*

"Because they're with Carrik?" says Aiya skeptically. "Isn't he the one who tried to kill Rain?"

"He wouldn't betray me again." I don't reveal the other, more certain yet less concrete reason I'm confident in Carrik: through all the backstabbing and heartbreak, no matter how hard I tried to hate him, I know beyond any doubt that we'd die for each other. There's no shaking the bond that comes with that knowledge.

"What is it you need, then? I'm assuming you want to save Hayes?"

"I'm here for a new *lairic* bracelet and the *nafini*. It's ready, right?"

Drina still looks wary, but she nods. "Yes. It should be the same kind of magic to bind souls as it is to unbind them. They require different spells, but the potion is the same."

To join another life to the barrier to strengthen it, or remove a soul to make it weak enough to tear down. This potion can do either. "How does it work?"

"Whoever is to have soul magic performed on them must drink the *nafini*. The effects will last for a few hours. A witch or warlock must perform a spell in that time to join or unjoin two souls. For your purposes, the barrier *is* a soul. It's a physical manifestation of a life—three lives—twined together. I must warn you, Saoirse, I'm fairly certain I brewed this potion correctly. I'm less certain I can perform this spell."

"I can do it," says J'siiri. "My mother knew the magic of souls better than anyone. She taught me well."

Drina nods, satisfied. "Love," she says gently to me, "would you like for me to accompany you anyway?"

I smile at her offer. It can't be easy for her to volunteer to journey to Vanihail—a sector notorious for hating witches, especially now. For me, she does it without thinking. I shake my head. "I want you and Aiya to get to safety."

"There's nowhere in Keirdre that's safe for witches anymore. Especially not in Ketzal. It's too far from the Palace. Your Hayes doesn't have any Enforcers loyal to him here."

It's the second time since I've been here that she's called him Hayes. It makes me suspicious. "You're being kind to Hayes. I know about the witch who died. You must hate him."

"People die every day. It's not every day that witches are allowed to come home. Your King has pardoned many, love. Including witches locked in Haraya and other prisons. They returned home after years of their lives were stolen. It infuriated the Enforcers. They hate him because he freed our people. I can't begrudge him that."

My heart warms with her words. "How many soldiers are here?"

"I'm not sure how many, but it's a lot. They conduct searches and raids at all hours, trying to catch us with contraband to justify arrests. We've had to be careful."

Aiya shifts and won't meet my eyes. My suspicions are piqued. My aunties' livelihood is contraband. They've made a living selling potions. If things are as bad here as they say, it must be nearly impossible for them to operate their business. Especially considering . . .

I'm on my feet and headed for the back door, hoping my hunch is wrong.

"Saoirse!" Aiya follows me, but I've already maneuvered through their tiny kitchen and shoved open the back door.

Drina and Aiya have lived here for as long as I can remember, in this teeny house bordering a massive garden of plants and herbs. Aiya grows the plants with her earth affinity, Drina brews the potions. That's how they work. A perfect pair.

As I step outside into what used to be the largest garden for illicit herbs in Keirdre, I'm met with a field of ash.

I should be used to this. The sight of black stretched wide over what should be green. But I'm not.

A frail piece of my heart shivers and cracks. Ash blows through the air like snow. It stings my eyes, but it's not the reason I'm blinking rapidly to hold in tears.

Drina and Aiya are behind me. I taste the cold, dry bitterness of Aiya's sorrow. They don't say anything. What is there *to* say?

"They torched the garden." My voice is hushed. As though raising it will disturb the charred remains of my aunties' lives. As if there's anything left here to destroy. "But then . . ." I turn to face them. "Why didn't they arrest you?"

"It wasn't the Enforcers," says Aiya. "Raids were getting more common. There was a smaller garden torched just a few roads away. We were terrified."

Understanding smacks me in the face. "*You* burned it?"

"We had to."

Decades of work. Up in smoke. "But it's your income."

"We have bigger issues than income, love."

She's right, even as my gut roils with fury. And guilt. Everyone told me Hayes shouldn't be King. I didn't listen. "I'm going to fix this," I say fiercely. "Once this war is over, things will be better. I promise." I blink harder, keeping the tears at bay. "I'm so sorry."

"This isn't your fault, love."

Then why do I feel so guilty? "All I've ever done is make your lives miserable. I made you waste *keil* beads to keep me safe because I'm a killer. I made you brew me illegal potions that put you in danger. I was selfish to keep Hayes on the throne. This wouldn't have happened if I—"

Drina stops me, enfolding me in a hug. We're standing on the edge of the grave of everything she spent her life building, and she's comforting me like I deserve it. "This. Is. *Not.* Your. Fault." She murmurs each word firmly into my ear, grip tightening.

"This is your life's work," I say.

"No. It's not. Not even close. Do you know what I'm most proud of?" She pulls away to look me in the eyes. "It's not the garden or this house. Those are replaceable. What I'm most proud of is the moment we found a little girl wandering outside our door, took her in, and gave her a home. I'm most proud of getting to watch that little girl grow up to be headstrong, fierce, loyal, annoyingly stubborn, and whatever else she wants to be. *You*, love, are my life's work. I've never regretted you. Not for a single moment."

I give up the losing battle against my tears. Sobbing, I throw my arms around Drina. Aiya comes up behind us and joins the hug. I always felt like a burden. I figured their lives were ruined the moment they learned I'm a siren. Feeling the truth of her words soothes an ache in me that's been steadily growing for seventeen years.

When my shuddering sobs have subsided, I wipe my eyes with the back of my hand. "I'm going to fix this." I look my aunties over. "Please leave here. I don't want anything to happen to you."

Aiya presses her lips to the crown of my head. "I could say the same to you."

It would be easy. Leave Keirdre, the kingdom I've always hated. Actually take Ikenna up on her offer. Return to Alkara with my aunties. Reunite with my family. The barrier would stay up, we could defeat Reyshka, keep J'siiri safe until the next transition of power, and start new lives in a world where we're *wanted*.

It sounds simple.

But . . .

"I am selfishly in love with you."

Over and over. I hear those words. Feel his lips on mine and the heat of his skin. See his smile, weary now from the weight of the crown. Melt under the force of those *eyes*. Hear him laugh. Feel the steady sound of his heartbeat against my cheek.

There are two truths I'm forced to reconcile. The first: Hayes isn't a solution. He asked me to trust him to fix Keirdre, but he *can't*. I can't put my faith in his ability to lead. If he won't bring down the barrier himself, I'll have to force his hand.

My second unavoidable truth: I'm selfishly in love with him too. Enough to break his heart to end this chaos for once and all.

I'm shaking my head. My mind is already made up. It was made up in Alkara, when I sent the letter to Ikenna.

Scratch that—it was made up the moment Hayes told me how he feels and I realized I feel the same.

Drina's smile is sad, but knowing. I don't respond, but she looks at me like she's read my thoughts. "I know, love. I know."

CHAPTER FORTY-SIX
OLD HABITS RENEWED

We ride with heavy cloaks obscuring our faces. We avoid pedestrian-heavy areas as best we can and move off the dirt paths when we hear people approaching. Days creep by as we travel from Ketzal to Vanihail.

We keep our hoods up as we slink through the streets headed for the tall gates that surround the Palace. J'siiri is smaller than me—and not a skilled climber—so I kneel and have her step into my cupped palm. With a grunt of effort, I push, hitching her up.

My arms burn, but I don't let go. "Pull yourself over," I grit out from between my teeth, struggling to keep my voice low and grip steady.

She grabs the gate's bars and pulls. It takes her a few tries, but eventually, she pulls herself up. Her minor accomplishment is immediately undercut by her loud shriek as she crashes to the ground on the other side.

Dammit.

I have no idea if anyone heard her. No time to wait and find out.

Quickly, I leap, catch the top of the gate, and climb, landing on my feet beside her.

I hear hurried footsteps making their way around the side of the Palace.

Dammit again.

J'siiri's still on the ground, grumbling to herself. I yank her to her feet and tug her forward. We sprint across the green space between the Palace wall and surrounding gate. A few neatly trimmed shrubs line the stone walls. J'siiri and I tumble behind one and wait.

Two guards come running around the Palace, searching for the source of the shriek.

I'm breathing deeply, but J'siiri is *wheezing*—she's going to get us caught if she doesn't learn to shut up. I slap a hand over her mouth, muffling the sounds of her labored breathing. I stay totally still, hoping to anything that matters that they don't think to look here . . .

A few moments that feel like hours pass before they grow bored and leave.

I exhale in relief.

And whack J'siiri on the arm.

She yanks her head away from my palm to give me a sharp look. "What?"

"You have to be quiet. We're not supposed to be here," I hiss.

"Well, *sorry*," she mumbles sarcastically. "I didn't realize when you asked me to come with you, I'd be expected to scale anything. I'm not good at climbing."

Obviously.

I hold in a groan of irritation. Usually when I sneak in, I climb the Palace wall and enter through my window. J'siiri could barely get over the gate—there's no way she's scaling a mostly smooth wall. She'd probably die trying. Or worse—get us caught.

"Stay here," I say. "I'm going to get myself in. I'll come back down and let you in through the side door. Don't move or make a sound until I come back. No matter what."

She nods obediently. Once she's crouched and hidden in the shrubbery, I start the familiar climb into my former chambers.

Everything is exactly as I left it. Mirror hidden beneath my bed. Rumpled sheets I never bothered to tidy. Most importantly, my guard uniforms are still in the wardrobe. I put one on and tuck another under my arm, along with the pin that identifies me as a Royal guard. I only have one of those.

I'm dressed like a guard again, but I don my cloak anyway. My face is still mine and I'm still a fugitive.

Creeping through these halls is another pattern I've missed. I keep to the shadows until I reach the side door Hayes used to use—back when he was just a Prince who liked to sneak out to visit pubs in the middle of the night.

I push open the side door and peek out. J'siiri is just as still and silent in the bushes as she was when I left. She looks relieved to see me.

We pause just inside the side door as J'siiri throws on the spare uniform and fastens the pin to her chest. She won't need a cloak. Unlike me, her face isn't recognizable here. Hayes is known for hiring odd choices for guards, like witches. She looks more like she belongs here than I do.

We return to my old room. I take off my boots while J'siiri looks around, brows raised. "You used to live here?"

"Yes." I motion her to the other side of the bed. "Get some sleep. We have a long day tomorrow."

Hayes told me Ikenna takes her meals alone in her chambers at seven, midday, and six after midday. It's after midnight now.

We have just under seven hours until her first meal of the day, when we can commence the next stage of my plan.

It's nearing seven. If Ikenna plans on eating when she normally does, her first meal will be brought to her chambers shortly.

Ikenna has to drink the *nafini*. She can't know she's drinking it—she'll refuse—and I can't sing to convince her to drink it. One, because it won't work on her. And two, because I don't want her knowing I'm back in Keirdre just yet.

Which is why J'siiri and I are outside the Palace kitchens, preparing to poison the former Queen of Keirdre's breakfast.

I'm wearing my cloak with the hood pulled low as always. J'siiri is dressed in my former uniform, pin on her chest, alerting all who see her that she's a Royal guard. Here, in the kitchens, it will give her authority with the servants.

Head high, J'siiri slams open the doors and enters the kitchens. The lunes she spent masquerading as her mother are useful. She looks as authoritative as a Queen.

I stay outside. Count silently, listening for—

Loud clangs from inside the kitchen.

Perfect. I slip inside, breath bated, hoping no one sees.

As planned, J'siiri has caused a commotion on the far side of the kitchen. She's knocked over a few pots and is screeching at the servants to clean it up. Everyone is focused on her. No one sees as I search the countertops for Ikenna's breakfast.

Sitting on a gilded tray on a countertop is a plate with buttery biscuits, a few hunks of smoked ham, and a bowl of porridge topped with sliced fruit. Breakfast fit for a Queen. Also on the tray: a cream-and-gold teapot. Ikenna's colors.

While the servants are occupied, I slip off the lid of the

teapot, tip over the vial of *nafini*, and release three drops before replacing the lid.

I expect to feel relieved as I leave the kitchens, task completed. We're one step closer to taking down the barrier. Once Ikenna drinks her tea, J'siiri can perform the spell to sever her connection to the barrier.

Instead of feeling relieved, I'm more anxious than I was before.

J'siiri will be out in a moment, but I don't wait for her. I stick to the shadows and traverse the halls, searching for a King, praying he finds it somewhere in his broken heart to forgive me for what I've just done. And for what I'm about to do.

CHAPTER FORTY-SEVEN

TEN MINUTES

Hayes's chambers feel different now that I'm no longer in a Dreamweave. Maybe that's just because of my nerves, wriggling painfully in my stomach.

He's not here yet, and I can't decide where to sit. I try the edge of his bed. It feels too invasive. I try the sofa in his sitting area. That feels too far from the entrance.

I settle for standing in the middle of the room, staring at the door.

My foot taps restlessly.

I have no idea where he is. No idea when he'll be back. No idea how furious he is with me.

The way we left things was messy. What I've just done is messier still.

But I had to, I tell myself. *I had to go behind his back again. I—*

The door opens and Hayes sweeps in, Jeune behind him. His head is down, and for a tick, he doesn't see me. His shoulders are hunched and he wears his exhaustion like a velvet cloak.

I open my mouth—nothing comes out.

So I just stand, staring.

His head comes up as Jeune closes the door behind them. Those ocean eyes land on me—his steps falter.

Surprise slashes across his face, and the citrusy flavor bathes my tongue. He's perfectly still, watching me, expression shifting through a myriad of emotions. I taste each of them. The peppercorn and brine of anger; the metallic taste of hurt—like blood when you bite down too hard on your lip. Something dry and cold and grainy, like a mouthful of frozen flour—heartbreak. Each of them hurts, but underlying it all is sweet and citrusy orange. He's hurt and furious, but there's a part of him that can't resist being happy to see me.

I cling to that. Before he can say anything and before I've fully worked out my next move, I'm rushing toward him. After not seeing him for so long, my limbs are no longer my own. They're all-consumed by the undeniable fact that I missed him.

My arms toss themselves around his neck with so much force, he staggers backward. Instinctively, he grabs me back, even as he's still trying to work out how he feels.

"Saoirse?" says Jeune in surprise.

Hayes whips around to look at her so quickly, I fear he's going to snap his own neck. "You—you can see her?" Without giving her a chance to respond, he snatches my hand and drags my bare wrist up so he can see it. No *lairic* bracelet.

"I'm here." I swallow, hoping the action takes my anxiety sliding down with it. It doesn't. "For real."

His surprise is back, this time flecked with that sweet longing I've grown used to. He looks me over, taking me in. I taste a new wave of emotions: surprise, most prominent; confusion, like oversalted stew; and something hazy—wariness.

I glance at Jeune. "It's good to see you."

"I bet." She smirks, eyeing the way I'm still wrapped around Hayes. "It explains the warm welcome."

I roll my eyes, grinning as I drop my arms. "I was going to greet you."

"Before or after you pounced on His Majesty?" Her tone is teasing. My face feels hot with embarrassment. Jeune laughs and holds up her hands. "How about I wait outside, and when you've finished . . . *greeting* the King, you can greet me as well. Maybe muster up some enthusiasm. A different kind, though. I don't need you groping me."

As soon as she's gone, I face Hayes again.

He's staring but hasn't spoken yet. Not to me, anyway. He addressed Jeune, but not a word to me.

A thousand coy or sweet ways to greet him flash through my mind, but his eyes are somehow bluer than I remember, and now that I'm here in person, his presence is packed with more heat than I can handle and the only thing I can manage to say is, "Hi."

Mentally, I slap myself. I make men fall at my feet on a daily basis, but when confronted with one I actually want, "Hi" is the best I can do?

"Hi?" Hayes sounds incredulous—and a little hurt. "That's what you have to say? What the hell are you doing here? *How* are you here? My mother showed me—" Something cracks in his eyes, and he shuts them for a moment. When he opens them again, they're ice. "I saw your letter. You don't speak to me for *weeks*. And now you're here? Why? I thought—"

His frantic confusion snaps my already feeble grasp on logic and autonomy. Without processing, I throw my arms around his neck. My intention is—I think—to hug him again. Maybe whisper in his ear how happy I am to see him. Instead, my lips are on his.

His response is instantaneous.

Before I've examined my own impulsivity, his hands slide down my back, traverse the curve of my ass, and hook onto my thighs. My legs are hitched up around his waist as he kisses me back, just as fervently.

Cinnamon.

Hayes is feasting on my mouth and I'm devouring the taste of his want of me. The spice of his lust burns. I let it. His hands shamelessly roam my backside. I welcome them.

I forget how to think, how to breathe, I think I forget my own sodding name. It's Hayes, all Hayes. The smell of him, taste of him, *feel* of him. Soft lips on mine, tongue diving relentlessly into my mouth, warm hands digging into my hips.

I don't even notice he's moving us until my back sinks into something soft and I realize he's laid me against his mattress. All the while, his lips don't leave mine.

I need to breathe. I wish I didn't. I could drown in him, drown in this moment, but I break away—just for a tick—to suck in air. He wastes no time. Drags his lips down the side of my throat, sucking on the soft skin of my neck as those hands burrow deeper into my waist.

I'm still breathless but I want *more.* I take hold of his face and try to drag it back up to mine. Instead, he rests his forehead on my shoulder, breathing heavily. "Wait."

The word freezes my actions, but I'm still on fire. "What's wrong?" I'm embarrassingly out of breath.

Hayes hovers over me, propped up on his elbows. With every breath I take, the rise of my chest brushes his, and the contact makes my body hum. His eyes search mine. "We have a lot to talk about, don't you think? What was that for?"

It takes a moment for the fog of my brain to clear enough for me to realize what he means. In the heat of everything Hayes, I forgot that I'm the one who initiated this. The one who returned from another world without so much as an explanation and threw myself at him. "I missed you," I say honestly.

He smiles. It's warm and beautiful, but also guarded and sad. "I like you missing me." He presses a soft kiss to my shoulder. "A lot. But what are you doing here?"

I reach a hand to trace the light stubble that's formed on his jaw since I last saw him. "That letter I wrote to Ikenna was a lie. I needed her to believe me so I could get back to Keirdre."

Doubt mars his brow. "You couldn't have told me? I thought . . ." His sentence trails and heartbreak swirls in his eyes. I know exactly what he thought.

I want to smooth the uncertainty from his forehead. Mend what I've broken. But even though my leaving then wasn't intentional, what I've done now *was*. "I couldn't contact you. The runes on my *lairic* beads faded."

For a tick, his face brightens. His head ducks—I think to kiss me again—but I stop him. "Wait! I have to tell you something."

He stops. Stares down at me. The creased brow is back. This time, it's confused rather than angry. He searches my face as though trying to read my thoughts.

After a long pause, his movements achingly slow, Hayes gently touches his lips to my forehead. Lingers there, savoring me, savoring this moment of peace. When he pulls away, he rolls over, lying on his back. He looks exhausted. "What did you do?"

I hesitate.

His head jerks over to me at my silence. "I'm not going to like this, am I?"

"I'm sorry."

Hayes's eyes slip closed. Seconds tick by as he takes heavy breaths, thinking. When he opens them again, he looks at me. "How long do we have before this ends badly?"

"Maybe ten minutes?" It's a guess, but it's about how long I imagine it will take J'siiri to wait for Ikenna to drink her tea, perform the spell, and make her way over to us. Subtracted from the time we've already lost.

Hayes considers this time frame with hooded eyes. "I have just two questions for you. First, do you want me?"

Cinnamon, cinnamon, cinnamon. I'm drowning in it. He's not even touching me and my body's on fire. I'm used to games and manipulation. Hayes is blunt and honest. He admits what he wants so freely.

Me on the other hand, I'm a coward. Admitting out loud that I want this—want *him*—wracks my insides with apprehension tense enough to hurt, but at the same time it burns me with longing so intense, it aches. "Yes, but—"

"Good." He rolls over, hovering over me once more, lips a gasp away from mine. "Second question: Do you *have* to tell me this bad news right now, or can it wait ten minutes?"

It's difficult to think when he's this close and looking at me like he plans to scorch me with his stare alone. Right now, I believe he could. "I—I guess I don't have to . . ."

"Then don't tell me." *Closer.* I didn't think it was possible for him to be closer without touching me, but Hayes manages. "Not yet. I want ten minutes with you. Ten minutes before you shatter me."

Each movement of his lips causes them to graze my skin, and I lose all sense of reason. "I'm—" *What was I going to say, again?* "I'm sorry."

Gently, gently, his hand cups the side of my face. His thumb caresses my bottom lip. His eyes follow the motion. He leans in, closer and closer. "Be sorry in ten minutes."

His lips descend over mine.

CHAPTER FORTY-EIGHT

ALL YOUR PROMISES BEFORE

Ten minutes later, we're interrupted by a knock on the door. At least, I think it's ten minutes. It could have been ten minutes or ten hours. Either way, it wasn't enough. Our time is up and I know what's coming is going to hurt.

Hayes peels his lips from the side of my neck. His hands slide away from my bare waist as he removes them from beneath my rumpled shirt. His chest heaves as he studies me with hooded eyes. "I'm guessing from your expression you know who that is?"

Without waiting for me to answer, he rises from the bed, grabbing his discarded shirt from the floor and tugging it on. "Who is it?"

My entire body is flushed as I climb from the bed to stand across from him. "Am I allowed to be sorry now?"

"Wait." He seizes my face and tilts it up, swooping in to steal one more searing kiss that makes my toes curl before he pulls away. His gaze is still heated, but I taste stale trepidation. "What did you do?"

"I poisoned Ikenna."

The hazy desire of his eyes freezes over. He stumbles away from me. "You—you *killed*—"

"No! Not killed. I gave her the *nafini* and had a witch perform the spell to remove her soul from the barrier."

"You *what*? Why would you do that? Each time you remove a life from the barrier, its defenses are weakened."

"I know."

He looks horrified. "We don't know how stable the barrier is now. If someone destroys it through force, *my* life is still tied to it. I'll die."

"You'll have to take it down before that happens."

Peppercorn spikes on my tongue with his brewing fury. "I told you why I can't do that. You're going to start a war. *Hundreds* of innocent people will die."

"I have a plan to keep that from happening."

"Your plan was going behind my back?" His gaze turns sharp. "Is this why you left? Did you lie about your beads dying?"

"Of course not."

"How can you say 'of course' anything to me? You just gambled my life—you gambled my entire kingdom. I told you why I don't want to bring the barrier down. I wanted to find a way to do it safely."

"When?" I demand. "*Eventually* isn't good enough. I knew you'd say no if I asked again. Now that Ikenna's no longer joined with it, it's vulnerable and you don't have a choice." I wince. That sounded harsher than I intended. "I'm sorry. I didn't mean it like that."

He laughs, but it doesn't sound like he thinks anything I've said is funny. He starts pacing, not looking at me. "That sounds exactly right. You forced my hand. You do whatever *you* want, and I deal with the consequences, right?"

"You knew I did something you wouldn't approve of when I got here."

"That means I don't have a right to be angry?" He paces past me. "Everyone is telling me I can't do this. The Enforcers and Vanihailians hate me. My mother thinks I'm a failure. My father never wanted me on the damned throne at all. *Everyone* is working against me, and I thought—" He looks at me, eyes flooded with hurt and tears. "I was foolish enough to think that, despite everyone else, I had *you*. One person in the world who believed in me."

My throat is dry. "Hayes—"

"How do you do it?" he asks softly. "How can you stomach to hurt me over and over again? The thought of hurting you makes me sick. Yet you do it like it's nothing. Like *I'm* nothing."

I reach out to lay a hand on his arm. "You're not nothing to me."

He jerks away as though my touch is poison. "I really hope that's not true. If this is your version of affection, I don't want it."

"You think your Prince will forgive you after this?"

I knew he'd be angry. I thought I was prepared for how much it would hurt. I was wrong. I don't think anything could prepare me for this. "I—"

Another knock at the door, more impatient than the last.

I want to scream at them to give us a minute, but I bridle my tongue. I give Hayes a pleading stare. "Please. Trust me. I have a plan."

Hayes shakes his head. "Stop asking for the impossible. Ask me to jump off a damned cliff into shark-infested waters. I'll do it. Sometimes, I hate myself for the things I'd do for you. But don't ask me to trust you. I can't. You never give me a reason to."

I'm a half tick away from bursting into tears, but Hayes crosses the room and pulls open the door without another word.

Jeune stands on the other side, smirking at the sight of

Hayes's still-rumpled shirt. "Did you not hear me knocking?" she asks with a wide, too-innocent grin.

Hayes ignores the question and looks over her shoulder to J'siiri. "Who's this?"

Jeune looks past Hayes and sees me. I'm coming undone at the seams, and when her brows draw together, I know she can tell. "Saoirse?" The teasing quality flees her tone, and she's softer now. "Do you want to introduce your friend? Or should I?"

"You've broken promises to me before."

"Don't ask me to trust you."

Each word is a stone hurled at me with enough force to bruise. They're each lodged painfully in my heart. I deserve each blow, but lune above, it *hurts*. Moments ago, I was lying in his bed and losing myself in kissing him. Now I'm falling to pieces and I can hardly look at him.

Jeune frowns when I don't say anything. "Saoirse?"

I drown it all. My thoughts, the memory of his hands traversing the curves of my body like he owns them, the taste of his disdain, and the sting of his too-true words.

I force a pinched smile. It lacks sincerity or warmth, but I know it's beautiful enough to bring any man to his knees. Except Hayes. I ensnare marks in pretty curses with my voice, my face. But Hayes fell for the rotten, putrid mess of my heart. My pretty smiles don't work on him because he sees through me.

"Of course." My voice is smooth and silky. I'm a siren, after all. Everything about me is lovely. Except for my twisted heart, which I foolishly gave away. "Allow me to introduce Queen—er—Princess J'siiri of Alkara." I nod to J'siiri. "J'siiri, meet His Majesty, King Hayes Vanihail of Keirdre."

CHAPTER FORTY-NINE
CHILLING AND CRUEL

J'siiri keeps eyeing the wrinkles in my shirt. Even though I've straightened it out multiple times, she keeps shooting me a knowing smirk. I'm trying to ignore her.

Unlike Jeune, she doesn't see that it's all wrong. That my smile is fake. That Hayes won't so much as look at me.

The four of us—Hayes, me, Jeune, and J'siiri—are in the sitting room in Hayes's chambers. J'siiri and I have explained our plan, and Hayes is massaging his temples to clear his confusion. "You want me to *what?*"

I have no idea who the question is directed toward, because he still won't acknowledge me, but J'siiri must assume he's talking to her, because she answers. "We want you to move the barrier so that it only surrounds the three groups going to war. The Keirdrens in Alkara who want to take over my kingdom. The *Resistance*," she spits out the name, "who killed my mother. And your Enforcers who oppose you."

"If the barrier surrounds them and only them," I say, "we can spare anyone else from getting caught up in it. They want war. So, we let them fight. But only each other."

Hayes is responding to me, but he's still only addressing

J'siiri. "Just because my mother is no longer joined to the barrier doesn't mean I know how to move it."

"That's why J'siiri is here," I say.

His expression is wary as he looks over J'siiri. I can't blame him. He doesn't even trust me and I'm telling him to put his faith in someone he's never met—for a decision that will impact the future of his kingdom. "You know how to move the barrier?"

"My mother was skilled at soul magic. I've known how to wield it since I was a child. If she could teach me, I can teach you."

"The plan is to give everyone exactly what they want," I say. "If we get all three armies to the same spot, you move the barrier and trap them inside. Alkara is prepared to fight the Enforcers. Once they're taken care of, you're free to rule Keirdre without their influence. The soldiers loyal to *you* can enforce laws as you see fit. J'siiri pretends to be her mother, and the two of you form a treaty between our two kingdoms. You can rule the way you want, without having to try and convince the Enforcers to side with you."

In theory, it's simple. The issue is that it's all contingent on Hayes's ability to one, move the barrier, and two, move it to surround the correct area. Both of which he's never done before. He doesn't get to practice. He gets *one* chance at this. One chance to master a kind of magic he's never used.

I can't dwell on that.

"I already told Reyshka to await Larster's signal," I say. "She's preparing for a battle at the doorway to the barrier. The Resistance is already convinced I've gotten you to agree to bring down the barrier entirely. They're waiting in place, prepared to fight. Reyshka is waiting for the signal to ambush them."

"How are you going to get the Enforcers in place?" asks Jeune.

"One of Ikenna's guards is a spy for Enforcer Arkin. Hayes has to tell Ikenna I'm coming back—with an army from the other side—in the presence of her guards. As soon as the spy reports to Anarin, she'll move her soldiers to the barrier to fight off any outsiders. At the signal, they'll attack."

Hayes is still silent.

Jeune glances at him, waiting for him to say something, ask a question. When he doesn't, she clears her throat. "What's the signal?"

"When the barrier moves."

Hayes addresses J'siiri. "Can you show me how I'm supposed to move the barrier?"

"You're the only person whose soul is tied to it now. All you have to do is feel for it. Then I'll show you how to work this ability as we travel."

"Travel where?"

"The barrier. We're going to get you as close as possible. It should make it easier." She sits cross-legged in front of him. "I'm going to show you how to *feel* for the barrier. Once you've felt the connection, it's easier to find it on your own." She raises a hand. "Do you mind if I touch you?"

Hayes wavers. After a pause, he nods. "Go ahead."

J'siiri presses her fingertips to either side of his temples. "Close your eyes."

He does.

Her own flecked eyes slip shut as she focuses. There's a pause—then her forehead creases and her lips tip into a frown. "That's odd . . ."

"What's wrong?" I ask.

J'siiri opens her eyes. Her hands fall away from Hayes's head. "There's someone else."

"What do you mean?"

"I can feel the barrier—but there are two forces joined to it. Hayes and someone else."

"Ikenna?" I say.

"No. I performed the spell correctly. It can't be Ikenna. There must've been someone else already connected with the barrier. Until they're removed, I don't think Hayes can move it on his own."

My chest is constricting. There's no way this was all for nothing. "You can't tell who the other person is?"

"It doesn't work like that."

My brain churns with whirring thoughts. Who else could be tied to the barrier aside from the Royal family? Larster and Finnean are dead. There are no other Royals.

The real question is who would King Larster entrust with such a responsibility while he was alive? His wife and sons, obviously. But who else? An Enforcer?

My first thought is Anarin. She's the water fae Enforcer of Vanihail. If there was an Enforcer that Larster trusted most, it could be her.

Or maybe not.

I think about that envelope Hayes found in his father's office right after he ascended to the throne. It said *Enforcer Reyshka Harker.*

At the time, it confused me, because Reyshka isn't an Enforcer for any sector in Keirdre. After the time I've spent in Alkara, it's clear she's the Enforcer for the Keirdrens on the other side.

I've heard stories about Reyshka Harker my entire life. I grew up believing she was a legend. So did my parents. There were hundreds of Keirdren soldiers in Alkara—presumably, their numbers have been growing for years. Reyshka's been there that whole time, and somehow, she's still alive.

I think about how Reyshka knew I was a siren the instant she saw me. Everyone else assumed I was just beautiful, but not her. She *knew*. As if she'd seen them before. Lived through Larster's creature cullings. Maybe she used to be an Enforcer. Maybe she helped Larster torch Szeiryna to the ground. And after she proved her loyalty, he rewarded her by promising her eternal life in a *new* world. It's just a hunch, but my hunches tend to be right.

Lune above . . .

"It's Reyshka," I say. "It has to be. How long have we heard stories of her? She's practically a legend, but she's still young. Larster trusted her enough to send her to the other side." The more I say out loud, the more sense it makes. Larster wouldn't have left it up to chance that he'd find a way to take over Alkara and expand Keirdre's territory within a single lifetime. This plan took years. I have no idea how long, but it's safe to say that when Larster sent over Reyshka, he didn't know how long she'd be there. He wouldn't want to risk her growing old and dying and having to trust and train someone else.

Larster needed someone who would live for as long as he needed them. I think about my time in Alkara, training with the Keirdrens. Everyone else left the safe house. Except for Reyshka. She stayed safe inside, in a house surrounded by an isi wood fence, at all times.

I look at J'siiri. "Hayes can still do it, right? Even if someone else is connected to the barrier?"

She looks wary. "It's . . . unlikely. Soul magic is extremely powerful. If another person's soul is still tied to the barrier, Hayes's power over it is essentially divided in two."

"Larster managed it," I say. "With Szeiryna. Ikenna's soul was joined to the barrier, and he still managed to move it."

"He had *decades* to practice—maybe even centuries. Magic is a skill, not a birthright. Especially not soul magic." She pauses. For a tick, I see something in her eyes. A spark of an idea. It flits over her face for a fraction of an instant before it's gone. She purses her lips and falls silent.

I perk. "What is it?"

"Nothing." She won't meet my eyes.

Even after lunes of playacting a stern-faced Queen, she still hasn't mastered how to mask her feelings. "Don't give me that. You just had a thought."

"I had an idea . . . I'm not sure it's a good one."

"Tell me anyway."

With a furtive look at Hayes, then me, she says, "If he was able to draw on *more* energy, it might be enough to overpower Reyshka's connection to the barrier."

"Perfect. How can he do that?"

"By tying his life to another."

Hayes's face mirrors my confusion. "Another barrier?"

"No. Not an inanimate object. A *person*. For best results, not a human. If his life were tied to another soul, he could pull from *their* energy when he moves the barrier."

It sounds like a perfect solution. "I thought you said it was a bad idea. What's the drawback?"

"For one thing, the energy he uses will drain whoever he's connected to."

That doesn't sound too bad. "Will their energy replenish?"

"Eventually. But the real issue is, unlike joining someone to the barrier, this connection is permanent. Connecting a soul to an object is one thing. It's reversible. Connecting two souls—two people—isn't. When souls are intertwined, there are consequences."

"Like what?"

"They feed off each other. When one person dies, so does the other."

I look at Hayes. Permanently tied to him. Souls connected for life. It doesn't even feel like a real decision. "I'll do it."

Hayes's head snaps up. He's been actively avoiding looking at me, but now his eyes hold mine. "What?"

"I'll do it." I shrug like it's not a big deal. "Of course I will."

Seconds pass as he stares at me.

Then, his eyes soften. For a tick, he's looking at me like he used to. Like he did when he was hovering over me in his bed telling me he wanted ten minutes.

The moment fades away, his eyes go hard, and he tosses his head back and *laughs*. Cackles without humor as if I'm absurd.

It's chilling and cruel. A piece of me breaks away to shatter on the floor.

His laughter dies and his eyes meet mine. What used to be ocean waves have hardened to steel. "Absolutely not."

I'm ice-cold. Hayes, full of warmth and light, is chilling me to the bone.

J'siiri looks at the two of us. For the first time, she seems to notice the tension between us.

Slowly, I reach for Hayes's hand. "Can we have a few moments—"

"No." He calmly and deliberately moves his hand away from me. Tucks it into his lap. "We don't need time. I have nothing to say to you." He stands. "We have to go to the barrier, right? That means we have at least a week of travel ahead of us. I'll figure out how to move the barrier within that time. You don't have to worry. I'll go along with your plan. I'll do what I'm told, same as always, but I will *not* tie my soul to yours."

He starts for the door. "Jeune," he calls over his shoulder, "I have some work to take care of, you coming?"

Jeune looks at me apologetically. Mouths, "I'm sorry," before following after him.

I flinch as the door shuts behind them.

"You think your Prince will forgive you after this?"

I didn't answer Zaire when he posed the question. I guess now I have my answer.

CHAPTER FIFTY

RECKLESS

Three days of traveling later, and Hayes hasn't gotten any better at feeling the barrier.

It's making J'siiri want to peel off his skin, me exhausted, and Jeune ready to hurl all of us out of the carriage.

Hayes told Zensen he was traveling to Kurr Valley for a formal meeting with the Enforcers one last time. A half-truth. Zensen tried to talk Hayes into bringing more guards than just Jeune, but Hayes refused.

J'siiri has spent pretty much every moment since our departure from Vanihail trying to help Hayes "feel" the barrier in his mind's eye. Unfortunately, nothing she says is helping. They've been going back and forth for what feels like forever.

"Maybe we should take a break," I suggest for the umpteenth time. Jeune is steering the carriage, so it's just the three of us, and I'm exhausted from listening to them bicker.

J'siiri ignores me. "You're not focusing," she tells Hayes. "Are you even trying?"

"Of course I'm trying. This isn't easy for me like it is for you. I'm not used to magic like this."

"It's the same as your water affinity."

"It's not. Water is natural. A piece of me."

J'siiri's eyes flash. "And magic isn't? Typical Keirdren. Assuming magic isn't natural while your affinity is."

"I didn't—" Hayes groans. "I didn't mean it like that. I have nothing against witches or magic. This kind of magic is just new to me."

J'siiri looks mostly placated by this, but they're still no closer to Hayes figuring this out.

"We should take a break," I say again.

J'siiri releases a huff of air from her nose. "Fine." She bangs on the wall of the carriage to get Jeune's attention.

We rock to a stop, and Jeune comes around to open the door. She immediately raises her brows, clearly sensing the hostility. "It's going well, I see," she says wryly. "Saoirse." She gives me a sharp look. "I need to stretch my legs. Come with me."

She leaves no room for argument. Not that I intend to fight her on this—I'm more than a little relieved to escape the carriage.

J'siiri looks panicked. *"Wait."* We've been trading off for night shifts. Two people sleep at a time, two keep watch over the carriage. She must assume she'll be stuck with Hayes for the night. "Don't leave me with—"

"Relax," says Jeune. "You're both royalty. There must be *something* for you to talk about." She closes the door in J'siiri's face before she can object further. She leads me a short ways from the carriage, close enough to keep guard, far enough we can't be overheard. Jeune rests her back against the bark of a tree, facing me. "This isn't working."

"I know. Hayes is being stubborn. He doesn't want to join his soul to mine." He hasn't spoken to me since we left Vanihail—he barely even looks my way. My tongue fiddles anxiously with the space behind my false tooth before I say what I've been fearing for the past few days. "I think he hates me."

If I expect sympathy, Jeune disappoints. Her face slackens and she bursts into peals of laughter like I've told the funniest joke she's ever heard.

I stare. "What part of this situation is funny?"

"Sorry." She's still chuckling. "Sometimes I forget you didn't know him before."

"Before what?"

"Before *you*. He's obsessed with you. Trust me, he doesn't hate you."

It's gratifying—slightly—but I can't shake the memory of the dark look in his eyes and the chilling sound of his laughter when he refused to bind our souls. "Maybe. He still won't listen to me."

"You're you. Make him change his mind."

I look at her incredulously. "I'm not going to sing—" I stop as Jeune whacks me on the arm. "*Ow!*" My hand flies to the place where she's struck me. I'm not in pain so much as I am surprised. "What the hell was that for?"

"I'm not asking you to sing to him, you lightbrain. He'd cut off his own hand if you asked him to."

"I already tried asking him."

"No, you tried cornering him to force him to do what you want."

I open my mouth to argue but let it close when I realize she's right.

Jeune keeps going. "You're used to using your voice or your face to control people. If you can't do that, you manipulate them. You make schemes and plot until they give in to you.

You're treating Hayes like he's just another man you have to trick to do your bidding. He's not. He loves you. You don't have to manipulate him. Just *ask*."

When we return to the carriage, Jeune grins at J'siiri. "Your Majesty, how about you and I take first watch?"

Hayes's brow furrows and he looks like he means to protest, so I quickly say, "That sounds great, thank you."

J'siiri scurries after Jeune like she can't get away fast enough. The carriage door *thuds* behind her.

Hayes and I sit on opposite benches, looking at each other.

Well, I'm looking at him. He's staring at anything *but* me.

"Hayes," I softly broach the awkward silence. "I'm sorry. I shouldn't have tried to force your hand." I pause, waiting for him to say something.

He doesn't.

I swallow. "The way I went about this was wrong, but the idea was right, and we're running out of time. In a few days, we're going to reach the barrier. You still don't know how to move it."

"I know that."

Finally, he speaks. I stop, expecting—hoping—he'll say something else. Nothing.

I keep going. "If we do what J'siiri suggested and let her join our souls—"

"No." Hayes has no preamble, no explanation. Just refusal.

I sigh. "I'm sorry. I'll keep saying it. I know you're still mad at me, but—"

His body stiffens and he looks startled. "Wait—you think I'm saying no because I'm *mad* at you?"

He seems insulted by the idea, but I have no idea what I've said to offend him. "Aren't you?"

"Of course not. I'm saying no because you're *reckless*."

I flinch.

He doesn't stop. "You run headfirst into danger. You seem to revel in your own self-destruction. You take absurd risks. Your life is constantly in danger." His voice rises with his anger. His hands are fisted in his lap and there's a vein pulsing in his forehead. For five beats of silence, he stares. Then, with a heavy sigh, the tension leaves his body and he sags in on himself. "And I was foolish enough to fall in love with you."

Each accusation was a slap to the face. But at his final words, the blows stop coming.

"It's like you don't care about yourself at all. But *I* do. I'd give my life for yours without even thinking about it. If your life is joined with mine, if our fates are intertwined, what am I supposed to do?"

Hayes slides to the end of his bench, knees pressing against mine. "If we do this, I can't protect you. Not even from yourself. You can't ask me to watch you get yourself killed. I'm not strong like you. I couldn't handle it."

I suck in a shuddering breath, so relieved it's hard to breathe. He still loves me. After everything. "You still . . ." I don't finish. It feels childish to say out loud.

His brow furrows, confused. "I told you how I feel about you."

"That was before."

A bit of his anger lessens with confusion. "Before what?"

"Before we got into a spat. Before you said you don't trust me."

"You thought that meant I no longer wanted anything to do with you?" He sounds bemused. "Saoirse, I am not one of your marks. Your spell on me does not fade over time. It's everlasting. I can be mad at you and still want you. Don't you know that?"

"I—" It seems like such a simple concept, and yet I'm floored now that he's said it. My whole life, I've been waiting for the moment I inevitably lose my family's affection. Waiting for the moment they see a part of me too monstrous to love. I withheld the darker parts of myself from Rain because she's good and I just *knew* if she saw what I'm really like, she'd be ashamed for loving me at all.

Hayes studies my expression like a book. His eyes shift, torn, before the anger drops from his shoulders and he holds out his arms to me. "Come here," he says gently.

Tentatively, I rise and move across the carriage. I stop, stooped over, just in front of him.

He pulls me onto his lap to straddle him. My hands instinctively brace against his chest and his hands settle on my waist.

Hayes meets my eyes. His own lose focus as he gazes steadily at me. A soothing warmth flares in my chest as we watch each other. I've seen his face before—countless times—but now I study his features, taking inventory of the things that have changed and the things that are comfortingly familiar. The dizzying effect of his ocean eyes. *Familiar.* Faint lines of exhaustion in their corners. *New.* Soft, sensuous lips. *Familiar.* Light stubble on his jaw. *New.*

Slowly, Hayes raises a hand. The movement is absent—like he's unaware he's doing it. The back of his hand grazes my cheek and trails down, feeling my skin.

I exhale, leaning into his touch. His hand twists around, palm against my cheek. Through his wrist, I feel his racing pulse. It matches my own.

My tongue sifts through his emotions. Stale anxiety, sweet

longing, and, beneath it all, *anger*. "I am *furious* with you." His words are harsh, but he pairs them with a soft kiss to my temple. When he draws back, he meets my eyes. "And I want you." The hand on my face glides down to trace along my collarbone, drawing a shiver. "I hate that you have no faith in me." Kiss on my shoulder. "And I want you. I hate that I can't trust you." Kiss on the corner of my mouth. "And I *want* you." Again, he pulls back to stare at me. "I'm going to get mad sometimes. Knowing you, I'm going to get mad a *lot*—that doesn't change how I feel about you."

Every part of me that he's touched feels scorched. My hands tremble where they rest on his chest. "I want to earn your trust. Ask me anything. I'll be honest. *Fully* honest. I promise."

His grip slides to my hips, but he doesn't say anything.

I take a breath. "I'll start by telling you a secret. When I first saw you, I thought you were beautiful."

The side of his mouth quirks into a sly smile. "Really?"

"Yes." My hands are still against his chest. I focus on them because looking into his eyes—which I'm sure have a teasing expression in them—is too much. "I mean, I hated you, of course. But lune above were you beautiful."

"That's a good secret." I can hear the grin in his voice.

"I'm an open book. Starting now. No secrets between us."

"All right. Do you think I'm a good King?"

Straight to the point. No skirting around it. I try to be equally direct. He deserves at least that much. "No," I say. "But I know you're a good person. Keirdre wasn't built for good people to lead. I love that about you."

"You love that I'm a bad King?"

"I love that you're *you*. Despite everything. The Enforcers didn't trust you, which made it impossible for you to do your job. Not because you're a bad King, but because they were loyal to someone awful and you weren't him. They didn't listen to you because you're *good*. The only way to be a good King to Keirdre is if you were Larster—that's the way he designed it. You're nothing like him. You're you."

"Then why didn't you tell me what you were planning with my mother beforehand?"

"I—" I stop myself before a lie slips out. Lying is instinct. For so long, it's been necessary for survival. But I don't have to lie to Hayes. No matter what faults he finds with me—and there are several—he loves me. I reach for the truth. "When you said no the first time, before I had a plan, I started thinking of you like a mark. I shouldn't have. I'm sorry."

He's quiet for so long I think he's finished asking questions. Until he says, "Did you enjoy killing Felix?"

It's a hard slap, but I don't flinch or look away. Hayes is the one who lost Felix. If anyone here deserves to be hurt by the question, it's him. Not me. I steel myself. "Yes," I say softly.

"And after? Did you regret it?"

"Not until I tasted how much his death hurt you."

Hayes swallows. "If— Do you think if you'd known who he was to me . . . would you have done it?"

I really want to say no. But it's not the truth. "Yes."

He flinches.

"I didn't know you then."

He's silent.

"I'm sorry." I don't know what else to say.

Still, he doesn't let go of me. "What did Felix's emotions taste like? At the end?"

"He was relieved. I was singing to him," I explain. "I walked into the river and he wanted to get to me. When he reached me, he was relieved." It sounds horrible when I say it out loud. Honesty *hurts*. But I lay it at Hayes's feet anyway, hoping it's enough. Hoping *I'm* enough.

"I asked you before if you ever sang to me," says Hayes slowly. "You denied it. Was that true?"

"I never sang to you. I never will."

His hands are still resting at my sides. He glides his thumb, drawing circles against my rib cage. "Promise?"

"I promise." My head falls forward until it's resting on his shoulder. "We need to talk about the barrier. You're right, I am reckless. But if my fate were tied to yours, I'd be careful." I take one of his hands in mine. Intertwine our fingers. "If your life was in my hands, I'd be careful. You know why?"

"Why?"

I shift in his lap. Wrap my arms around his neck. Press my forehead into his. "I have another secret to tell you."

His ocean eyes search mine. "What?"

My voice drops to a whisper. "I love you too."

He jerks his head back, eyes wide as they rove my face with disbelief. The corners of his mouth lift, and he tastes like oranges—happiness—tinged with something murkier. Doubt. "Yeah?"

I hold his gaze, willing that flicker of doubt to go away. "Yeah." For a few brief, eternal moments, I stare into the endless sea.

My every instinct: kiss him.

So, I do.

Hayes responds immediately. His hands slip around my waist. He pulls me closer, closer, closer, until the fronts of our bodies meld into one. His head tilts, slanting against mine. I kiss him with everything in me, willing him to taste the sincerity of my words the way I can taste his. His doubt burns away, like it was never there at all.

I've kissed my marks before. I've kissed Hayes before. It's never been like this. I feel exposed. I've shown him the darkest corners of my soul, and still, he's here, wanting me.

One hand slides up and up, over my back, fingers dancing over my spine, making me shiver. His fingers curl around the back of my neck and angle my head just where he wants it, pulling me closer. Delving deeper into the kiss.

With every breath we share, I grow more and more addicted to the taste of his love for me. I always thought love would be sweet like candy, but I was wrong. It's savory. Smoky. Rich and flavorful. Intense and burning. But not sweet. Sweet, I realize now, is too shallow. Sweet is fleeting. Dances across the tongue and flees a few ticks later. *This*—Hayes—is fulfilling. Eternal. The cinnamon is still there, but it's in the back of my throat, an aftertaste. He wants me—mouth on mine, hips pressed together, hands sliding over my skin—but he also wants *me*—long conversations, stretches of silence where words aren't needed, and smiles like sunshine.

His tongue dips into my mouth, and I let him devour me. I wonder if this is how my marks feel. Knowing I have the capacity to destroy them, and handing me their souls anyway. I thrust mine to Hayes willingly.

His hands slip down until they're resting on the curve of my ass. My greedy hands fiddle with the hem of his shirt in a wordless question. Impatiently, he pulls away just long enough to yank it off himself. He does it so quickly, I've barely processed that he's now bare from the waist up before his mouth is back on mine.

My palms drag over his torso, reveling in the feel of him.

He's sculpted to perfection. I've seen glimpses of his chest, his stomach—lune above, his *arms*—before. But feeling him beneath my palms is an entirely different experience.

His hands burrow deeper into my ass, and my hips start to move against him of their own accord. He groans into my mouth. His thumbs slip under the hem of my shirt, brushing the bare skin of my midriff, just enough to tease.

It's only after I realize that I'm seriously considering the best way to have him on this carriage bench that I break away, gasping for air that wasn't important a half tick ago.

"We should—er . . ." Now that my face isn't against his, I have an unimpeded view of his bare torso. My sentence trails as I lose my thread of thought.

Hayes smirks at me. "Something wrong?"

It takes me an embarrassingly long time to find my voice. "You should put your shirt back on." My hands, resting on his chest, don't move, and I sound more dazed than assertive. "We're supposed to see if you can feel the connection to the barrier."

"I can feel a lot of things right now." His hands, still on my ass, give a squeeze.

I emit a squeal—a sound I don't think I've ever made before. "*Hayes.*" I mean it to sound reprimanding, but it comes out sounding more needy, and I accentuate the noise by inadvertently sliding my hands down his chest to rest on his abdomen. The taut muscles of his stomach flex beneath my palms and my control snaps.

My head dives toward his again. His ocean eyes are dark like storm clouds. His body is tense under my touch. Exhibiting more restraint than I think I've ever had, he leans forward and gently kisses my forehead. "I intend to spend a significant portion of the rest of my life kissing you," he murmurs against my forehead. "But I think now it's time for us to get J'siiri."

He's speaking, but I'm still lightheaded from kissing him. "J'siiri," I repeat back, sounding frazzled.

Those soft lips still caressing my forehead smile. "Yes. J'siiri. The witch you brought with you. Remember her? We need to speak with her, and I think that will be less awkward if I'm fully dressed and you're not on top of me. Not that I'm complaining."

My face feels hot. I climb off his lap and sit on the bench across from him. Somehow, despite everything, I'm still unsure where we stand. "Why do we need J'siiri?"

"So she can join our souls." He smiles at me as he pulls his shirt back over his head. "It's how I'm going to move the barrier, right?"

"You're going to let her do it?"

He laughs. "A very stubborn girl I know told me it's the only way I'll be able to move the barrier in time. I was reluctant at first but . . ." His eyes spark with mischief. "Let's just say that her methods of persuasion are *very* convincing."

CHAPTER FIFTY-ONE

SPARK TO LIFE

Hayes and I sit facing each other, legs crossed, knees brushing.

"Once done, this cannot be undone." J'siiri stands between us. "Are you *sure* you want to do this?"

I meet Hayes's steady ocean gaze. "I'm sure."

J'siiri looks to Hayes for confirmation. He doesn't say anything. Just stares at me with a look so intense, her eyebrows shoot up and she clears her throat. "I'm taking that as a yes." Her hands shake as she passes me the *nafini*. "Just a sip."

The potion is turquoise like the sky and smells like ginger. I tilt the vial, taking just a bit. Immediately, I gag on the taste. It's acrid—like drinking charred firewood. I pass the vial to Hayes and he coughs, his face screwing up as he sips it.

"Sorry." J'siiri grimaces as she pockets the vial. "Probably should've warned you it tastes awful." She licks her lips nervously as she places one hand on each of our foreheads. Her eyes close. There's rapid movement behind her lids, and I'm reminded of a time, forever ago, when Hayes and I sat on pub stools. Laa'el was pulling an image of me from a pub owner's mind. Her eyes were closed, moving the same way J'siiri's are now.

"It's going to be intense. You might want to close your eyes," she murmurs.

My eyes close.

For a few ticks, there's nothing. Then, something flickers. A spark. Like someone sharply rubbing two flint rocks against each other in my mind.

My body hums with a faint sensation I can't place.

Behind my lids, there's a flash of silver sparks.

Hiss.

The thrum of my body grows more intense, like I'm standing too close to someone pounding on bass drums. I feel the heavy reverberations in my chest.

Another spark dances across my field of vision, this one brighter. Longer-lasting.

Another hiss. Another spark.

Something crackles, like dripping bacon grease sizzling over an open flame. Each sputter is accompanied by a scattering of sparks. At first they're silver, but as they grow and the feeling of drumbeats in my chest intensifies, the color becomes more vivid. Blue. Like the ocean. Like Hayes's eyes.

The ocean-colored sparks come faster, larger, until all I can see is a wall of sea. All I hear is sputtering.

I become hyperaware of the feel of Hayes's knees lightly grazing mine. The sensation of J'siiri's hand pressed to my forehead fades away. I can't even be sure she's still touching me. All I feel is Hayes. He's radiating enough heat to burn, but I bask in the glow.

Thump. Thump.

The bass drums are slowing down. It takes me a moment to realize the feeling is my heart. Well, mine *and* Hayes's. They beat the same, deep rhythm.

Slowly, the sound fades until it's a sensation in the back of my mind. The feeling of another heartbeat, beating in tandem with mine.

The sparking ocean dissipates. My mind is quiet.

I can once again feel J'siiri's hand on my head, and Hayes is no longer burning me.

". . . open your eyes now," J'siiri is saying.

My eyes fly open.

It felt like only a few minutes passed, but the sky is flushed with oncoming dawn. It was pitch night when we started.

J'siiri looks spent. She slumps to the ground, barely managing to keep her eyes open.

Hayes glances at me, then J'siiri. "Did it work?"

"You tell me." She sounds half-asleep already.

I study Hayes. He looks more . . . *vibrant*. Like the colors of his existence have intensified. I feel the thumping drumbeat of his heart, like an internal compass, pointing me to him. It's not overwhelming like it was when J'siiri was performing the spell, but it's *there*. Comforting.

He smiles. "It definitely worked."

"Good." J'siiri sits on the ground, legs sprawled in front of her, as she nods to Hayes. "We're going to see if you can feel the barrier now."

"How?"

"You feel that connection to Saoirse?"

"Yes," he says without pause.

"Reach for the barrier the same way."

A flare of lemon-fused surprise hits my tongue a split second before Hayes's face lights up. "I can feel it." He looks awed. "It's all around me. I don't know how I didn't feel it before."

"Perfect." J'siiri yawns.

"What should I do with it?"

"Nothing. You don't want to move it yet. Not until we're in position, or it might tip off Reyshka something's wrong. Don't worry. This was the hard part. Moving it should be like using your water affinity. You feel confident in that?"

"Yes . . ."

"Then you'll be fine." She smiles weakly. "Now, if it's all the same to you . . ." She doesn't finish her sentence. Just keels over, snoring, fast asleep.

CHAPTER FIFTY-TWO
CURTAIN OF STARS

We abandon the carriage as we get close to the Enforcers—they'll see us immediately.

Their camp is easy to spot. They're not hiding. They *want* people to see and fear them. They *want* to be imposing, with their massive navy tents, soldier uniforms, and plainly visible blades.

Their tents are set up in a field in Kurr Valley, not far off the road. A handful of soldiers are here, keeping watch over the main camp or taking breaks. Most of the soldiers lie in wait closer to the barrier, in the trees where Carrik and I trekked along the river when we left Keirdre.

The four of us slink through the forest up that damned incline, stopping when we hear the sounds of soldiers up ahead. We need to be close enough to trap them within the barrier without any outsiders getting caught inside, but far enough away we're not seen.

Somewhere up ahead is Anarin Arkin. She caused this. Killed Thannen, framed me, plotted to usurp Hayes. I despise her. Soon, when the barrier moves, she'll find herself trapped inside a war she created. She dreamed of war. I hope she drowns in it.

The Jeune River rushes beside us. Drops of water sail through the air, landing against my skin, invigorating me as I sit on the ground. J'siiri insisted. According to her, once Hayes starts drawing energy from me to move the barrier, I'll be too weak to stand.

"You've done this before, right?" says Hayes nervously.

"Yes." J'siiri guides Hayes to stand next to me. "We've done lots of experiments with soul magic."

"How did they turn out?" asks Hayes.

"Remember, you want to move the barrier so that it's in between us and the Enforcers. It'll wrap around them and the armies on the other side, and we'll be out here."

"You didn't answer my question. What happened when you tried this before?"

She licks her lips. "Nothing."

It's clearly a lie.

"J'siiri." Hayes folds his arms. "I'm not doing anything with this barrier until you tell me what happened."

"Usually, nothing happened. There was only *one* time some-one didn't make it."

"Didn't make it as in *died*?" Hayes vehemently shakes his head. "I'm not—"

"It's fine." I grab his arm and hold him in place. "Do it. I trust you. You're not going to kill me." Even if I didn't trust him, it doesn't matter. We're out of time. As we speak, forces from both the Resistance and Keirdre are gathered on the other side of the barrier, preparing for war.

My nerves are frayed past the point of repair. This is going to work. It has to.

"Hayes." J'siiri's voice is low and soothing. "This is just like your water affinity. You're going to *feel* for your connection to the barrier. Envision warping it to your will, just like with water. Right now, don't move it. Just make it twitch—so you know you can do it. If you need more energy, use Saoirse. Draw energy from her, push it into the barrier."

Hayes's stale unease is all I taste as he places a hand on my head.

There's a tug in the back of my mind. The bass drumbeat of Hayes that lives there pulses.

As it does, I start trembling.

Scratch that—it's not me, it's the *ground*.

Hayes jumps. "Was that—"

"The barrier." J'siiri grins. "You did it. When you start to actually move it, do what you just did, but *more*."

Hayes nods. Looks at me. "You're feeling all right?"

"I'm good. I'll be better when you move the barrier."

He swallows, but with a quick nod, he closes his eyes, preparing to physically move the barrier this time.

I feel the ground rumble again, more intense than when he was practicing before.

The pulsing drum emanates warmth that starts in my chest and radiates through my entire body.

The world shakes harder.

What started as gentle warmth in my body tightens around me. Until it's so stifling, so constricting, it's like I'm sitting in a locked room filling with smoke. Sweat drizzles down my forehead. It dampens the undersides of my arms. Slides down my back. It's *hot*. Too hot.

My breaths get shallow, as though I'm sprinting uphill.

Hayes's eyes flicker open. "Saoirse, are you—"

"I'm fine." I'm out of breath. Talking *hurts*. It's a waste of what little air I have left. "Keep going."

Someone takes my hand. Jeune squats next to me. Water *moves* from the river to me, dousing me. It's soothing. Not enough to cool the stifling heat, but enough so I can breathe.

The earth around us growls, the sound getting louder. The more it shudders, the weaker I feel. Jeune is still drenching me in river water, but it's not enough. I'm too tired to stay upright, even just to sit. My body crumples, eyes closed, and I fall back, lying on the quaking forest floor.

I taste a surge of Hayes's panic. It's faint. Everything is faint now. Muted. Like I'm looking through murky water. Tasting everything watered down and tepid.

"Saoirse." Hayes sounds terrified. "Keep your eyes open. I need to know you're alive."

I force them open. "I'm fine." My words are garbled.

Trees shudder around us. In the corner of my shrinking vision, I see something glaringly bright. My head falls to the side to look.

A brilliant ring of glowing silver. Like a wall made of stars. It approaches from all directions, hurtling toward us in a ring. The closer it gets, the more the world quakes.

The barrier.

The force that surrounds us is *moving.* The glow where it once rested along the Jeune River flies away from us—ensnaring the Resistance and Reyshka's army in Alkara. That same glow races toward us from the other direction. As it moves, it obscures the outside world behind a curtain of stars.

As the barrier descends upon us, fields and homes and trees disappear as they're left out—free of this new barrier's confines.

Hayes releases a deep yell—I don't think he can help it—and

the tremors intensify. Leaves and branches tumble from trees, piling around us. Squawking birds take flight and flee.

In the back of my mind, I hear footsteps. Lighter than the rumbling of the thunderous barrier, but loud enough I can guess their source: soldiers. The ones working for the Enforcers. They heard Hayes yell and are making their way toward us.

"Dammit," Jeune mutters. "Hayes, there are soldiers coming for us. Any chance you can move the barrier any faster?"

He yells again, louder this time. I gasp—it feels like something heavy has thudded into my chest, winding me. I lose sensation in my arms, my legs. I'm battling my instincts just to keep my eyes open.

The barrier is a few paces behind us, steadily approaching, when a wave of soldiers bursts into the clearing.

I have no energy to fight them off. Fortunately, in a few ticks, before they reach us, the barrier will swoop past us, surround them, and trap them inside.

The silver stars that make up the barrier move closer.

The soldiers race toward us.

The barrier is less than a pace away—

When it stops.

On the other sides, the barrier continues to shift, but the part that's nearest us *stops*, half a pace away.

Hayes's brow clenches. I feel another jolt as another breath of air is knocked from me. Still, the barrier doesn't move.

Jeune grabs her blade and steps in front of us. "Hayes . . ."

The soldiers are closer. In a few ticks, they'll be upon us.

"The barrier is stuck," says Hayes frantically.

"What the hell do you mean, stuck?"

The rumbling stops. The barrier halts on all sides. In its wake, I hear a roar followed by the sound of clanging metal. The war on three fronts has started. Keirdren soldiers are running right at us.

And we're trapped inside the barrier.

CHAPTER FIFTY-THREE

BREATHLESS IN THE DOWNPOUR

Jeune charges forward. There are five approaching soldiers and four of us—except I can't move and neither Hayes nor J'siiri are trained soldiers. Which leaves Jeune. One against five.

Apparently undeterred by this, Jeune swings her blade, striking it against the sword of the first attacker.

Two more soldiers swipe at her from either side. She ducks both blades, kicking out and catching the first soldier off-balance. He topples as Jeune springs back, still holding her blade, glancing between them, waiting to see who will pounce next.

"*Ow!*" The soldier closest to her drops his blade. It clatters to the ground, glowing red—like someone held it in a flame.

My brain is working slower than usual, so it takes me a second. *Magic.* J'siiri used magic to heat the blade's metal.

Jeune doesn't pause. Just plunges her blade into the soldier's stomach, killing him instantly. She whirls, swiping the arm of another soldier, drawing blood.

Two of the other attackers also drop their swords, palms blistering from the heat. Since they're disarmed, Jeune makes quick work of them.

Just two soldiers remain.

River water comes at Jeune, a large enough wave to drown her where she stands. She throws up her arms, using her own affinity to stop the water from crashing down on her. With her hands occupied, she can't use her blade.

I try and force myself to sit up. To move my arms, to move the water.

My body is full of lead. No matter how many times I give my arms the instruction to move, I *can't*. I'm empty. No strength left.

The soldier not moving the water darts toward Jeune, sword raised, prepared to strike.

Like his comrades', the sword glows red with heat. He grits his teeth, trying to hold on to it before he, too, is forced to drop it as his hand blisters.

Hayes swoops in, moving faster than I've ever seen him. Drags a blade across the soldier's chest, drawing blood and leaving him dead.

The last soldier—still struggling with the water and Jeune—doesn't have time to react before Hayes stabs him in the side.

He keels over.

Jeune flings the water overhead away, back into the river.

We're all breathing heavily. Jeune leans forward, resting her hands against her knees with a nod to J'siiri. "The heated blades was a nice touch, thanks."

J'siiri smiles. "Anytime."

Jeune is still panting. "Now, can you please explain why the hell we're inside the barrier?"

"I'm sorry," J'siiri says. "I forgot. I—I think it's because Hayes is tied to it. While he's moving it, he has to be *inside*."

"That can't be true," says Jeune. "Reyshka's joined to the barrier, and she left Keirdre."

"You can cross through the doorway, but you have to be inside while it moves."

"Good." Hayes crouches at my side. "We can use the doorway to get Saoirse out of here. There's a war happening, and all three sides would love to see her dead." Gently, he touches the side of my face. "Saoirse? Are you all right? We're getting you out of here."

My head is throbbing. It's just about the only sensation I have. Pain. The dull, sore kind that lingers in every part of you. "I can't stand." My tongue is heavy so my words sound off, but Hayes understands anyway.

"You don't have to." It's not until the world tilts that I realize he's lifting me, one arm under my bended knees, the other behind my back. "Where's the doorway?"

"It *was* at the barrier near the river," says J'siiri. "But you just moved the barrier to surround Reyshka's army. So now it's—"

"On the other side of the battlefield," Hayes mutters. "Perfect."

"You can't carry her through a war zone," says J'siiri.

"Watch me." Hayes tightens his hold on me. "We'll stick to the perimeter of the barrier. Try to avoid the main fighting in the middle."

Jeune nods. "J'siiri and I will stay on the outside of you and Saoirse. If anyone attacks, I'll fight them off and J'siiri—"

"—will heat their weapons like I did before," J'siiri says.

Satisfied with this plan, we start moving.

I'm weary all over. My arms and legs are slack. My head lolls back against my will. The small bit of energy I have goes toward breathing, and even that small act is draining. I want to close my eyes. Curl up and turn off the world. Unfortunately, that's not an option. Not yet.

Every once in a while, Hayes splashes me with river water. I appreciate it and it gives me small bursts of energy, but just enough to make breathing easier for a few ticks. I'm still completely useless.

I can tell we're moving quickly—the trees are a blur as we pass—but everything is still muted around me. My head sags against Hayes's chest, and every time my eyes give in to my exhaustion and close, he rouses me. "Keep your eyes open." Even in my dulled state, I hear the terror in his voice. "I know you're tired, but I need to know you're still breathing."

"I'm fine," I say with a roll of my eyes. Except all that comes out is, "Mm fine." And my eyes don't roll—they just slip into a dazed, half-closed position.

Hayes mutters something under his breath that sounds like, "So damned stubborn," and kisses my forehead affectionately. His arms must ache from carrying me, but he doesn't complain.

Two soldiers burst out from behind a tree. Alkaran. I can barely see, so I can't place what kind of creatures they are until thick tree roots burst from the ground and reach for us.

Jeune hacks at one, sawing her blade back and forth. The dryad on the right screeches with pain.

J'siiri presses her hand against the one on the left. He lurches away from her. There's a burn the shape of a hand on his bark-like skin. With a snarl, he raises a blade and slices at her—

Clang.

It's blocked.

Another soldier jumps in between J'siiri and the impending blade, fighting the dryad off with a sword of his own.

The ensuing battle is brief. The victor is the new soldier. I'm too weak to identify him. At least until Hayes inhales sharply in surprise. "Spektryl?"

Carrik doesn't react right away. Instead, he turns and joins Jeune in fighting off the second dryad. When they also drop to the forest floor, dead, Carrik turns to face us. His green eyes immediately land on me. "Sorkova."

I strain to lift my head. "What . . . ?" It's all I can manage, but he can tell that I'm wondering what the hell he's doing here.

"Lex and Zaire would've thought it was suspicious if I didn't fight with them. I've been trying to stay to the perimeter to keep out of the thick of it."

Only one thought comes to mind. "Where's—"

"Fine." He instantly guesses the direction of my thoughts. "Your family is safe. Nowhere near here. What the hell are *you* doing here? Why do you look like cow cud?"

"We're trying to get out," says J'siiri. "We're looking for the doorway."

Carrik's still looking at me. "What did you do to Saoirse?"

"It's a long story," says Hayes. "But she can't move. Jeune and J'siiri are keeping guard and I'm carrying her."

Carrik raises his blade. "I'm coming with you. I'll guard her too."

Nobody argues. We now have two trained soldiers instead of just one. Together, we start moving. At first, staying to the perimeter is a good strategy. We're in the trees, and aside from a few clearings where Jeune and Carrik are easily able to pick off the handful of soldiers that attack, we're mostly left alone.

Unfortunately, the forest doesn't continue forever. When we reach the edge of the tree line, we're in the grassy valley between the forest and Pennex. I can't see the city up ahead, which means the barrier cuts through the valley.

If we get through the valley, we reach the barrier. Easy enough.

Except for the fact that the battle is thickest here.

"Same strategy." Jeune squares her shoulders to convey confidence, but the back of my throat burns with her fear. "Stay on the perimeter. Work our way around."

She's barely taken one step out of the trees before an arrow soars overhead, narrowly missing her.

The next one hits true—Carrik. Right in the arm.

He cries out and drops his sword just as two soldiers rush for him. Short and carrying long, curved blades that are *on fire*.

Goblins. Lex told me they can withstand intense heat. They descend upon Carrik, but Jeune fights them off. I'm not sure what kind of magic their blades are enchanted with, but no matter how many times Jeune and Carrik douse them with river water, they keep igniting again.

It doesn't matter. Jeune and Carrik move together like they've been fighting side by side for years. In a matter of seconds, both goblins are dead. The flaming swords extinguish with them.

We advance a few paces before we're met with another wave of soldiers.

Again, Jeune and Carrik are a perfect match, blades swinging in sync, water flowing in harmony, their movements smooth as though choreographed.

Until Jeune starts choking.

One moment she's fine, the next, she freezes in place, hands flying to her throat. An air fae stands a few paces away, hands out. He tightens the air coiled around Jeune's throat like a noose. Carrik is still fighting, too busy staying alive to stop the air fae.

My hand moves weakly, trying to move water from the river. All I manage is a few useless flaps of my arm before it falls still at my side.

Jeune is making garbled choking noises.

Hayes quickly sets me down on the forest floor. "I'll be right back." He grabs hold of one of the fallen goblins' curved swords and charges at the air fae. He's not a skilled fighter, but fortunately, all he has to do is disorient the air fae long enough for Jeune to breathe again. She can handle the rest.

I just barely manage to lift my head to watch their battle unfold when I'm hit with a surge of water so intense, I'm thrown backward. My body slams into something solid—the barrier.

I scream as I fall to the ground.

It's water, so it gives me a bit of energy, but I'm dazed, on my back, and straining to sit up to see who attacked—

"Siren!" a familiar voice screeches.

Reyshka's face is screwed in knotted fury as she storms toward me. She's *furious*. So much so, I sense it even with my limited capacity to feel. It's more than anger. It's hatred, scorching enough to rival the sun.

"Saoirse!" Someone calls my name, but with all my attention on Reyshka, I can't tell who.

Reyshka glares as she approaches me, each step slow and deliberate. "Siren." She spits out the word. "I encountered Keirdren soldiers here. Imagine my surprise when they informed me"—her arm jerks, bludgeoning me with more water that slams me into the barrier—"that King Larster is dead. Killed by a *siren*."

I moan, sore all over. "I didn't—"

Her hand flies to the blade strapped around her hips. "I *knew* better. I *knew* you were a liar. I *knew* it."

I'm exhausted, but I force myself to sit up. That small action has me winded. Each breath I inhale, I immediately lose.

My lips part—trying to sing—but my throat is dry and my lungs are burning. Nothing comes out.

"This—" Reyshka gestures to the battlefield behind her. "This was your doing."

"Yes."

"You lied to me."

Obviously. "Yes."

She snarls, and before I can react, she's raised her sword.

I'm not armed. I have no voice. I can barely move. My back is pressed against the barrier, so I can't even scramble away. I'm completely defenseless.

I focus on the feel of the water on my skin. I need it to give me just *one* burst of energy.

It takes everything in me, but as Reyshka raises her blade, I *lurch* to the side. It's all I can manage.

Her sword grazes my ankle, but with my dulled senses, I barely feel it.

I wonder why she's fighting so gracelessly until she kicks my leg. "Get up," she demands. "And fight."

Wish I could.

My head swivels, searching for something I can use—anything. To my right, there's a soldier lying dead next to his discarded blade. I crawl backward, barely propped up by my weak, quivering arms.

Reyshka follows as I crawl back. *"Get up."*

My fingers curl around the blade's handle as Reyshka swings down.

She's going to kill me. I have no way to defend myself. In this state, she's stronger than me. And I barely have a grip on this damned—

A sword slices in front of me. It meets Reyshka's and shoves, forcing her to back up.

Carrik. He stands between us, fierce and poised.

Reyshka glares. *"Move."*

"I'm not going anywhere. Neither is Saoirse. I don't mean to boast, but I'm a fairly decent swordsman."

Her lips curve into a smirk. "I'm better."

"You want to test that theory?"

Her smirk widens in answer.

Carrik shoots me a look over his shoulder. I read the concern on his face. He holds my gaze for two ticks before spinning back to Reyshka.

Their blades clang in the familiar rhythm of battle.

It's my first time seeing Reyshka fight. I immediately understand why she's a legend. It's a title well earned. She's skilled. Her movements are quick and efficient, her eyes sharp and calculating. She sees each of Carrik's moves and anticipates.

Fortunately, Carrik Solwey has a reputation of his own. A swordsman so talented, a kingdom built on the backs of humans was willing to overlook him being half human and make him a guard.

Reyshka's eyes glint as they dance. She feints right—so skillfully I don't realize it's a feint until it's too late and her blade is slashing across his chest.

I see the blood before I hear him cry out.

His blade clatters to the ground. Carrik lurches for it—but Reyshka is faster.

My throat is dry, but it's startled into response as Reyshka slices her blade again.

The world slows. Like she's moving through honey and I'm watching from a distance, immobile. In this sluggish new world, the sword drags across Carrik's chest, leaving a trail of deep red in its wake.

This wound is deeper than the last. Yet I'm still in complete disbelief when Carrik Solwey crumples next to his blade.

He's not moving.

Why isn't he moving?

He's not dead. I know he's not. He can't be, he can't be, he can't—

I'm screaming. I don't remember when the scream started, but at some point I become aware of my surroundings again and I'm in the middle of a scream. It fills the air. Fills the entire confines of this new barrier.

My throat was dry before. It still is. The scream rips it raw, and it *hurts* but everything hurts so I don't feel it.

Reyshka steps over Carrik's body. It's a callous move. I feel like I'm watching her cut him open all over again. She doesn't even glance at him, just moves toward me with a determined grace I hate.

The sky darkens with my grief. I don't know if Carrik is alive. I don't know if I'll ever feel all right again. The rain answers my pain.

Water pours from above. I'm soaked in moments. I take it all in. The rain, the cold, the heartbreak. The water brings me back to life.

Now's not the time for tears. I don't need the water to soothe my sorrow. Instead, I let it fuel my fury.

My mouth opens again—to do what, I'm unsure. Maybe to taunt her? Call her something vile—but all I manage is another scream. No words, just a screech, loud enough to shatter eardrums and drown souls.

There's a melody hidden in this scream. One of haunting and rage and hatred.

My eyes are bright and silver, and the world is on fire. *I'm* on fire. Set ablaze by the water. I dart around Reyshka and land beside Carrik. I want so badly to check if he's still breathing—if he has a pulse—but there's no time.

His blade is beside him, soaking in the downpour. I ignore it, reaching instead for the dagger in his boot. The one he always kept with him for luck. His mother's.

Keeps. The one he always *keeps* with him for luck.

I'm going to kill her. I've never been more sure of anything. I'm going to kill Reyshka Harker, and when I do, I want to be up close and personal. I want to watch the light fade from her eyes and I want it to be with Carrik's dagger.

I hurl myself at Reyshka. My exhaustion is long gone. Drowned. Dragged beneath the waves of the ocean of my grief.

My song has frozen her in place. She's perfectly still—transfixed—at the sound of the screeching song she can't resist.

I drive the dagger into her gut with enough force to leave a bruise on her stomach. I twist, digging it in deeper. I pull it back and drive it in again, just because I can.

I've never fought Reyshka before. I'll admit, she's a great instructor.

But she's never fought a siren before. Much less a siren in anguish.

She stormed over to me earlier, demanding I fight. And yet now, she never raises a hand to fight back. Even as the light drains from her eyes and she falls, she doesn't fight me.

Her mouth opens. I think maybe she's speaking, or maybe she's groaning from the pain, or maybe that's just how people die. It doesn't matter, she doesn't matter, nothing matters.

I pull out the knife. That wound, left untreated, is more than enough to kill her. I have no intention of treating her, but I also have no intention of only cutting her open once.

She meets my eyes. I have no idea what she sees in them, but I'm still screech-singing, my eyes are still silver, and inexplicably, she still looks spellbound. She's too entranced by me to be afraid.

It infuriates me. I want her final moments to be of complete horror. I want her to feel a fraction of the hurt that soaks my entire being.

So, I stop singing.

Force the silver to fade from my eyes until they're back to amber. Back to me.

Water drips down her face as it contorts with confusion. Without the spell of my song, the pain of the wound in her gut is settling in. Her fear burns my throat, her panic is sharp like fresh lemon juice, and her horror—ripe with the realization that she is about to die—is sweeter than any candy.

Taking her indisposition as an opportunity, I snarl at her, "That was my best friend."

I hold her quickly dulling eyes as I draw Carrik's dagger across her neck. Scarlet blooms behind the dagger's path.

I usually look away when I make a kill. Before the body

slams against the ground or the river sweeps it away. I don't look away now. I savor this moment. A life for a life.

It's not enough. It will *never* be enough.

For a few ticks, she rocks back and forth on her feet, eyes dazed as though she can't believe what just happened.

Her grip on the blade loosens. Her arm goes slack and she slumps forward, arms extended as though she expects me to catch her.

I don't.

Reyshka Harker, a legend brought to life, tumbles to the ground in a splash of blood, rainwater, and tears.

CHAPTER FIFTY-FOUR

OUT OF TEARS

Carrik lies face down on the muddy ground. I roll him over onto his back and immediately regret it. When I couldn't see his face, I could play pretend. Looking at him now, my heart drops.

His chest is completely still. Green eyes slightly open, but glassy and empty. It's more horrifying than if they were closed.

He's—

I refuse to finish the thought. I don't accept it. I rip open his shirt and pound on his chest. "Carrik." My voice trembles with broken sobs. "Wake up!" I shout each word like a command. Like he's one of my marks, under my spell, who will do what I say just because I ask him to.

He doesn't move.

"*Wake. Up.*" I accentuate each word by beating his chest. Like pummeling his body is going to heal a blade wound.

"Carrik!" I scream again. Pound harder. "I don't hate you. I never hated you. *Please.*" My hands are covered in the red of his blood as they skim over him, searching for some way to heal this. My voice softens. I drop my head to hover near his. "You have to wake up," I whisper. "So I can tell you I forgive you. *Please.*"

He doesn't move.

My vision blurs with more tears. He saved my life. Stepped between me and Reyshka and fought her off.

But he saved me long before that. At the Barracks, when I was drowning in loneliness and self-hatred. In Alkara, when I needed to rise to the top of Reyshka's soldiers. And my family. He took them to safety without asking for anything in return.

Anything but forgiveness. I never gave it to him. Instead, I'm sobbing out promises to a corpse because I'm too late and it's too late and he's—

Dead.

My fists stop beating at his chest. He's not going to wake up.

My head falls forward, landing on his chest. My hair mixes with blood and rain and tears. My lips part, and I scream. It's like screaming with Carrik in the ashes of Szeiryna, except he's not by my side this time. He'll never be by my side again. That knowledge forces the scream out, louder than it's ever been before.

In Szeiryna, I mourned a family I never met. Now, I mourn a family I cast aside. Over and over again.

I remember that moment on the pier. Singing into an asterval on the deck of the *Sea Queen*. Remember the moments after, when I no longer needed an asterval to carry my voice.

My scream grows louder.

I think about all the times Carrik trained with me, in Keirdre and Alkara. All the times he encouraged me to use my water affinity. To shirk my fear of myself.

Louder, still.

I think about his rage. How his parents were killed and he could do nothing about it. Think about how I'm filled with that same rage, same brokenness.

I never told him that.

My scream echoes off the walls of this new barrier, filling the space with grief and fury. This scream is a song. Darker and more devastating than anything I've sung before. And yet still infuriatingly beautiful. It fills this new barrier, resounding off the walls of this space around us.

I don't know when I stop screaming, but when I do, Hayes is standing over me and three armies are before me, frozen in place. They're enchanted, staring at me in awe.

Kill them. Kill them all.

Carrik's anger made him want to burn the world down. I can understand it, because right now, I want that too. I want to set them all aflame and gleefully watch as I punish them for everything I've lost.

I've played this game before. Let retaliation sate my instincts. The thing is, it's never actually fixed any of my problems.

I think about Finnean. According to Ikenna, he was killed by a siren he loved. In retaliation, Larster set fire to Szeiryna. According to Carrik, that was a lie. Larster killed the siren and, in turn, her family killed Finnean.

I suppose I'll never know the full truth. But it doesn't matter, because either way, the tale ends in revenge and loss. Either way, Finnean and Szeiryna are gone.

I'm tired. Tired of repeated history and cycles of war.

Carrik's gone. My rage wants me to kill all three armies before me in punishment. Maybe I'll always want to kill. Maybe it's because of my siren instincts—or maybe it's because of *me*. It doesn't matter why. There's power in resisting your instincts. Power in choosing *not* to seek retaliation.

I raise my voice to the crowd. "Lower your weapons."

Clattering as several weapons drop immediately to the ground. Not enough. *"Now."*

More weapons drop.

I sing a few more notes—ensuring I've successfully captured everyone's attention, even those who stubbornly hold on to their weapons.

I feel Hayes beside me. His head is held high, the set of his chin looks regal. He raises his voice so it echoes over the battlefield. "I am King Hayes Finnean Vanihail. I am the King of Keirdre, as is my birthright. Any Keirdren who raises a hand or weapon against any Alkaran will be found guilty of treason. And they will be penalized."

J'siiri moves to stand beside Hayes. With her *keil* bead, she looks like I'llyaris again. "I am Queen I'llyaris, Queen of Alkara. Any Alkaran who raises a hand or weapon against any Keirdren will be found guilty of treason and properly punished as well."

Murmurs break out in the crowd.

Anarin shoves her way forward. Her eyes are sharp with defiance, lips twisted in a snarl directed at Hayes. "I will *never* bow to you."

I expect Hayes to flinch. He doesn't. Just regards her calmly. "I don't remember asking you to bow. Regardless, Enforcer Arkin, I am formally stripping you of your title and charging you with treason."

She chuckles darkly. "I don't answer to you. You are a child throwing around words you don't understand. You *never* should've taken the throne."

Still, Hayes remains calm. "Fine. If you're so eager to fight, go ahead. Just know, there are consequences. Raise your weapon if you wish." He glances at me. "Saoirse, do you have a problem with Anarin keeping her weapon?"

His eyes, cool as they regard Anarin, are brimming with

meaning as they look at me. I read his intention in his gaze. He's asking for my help to make an example of her.

I smirk and slink toward Anarin, singing a soft melody. She trembles as I stop a few paces away. "You want to use your weapon so badly?" I say sweetly. "Fine. Raise your blade."

She doesn't hesitate. She lifts her sword, staring at me with cow eyes soaked in longing.

"Stab it into your thigh," I tell her.

Again, she does it without thinking.

Blood flows and her gaze snaps down for the first time, blinking to clear the fog my song has created. "*Ow.* W—"

"*Again,*" I say.

She drives the blade into her thigh a second time.

Behind me, I sense Hayes's distaste with this display. He never wanted to be his father—never wanted to be the kind of King who makes violent examples of others. Still, these soldiers are loyal only to Larster. If Hayes wants their obedience, he'll have to pretend. At least for a bit.

"Enough. I think she understands." Hayes raises a hand, stopping me. Even though I see the pulse jumping nervously in his throat, outwardly, he's stoic.

"You can stop," I tell her.

Anarin's eyes glitter with hatred as she obediently drops her blade.

"Keirdrens," says Hayes again, "*lower your weapons.*"

The remaining soldiers who weren't under my spell before heed him now. Their weapons clatter to the ground.

"Anyone who chooses to fight against Alkara or myself will be punished. If not by Saoirse, then they will stay inside this barrier, unable to leave until I've determined they've reconciled." He takes a breath and glances first at me, then at J'siiri.

We planned what's to come. The King of Keirdre and Queen of Alkara publicly announce they've formed an alliance. Together, we'll work to keep the peace between our two kingdoms and usher Keirdre into a better future.

"Anarin Arkin is guilty of treason," Hayes announces. "But she was not wrong. I should not have taken the throne. I wasn't ready. I'm still not."

What?

I twist to face him, just as stunned as the rest of the crowd. The soldiers before us erupt with exclamations of shock.

Hayes faces them, not looking at me. "For too long, Keirdre has suffered under the weight of a King unfit to rule. I refuse to continue this legacy. My father divided this kingdom from Alkara. And then he divided it further from within. He shouldn't have. Keirdre doesn't need a King, it needs unity. Under the reign of Her Majesty Queen I'llyaris and the rest of the Alkaran council, we'll have it."

He turns to J'siiri. In front of three armies, the King of Keirdre drops to one knee before her. He ducks his head. "Keirdre has much to learn from your leadership, Queen I'llyaris. I, for one, am eager to learn."

Silence.

Slowly, Hayes rises and faces the Keirdrens again. "I did not ask you to kneel to me. And I will not. I am no longer a King, so I no longer have the authority to ask anything of you. I cede my crown and my title. Those who want peace will follow the command of Queen I'llyaris. Those who do not . . . well, that's for her to decide."

J'siiri's eyes remain wide with shock for a tick before she clears her features, donning a mask of calm authority. She holds her head high, looking regal. Like a Queen. "Anyone who wishes to continue fighting is welcome to. But, as Hayes said, if you do, you will remain trapped here indefinitely, at the mercy of a siren until you kneel before your Queen."

No one moves for so long, I fear no one is going to.

Then, a soldier makes his way to the front of the crowd. Slowly and deliberately, he sinks to one knee. "Queen I'llyaris."

Three armies slowly drop to their knees and echo the same.

CHAPTER FIFTY-FIVE

MARKED GRAVES

Carrik Solwey's funeral is in Sinu. It's small, just people who knew him. Hayes offered to have a larger service, like one for prominent soldiers slain in battle. It's not what Carrik would have wanted. He loved being a soldier, but he hated Keirdre and its traditions. He would've wanted something small and intimate.

I cry into Hayes's shoulder. I've been doing that a lot over the past week. Each time, no matter where we are, he's there. He hugs me freely, presses soft kisses to my hair, murmurs words in my ear that mean nothing and everything.

We sit in the front row, right in front of the stage. I'm tucked into Hayes's side, and Rain is curled against mine.

Lex speaks first. Zaire and Lex begged to come, and I relented. They're going to spend the next several years in prison, but they knew Carrik for years. Passed letters that helped him recover from the loss of his family. In many ways, they were better friends to him than I ever was.

Lex might be a liar who orchestrated a war, but they genuinely cared for Carrik. I think he would've wanted them here.

I'm supposed to speak next, but when Lex sits down, my throat closes and I can't move. My sobs come harder, louder. I don't want to speak. If I do, he's gone. If I do—

Rain stands and moves to the front.

What is she doing?

My heart swells as my Beansprout meets my eyes and speaks. "Carrik Solwey was a friend. A really good one." A tear slides down her cheek. She wipes it away and keeps going.

Rain truly is better than me. In every sense. He blackmailed her, kidnapped her, and hurt her—and she's standing at his funeral telling a room full of people how much she cared for him.

"He liked to tell jokes. He always remembered my birthday. He'd give me gifts. Nothing expensive, but he'd whittle something out of wood or find a crystal and make it into jewelry." She sniffles. Wipes away more tears. "He gave me all kinds of gifts. My *favorite* was five years ago. My sister used to train at the Vanihailian Barracks. She came home all the time and she was always miserable. One day, five years ago, she came home smiling."

The tears are coming faster now. "It was because she made a friend. Carrik. That was the best gift he ever gave me. He made her happy. He made a lot of people happy." She chokes on a sob. "I'm going to miss that."

When she's finished, she stumbles into my arms. I cry into her hair, and she sobs into my chest.

We bury him with the letters his father never got. I figure if there's an afterlife and they're both there, he can finally deliver them.

On either side of his tombstone are gravestones for his parents, Mykah and Aylix. Their bodies aren't buried here, but I think Carrik would be happy to know they finally have marked graves.

CHAPTER FIFTY-SIX

HAYES

"Ow," Rain whines as I braid her hair.

I roll my eyes. "Oh, please. I didn't even pull that hard."

"You don't have to make it so tight."

"I do if you want it to last all night." She's sleeping over at a friend's house tonight. It's the first time she's done that. The first time I've *let* her do that.

She practically *begged* me to braid her hair before she leaves so she doesn't have to deal with it in the morning. I picked some kylith flowers from the yard, and I work them into the braid, giving her hair a splash of blue. I've missed this. Sitting on the sofa that smells like grass while she sits in front of me on the rug made of rose petals in our old home. The mill house.

The past two weeks have been chaotic—and I've an inkling they're only going to get more so—so I cling to these rare moments of normalcy. A lot of people were imprisoned after the war on three fronts. The Enforcers, their soldiers, the Alkaran Resistance, and anyone in Reyshka's army who refused to swear allegiance to the Queen of Alkara.

Given the treaty, J'siiri as Queen I'llyaris's reign was extended for one more lune to give her time to discuss the details of the treaty before the next monarch ascends to the throne. In the past two weeks, J'siiri and Hayes have been in frequent communication.

Hayes ceded his throne to Alkara, but the process of actually uniting Keirdre and Alkara is a joint effort. Hayes and his advisers and J'siiri with her advisers have meetings just about every day about next steps, especially how to deal with those who were less than thrilled about the end of Keirdre's monarchy.

Seemingly overnight, dozens of wealthy Vanihailian families fled their homes. Apparently, they'd rather leave Keirdre than stay under its new regime. Hayes and J'siiri have teams searching for them, but given their vast resources, I doubt they'll be found anytime soon.

"When you're done, would you like me to braid your hair?" asks Rain.

"No, I like to keep it down."

"You sure?" Rain twists around to grin at me, eyes mischievous.

"Yes . . . why?"

"You're braiding my hair because *I'm* having a sleepover. And since you're having a sleepover too . . ."

Lune above.

My face is hot.

In Alkara, I developed the habit of sleeping in Hayes's bed. As the details of the union between Alkara and Keirdre are worked out, Hayes still lives in the Palace. Which means I sleep there as well, every night.

"Shut up," I grumble to her.

She laughs. "I told you he's pretty. Don't you think he's pretty?"

"Shut up," I say again.

A knock at the door cuts off her laughter and spares me

from being teased by my twelve-year-old sister. I'm relieved to tie off the end of her braid and go open the front door.

I'm met with ocean eyes.

I smile. "Hey. We were just—" I stop. If I tell him we were talking about him, he'll want to know what we were saying. I have no intention of sharing. "Come in." I move aside for him to enter.

Rain sidles up beside me. "Hi, Hayes." She angles her head pointedly so he can't miss the flowers in her hair.

He grins. "Hey, Rain. Your hair looks nice."

"Thank you." Satisfied with the compliment, she tilts her head back to its usual position. "Are you stealing my sister again?"

He chuckles. "Guilty." He sounds oddly nervous as he looks away from her to me. "You have a moment to talk?"

I'm fairly certain I already know what he wants to talk about. "Sure." I squat in front of Rain. "I'll be right back, Beansprout. Then I'll walk you over to Nyrell's, all right?"

"Or I could walk by myself . . ."

I laugh. "Not a chance." I've been slowly loosening my iron grip on my sister and letting her have fun—but there's *no* way I'm letting her walk thirty-five minutes through Vanihail, two weeks after a war, alone. With a parting smirk at my sister, I lead Hayes upstairs to my room. Former room, I guess, since I haven't actually slept here in ages. "What's wrong?"

"Nothing." He says that, but his emotions are stale with his nerves. He grabs one of my hands and plays with my fingers, not looking at me. "I intend to marry you someday."

I blink, stomach fluttering. I thought I knew what he wanted to talk about—this isn't what I expected him to say. "Is this a proposal?"

"A proposal is a question. That was a statement."

I quirk an eyebrow. "You're ordering me to marry you?"

"If I remember correctly, you were never very good at following orders, even when I was a Prince or a King." Some of the anxiety he was clearly carrying around disappears as he looks at me with an easy smile. "It's not an order. I just want you to know that I'm serious about you."

I can't help laughing. "Considering our souls are permanently bound together, I figured as much. Where is this coming from?"

"I got a letter from J'siiri today."

Ah. So this is what he wants to talk about. "I know."

Hayes frowns. "You do?"

"Yes." I move past him to retrieve something from my dresser—a letter. "I got one too."

Brow knitted with curiosity, Hayes reaches for my letter, but I hold it out of reach. "Wait. She told me she offered you a position on the council. Are you going to take it?" One of her last acts as Queen. If Hayes accepts, he'll serve on the Alkaran council, as a liaison to help facilitate the union of Keirdre and Alkara.

Hayes's nerves are back. "That's what I wanted to talk to you about. I want to take it. I want to learn how to rule so that someday, I'm worthy of a title. But if I accept, I'll have to move to Alkara. I want you to come with me. And your family, of course."

Is this why he was nervous? *Lune above, he's adorable.* "Sure."

He looks stunned—and ecstatic. "You're serious? Just like that?"

"Just like that," I agree. "I'll get to show Rain all the creatures we used to read about. Maybe we'll travel outside of Alkara. There's a whole rest of the world out there. She'll love it. Besides . . ." I grin coyly. "It was my idea."

"You told J'siiri to offer me a spot on the council?"

By way of answer, I hold out the letter I received from J'siiri just this morning.

His eyes jump quickly as he reads it over. A wide smile threatens to split open his face. "You told her to offer *both* of us positions on the council?"

"It's Alkaran law," I say. "All creatures are supposed to be represented on the council. Since I'm the only siren they have, I need someone to represent *my* interests."

He laughs. "You could have told me that."

"Where's the fun in that?" My smile turns into a smirk. "You know, all these changes are going to complicate things."

"Why?"

"We're equals now. I'm not sure what to call you," I muse. "I can't call you 'sir.' Can't call you 'Your Majesty.' I *definitely* can't call you 'Your Highness' . . ."

He throws back his head and laughs in a way I haven't seen him do in a while. "Hmm . . ." He pretends to think about it, but the mischief dancing in his ocean eyes and the amusement twitching in the corner of his mouth tell me he already has an answer. "How about Hayes? Have you tried that name yet?"

"Hayes?" I raise a teasing eyebrow at him. "You know, I guess I kind of like the sound of that." I hold out a hand for him to shake. "Nice to meet you, *Hayes*."

He grabs my hand. Instead of shaking it, he uses it to yank me to him, wrap his free arm around my waist, and kiss me.

ACKNOWLEDGMENTS

So many people helped shaped this book into existence, either through feedback and writing help, unwavering support through my debut year, or steadfast friendship. Writing *Drown Me with Dreams*, my sophomore novel and the conclusion to a story that means so much to me, was hard. For everyone who played a hand in this book, I am so incredibly grateful. First, I want to extend a massive thank you to my endlessly supportive parents. You both cheered me on through my debut's release, took time out of your busy lives to fly to my book event(s), and you've listened to me talk about publishing for hours, even when you have no idea what I'm talking about. Thank you both so much!

Thank you to my unicorn agent, Naomi Davis, for getting me through the release of Book 1 and hyping me up for Book 2. I honestly don't know how I would've gotten through my debut year without your guidance through this process. Additionally, I am so, so grateful to my editor, Camille Kellogg. Thank you for every response to my frantic emails and for always being open to brainstorming with me. This book wouldn't be what it is without you.

Working with the team at Bloomsbury has been a dream come true. Thank you to: Alexa Higbee, Briana Williams, Erica

Barmash, Faye Bi, Phoebe Dyer, Beth Eller, and Kathleen Morandini in Marketing and Publicity; Jennifer Choi, Andrew Nguyễn, and Stephanie Purcell in Rights; Donna Mark and Yelena Safronova on the design team; Alona Fryman and Erica Chan on the marketing design team; Laura Phillips, Oona Patrick, and Nicholas Church on the managing editorial and production team; Sarah Shumway and Mary Kate Castellani in the editorial team; and Valentina Rice and Daniel O'Connor in sales. Thank you all for everything you do!

I was blown away by this stunning cover art, courtesy of the talented Fernanda Suarez. Thank you so much for bringing these characters to life and working with the design team to make such a jaw-dropping cover I'm completely obsessed with.

Drown Me with Dreams has had love and support from across the pond as well. Thank you so much to the entire team at Hodderscape for all you do. Massive thank you to Molly Powell and Sophie Judge in the editorial team; Kate Keehan in publicity; Laura Bartholomew in marketing; Claudette Morris in production control; and Will Speed in design. I am appreciative of all you do to put books in the hands of UK readers.

I have so many thanks to dole out to people within the writing community. I can't imagine going through publishing without the support of my amazing author friends. Thank you to Karen Sapiro, Amanda McBride, Eliza Luckey (and Lucy, of course), Emily Emmett, Jennifer Risi, and Laura Samotin. Special thanks to the incredibly talented Joan Reardon, whose debut *The Grimsbane Family Witch Hunters* is out today! You ladies are amazing and I am forever grateful for our friendship.

To my friends in the Lit Squad: y'all are sometimes the only thing keeping me sane. Thank you to Camille Baker, Bethany Baptiste, Sami Ellis, Elnora Gunter, Jas Hammonds, Allegra

Hill, Deborah Kabwang, Avione Lee, Britney Lewis, Shauna Robinson, and Melody Simpson. Honestly don't know how I'd do this author thing without you.

I am very grateful to my fellow authors who offered blurbs for *Sing Me to Sleep*, including Natasha Ngan, Deborah Falaye, Alechia Dow, Adrienne Tooley, and Kate Dylan. For helping me get through my debut year, special thanks to Riss Nielson, Rachel Menard, and Jean Louise for being fabulous conversation partners for the release of *Sing Me to Sleep*, and for generally being amazing, kind, and encouraging. To Alechia Dow, thank you for your words of wisdom, friendship, and outstanding food recommendations.

Special thank you to Taylor Grothe, Yusof Hassan, Bayana Davis, and Andrea Aquino for your friendship, and my ride or dies, Yume Kitasei and Ehi Okosun. There are too many friends in the writing community to thank you all, but so many authors have touched my life, and I can't thank you enough for the endless love and support.

To my friends outside of writing, thank you for your encouragement and for those of you who came out to launch events. I'm especially grateful to Emilie Barrett and Pippa, who flew out from St. Louis for my debut launch event. And special thanks to Annabel Winterberg for her help copyediting this book.

Finally, a massive and heartfelt thank you goes out to my family. I can't stress enough how fortunate I am to have such an amazing family who has gone out of their way to shower me with love through my debut year and beyond. Thank you so, so much for years and years of being a rock I can always rely on.